A MOTHER'S SECRET

Tess Stimson is the author of ten novels, including top
ten bestseller *The Adultery Club*, and two non-fiction
books, which between them have been translated into
dozens of languages.

A former journalist and reporter, Stimson was
appointed Professor of Creative Writing at the University
of South Florida in 2002 and moved to the US. She
now lives and works in Vermont with her husband Erik,
their three children, and (at the last count) two cats,
three fish, one gerbil and a large number of bats in the
attic.

A
MOTHER'S
SECRET

TESS STIMSON

avon.

Published by AVON
A division of HarperCollins*Publishers* Ltd
1 London Bridge Street
London SE1 9GF

www.avonbooks.co.uk

This paperback edition 2020

First published in Great Britain by HarperCollins*Publishers* 2019

A catalogue copy of this book is available from the British Library.

ISBN: 978-0-00-838461-6

20 21 22 LSC 10 9 8 7 6 5 4 3 2 1

Typeset in Meridien by Palimpsest Book Production Limited,
Falkirk, Stirlingshire
Printed and bound in the United States of America by LSC Communications.

For more information visit: www.harpercollins.co.uk/green

For my nephews,
George, Harry and Oliver.
Your Daddy would be so proud of you.

Charles Michael Francis Stimson
1974–2015

Yet each man kills the thing he loves,
By each let this be heard,
Some do it with a bitter look,
Some with a flattering word,
The coward does it with a kiss,
The brave man with a sword!

The Ballad of Reading Gaol
Oscar Wilde (1854–1900)

Now

I crawl back into bed and stare blindly up into the darkness. I won't sleep; not tonight, not for many nights to come. I doubt I'll ever sleep soundly again.

I start to shake. The adrenalin that brought me this far suddenly drains away and I begin to shiver so violently my muscles cramp. I press my fist against my mouth to still the chatter of my teeth. If I had anything left in my stomach, I would be sick again.

I've always thought of myself as a fundamentally good person. I'm not perfect, but I've spent a lifetime trying to do the right thing. I rescue spiders from the bath; I stop traffic to let a mother lead her row of ducklings across the road. I literally wouldn't hurt a fly. A month ago, I'd never have believed myself capable of killing a mouse, never mind murdering another human being in cold blood.

But human nature has an infinite capacity to surprise.

We teach our children to fear dark alleys and strangers, but the real danger is much closer to home. You're more than twice as likely to be murdered by someone you love than by someone you've never met. If you're a child, it's

1

nearer three times. If you want a reason to be scared, look in the mirror.

Evil doesn't have two horns and a tail. It's ordinary, just like me.

Those jealous husbands who bludgeon their wives to death, the women who smother their babies, the estranged fathers who lock their children in the car and connect the exhaust. Ordinary men and women, all of them.

Just like me.

Four weeks earlier

Chapter 1

Monday 11.00 p.m.

Maddie opened her eyes. It was dark; she struggled to orient herself as her vision adjusted to the gloom. She was in the nursery: she could just make out the silhouette of Noah's cot. She had no idea how she'd got here. When she groped for the memory, it'd been wiped clean.

Her throat felt raw and hoarse, as if she'd been screaming. She moistened her lips, and tasted blood. Shocked, she touched her mouth, then looked down to see a dark smear on her fingertips. Had she fallen? She and Lucas had been arguing, she remembered that, though she couldn't remember what the row was about. Had she stormed out of the room? Walked into a door?

She closed her eyes again and thought back to the last thing she *could* remember. She and Lucas had been upstairs, in their bedroom; her husband had just come out of the shower, spraying her with water as he towelled his thick, dark hair. Her heart had skipped a beat, as it always did when she saw him naked, even after six years of marriage, the intensity of her craving for him almost frightening her as she'd pulled him hungrily onto the bed.

She suddenly remembered: with perfect timing, the baby monitor on the bedside table had flared into life, an arc of furious red lights illuminating the bedroom. Not that the alarm had been necessary; Noah's screams had echoed from the adjoining nursery, loud enough to wake everyone in the house, and probably everyone on the street, too.

Lucas had told her to let the baby cry. *That's* why they had been arguing. Lucas had told her to leave Noah. It was just colic, he'd grow out of it – *Come on, Maddie, just leave him* …

And then her memory simply snapped in half, like a spool of tape at the end of the reel.

She exhaled in frustration. She had no way of knowing if she and Lucas had argued five minutes or five hours ago. The doctor said her memory lapses were normal, the product of exhaustion and the pills she was on. Nothing to worry about, he said. Nothing to do with what had happened before. She had three children, two of them under three: of course she was tired! Of course she forgot things! It'd all sort itself out if she was patient.

But it was happening more and more often: whole blocks of time, lost for good. It'd started around the time she'd found out she was expecting Noah, and had got worse in the nine weeks since his birth. No one watching her would notice there was anything wrong. She didn't collapse or black out. But suddenly, in the

6

middle of doing something, she would find she couldn't remember what had just happened. A few seconds, or a few minutes of her life, gone forever. Her memory stuttered and skipped like a home movie, with blank spaces where pivotal scenes should be.

All she could remember tonight was the baby screaming, Lucas rolling away from her in frustration …

Noah wasn't screaming now.

Galvanised by fear, she sat up and switched on the nightlight. She'd been holding him in her arms, but they were empty now. He wasn't in his cot, he wasn't on the floor. She couldn't see him. She leaped up from the chair in panic, and then she saw him, crushed against the back of the seat. Somehow, he'd slipped out of her arms and become wedged between her hip and the side of the rocking chair, his vulnerable head pressed against the wooden spindles. Terror flooded her as she crouched on the floor and pulled his limp body onto her lap. His eyes were closed, his face still and pale, except for the vivid red imprint of the chair on his cheek.

She put her ear to his chest, praying for a heartbeat, pleading with a God she didn't believe in. *Please let him be OK. Please let him be OK.*

Abruptly, Noah squirmed in her arms and let out an indignant but healthy cry. Maddie gave a strangled half-sob, half-laugh and snatched him up against her shoulder, her throat clogged with grateful tears.

'Mummy?'

She practically jumped out of her skin. Nine-year-old

Emily stood silhouetted in the doorway to the hall, her long nightdress giving her the air of a Victorian ghost.

'Emily! Did Noah wake you?'

Her daughter nodded sleepily. 'Can't you make him stop, Mummy? I'm so *tired*.'

Maddie felt thick-tongued and groggy, as if she'd awoken from a drugged sleep. 'Me, too, darling.'

Emily leaned against the rocking chair, her long, fair hair brushing against her brother's furious scarlet face. The screaming baby grabbed a fistful in his tiny hand. 'Can't you give him some medicine or something?'

'It doesn't really help.' Maddie gently freed her daughter's hair from Noah's grasp. 'Go back to bed, Em. You've got school in the morning.'

'I feel hot.'

She felt her daughter's forehead. A little warm, but not enough to worry about. 'Get some sleep, and you'll be fine.'

'I can't sleep. He's too noisy.'

'I'm sorry,' Maddie sighed, standing up and switching Noah to the other shoulder. 'There's not much I can do. Why don't you try putting a pillow over your ears?'

'Nothing blocks *that* out.'

Maddie closed the door as Emily stomped back down the corridor to her own room, praying the noise didn't wake two-year-old Jacob too. She paced the small nursery, shushing and rocking the baby, so bone-tired she was almost asleep on her feet. She felt ninety-two, not thirty-two. Her back ached, and her eyes were raw and gritty. Her breasts throbbed with the need to nurse, but when she sat down to try, Noah stubbornly refused to feed.

She got up again and pressed her forehead against the cool glass of the nursery window, looking down into the inky garden as she jiggled Noah up and down in an attempt to soothe him. There was nothing lonelier than being awake when everyone else was asleep.

Unplanned isn't the same as unwanted, Lucas had said. But he was wrong. Noah hadn't been a happy accident, not for her.

Oh, she loved him beyond words now he was here, there was no question of that. She'd walk over hot coals for him, of course she would. She was his mother; there was nothing she wouldn't do for any one of her children. But it'd taken everything she'd had to put herself back together after Jacob, and she hadn't been sure she'd had it in her to do it again.

Emily had been an easy infant; even though Maddie had, quite literally, been left holding the baby when her daughter's father had been killed five months into the pregnancy, she'd coped better with single motherhood than she'd expected. It'd helped that Emily had apparently read the textbook on how to be the perfect newborn. She fed every four hours. She smiled on cue at six weeks. She put on exactly the right amount of weight and hit all the correct percentiles for her age. Maddie had taken Emily to the animal sanctuary where she worked, and her daughter had cooed beatifically in her pram in the sunshine for hours while Maddie groomed horses and mucked out stables. She'd listened to other mothers at her postnatal classes complaining about mastitis and sleepless nights and wondered what their problem was.

Her mistake, she'd realised when Jacob was born, had been having her easy baby first. She'd confidently assumed motherhood would be just as straightforward second time around, especially since this time she didn't have to do it all alone.

She couldn't have been more wrong.

Chapter 2

Lucas noticed the red marks on Noah's face as soon as he came into the kitchen. He crouched down beside the baby's bouncer, stroking Noah's cheek with his thumb. 'What happened to you, kiddo?'

Maddie busied herself with Jacob's Weetabix so her husband couldn't see her face, too afraid to admit she'd flaked out last night with their baby in her arms. Thank God Noah was none the worse for wear, apart from the marks, which were already starting to go. 'I think he got himself wedged in a corner of his cot,' she fibbed. 'He must've pushed his face up against the bars.'

'Poor little bugger.'

'It'll fade.'

Lucas dropped a kiss on Noah's head, then straightened up and started emptying the dishwasher. Maddie surreptitiously watched him as she stirred Jacob's cereal. She never tired of seeing her husband do simple domestic tasks like make coffee or empty the bin. Part of it was sheer novelty; her mother, Sarah, had raised her alone

11

after her father's death when she was two, so she wasn't used to seeing a man help out around the house.

She also found it strangely erotic to watch her big bear of a husband wipe down a kitchen counter or neatly fold tea towels. At six-feet-five, he dwarfed everything he touched; the plates seemed like toys from Emily's tea set in his huge hands. She and Lucas were a marriage of opposites on many levels, not least of them physical. She barely scraped five-feet-two, the top of her head just level with his broad chest. He was dark-haired to her sandy blonde, brown-eyed to her blue. He could have picked her up and tucked her under one massive arm. She couldn't even get him to roll over in bed when he snored.

But despite his mountain-man appearance, Lucas was actually a cerebral, dreamy, indoor sort of man; his weekdays were spent at a drawing board, designing buildings for a small, local architectural firm, and in his downtime at weekends he did crosswords or read obscure Russian novels. For Maddie, on the other hand, there was no 'weekday' or 'weekend'; she ran an animal sanctuary, which was a twenty-four-seven commitment. She didn't have time to worry about what to wear, never mind what to read; most mornings she flung on the same filthy jodhpurs from yesterday and dragged her hair back into an unwashed ponytail. Her hands were callused from years of mucking out stables and lunging ponies, her fingernails broken and dirty. If she put on a skirt, it was a noteworthy event.

No one who met Lucas and her separately would match them as a couple. And yet theirs had been a whirlwind romance, love at first sight. Four months after meeting in the jury room at Lewes Crown Court, they were married. Six years on, in defiance of the friends who'd said she had no idea what she was rushing into, they were as much in love as ever.

She'd known, of course, that Lucas must have baggage; as her best friend Jayne succinctly put it, no one got to thirty-four without a few fuck-ups along the way. But, recklessly, she hadn't been interested in his past; only in their future, together. Even now, she still knew very little about his life before they'd met. He rarely talked about his childhood or adolescence, for good reason. When he was just thirteen, he'd rescued his four-year-old sister Candace from the house fire that had killed both their parents. Looking back now, Maddie wondered if their shocking bereavements had been part of what drew them together. She understood better than most that to survive tragedy, sometimes you had to close the door on the past.

But her first instincts had been right. He was a good husband, a wonderful father and stepfather. He brought her a cup of tea in bed every morning and rubbed her feet at night when she was tired. And they'd made beautiful children together, she thought fondly, as she put Jacob's breakfast on the high chair in front of him. Both their sons were a perfect blend of the two of them, with ruddy chestnut hair and hazel eyes. Only Emily looked like she didn't belong. She was growing more like her biological father with every passing year.

As she stirred the lumps out of Jacob's cereal, Maddie felt an unexpected rush of tears. She blinked them back, cursing the pregnancy hormones that left her so vulnerable. Emily's father, Benjamin, had been her first boyfriend, a veterinary student in his final year at the same college as she when they'd met. Quiet and painfully shy, Maddie had always found it hard to make friends, having been raised by a widowed mother too busy with her charitable causes to have time to show Maddie how to have fun. At twenty-one, she'd never even been on a date until Benjamin asked her to join him at a lecture about animal husbandry.

Somehow, Benjamin had got under her skin. Theirs had been a gentle, low-key relationship, a slow burn born of shared interests and companionship. It wasn't love, exactly, but it was warm and reassuring and safe. Eight months after they'd met, she'd lost her virginity to him in an encounter that, like the relationship itself, was unremarkable but quietly satisfying.

The pregnancy a year later had been a complete accident. To her surprise, Benjamin had been thrilled. They'd both graduated college by then, and while she made next to nothing at the sanctuary, he was earning enough as a small animal vet to look after them both. He bought dozens of books on fatherhood and had picked out names – Emily for a girl, Charlie for a boy – before Maddie had been for her first scan. He was so excited about becoming a father, his enthusiasm was contagious.

He'd died in one of those stupid accidents that should never have happened, skidding on wet leaves on a country road one dark November afternoon. No one else was even involved. Maddie herself had been out shopping for baby clothes when it happened. She would never forget turning into their street and seeing the police car parked outside their flat. She'd known, instantly, that Benjamin was dead.

She hadn't fallen apart, because she'd had the baby to think of. She'd put her head down and concentrated on Emily and the sanctuary, never permitting herself to think about what could have been. She had her daughter, and her horses. For four years, it'd been enough.

And then she'd met Lucas, as unlike Benjamin as it was possible to be. Their relationship had been a *coup de foudre*, stars and fireworks and meteor showers. She fell in love not just with him but with the person she became when she was with him: confident, witty, amusing. When he asked her to marry him, she didn't hesitate. Lucas had saved her, in every way a person could be saved.

Maddie spooned a mouthful of Weetabix into Jacob's mouth and wiped his chin. She'd been so excited at the thought of having his baby, of seeing what the combination of his and her genes would produce. When Jacob was born, three years after they married, she'd expected him to slot into their lives without a ripple, the way Emily had. But from the start, he'd been hungrier and more fretful than his sister. He'd refused to latch on properly and had quickly lost weight. Then she'd developed mastitis. At the midwife's insistence, she'd switched to formula, feeling like a failure, her anxiety and exhaustion unsettling Jacob even further in a vicious circle. And then, just as suddenly, her agitation and nerves had been replaced by an emotional numbness that was far more troubling.

It was obvious, even to her, that there was a huge difference between not caring about anything and not being *able* to care. But she found herself incapable of doing anything about it. There'd been days when Lucas had left to take Emily to school in the morning, kissing her cheek as she sat on the edge of the bed, only for him to return home from work ten hours later to discover her still sitting there, Emily at a school friend's and Jacob screaming in his cot.

Her mother had recognised her postnatal depression for what it was and done her best to help, encouraging her to get out more, to relax; she'd taken care of the children and sent Maddie to the hairdresser, for a massage, a girls' night out. But months had oozed by, and she hadn't got any better. In the end, her mother had forced her to see the doctor. For a long while, even Dr Calkins hadn't been able to help and there had been frightening talk of inpatient care and electroconvulsive therapy. But finally, *finally*, just as Jacob reached his first birthday, the counselling and the pills had begun to work. Her feelings had gradually returned; mainly negative emotions to begin with, like hate and self-loathing and sadness, prickling sensations returning to a limb that had been numb for a long time. She'd been angry for quite a while, too, but everyone had been so glad to see her feel anything, they hadn't minded. There had been tears, lots of tears, but eventually the good feelings had come back. Things had started to matter again. She started to care.

Through it all, Lucas had been steadfast in his support. Many men would have given up on her, but not Lucas.

She liked to think of herself as independent and self-sufficient, but the truth was, she didn't know what she'd have done without him.

His competence with the baby had surprised her. He'd been a hands-on stepfather with Emily from the very beginning, taking her to nursery school and teaching her to tie her own shoelaces. But Emily was a little girl; babies were a different kettle of fish. Lucas was so bookish and academic, Maddie hadn't really expected him to get his hands dirty when Jacob was born. But he'd changed nappies and soothed tears, as if born to it. Even now, he was the one who comforted Jacob when he had tooth-ache, sitting beside his cot and stroking his back for hours until he settled. On the nights Noah was truly inconsol-able, it was Lucas who strapped him into the back of his car and drove around for hours until he fell asleep.

He ruffled Jacob's hair now as he crossed the kitchen to put the milk away. His son slammed the palm of his chubby hand against the tray of his high chair, impatient for his breakfast. Maddie jumped and stirred the bowl of Weetabix again as Emily appeared in the kitchen doorway, still wearing her nightdress.

'Why aren't you dressed?' Lucas demanded. 'We have to leave in ten minutes or you'll be late for school.'

Emily ignored him, lolling against her mother's chair and chewing a rat-tail of long blonde hair.

'Lucas asked you a question,' Maddie said sharply.

Imperceptibly, Lucas shook his head. *Not now*. It was an argument they'd had more than once over the years. She was loath to admit it, but the truth was, the joins

17

in their blended family showed, however much she tried to pretend they weren't there. Emily had had her mother to herself for the first three years of her life. Together with her grandmother, Sarah, they'd formed a tight little family unit. And then Maddie had met Lucas and brought first him, and then Jacob and Noah, into their feminine circle. Sarah adored Lucas, she thought he was the best thing that could have happened to her daughter, but Emily had been slow to thaw. Even now, her relationship with him was painfully polite at best. Lucas accepted it for what it was, but Maddie bridled on his behalf every time her daughter snubbed him.

'Go and get dressed,' Maddie said, giving her daughter a chivvying push. 'You'll make everybody late.'

'But I don't feel well.'

'What sort of not well?' Maddie asked.

'I feel hot, and I've got a headache,' Emily whined. 'And I'm so *itchy*.'

'Don't scratch,' Lucas and Maddie said simultaneously.

She handed the cereal bowl to Lucas so he could take over feeding Jacob. 'Come here, Emily. Let me see.' She peered down the back of her daughter's nightdress and immediately felt guilty for her brusqueness. 'Chickenpox. That's all we need.'

Lucas looked alarmed. 'Shit. Am I going to catch shingles?'

'Don't panic,' Maddie said. 'You can get chickenpox from shingles, but not the other way round.' She tugged Emily's nightdress back into place and made a quick decision. 'I'll see if Jayne can have her today.'

'Can't I stay home with you?' Emily asked.

'Sweetheart, I wish you could, but we have a new horse arriving today and I have to be there. You could come with me, if you like?'

Emily shook her head. She was terrified of the horses: their sharp hooves, their huge yellowing teeth, the sheer size of them. Maddie blamed herself: when Emily had been two, she'd put her on the back of one of her most tranquil sofa-ponies, Luna, a wide-backed, sweet-natured grey who'd taught a generation of children to ride. But that particular day, something had spooked her and she'd bolted and thrown Emily off. Her daughter hadn't been hurt, but the episode had given her a lasting fear of horses.

'Do you think Jayne could keep Emily overnight?' Lucas asked Maddie.

'I doubt it. It's Steve's birthday and Jayne's taking him out for dinner to celebrate. Maybe Emily could spend the day with her and go to Mum's tonight. I really don't want Noah getting sick, especially when it's only his second week at daycare. He's just got used to his new routine, and I don't want to disrupt it if we can help it. When you drop the boys off this morning, Lucas, tell them to keep an eye out for spots and call me if either of them run a temperature.'

'I can sleep over at Manga's?' Emily said, brightening. 'Can I stay there till I'm better?'

'Yes, good idea,' Lucas said hastily, thrusting Jacob's breakfast back into Maddie's hands. 'I can't be getting sick, not with all I've got on at the office.'

He was already halfway out of the door. Maddie

suppressed her irritation. Lucas was irrationally phobic about illness. A single sneeze was enough to send him into meltdown. Maybe it had something to do with what had happened to him as a child, an association with doctors and hospitals. A trauma like that had to have left emotional scars. Generally speaking, her husband had emerged from the tragedy remarkably sane and well-balanced, but Candace had fared less happily, even though she'd been so much younger when the fire had happened. Lucas was naturally very protective of her, but there was only so much he could do. Maddie didn't resent their closeness, of course; as an only child, she actually rather envied it, and she adored her eccentric sister-in-law. But Candace had cost her husband many sleepless nights over the years, and there were times Maddie felt that her marriage was rather crowded.

Guiltily, she pushed the thought away. Despite his issues, Lucas had been undeniably supportive when she'd had postnatal depression; she could hardly turn around and complain about his loyalty to his sister now. It was one of the things she loved about her husband: once earned, his support was absolutely steadfast.

But there was only so much any man could take, even one as devoted as Lucas. Maddie had already put him through the wringer once. She couldn't bring herself to tell him about her strange memory lapses and have him worry he couldn't trust her with the children. She was sure the doctor was right, anyway. They were bound to stop once Noah started sleeping through the night.

Chapter 3

Tuesday 10.00 a.m.

As soon as Jayne opened her front door, Emily pulled away from her mother and ran down the hall to the kitchen. Jayne's house had an identical layout to their own, although her garden was bigger because she was on the end of the modern housing estate in East Grinstead where they both lived. The resemblance stopped there, however; whereas Maddie's decorating style could best be described as working-mother-meets-couldn't-care-less, Jayne's home was exuberantly themed. She and her husband Steve had gone on a safari in Lesotho to celebrate their twentieth wedding anniversary the previous year; the living room was now filled with African masks and zebra-print cushions. Both her adult sons had recently left home and Jayne had turned one bedroom into a Moroccan souk and the other into a minimalist Swedish spa. It was an interesting look for a four-bed semi, but if anyone had the personality to pull it off, it was Jayne.

Maddie dumped Emily's pink backpack on the retro fifties kitchen table. 'You're a total star,' she said. 'I literally don't know what I'd have done without you.'

'Forget it. I literally can't think of anything I'd rather do.'

The two women grinned at each other. She and Jayne had met eight years ago at a council meeting about a proposed bypass that would cut through a beautiful section of their West Sussex green belt. The main speaker against the development had had an irritating habit of adding 'literally' to almost every sentence; sitting next to each other, she and Jayne had got the giggles and had eventually been asked to leave the meeting, as if they were naughty schoolgirls. They'd been firm friends ever since.

'Seriously, though, you're a lifesaver,' Maddie said. 'I owe you one.'

'Don't be daft. If it wasn't Steve's birthday, I'd have her overnight. I've got more than enough time on my hands.'

Maddie gave her a sympathetic smile. Jayne had quit her job as a receptionist at a law firm a couple of years earlier to look after her widowed father and his death four months ago had left her at a bit of a loose end while she searched for a new job.

'Time for a quick cuppa?' Jayne asked, putting on the kettle.

Maddie glanced at her phone. 'Go on, then. I've got half an hour before I have to leave.'

'Do you want me to put on a DVD for you, Emily?' Jayne asked. 'Or would you rather play in the garden?'

The little girl looked hopefully at her mother. 'Can I watch Netflix on my phone?'

'I suppose, since you're theoretically sick. But not all day,' she added helplessly, as Emily grabbed her backpack and shot off towards the sitting room.

Jayne got out a couple of mugs. 'You'll be telling me next Jacob has a Snapchat account,' she teased.

'Oh, God, am I an awful parent for getting her a smartphone?' Maddie exclaimed. 'I am, aren't I? Lucas was dead set against it, but I wanted her to be able to reach me if there was an emergency—'

'Give over. You're a great parent. I was just teasing.'

'It's not funny,' Maddie groaned. 'I can't keep up with it all. I've only just got to grips with Facebook, and now they're all on Instagram or Pinterest or God knows what instead.'

'Listen to you. You sound like your own grandmother. You realise you're technically a millennial, don't you?'

'You know you're way more on the ball than me.'

Jayne set a mug of tea in front of her. 'That's a low bar, love.'

At first glance, theirs was an unlikely friendship. Jayne was nine years Maddie's senior, an energetic, outgoing woman who'd grown up with four brothers and was the life and soul of the party. She'd married and had children young and had been the kind of mother who threw end-of-term parties for the entire class and was everyone's favourite chaperone on school trips. Maddie never even went to parent–teacher conferences without Lucas as a protective buffer. But she and Jayne had both grown up in homes where money was tight and dessert a treat you only had on Sundays. They'd learned the value of thrift and hard work.

'You all right?' Jayne asked. 'No offence, love, but you look shattered.'

Maddie sighed. 'I'm fine. Just tired. Noah's still not sleeping. I know it's just colic, but it never seems to end.'

'I hope that lovely bugger of yours is pulling his weight.'

She shrugged. 'He has to get up for work in the morning. I'd bring Noah into our room, but there's no point both of us being up all night. The horses don't mind if I fall asleep on the job, but if Lucas does, a hotel will end up with no windows or something.'

'Screw his hotels. You're more important. It's easy for things to get you down when you don't get enough sleep—'

'It's OK,' Maddie interrupted, knowing what her friend was driving at. 'I'm OK. I'm still taking my pills. Dr Calkins even said I can start tapering down soon. I'm not depressed.' She summoned a tired smile. 'Exhausted, but not depressed.'

'Any more funny turns?' Jayne asked lightly.

Maddie hesitated. Jayne had been with her the first time she had one of her memory lapses, not long after she'd found out she was expecting Noah. They'd been at the garden centre, looking at lavender bushes for Jayne's new landscaping project. One minute she'd been crushing a soft purple stalk between her fingers, inhaling its aromatic scent, and the next, she'd been

24

eating cheddar-and-kale quiche at Stone Soup two miles away with absolutely no idea how she'd got there.

Jayne had laughed when she'd told her, said it was typical baby brain, to forget about it. She'd left her car in the multistorey at the shopping centre when she'd been expecting Adam, Jayne said – she'd actually got the bus home before she'd realised!

But then it had happened again, three months later, when Maddie was collecting Emily from school. This time she'd lost a whole afternoon. It was like someone had simply wiped the slate clean. She could remember turning into the crescent-shaped drive in front of Emily's primary school for afternoon pick-up; she could see Emily standing on the front steps, chattering to her best friend, Tammy, windmilling her arms as she demonstrated some sort of dance step. And then suddenly Maddie was upstairs in the bathroom at home, kneeling next to the tub as Jacob splashed fat hands on the water, giggling. It was dark outside; she'd lost four hours, hours in which she'd driven her children home and fed them and helped out with homework and changed nappies. And she couldn't remember any of it.

It wasn't baby brain. This was something different and it scared her. She hadn't done anything odd or out of character during one of her episodes – at least, not yet – but just the thought was frightening. She hadn't wanted to go back to her psychiatrist, Dr Calkins; he was a good man and he'd done his best to help her when she'd had postnatal depression, but he'd also been the one pushing for her to be admitted to a psych ward

25

and suggesting ECT. She knew he'd only had her best interests at heart, but the idea of electric shock therapy had terrified her. She'd worried that if she'd told him she was literally losing her mind, he'd definitely have wanted to admit her, and if she'd refused, she might have ended up sectioned.

Nor did she want to tell Lucas; it would only worry him. And she couldn't talk to her mother, either; Sarah wasn't the kind of woman who did reassurance and sympathy. She solved problems, found solutions. She'd parented Maddie efficiently when she was a child, ensuring she was clothed and fed and nurtured, but although Maddie had always known she was loved, she'd never felt Sarah *liked* being a mother very much. Even when Sarah played with her, getting out the finger paints or making jam tarts, she'd always had the sense her mother was ticking off a good-parenting box rather than actually enjoying spending time with her.

But the third time she'd had a memory lapse, four weeks after Noah was born, Maddie had been so frightened she'd had to tell someone. Jayne might only be a little older than Maddie, but she made her feel mothered in a way Sarah never had. It was Jayne who'd finally talked her into going back to Dr Calkins, even offering to come with her. With Jayne beside her, she'd told the doctor everything and had been surprised, and immensely reassured, when he'd explained it was nothing more than a side effect of the antidepressants she'd been on since Jacob's birth. Once Noah was a little older, he said, they'd scale back her meds and everything would be fine.

She hoped he was right, but last night had shocked her to the core. She'd never knowingly put the children at risk before. It was only luck Noah had just ended up with a few red marks. What if she didn't simply lose her memory next time? What if she had a proper blackout, when she was driving or carrying the baby? Or what if she did something she couldn't remember, like leaving the gas on or the bathwater running? She could burn the house down, and never even know it.

'Well?' Jayne teased, flicking the kettle back on. 'Or have you already forgotten the question?'

Maddie was about to tell Jayne what had happened. But then Emily came running back into the kitchen, asking for something to drink, and Jayne noticed some of her chickenpox blisters were weeping and went off to get some calamine lotion, and so in the end, Maddie said nothing at all.

Lydia

She wriggles uncomfortably in the dark. She badly needs to pee, but if she comes out of the cupboard, Mae will be very angry. Mae told her to stay in there till the lady has gone or she'll be sorry. She knows better than to disobey Mae. Last time, Mae beat her so hard, she knocked out two of her teeth and she couldn't move her arm properly for ages. *Let that be a lesson to you.* Sometimes her shoulder still hurts.

Mae says she's a wicked little cow who'll get what's coming to her. She says one of these days she'll end up hanging from a hook in the shed, like the rabbits, with her gizzard slit. She doesn't know what a gizzard is, but she doesn't want hers slit. It sounds like it would hurt.

She really *really* needs to pee. She squeezes her legs together tight. It's so hot in the cupboard and she's thirsty, too. She doesn't know why she has to hide, but she thinks it's probably because she was so naughty yesterday. Mae had to punish her and now she has big red and purple bruises all over her legs. She didn't mean to be a greedy little brat, but she was so *hungry*. Sometimes Mae forgets to feed her, and so after Mae has gone to bed, she sneaks back downstairs and eats whatever she can find in the kitchen, like she was last night when Mae caught her.

She wishes Davy was still here. Her brother was nearly as big as Mae and Mae didn't get as cross with her when he was around. But Davy left. He told her he'd come back for her, but he hasn't yet. *Good riddance*, Mae says.

She doesn't think it's good riddance, though. She misses Davy.

She can't hold the pee in any longer and it starts to trickle down her leg. Mae will be angry that she wet herself, but it's better than coming out of the cupboard and having the lady see her. Last time a lady came to the house, Davy had to leave. It was her fault, because the special sweets made her sick. They were blue and came in a little bottle. They didn't taste very nice, but Mae told her to eat them all, *a special treat*, so she did. They made her feel funny. She got all sleepy and Mae let her curl up on the sofa, which is something she never usually does. But then Davy came home early from school and found her and he gave her a glass of warm water with salt in it, which tasted disgusting and made her sick. She doesn't know why that made Davy so happy, but he hugged her and kissed her and made her promise never to eat Mae's sweets again.

The next day, the lady came and asked her lots of questions about Mae (the lady called her 'your mummy' and Mae didn't say, *Don't you bloody call me that, you little bastard, if I'd had my way I'd have got rid of you, you can blame your father, fucking bastard I should have known he wouldn't stick around*). Mae sat on the sofa next to her with her arm round her and pinched her hard when the lady wasn't looking, to remind her to keep smiling and be a good girl. Mae didn't get cross with Davy in front of the lady, she laughed and said Davy had got the wrong end of the stick, it was a silly accident, she was very careful about where she kept her pills, especially when there were kiddies about, but you know what they're like, you have to have eyes in the back of your head. She didn't understand what Mae meant about the stick, but she hoped it wasn't a big one.

The lady wrote all this down and then she went and Mae stopped smiling and dragged Davy upstairs and she heard Mae shouting and Davy shouted back, and there was lots of banging and yelling and screaming. She didn't see Davy for a few days after that and then one night he sneaked into her bedroom and crouched down by her mattress on the floor to shake her awake. His face was all purple and bruised and one eye was swollen shut. He told her he was going to track down his own dad and he'd get him to speak to the lady and *make* her listen this time. You poor bloody cow, he said. If you was a dog, they'd take you off her, they wouldn't let her treat you like this.

But Davy never came back. Mae said good riddance, just like your father, they're all the same. Mae said it's your fault he left, you wicked evil little bastard. Mae

30

must be right, or else why hadn't he come back for her like he promised?

She hears the door slam now and Mae stomping up the stairs. She scrambles back away from the cupboard door, trying to make herself small in the corner. Even though she didn't come out of the cupboard, she knows she's going to be in trouble anyway because of the pee and because she's a bad lot who's got it coming to her.

The door flies open and she blinks in the sudden light. Mae reaches in and grabs her arm and yanks her out, and she tumbles onto the bare boards, scraping her knee. Mae doesn't give her time to stand up. Her arm feels like it's being pulled out of its socket as she's hauled along the hallway, and she has to bite her lip hard to stop from crying.

Mae stops suddenly and flings her into a heap against the wall. You dirty little bastard! she screams. Four years old and you're still wetting yourself! You little cunt!

She curls into a ball as Mae aims a kick at her, trying to protect herself. She didn't know she was four years old. There are so many things she doesn't know, including her own name. Davy called her peanut and Mae calls her little bastard and dirty bitch and fucking slag, but she doesn't think any of those are her name.

Mae grabs her arm again. She just has time to scramble to her feet as Mae drags her down the stairs. She is shocked when Mae hauls the front door open and yanks her outside. She's hardly ever allowed outside.

There are so many things she wants to look at as Mae pulls her down the street, but she's too busy trying to keep up with her. Then they get on a bus and she bounces up and down in her seat, so excited she forgets to be scared. A bus! Davy used to get a bus to school every day, sometimes she watched him from the window, but she's never been on a bus! She wonders where they are going. Maybe Mae has found Davy at last. Maybe she's not angry with him anymore and they are going to get him and bring him home.

She is sad when they get off the bus, but Mae grips her hand and marches her down a big street, much bigger than the one where they live. It is filled with shops with big glass windows with plastic people standing in them, wearing the cleanest clothes she has ever seen.

Suddenly Mae halts by a black door with gold writing on it and pushes her through it. There are no plastic people in this shop, just a pretty lady with long yellow hair sitting behind a desk. Opposite her is a lady in a blue hat, and an old man with a shiny bald head. The lady with the blue hat is crying.

You want a kid? Mae says roughly. Here. You can have this one.

Chapter 4

Wednesday 7.30 a.m.

Emily looked much better the next morning when Maddie stopped at her mother's house, where Emily had spent the night, to see how she was doing. Her daughter's spots had started to scab, which her mother said was always a good sign with chickenpox, and her temperature was almost back to normal.

'You didn't have to come over,' Sarah said briskly, putting the kettle on to boil. 'I told you last night we're fine. Emily's helping me make some posters for my sale this morning, aren't you, darling?'

Emily nodded. 'We've got glitter pens,' she announced. 'And special stickers.'

'Another fundraiser?' Maddie asked, surprised. 'Didn't you have one just last weekend?'

'That was for Child Rescue. This is the Mercy Foundation.'

Maddie kicked herself for even asking. She'd long since given up trying to keep track of her mother's good causes. Sarah was an indefatigable do-gooder; Maddie had grown up surrounded by boxes filled with cast-offs destined for jumble sales and had learned to sort china and check pockets almost before she could talk. When her mother wasn't volunteering at the local soup kitchen, she was helping out with Meals-on-Wheels. It was impossible not to admire the energy and commitment she put into her charitable work, but Maddie had always felt slightly resentful. Her teenage Saturdays had been spent sorting jumble or posting flyers through letter boxes, while everyone else at school had been out shopping and having fun. It was no wonder she'd found it so hard to make friends. Even now, Sarah's diary was twice as hectic as Maddie's own. Unless Maddie was in crisis, she had to book lunch with her mother a month in advance. There was always another cause more worthy of her attention.

No, that was petty and mean. Sarah was the first port of call for a dozen local charities and a lifeline for many of them. Her mother wasn't given to self-pity, but Maddie knew she hadn't had it easy, losing her parents while still in her late teens and then being widowed when Maddie was just two. Maddie's father, who had been nearly twenty years older than Sarah, had ensured his wife and child were provided for; their bungalow had been paid off and there'd been just enough money that Sarah didn't have to work, as long as she was sensible. She'd chosen to pay it forward by volunteering and fundraising.

At fifty-four, she was still an attractive woman, with a neat figure and the same rich strawberry-blonde hair Maddie and Emily had inherited. She'd have no shortage of eligible suitors, should she choose. But she'd never looked at another man since Maddie's father had died. 'I've already been luckier than most women,' she said, whenever Maddie raised the subject. 'I have you, and the children, and my charity work. That's all I need.'

Maddie finished her cup of tea and stood up. 'I'll come back and pick Emily up this afternoon, after work,' she said. 'The nursery rang this morning, and said half the children are out with chickenpox, so I'm sure the boys will get it too. I know Lucas will hate it, but there's not much point keeping Emily in quarantine with you if they're all going to come down with it anyway.'

'Oh, please, can't I stay with Manga?' Emily exclaimed, using her childhood name for her grandmother, which had evolved when she'd mangled 'Grandma' by saying it backwards. 'I'd much rather be here.'

'How about you come back and help me with the sale on Saturday afternoon?' Sarah said. 'Your spots should be nearly gone by then, and I could really use some help setting up the stalls. It'd just be you and me. The boys can stay with Mummy and Lucas. How does that sound?'

'Could we go to the Lucky Duck afterwards?' Emily said eagerly. 'Can we order burgers? The ones with the special thousand island dressing?'

'I don't see why not.'

Emily cheerfully opened a bag of silver foil stars and emptied them onto the kitchen table alongside her poster, good humour restored.

Maddie hugged her daughter goodbye, and put her

empty mug in the sink. 'I'd better get going,' she said. 'Izzy's arranged for a photographer to come and do some PR shots for the *Courier*. I promised I'd help her set up some jumps for the horses.'

'Hang on,' Sarah said. 'I'll come and see you off. I've got to put the recycling out.'

'I can do that for you.'

'No, I've got it.'

She slipped her feet into her gardening clogs and followed Maddie out, wheeling the recycling bin to the kerb. Maddie unlocked her twenty-year-old Land Rover, jiggling the key carefully in the sticky lock. It'd already had a hundred and fifty thousand miles on the clock when she'd bought it, eight years ago; one of these days, it was just going to collapse into a heap of rust.

'Are you OK, darling?' Sarah asked as she walked back towards her. 'You look awfully tired.'

'Not you as well,' Maddie sighed. 'I *am* tired, Mum. What do you expect? I have a nine-week-old baby to look after. Noah was up all night again last night. I finally got him to sleep around three, and then Jacob woke at five and climbed into bed with us.'

'And Lucas slept right through it all, of course.'

Maddie paused, half-in and half-out of the car. 'What's that supposed to mean?'

'Nothing, dear.'

'No, if you've got something to say, Mum, spit it out.'

'I've got nothing against Lucas, darling, you know that. I think he's been very good for you in lots of ways.'

36

'But?'

Sarah hesitated. 'He has been very good to you,' she said again. 'But you've been very good to him, too, Maddie.'

Maddie bristled. First, Jayne implied Lucas wasn't pulling his weight, and now her mother. They had no idea how hard he worked. He wasn't as hands-on with Noah as he had been with Jacob, admittedly, but he was working hard towards making partner at his firm. And sometimes he could be a bit bossy, a little bit controlling, especially when it came to the children, but that's because she was too soft. He was an incredible father. She refused to hear a word against him.

'He's my *husband*,' she said firmly. 'We're in this together, Mum. We don't keep track of who does what. And to be honest, if we did, I'd be the one in the red, not him.'

'I'm not criticising him, Maddie. I'm just worried about you. You've got a lot on your plate. Three children and the sanctuary to manage, on top of everything else.' She laid a cool hand on Maddie's arm. 'If you don't get enough rest, it's easy for things to become overwhelming.'

Maddie shook her off. 'I'm fine, Mum.'

'Asking for help isn't a sign of weakness—'

'I said I'm *fine*,' she snapped, and then instantly regretted it. 'Sorry. I didn't mean to bite your head off. I just wish everyone would stop *watching* me all the time. Don't worry. I'm taking my pills. I've been checking in with Calkins. I'm just tired, that's all.'

'Remember. I'm here if you need me,' Sarah said.

Maddie buckled her seat belt and backed the Land Rover out of the driveway, glancing briefly in her rear-view mirror as she paused at the junction with the main road. Emily had come out to find her grandmother, and as Maddie saw the two of them standing together, she was suddenly struck by how very much alike they were.

And the resemblance went beyond the physical; at nine years old, Emily already had the same quiet, self-contained composure as her grandmother. She and Sarah were made of the same unbreakable steel. Even as a baby, Emily had never seemed to need Maddie the way Jacob and Noah did. She'd lie outside for hours in her pram at the sanctuary, placidly playing with her own fingers and toes. When Maddie had been at her lowest ebb after Jacob's birth, Emily had quietly found ways to amuse herself, never complaining or demanding attention. She lived in a world of her own, perfectly content with her own company.

Maddie never had to worry about Emily. It was the boys she found so exhausting, and so hard to manage. There were times, although she would never admit it out loud, when she couldn't help thinking how much easier life would've been if she'd stopped at one child, like her mother.

Chapter 5

Wednesday 10.00 a.m.

Later that morning, Maddie leaned on the split-rail fence along the edge of the bottom paddock, watching as Izzy took Finn over a five-bar jump and landed him neatly on the other side. Both horse and rider had seen better days, but they were still poetry in motion.

On the far side of the jump, a photographer with a floppy boy-band fringe snapped away.

'Did you get what you need?' Izzy called, as she pulled Finn up.

The photographer fiddled with his lenses. 'One more time?'

Finn's chestnut flanks rippled in the sunshine as Izzy took him over the jump again. He was a former show-jumper, one of the most beautiful horses Maddie had ever seen. He'd probably earned a great deal of money for his owner, before the trophies had stopped coming and he'd been sold and then resold and finally dumped by the side of the road by an unscrupulous dealer, abandoned without food, water or shelter. When he'd arrived at the sanctuary, Maddie had been able to count his ribs, and his feet were in such a bad state, he could barely walk.

The photographer snapped away as Maddie fed Finn some Polos. She was grateful when he left.

'Please tell me we don't have to do that again soon,' she grumbled to Izzy, as they led Finn back up to the yard.

'Play nice,' Izzy chided. 'The *Courier*'s promised us two pages if they like the photos.'

They certainly needed the publicity. The sanctuary's finances were in a perilous state; when Maddie had first started working here full-time eleven years ago, there had been seven members of staff, plus a couple of pony-mad teenage girls trading riding lessons for sweat equity. Now they were down to just three: Bitsy, the last remaining stable-hand, a gruff, weather-beaten woman who'd worked at the sanctuary since she was sixteen; Isobel Pyne-Lancaster, who spent most of her time circulating the begging bowl around her smart friends; and Maddie herself.

It was a daily battle just to keep their doors open. Maddie couldn't bear to turn any horse or pony away, no matter how short of funds they were. But it cost thousands of pounds a month just to keep the sanctuary running. Some of the money came from riding lessons and the odd gymkhana, but the rest came from donations. Maddie might find it difficult to ask for something for herself, but when it came to her horses, it was a different matter. In that, she supposed, she was just like her mother.

Maddie fell in love with horses the way most women fell in love with men. Ironically, she'd never been a horsey child; Sarah had never had the kind of money that supported ponies and riding lessons and gymkhanas, and even if she had, it wasn't the kind of posh, braying world they mixed in. But when she was eleven, her mother had dragged her along to a fundraiser at a local stable yard for people who'd been severely injured in riding accidents; not the most auspicious introduction to the equestrian world. She'd been absolutely terrified: of the stamping and whinnying, the huge, iron-clad feet that looked like they could crush her in a heartbeat, of the horses' sheer size.

But then one of the stable girls had given her a carrot and led her over to a vast, orange sofa of horseflesh called Paul. 'Hold your hand flat,' the girl had instructed, as the horse snorted and nuzzled her shoulder. 'He won't bite.'

Paul had bared his great yellow teeth as if laughing at her. Maddie had frozen, too petrified to move, as his huge velvety nose snuffled against her hand. With the delicacy of a dowager selecting a cucumber sandwich, he'd taken the carrot and whinnied with pleasure, butting against her arm as if in thanks.

Maddie had gazed up at him in rapture, her heart swelling with joy. He liked her! *He liked her!*

It had been the start of a love that'd had no equal until Emily was born.

Maddie had spent her teenage years in jodhpurs, with straw in her hair and dirt under her nails, mucking out stables at a nearby horse sanctuary in return for riding lessons. At one point, she'd dreamed of being a jockey. She was the right height and had the necessary slim, wiry build, and over time, she acquired the technical skills, but eventually she'd had to accept she just didn't have the killer instinct. It took strength and guts to hold on to 1200 pounds of horseflesh thundering along at forty miles an hour. Horses could smell your fear, and she'd never quite mastered hers. Instead, she'd got a degree in animal welfare and started working full-time at the horse sanctuary. Later, after Benjamin's death, she'd used her small inheritance from her father to buy out the owners, two retired vets, when it'd become too much for them to manage.

Finn had been her first rescue horse. He'd obviously been viciously abused as well as shamefully neglected, and when he'd arrived at the sanctuary, he'd had no idea how to respond to affection, backing away in fear when she tried to stroke his nose. He'd circled his stable endlessly, grabbing mouthfuls of hay and spitting them out over the door and biting his own shoulders. She'd had no idea horses could self-harm until then.

It'd taken months of persistent, loving patience to calm him enough to even get a saddle on him. But, in the end, he'd become her greatest success story. She always put her most nervous riders on Finn. He was like a huge armchair. He understood their fear, because of what he'd been through himself.

Izzy led Finn into his box. 'Mads, I need to talk to you,' she said, as she came back outside and bolted the stable door behind her.

42

'That doesn't sound good,' Maddie said, with a lightness she didn't feel.

'Look, I know you don't want to hear this, but I think we should consider selling the lower meadow,' Izzy said, as they crossed the yard. 'Our cheque for feed this month bounced again. The south stables are leaking, and if we don't fix the roof soon, it's going to come down. Bitsy hasn't been paid for two months, and I know you haven't taken a penny in almost a year. We have vet bills, hay bills, the rates are due.' She stopped as they reached the small Portakabin that served as the sanctuary's offices. 'We're sinking, Maddie.'

Maddie frowned. 'If we start selling off bits of land to pay bills, we'll end up with nothing left. We'll have another fundraiser. I'll talk to my mother, see if she can help.'

'That might see us through this crisis, but what about the next one?' Izzy said. 'We need to increase our donor base and find new sponsors, so we can get some kind of regular income coming in. Otherwise, we're just putting our fingers in the dyke.'

Maddie knew her friend meant well. Izzy and Bitsy loved every blade of grass, every stone and split-rail fence of the sanctuary as much as she did. Like her, they considered it their second home. They'd been at the sanctuary even longer than she had and she'd known them since she'd first started mucking out stables there as a teenager. It was Izzy who'd suggested a degree in animal welfare when her mother had

43

insisted she go to college, and Bitsy who'd encouraged her to buy the sanctuary when the vets could no longer manage it, promising to stay on at the stables as long as Maddie needed her. Izzy had even given Lucas a couple of riding lessons, before they'd concluded, by mutual assent, that horses weren't for him. She and Bitsy had organised Maddie's hen weekend on the Isle of Wight with Jayne and Lucas's younger sister, Candace, where they'd all got outrageously drunk. Sixty-two-year-old Bitsy had been arrested for indecent exposure after she'd dropped her trousers and peed behind a postbox; somehow, Candace had sweet-talked the arresting officer, a baby-faced policeman barely out of his teens and a full head shorter than she, into dropping the charges in return for her phone number. Bitsy and Izzy were her family. They knew the sanctuary meant the world to her, as it did to them. Losing even a part of it would break all their hearts.

Izzy would rather cut off her own arm than sell the lower meadow. If she was suggesting it now, they must be in real trouble.

Maddie leafed through the bills on her desk after Izzy had left. *Overdue. Three months in arrears. Immediate payment is required.*

Izzy was right. They couldn't go on like this. Lucas had told her the same thing. And he didn't just want her to sell the lower meadow; he'd actually asked her to consider selling the sanctuary itself.

She understood his reasoning: the sanctuary was a financial black hole that had long since swallowed every bit of her legacy, and more besides. As Izzy said, she hadn't paid herself in more than a year. If she sold the land to a developer, she'd make enough for Lucas to buy into a partnership with his architectural firm and enable him to take on some of the projects he longed to do which were currently no more than a pipe dream.

But the sanctuary wasn't just a hobby or even a good cause, not to her. Maddie felt hurt that Lucas could even ask her to sell it. The horses were her *family*. She loved Finn second only to Lucas and the children. Of course she didn't want to stamp on Lucas's dreams, but closing the sanctuary to facilitate them was inconceivable. It'd be like selling Noah to a baby trader!

She'd sacrifice a kidney rather than let one single horse go.

Chapter 6

Friday 11.30 a.m.

Maddie's hair smelled of vomit, and her jeans of urine. She'd already changed her T-shirt three times before giving up and accepting the noxious stains as the scars of battle. Her nails were caked in pink calamine lotion, and she strongly suspected the suspicious marks on her socks had something to do with Jacob's foul-smelling nappy earlier.

'Of course it's not a bad time,' she lied, opening the front door wider. 'Please, come in.'

Candace thrust a Tupperware box at her as she came in. 'I made scones. They're a bit burnt, but you can kind of scrape that off.'

'Sorry about the mess,' Maddie apologised, clearing a heap of dirty washing off a kitchen chair so Candace could sit down.

'You should see my place,' Candace said cheerfully, lobbing a pair of dirty knickers onto the pile in Maddie's arms. 'Lucas told me Jacob's come down with the pox, too. I thought you might need some moral support.'

Maddie shoved the dirty clothes into the washing

machine and jammed the door shut. 'You have no idea. Your brother practically ran screaming from the room when Emily came out in spots. You know what he's like about getting sick. I'm amazed he hasn't made us fumigate the place.'

Candace picked up a piece of leftover Marmite toast from one of the kid's plates and took a huge bite. 'I was a bit surprised when Lucas's office said he was home today,' she said through a mouthful of crumbs. 'I thought maybe you'd gone down with it too, that's why I came round.'

'That's sweet of you, but I'm fine. I've already had it.' Maddie looked puzzled. 'I don't know who you spoke to at his office, but they've got their wires crossed. Lucas has a meeting in Poole today, and then a late work dinner. He won't be back till tomorrow morning.'

Candace snorted. 'That sounds more like my brother. If you were relying on him for the "in sickness" bit of things, you're out of luck.' She took another bite of toast. 'Are you all right, Mads? You look exhausted.'

'So everyone keeps telling me.'

'Sorry, darling. But you *do* look a bit ropey.'

'That's nothing to how I feel.' Maddie collapsed onto a chair. 'Thank God Noah hasn't gone down with it yet, though it's probably only a matter of time. Jacob's been throwing up all day – this is the third set of laundry I've done today.'

'How's Emily?'

'Fine, apart from the itching. I had to cut her nails right back to stop her scratching.'

'The older you are when you get chickenpox, the worse it is,' Candace shuddered. 'I was only five when I had it, and I was hardly ill at all, but Lucas was fourteen and he had an awful time. I remember Aunt Dot had to tie mittens on him in the end to stop him scratching himself to pieces.' She lowered her voice and grinned conspiratorially. 'Apparently he even had spots on his willy.'

Maddie laughed. She loved Candace; she might be a little tactless at times, but she didn't have a mean bone in her body. At thirty-one, she was only a year younger than Maddie, but she seemed to have settled into a happy spinster groove, content to play the eccentric maiden aunt to her niece and nephews. It was unfortunate: the same strong, masculine features that made Lucas so ruggedly handsome were significantly less flattering on his sister. She must have been six feet and was built like a rugby prop forward. But beneath it all, she was emotionally fragile. She'd never managed to maintain a serious relationship and Maddie wondered if it was another legacy from the terrible tragedy that had shaped Candace's childhood: the fear of letting anyone get too close.

Lucas had introduced her to his sister just a couple of weeks after they'd started dating. The three of them had met at a rooftop bar in London overlooking St Paul's, near where Candace worked as an IT consultant, and Maddie remembered feeling sick with nerves as she'd got into the lift with him, terrified that if Candace didn't like her, it would be the end of everything. Lucas himself had been uncharacteristically subdued and Maddie had assumed it was because he, too, was anxious she met with his sister's approval. It was only later she'd found out he'd been far more worried what she'd think of Candace.

The evening had gone well, although she'd been a little taken aback by quite how much vodka Candace had managed to put away. But it'd been a Friday night and Candace had been celebrating landing an important new client. They'd left her at the bar around ten, waiting for some friends, and Maddie had fallen happily asleep in Lucas's arms, thankful she'd passed the biggest test of their relationship so far.

At 3 a.m. the next morning, Lucas had been awakened by a phone call from the police. Candace had been arrested after drunkenly crashing her Mini Cooper through the plate glass window of a car showroom in Berkeley Square. She'd been more than three and a half times over the legal limit.

She'd lost her licence and her job. It was the start of what was to become an all-too-familiar pattern. Candace would promise the moon and stars, swearing to cut back on her drinking, and for a while she'd succeed, before falling off the wagon in spectacular fashion. Lucas had paid for her to go to rehab several times, until finally, four years ago, Candace had got her life back on track and moved down to Sussex to be near them. Maddie didn't hold her problems against her. She knew better than anyone the demons that were fought in private.

There was a loud wail from upstairs, and Maddie

wearily shoved back her chair. 'Sorry, that's Jacob. I'd better go to him before he upsets Emily. She's hyper-sensitive to noise at the moment. She hasn't even wanted to watch any television, because she says it's all too loud.'

'She must be ill. Well, I won't keep you, darling.' Candace stood and enveloped Maddie in one of her brother's bearlike hugs. 'Let me know if there's anything I can do. Happy to mind the little buggers if you need a break.'

Noah suddenly started crying too, woken by his broth-er's yells. Maddie almost burst into tears herself.

'Let me see to Noah,' Candace offered. 'Probably just lost his dummy. You go and sort out Jacob.'

Maddie hesitated.

'Go on,' Candace said. 'I'm not going to drop him or feed him gin.'

Instantly, she felt guilty. Candace had never given her any reason to worry when it came to the children. She might not let her get behind the wheel with them in the car, but Candace had babysat for them numerous times.

'There's a clean dummy on the bookcase by the window,' she said, shrugging off her misgivings. 'Let me know if he needs changing.'

She followed Candace upstairs and went into Jacob's room. The little boy was standing up in his cot, arms outstretched to the stuffed dolphin that had fallen on the floor. Maddie gave it back to him and settled him down, stroking his back until he fell asleep again. She could hear Candace singing to Noah through the thin walls. Led Zeppelin, if she wasn't mistaken.

Her mobile phone suddenly buzzed in her jeans pocket. Quickly, she tiptoed out of the room to take it.

'I got your email,' her accountant, Bill O'Connor, said, without preamble. 'Is now a good time?'

There was no such thing as a good time today, but Maddie headed downstairs to the tiny study she and Lucas shared. 'What are your thoughts, Bill? I know the figures aren't great, but we're behind on the Gift Aid paperwork, so if you take that into account—'

'This isn't about that,' Bill interrupted. 'You asked me to look at a second mortgage on your house.'

'It'd just be for a couple of years,' Maddie said quickly. 'I'm sure we can get back in the black soon. Izzy's got some wonderful fundraisers planned, and she's talking to a couple of big donors, so it's not like I'm pouring good money after bad, I do have a plan, if we can just get enough to tide us over—'

Her accountant cut across her babble. 'Putting aside the wisdom of using your personal funds to prop up the business, I have another concern. Whose name is the house in?'

Maddie was taken aback by the question. 'Lucas and I bought it together. It's in both our names. Why?'

'So, both your signatures would be required to take out a second mortgage?'

'I suppose so, but I'm sure Lucas would agree—'

'I'm not worried about Lucas agreeing, but you already have a second mortgage, Maddie.'

The front door banged suddenly. Through the window, she watched Candace lever herself into the tiny front seat of her sports car and shoot out of the drive with a spurt of gravel. She was a little surprised her sister-in-law hadn't bothered to say goodbye, but Candace was always a bit unpredictable.

She switched her phone to the other ear. 'Sorry, Bill. What did you just say?'

'A second mortgage was leveraged against your house just over six months ago.'

'That can't be right. You must be confusing it with—'

'I'm not confusing it with anything. I'm looking at the paperwork right now. Eighty thousand pounds, using the house as collateral. I have your signature right here. At least,' he added ominously, 'I assume it's your signature.'

Maddie sat down abruptly. For once, she was speechless.

'Maddie,' Bill said heavily. 'You're my client. I have to consider your interests first. I hate to ask you this, but did Lucas take this loan out without your knowledge?'

'Of course not!'

'So you *did* know?'

She hesitated. Did she? Her memory hadn't been exactly reliable recently. But she found it hard to believe she could have forgotten something this big. Eighty thousand pounds! A loan like that didn't happen overnight. They'd have discussed it, and signed paperwork.

Her memory was bad, but it wasn't *that* bad. She couldn't possibly have forgotten everything.

But Lucas would never have taken it without telling her, she was equally certain about that. Five thousand, perhaps; he'd lent Candace quite a bit of money to help get her new IT consultancy off the ground last year and it was possible he might have borrowed a bit more without running it past Maddie first. But eighty thousand pounds? It simply wasn't possible.

Why would he even need that kind of money in the first place?

Chapter 7

Saturday 2.00 a.m.

Maddie couldn't sleep. The first night since he was born that Noah hadn't been up with colic and she was awake anyway, tossing and turning in bed, wishing Lucas wasn't away tonight of all nights, so she could simply ask him, face-to-face, about the loan.

She needed to look him in the eye when she asked him why he'd done it. Because there was no getting around the fact that her signature on the mortgage application form had been forged. She'd seen it with her own eyes. It was a competent attempt, but the signature on the paperwork Bill had sent her clearly wasn't hers.

Until now, she'd have said she knew her husband inside out. Maybe not his entire personal history; there was much about his life before they'd met that she didn't know. But they'd survived some testing challenges in the six years they'd been together and she had a pretty good idea of the mettle and character of the man she'd married. That'd been evident from the day they'd met in the jury box at Lewes Crown Court.

They'd been empanelled for the trial of a haulage

contractor accused of murder. It hadn't been the glamorous *Law & Order* melodrama she'd secretly hoped for when she'd been called for jury service, but a rather pedestrian tale of embezzlement, bad luck and bad choices that had ended with a blow to the head from a wrench in a half-built swimming pool.

Maddie, along with the rest of the jury, had initially been inclined to side with the prosecution. The haulage contractor had admitted he'd been on the building site where his auditor's body had been found. He'd acknowledged they'd had a blazing row on the morning of the day of the murder. The wrench had come from his own set of tools and bore his fingerprints. As they started their deliberations, the foreman, a retired doctor, had repeated everything the Crown had laid before them as if it were undisputed fact, and sat back, job done.

It was Lucas who'd made them all think again. 'Where's the forensic evidence?' he'd demanded. 'Where's the motive?'

'Fraud,' the foreman said, folding his arms. 'It's obvious.'

Lucas had looked round the jury table, holding each of their gazes in turn. They were a pretty uninspiring crew, Maddie had to admit, seeing them through his eyes. Five men, seven women, all but two of them white, most on the fringes of what her mother called the 'real' working world: the unemployed, the retired, stay-at-home mums. Lucas had been the exception. She later learned he'd passed up the chance of a major design commission to do his jury service, and he'd taken the responsibility seriously.

'Where's the proof?' Lucas had asked. 'The police investigation found nothing to back up the prosecution's fraud theory. I'm not saying the man's innocent, but it's not enough for us to think he *probably* killed his auditor. The prosecution has to *prove* it. The question is, have they done that?'

Lucas had achieved what the defence had signally failed to do and made them put aside their prejudices and actually consider the case before them. The evidence was all circumstantial, he argued eloquently, and set against it was the accused's previous good character. This was a man who'd never had so much as a parking ticket, a committed churchgoer and family man. To convict him of cold-blooded murder, of picking up that heavy wrench and smashing in the skull of another human being, they had to be sure. Not just fairly sure. Not just on-the-balance-of-probabilities sure. They had to be absolutely sure beyond *any reasonable doubt*.

His reasoning was calm and logical, but he'd exuded a fierce, suppressed energy Maddie found mesmerising. She could almost see the neurons firing in his brain. She hadn't been the only member of the jury to fall a little bit in love with him.

Thanks to Lucas, the haulage contractor had been found not guilty, and less than three months later, an ex-boyfriend of the victim had been picked up in a routine traffic stop and confessed to the crime.

Lucas deserved the same benefit of the doubt as the haulage contractor, Maddie told herself now, tossing onto her back and staring up at the ceiling in the dark, her eyes dry with exhaustion. Thank God Noah was giving her some peace, for once. She didn't have the energy to deal with his crying.

Lucas was the most honest, principled man she'd ever met. She had never once caught him in a lie in all the years they'd been married; not even a little white one. He'd lost commissions because he refused to compromise his principles and use sub-standard materials to cut costs. He'd stood by the head of the local junior school when the man had been falsely accused – in a venomous and anonymous poison-pen letter – of sexually abusing a child, insisting the school board not rush to judgement without proof.

Maddie rolled restlessly onto her side. She was desperate to sleep, but her mind raced frantically, like a rat seeking its way out of a trap. Was it possible there was a darker side to her husband? How did she even know he was in Poole, as he'd said? His own secretary had told Candace he was working from home. You read stories in the papers about people who led secret lives – men with two wives at opposite ends of the country, serial killers who prowled the streets picking off prostitutes before going back home to eat Sunday lunch with their families. Their nearest and dearest always claimed to have had no idea what was really going on. Maybe the signs had been there, but they'd been too blind and too trusting to see them. In the end, how much did you ever really know anyone?

Lucas was forty years old, and she had only been part of his life for six years; of course there were things she didn't know about him, just as there were things about her life that she hadn't shared. Maybe there were aspects of his past he wasn't proud of, things that had no bearing on the man he'd become. She could only speak to the Lucas Drummond she knew, and she didn't believe that man would ever deliberately deceive her.

But she was beginning to wonder if she knew him as well as she thought. The subtle pressure he was putting on her to sell the sanctuary, for example, so that he could buy into a partnership with his architectural firm. It had started to feel like emotional blackmail. And he'd been wonderfully supportive when she'd been depressed, but during her illness he'd been very firmly in charge, and she couldn't help noticing that's the way it'd stayed, even when she'd got better. He'd decided to take Emily out of her private primary school, for which Sarah paid, and send her to the state school down the road, so that Emily and the boys would have exactly the same education. Maddie didn't know why, but he wasn't terribly fond of Jayne, either, and had quietly vetoed dinners and get-togethers with her husband for so long that she'd stopped even suggesting them. It was almost as if he didn't want her to have any friends, and for the first time, Maddie wondered why.

She sat up again and punched her pillow into shape. Maybe there was a perfectly good reason why Lucas had faked her signature and taken out a loan without telling her, though she couldn't think of a single one. But in the end, it didn't matter *why* he'd done it. It meant she couldn't trust him; she'd always be wondering what was going on behind her back. It'd be like taking back a man who'd cheated on you. Wouldn't you always be wondering when he was going to do it again?

Chapter 8

Maddie woke with a start. It'd been almost light when she'd finally fallen asleep, utterly exhausted. She was grateful Noah had slept through the night, but she'd almost have welcomed the distraction. At least it might have stopped her mind spinning.

She reached for her phone on the bedside table and gasped when she saw the time. Seven-thirty! No wonder her breasts felt like they were going to explode. Noah had gone for nearly eight hours without a feed. He must be absolutely exhausted himself to have slept for so long. However awful his colic was for her, it was worse for him, because he had no idea why he was in pain.

She struggled out of bed, grabbing her dressing gown and jabbing her arms into it as she stumbled across the room. Jacob had slept longer than usual, too, probably because of all the Calpol she'd given him yesterday to bring down his temperature. She needed to get the kids all up and moving; Lucas would be home any minute. She wanted to get her head together before she talked to him.

She heard the crunch of tyres on gravel and peered out of the bedroom window. Lucas was already pulling into the driveway. Her stomach churned with nerves. She ached to nurse Noah, but she needed to talk to Lucas more. She had to confront him and get it over and done with. She cracked the door of the nursery to check on the baby. He didn't stir, so she carefully shut the door again and turned towards the stairs.

Afterwards, she could never say what made her stop and go back. Some sixth sense, perhaps; a mother's intuition. Or maybe she'd known the moment she'd seen her son's arm, but her mind, fighting to protect her for just a few more seconds, had refused to process it.

As soon as she re-opened the door, she knew something was very wrong.

Lydia

She's never been so happy in her life. She was frightened at first when Mae abandoned her with strangers, because even though she's scared of Mae, at least she knows her, she knows where she is.

But then the lady with the yellow hair came out from behind her desk and talked to the crying lady in the blue hat and the old man with the shiny bald head for a long time, and then the crying lady stopped crying and came over and crouched down beside her and said, my name is Jean and this is my husband Ernie and what's your name? She didn't want the lady to be cross with her because she couldn't remember her own name, so she said Mae, because it was the only name she could think of. And then the not-crying-now lady said, how would you like to come home with me, just till everything gets sorted out? And so she did.

She's been here for weeks and she still can't believe how *big* their house is. There is an entire room with a table and chairs just for eating in and another room with a big green bath for washing yourself. There was a bath at Mae's house, but no one ever used it for washing themselves. Once, one of Mae's special friends stayed with them for a while and he kept his two pet ducks in it. When he left in the middle of the night without saying goodbye, Mae was so angry she wrung their necks with her bare hands.

Jean lets her have a bath every day. She has a bed, too: a real bed, not just a mattress on the floor, and it has pink sheets on it. She didn't know what the sheets were to begin with. Clothes for a bed! It seemed such a funny idea. The first night she slept on the floor, so as not to get them dirty or wrinkled. But when Jean came in the next morning, she laughed and said it was OK if she messed the sheets up, that's what they were for. Then Jean jumped on the bed *with her shoes on*, laughing until she climbed on the bed herself and jumped up and down, too.

And there is food, so much food! It seems it's always time for one meal or another. Slow down, Jean laughs, as she crams toast into her mouth at breakfast and shoves more in her pockets for later. You'll make yourself sick. She does, too, her belly isn't used to feeling this full. It takes her a few days to realise that the gnawing pangs in her tummy have gone. She still fills her pockets with scraps when she leaves the table, she can't help it, but Jean doesn't seem to mind. You poor love, she says. We'll soon fatten you up.

Jean takes her shopping and buys her new dresses as clean and fresh-smelling as the sheets and her very own shoes that don't pinch or slop around on her small feet. Jean shows her how to wash her hair with shampoo and how to braid it neatly into two plaits, and she never hits her, *not ever*, not even when she has an accident because she's too shy to say she needs to pee and has forgotten how to find the bathroom in this huge house. Jean doesn't even shout. Jean strokes her hair and hugs her and says it doesn't matter, it was an accident, we'll fix it in a jiffy, don't you worry.

She doesn't ask how long she's going to stay here. She doesn't miss Mae at all, which proves just what a wicked little girl she really is. But she doesn't want to think about Mae. She's in the middle of such a lovely dream and she doesn't ever want to wake up. Sometimes, she hopes she's dead so she won't have to.

But then one day Jean answers the telephone and when she comes off she's crying again. Ernie asks her what's the matter and Jean collapses in his arms, I'm not going to let them take her, she says. What do they know, these social workers, I'm not giving her back to that wicked woman, over my dead body.

But Jean won't be able to stop Mae. No one can ever stop Mae when she's made her mind up about something.

Jean does her best, she writes letters to important people and she begs and pleads, but it's no good. The night before Jean has to take her back, she cooks her favourite macaroni and cheese followed by chocolate ice cream. Jean brushes and plaits her hair and reads her a story and tucks her into her nice clean warm bed with the pink sheets for the last time and her face gets that strange look people have when they're trying really hard not to cry. Jean kisses her cheek, I'll never stop fighting, I'll make them listen, I'll come back and get you, just you wait and see. But she knows deep down it'll never happen. Davy promised he'd come back for her, too, but he never did.

Mae is waiting for them at the shop where she left her, looking so different in a normal mummy dress instead of the low tops and short skirts she normally wears that she almost doesn't recognise her. Mae bursts into noisy tears and throws her arms around her in a suffocating hug, my baby oh my baby thank goodness you're all right!

She doesn't want to let go of Jean's hand, but Mae is holding on to her so tight she can't breathe, pulling her away. You've been very kind, looking after her while I was under the weather, she says, but I'm right as rain now, few pills, bit of rest, just what the doctor ordered. Mae's fingernails dig into her shoulder, but her mother's bright smile doesn't slip.

She wants to beg Jean not to let her go, she wants to run right out of the shop and keep on running as far away from Mae as she can get. Her heart is beating loudly in her ears and she feels hot and shaky and sick in her tummy. Her little hands clench into fists by her sides. She wants to hit something, she wants to hurt someone as much as she is hurting, and she realises, in a kind of dazed surprise, that this is what *angry* feels like.

She doesn't know why Mae even wants her back. Mae says she's never been no good, nothing but trouble since the day she was born. Should have got rid of you when I had the chance. But maybe Mae has missed her after all, she thinks hopefully. Maybe things are going to be different now.

It's only when Mae is marching her back down the high street, towards the bus stop, the grip on her shoulder so tight she knows she'll have bruises tomorrow, and leans into her and says, you think I wanted you back, you little cow, they was going to take the house off of me with you and Davy both gone, now you're going to fucking well earn your keep, that she understands Mae hasn't missed her at all, and if she thought it was bad before, it's going to be a hundred times worse now.

Chapter 9

Fear and loss seeped like moisture from the room's neat beige walls. This was where they brought you when there was nothing more they could do. Maddie stared at a cork board covered with leaflets. *What To Do After Someone Dies. Living With Grief. After Suicide: A Guide For Survivors. Coping With A Terminal Diagnosis. Palliative Care: What You Need to Know.*

She turned away, her stomach churning. So much pain and misery in the world. How had she ever thought she'd be lucky enough to escape?

She felt strangely disconnected from everything, as if she was moving underwater, or trapped behind a thick glass wall. She knew her baby was dead. She could still feel his chilling weight in her arms, and yet she couldn't take it in. The reality was so monstrous, her mind refused to accept it.

She'd known Noah was gone the second she'd seen his arm dangling through the bars of his cot, his body strangely still. If she lived to be a hundred, she would never forget the thousand years it'd taken her to rush to his cot and pull the blanket away from his cheek. His face had been waxy and deathly pale, his lips a deep mottled blue. When she'd touched his cheek, he'd been cold.

She had no memory of rushing to the window and screaming down at Lucas, though she supposed she must have done. Her throat was still raw. She didn't remember scooping her baby out of his cot, either, but she would remember forever the cold, dead weight of him in her arms. She could feel it still. The back of his head, where she had always put a steadying hand, like a ball of stone. Her precious, warm, milky son, now a stiff, cool statue, a porcelain doll. Already she couldn't remember what he looked like alive. When she tried to picture him, all she could see was his face, deadly white but for his indigo lips and the purple blotches on his skin where the blood had settled.

She supposed Lucas had called the ambulance and her mother. She didn't know how long it'd taken for the paramedics to get there. She hadn't wanted to let Noah go, refusing to let anyone take him from her arms. It was Sarah who'd finally persuaded her. Maddie had handed Noah's cold little body to her mother, watching as the paramedics briefly examined him and then wrapped him tenderly back in his blanket. She'd felt the emptiness of her arms and had known instinctively the feeling wasn't ever going to go away.

'Maddie, stop that. You don't take sugar. Maddie! Stop!'

She jumped and glanced up. She was standing at a

counter at the side of the room, spooning sugar into an empty coffee mug. It was already a quarter full; she must have added at least six spoonfuls without even knowing what she was doing.

'I'm sorry,' she said, dropping the spoon so that it clattered onto the counter. 'I don't know what I was thinking.'

She sat on the tan leather sofa, pinning her hands under her thighs to stop herself from plucking at her clothes. It didn't matter what anyone said. It was her fault Noah was dead. She'd wished him gone. She hadn't meant it, of course, but she'd got exactly what she'd asked for. Maybe, deep down, in a corner of her mind too dark for her to see clearly, this *was* what she wanted.

Maybe she'd even made it happen.

'He kept crying,' she burst out suddenly. 'No matter what I did, I couldn't make it stop.'

'He had colic, Maddie,' Lucas said hoarsely. 'He couldn't help it.'

She stared down at her lap. Her legs were jiggling, but she seemed powerless to stop them. 'I could hear it in my head, all the time. The non-stop screaming, on and *on*. Sometimes I didn't know if it was him crying, or me. I tried to be patient, I did my best for him, but nothing made him happy. No matter what I tried, it didn't make any difference. He never stopped *screaming*.'

'It wasn't your fault, Maddie.'

'I couldn't make him better. I'd feed him and change him and cuddle him and nothing helped. I couldn't stand it anymore.' She covered her face with her hands. 'I just wanted it to *stop*.'

When Lucas spoke again, he sounded wary. 'Maddie, what are you trying to say?'

'I wished he hadn't been born,' she said bleakly. 'I wished he wasn't here. Sometimes ... sometimes I even prayed he'd just disappear. That someone would just ... *take* him.'

'Maddie—'

'Didn't you hear me?' she cried wildly. 'I wanted someone to take my baby! What kind of mother would fantasise about something like that?'

'It's not your fault,' Lucas said again, but his voice sounded less certain.

He sat next to her and put his arm around her, and she leaned into the familiar bulwark of his shoulder, but it no longer seemed comforting or safe. He was like an oak that had been hollowed out, as vulnerable as she to the coming storm.

Chapter 10

Saturday 10.00 a.m.

The door opened. One of the doctors who'd met them from the ambulance came into the room, followed by a middle-aged woman wearing round gold spectacles and a painfully sympathetic expression.

'Mr and Mrs Drummond, first let me offer you my deepest condolences,' the doctor began, pulling up a hard plastic chair opposite the sofa and placing a file on the coffee table. 'I am so very sorry for your loss. I can't begin to imagine how you must be feeling.'

Maddie stared at him blankly.

'My name is Leonard Harris, and I'm the duty doctor at A&E today. This is Jessica Towner,' he added, as the older woman took another chair beside him. 'She's our family liaison and bereavement counsellor. She's here to help you through the process and explain everything that will happen next.'

'I'm also very sorry for your loss,' the woman murmured, her voice a respectful whisper. Maddie had to strain to hear her. 'I'm here to help you in any way I can. I know what a distressing time this is, so if there's anything I can do to make things a little easier, please ask.'

The doctor leaned forward, his clasped hands dangling between his knees. 'I know you must be in a state of shock right now,' he said, 'but there are a few questions I have to ask. There are certain procedures we have to go through, and a few decisions you need to make, which Jessica will discuss with you in a moment. If we can sort some of these things out now, you'll be able to go back to your family and grieve without any more interference.' He waited a moment for this to sink in, and then reached for his file. 'We just need to check a few facts first. Your son's name is Noah Michael Drummond, correct?'

'Michael was after my father,' Maddie said automatically. It was suddenly important they understood her son wasn't just another statistic, a name on their forms. He would never have a chance now to show the world who he was. She had to speak for him. 'We both liked the name Noah. We wanted something old-fashioned.'

'And he was born on the third of February this year?'

Lucas nodded.

'There were no problems with the pregnancy or birth? No complications during labour or delivery?'

'No, none.'

The doctor ran through a series of routine questions about Noah's birth and the first few weeks of his short life. Maddie tuned him out, letting Lucas answer all of them. She found herself unable to concentrate on what the doctor was saying. The questions were pointless anyway. Apart from colic, Noah had never had a single thing wrong with him, not even a cold. Her pregnancy had been ridiculously easy, and Noah had had a normal birth, her labour taking less than four hours from her waters breaking to his delivery. She hadn't even needed an epidural. She was good at having babies. Shelled them like peas, her mother said.

'Maddie,' Lucas murmured, squeezing her hand.

They were all looking at her. Clearly, someone had asked her a question.

'I'm sorry,' she said thickly. 'Could you say that again?'

'I know it's difficult, Mrs Drummond. I'd just like you to walk me through the last time you saw Noah alive.'

Oh, God, Maddie thought, spots dancing in front of her eyes. *Oh, God.* She was never going to see him open his eyes again. Never see him smile ...

'Maddie,' the bereavement counsellor interjected suddenly. 'Would you like to step into the bathroom for a moment to tidy up?'

'You're leaking,' Lucas murmured.

She glanced down. The entire front of her T-shirt and fleece were soaked with breast milk.

The counsellor led her to a small en suite bathroom at the back of the room and shut the door behind them. Maddie stood mutely as the older woman unzipped her fleece and gently pulled her soaked T-shirt over her head as if she were a child. It was like her body was crying, the milk running down her skin in an unstoppable flood of tears.

'Here, love, use this towel,' Jessica said, as Maddie unhooked her sodden maternity bra. 'I'm going to find you a clean T-shirt and bra from our donations box. Would you like me to see if I can find you a breast pump, so you can express a bit, just to tide you over?'

Maddie nodded. When Jessica slipped discreetly out of the room, Maddie sank onto the closed lavatory seat, pressing the towel against her chest. What was she supposed to do with all this milk now? You couldn't just stop breastfeeding overnight. When Jacob had been nine months old, he suddenly refused to nurse and she'd ended up with mastitis. It'd been agony. Emily had been so much easier. She'd been able to wean her gradually, tapering the number of her feeds over a period of weeks. She'd have to do the same now, she supposed, expressing just enough milk to keep from getting engorged, until her milk flow dried up naturally. She realised with a nauseating sense of horror she'd effectively be weaning a dead baby.

The counsellor returned a few minutes later with the promised clothes and a hand-held plastic breast pump. 'If you're wondering what to do with it, there's a milk bank here at the hospital,' she said gently, as if she'd read Maddie's mind. 'They use it for premature babies in the NICU. You could donate your milk, if you wanted. It wouldn't be wasted.'

Maddie nodded, not trusting herself to speak. The idea of expressing milk for a dead child was more than she could bear.

Jessica left her alone in the bathroom and she pumped off just enough to relieve the fiery heat in her breasts. When she was done, she put on the bra and plain white

T-shirt Jessica had found for her and returned to the grief room. Another man had joined the doctor and Lucas while she'd been gone. She knew immediately he was a policeman, despite the raincoat he'd tactfully buttoned up to hide his uniform.

'PC Tudhope is going to sit in, so we don't have to go through the same questions again later,' Lucas said.

'It's just a formality,' the constable added quickly. 'Please, it's not my intention to intrude on your grief or suggest any wrongdoing on your part at all.'

'It's fine,' Maddie said dully.

'Mr Drummond has explained that he was away for work until this morning,' the doctor said, picking up his file again. 'So perhaps you could start by saying how Noah seemed to you yesterday?'

'He seemed fine,' she said helplessly.

'Was he eating normally? Did he show any signs of distress at all? Did you notice if he had a temperature?'

'His temperature was normal. I know, because I checked it twice. Emily and Jacob – our other two children – they both have chickenpox, so I thought he might get sick, but he didn't have a fever and he took all his normal feeds. He seemed fine,' she said again.

The doctor looked up from his notes. 'Your other children have chickenpox?'

'Emily came down with it a few days ago, and then Jacob the day before yesterday. Why? Is that what—'

'We can't rule anything out at this stage,' the doctor said, gently cutting her off. 'So, what time did he go down for the night?'

'His last feed was around ten. He doesn't usually settle properly after it, because he has colic. I'll put him down, but he doesn't really sleep for more than a few minutes at a time. He cries for hours, sometimes. Nothing seems to help.' She glanced at Lucas as if for confirmation, and he took her hand and squeezed it. 'We've tried everything: colic tablets, gripe water, rubbing his back, a warm hot-water bottle on his tummy, massage, everything. I've even tried changing my diet and cutting out dairy and anything spicy, in case it's something in my milk upsetting him. I asked my doctor if it might be my antidepressants, but he said they wouldn't affect it. The only thing that seems to help Noah is walking up and down the corridor with him. You can't even sit down, or he starts crying again.'

It suddenly occurred to her she was still speaking about her son in the present tense. But she didn't have to worry about Noah crying anymore. Nothing would ever upset him again.

The policeman's expression sharpened. 'You're on antidepressants, Mrs Drummond?'

'I had postnatal depression after Jacob,' she said, wondering if he would judge her for it. 'I've been on them ever since.'

'My wife hasn't had a depressive episode in nearly two years,' Lucas interjected quickly.

The doctor made a notation on his pad. 'Was Noah's colic worse than usual last night?' he asked.

'No!' Maddie exclaimed. 'That's the thing! He didn't have colic! He didn't cry at all!'

'Did you think that odd?'

'I thought maybe he'd finally outgrown it. Doctors call it hundred-day colic, don't they?' she asked desperately. 'He's not quite ten weeks old, but I thought maybe he was growing out of it a week or two early, like Jacob did. I didn't go in to check on him because I didn't want to wake him. Jacob's colic was never as bad as Noah's, but—'

'You didn't check on him?' Lucas interrupted. 'All night?'

Maddie hesitated. How could she admit she hadn't checked on their son because she'd been worried sick about why her husband had borrowed some money without telling her? How utterly trivial and unimportant it seemed now. 'I was just so grateful he'd stopped crying, I didn't even think why,' she said wretchedly.

'In most cases like this, there's nothing you could have done even if you'd checked him every ten minutes,' the doctor said gently. 'I know it's easy for me to say, but please don't blame yourself.'

The constable leaned forward. 'Mrs Drummond, just so I can be absolutely sure of the timeline: you put him to bed around ten last night, and he seemed perfectly fine, everything normal. And then you didn't look in on him again until this morning, at around seven-thirty, when you found him?'

It didn't matter how nicely they said it. She hadn't bothered to see if her baby was all right because she'd been too thankful he wasn't crying. All that time she'd been praying he wouldn't wake up, he'd been lying in his cot, cold and dead.

'I didn't set my alarm, because Noah usually wakes me long before I need to get up,' she said, anguished. 'As soon as I woke up, I went to check on him, but—'

'No one's blaming you,' the doctor said again.

'You were the one looking after the children yesterday? They weren't with a childminder or relative?' the constable asked.

'No, I stayed home with them because Emily and Jacob were sick.'

The constable glanced briefly at Lucas, his expression considering, and then back at Maddie. 'No one else was there to help you, Mrs Drummond?'

'Candace – that's Lucas's sister – she stopped by for about half an hour mid-morning. She helped settle Noah down when he woke up, actually, but other than that, it was just me all day.'

'We'll need to speak to your sister, sir,' the constable said.

Lucas nodded. 'I can give you her number.'

There was a knock at the door. A woman with dark red hair peered in and signalled to the constable, who got up and exchanged a few words with her in the doorway.

'Can we see Noah now?' Maddie begged the doctor. 'Please. I can't bear to think of him on his own.'

'He won't be on his own,' Jessica reassured her. 'I'll take you to him in a few minutes, as soon as we're done.'

Maddie saw the constable glance over his shoulder at them. He finished his conversation with the red-haired woman and she left. Something in the constable's demeanour had changed when he took his seat again; a subtle professional shift which reminded Maddie that beneath the tactful raincoat, he still wore a police uniform.

'It seems a doctor has examined your baby and found considerable bruising to the side of his head,' he said, his tone carefully neutral. 'Would you mind explaining that?'

Chapter 11

Saturday 11.00 a.m.

The policeman had addressed both of them, but Maddie felt as if every pair of eyes in the room was directed at her.

'What bruises?' she exclaimed, knowing exactly what they meant.

'On his forehead and left cheek,' the constable said, indicating their location on his own face. 'Two long heavy marks running in parallel, quite clearly delineated. They would have been obvious to you, I'm sure.'

Lucas's expression cleared. 'Oh, that. He got wedged against the side of the cot a couple of days ago.' He looked at Maddie. 'Remember? Those red marks on the side of his face from the bars?'

She felt like she was going to be sick. She'd lied about those marks on the spur of the moment, because she hadn't wanted Lucas to think she was getting ill again. It'd taken so long for him to trust her properly again. Even after her depression had finally lifted, she'd seen the flicker of doubt in his eyes every time he left her alone with the children. She simply hadn't been able to face putting it there again.

How could she have known that one stupid, pointless lie might return to haunt her? But if she admitted it now, Lucas would never forgive her. And what did it really matter, in the end? It had nothing to do with what had happened to Noah.

'They'd almost gone,' she protested. 'They weren't really bruises, anyway, just pressure marks. You could hardly see them.'

'There may have been considerably more bruising beneath the skin,' the doctor said. 'It might not have become evident until after death, when the body stops healing itself. It's certainly possible the marks could have become more pronounced post-mortem than you remember.'

'But it happened days ago!' Maddie cried, aghast. 'He's been perfectly fine since then. That couldn't have caused ... it couldn't have caused ...'

The doctor's eyes filled with pity. 'We won't know until we've had a chance to examine him properly, I'm afraid.'

Maddie felt like she was going to pass out. She'd killed her baby. She'd dropped him and then she'd covered it up. She'd lied to her husband and slept while her baby died alone.

The policeman wrote something down in his note-book. 'Can you tell me exactly what happened for him to get those marks, Mr Drummond?'

'I wasn't there. Maddie told me what had happened the next morning.'

'Perhaps you could explain, then, Mrs Drummond?'

There was no inflection in his voice, but again Maddie felt the weight of the unspoken accusation. She had to tell them the truth. If there was any chance at all that Noah's accident had killed him, she had to admit what had really happened now. They'd understand she hadn't meant to hurt him. Even if they didn't, what was the worst they could do? Throw her in jail? It didn't matter. Nothing mattered now.

Except her children. She thought suddenly of Emily and Jacob, waiting for her to come home, scared and anxious. Jacob might not understand what was happening, but Emily would. They needed her. She should never have lied in the first place, but there was no going back now. If she told this policeman the truth, how did she know they wouldn't arrest her, there and then? She couldn't help Noah now, but she could help Emily and Jacob.

'He got himself wedged in the corner of the cot during the night,' she said, trying to still her nerves. 'He gets very restless at night because of his colic. He was perfectly fine,' she added quickly. 'His cheek was just a bit red for a day or so, that's all.'

'Was his neck or head constricted at any point? Between the bars or in the gap between the side of the cot and the mattress, for example?'

'No. He'd just wriggled himself into a corner, that's all.'

The constable nodded. Maddie had no idea if he believed her or not.

'I realise you all have a job to do, but my wife has explained what happened,' Lucas said, with quiet dignity. 'We've just lost our son. We need to get home to our other children. If you have any more questions, we'd be happy to answer them another time, but for now, we just want to say goodbye to our baby and go home to grieve with our family.'

The police constable got to his feet. 'Of course. My sergeant says they've finished at your house, so you're free to return. Again, Mr and Mrs Drummond, my very deepest condolences on your loss.'

'I'm afraid I have to return to my rounds,' the doctor said. 'Jessica will take you to see Noah and explain the procedure from here. If you have any questions, please feel free to come and find me at any time.' He extended his hand first to Lucas and then Maddie. 'I really am so very sorry.'

'Can you just tell me ... would he ... would he have suffered?' she asked quietly.

'No. No, it would have been very quick. I doubt he'd even have woken up. He wouldn't have felt any pain.'

Maddie flinched. He might not have felt pain, but he'd died alone. The thought shredded her heart. She should have been there with him. She'd failed him when he'd needed her most.

Once they were alone, Jessica opened her folder and handed Lucas a small booklet. 'I'm afraid there's an awful lot of paperwork associated with death,' she said apologetically. 'This should help you through the majority of it. Unfortunately, you won't be able to register Noah's

83

death until after the inquest.' She gave Maddie another leaflet. 'The Lullaby Trust offers support to families after the death of a child. They're wonderful, and I recommend getting in touch with them when you feel ready. You can call their helpline any time and they have a number of online forums for parents who are in the same situation as you. They also have a network of parents who have lost a child in the past and have been trained to offer support to those similarly bereaved.'

'There's so much to take in,' Maddie said.

Jessica smiled sadly. 'I know. The review booklet in your packet outlines the steps you have to go through and will answer many of your questions. I'll give you my contact details and, of course, you can get in touch any time.'

'What about the funeral?' Lucas asked. 'When can we arrange that?'

'Not until after the inquest, I'm afraid.'

Maddie felt the room swim. 'He has to stay here till then?'

'I'm afraid so.'

'Can we at least bring our other children here to say goodbye to him?' asked Lucas.

'No!' Maddie exclaimed.

'Actually, Maddie, we do recommend siblings be allowed to see their brother or sister,' the counsellor said gently. 'Children are very literal. They need to see what death means. It helps them understand what's happened and that the baby has really died and isn't coming back.'

Maddie choked back a sob. Lucas reached for her hand and she gripped his fingers, too distraught to speak.

Jessica picked up her folder. 'If you'd like, I can also make footprints of his hands and feet, as keepsakes. Would you like a lock of his hair as a memento? I can arrange that, too.'

'Yes, we'd like that,' Lucas said hoarsely, as Maddie nodded.

'I'll have everything sent on to you,' Jessica said. 'If you're ready, I'll take you to see him now.'

Maddie clutched Lucas's hand as they followed Jessica back through the hospital foyer towards the lifts. All these people going about their normal daily lives. Queueing for coffee, reading newspapers, checking emails, as if nothing had happened. As if her baby hadn't just died. That woman dragging her screaming toddler away from the sweet counter in the hospital gift shop had no idea how lucky she was that her little girl was still alive. Right now, she was probably wondering why she'd bothered having children. She didn't realise the happiness she took for granted could be snatched away in an instant.

A couple with a newborn in a plastic car seat followed them into the crowded lift, wearing the proud, self-conscious expressions of new parents. The young mother fussed with the baby's blue blanket, tucking it tightly around his crumpled red face. *It doesn't matter what you do*, Maddie wanted to tell her, *you can't keep your baby safe. You can do everything right: you can keep his head warm*

85

and test his bathwater with your elbow and put him to sleep
on his back and keep small parts out of reach and it still won't
be enough. It will never be enough, because while you're
sleeping, death can steal your baby without you even knowing.

Lucas saw her staring. He moved to block her view and she buried her face in his chest. Her legs shook and she would have fallen if he hadn't held her.

When the lift doors opened, Jessica led them along a labyrinth of hospital corridors and then stopped by a plain, unmarked door. 'I want you to prepare yourselves,' she said quietly. 'It's going to be a shock, seeing him again.'

'Can we hold him?' Lucas asked.

'If you'd like to. It can be very upsetting for some parents. He won't be warm, the way you expect. But you can spend as much time with him as you need. After you've gone, I'll take the hand and footprints and a lock of his hair. You can bring your other children back later today or tomorrow to say goodbye to him. There's a very helpful leaflet in the packet I handed you about explaining death to very young children.'

Lucas turned to Maddie. 'Are you sure you want to do this?'

She nodded bravely, her chest suddenly tight. Her breath was coming in shallow gasps. It took every ounce of her resolve not to turn and run away.

Jessica opened the door. The room was bright and well-lit, painted a soft lilac with a frieze of white lilies running midway around the wall. A matching blind filtered sunshine from the small window. It reminded

Maddie achingly of the hospital room she'd had when Noah was born.

Summoning all her courage, she gripped Lucas's hand and approached the small transparent cot in the centre of the room. It looked exactly like the ones in the maternity ward. A tiny figure lay swaddled in the middle of it. The stillness in the room was tangible. This wasn't a child who was sleeping. The essence that had been Noah had palpably gone.

Maddie gazed down at the pale white face, as cold and inanimate as a carving. Two livid purple bruises stood out shockingly against his blue-white skin and she wondered how she could have not noticed them before. He looked like a little waxwork doll, not human at all.

And finally she understood her baby was dead.

Lydia

She's never seen Mae this angry. Her mother shouts so loud that spit comes out of her mouth and her eyes almost pop out of her head. Do you know what you've put me through, you little cunt? Bowing and scraping to them stuck-up bastards to get you back. Just to keep a bleeding roof over me head!

Mae makes her take off the dress Jean gave her, and the shoes, and refuses to let her put on her old clothes, so she has to sit, shivering, in the corner of the room in her underwear. You think you're better than me, do you, with your fancy airs and graces and your posh dresses, you'd better think again, you're nothing without me, nothing, do you hear me, you little piece of shit?

The gloomy house seems even darker and more scary now. It smells bad and there are mice and spiders everywhere. Every night, she cries herself to sleep on the bare scratchy mattress, trying not to think about the pink sheets or the way Jean used to stroke her hair and tuck her into bed. It doesn't take long for the hunger pangs to come back, gnawing away at her insides. When Mae beats her for sneaking downstairs for a drink of water, she doesn't even bother to protect herself. She just wants it to be over.

Mae has so many special friends these days, she can't keep track. They don't just come at night, now, they come at all hours, with their big bellies and greasy hair and their way of looking at her that makes her skin feel itchy like it's covered with bugs. She sees them giving Mae money sometimes and cigarettes.

One day, she goes to the bathroom and walks in on one of the men, bare-chested, doing up his trousers. She sees his *thing*, it's all white, unnaturally white, like a strange pale worm curled up in a nest of brown hair, and she can't stop staring even though it makes her feel sick to look at it. He laughs, do you want some girlie, you want some of this? and she turns and runs out of the bathroom.

But Mae is waiting. How much? Mae asks the man. He laughs again, but Mae doesn't laugh, her eyes narrow and her face gets that *look*, like when she strangled the ducks in the bath with her bare hands. Come on Jimmy, how much?

Time to earn your keep, Mae tells her. She drags her by the hair into her bedroom, and it smells bad in here, sweaty and damp and something else, something that makes her wrinkle her nose in disgust. Mae's never let her come in here before. There is a red scarf thrown over the lamp on the dresser and strange pictures on the walls. She tries to free herself from Mae, she has a really bad feeling in the pit of her stomach – *danger*

danger – but Mae smacks her around the head so hard her ears ring and she feels dizzy, and the man is here and the two of them pick her up and toss her on the bed as if she is as light as a kitten.

Then Mae leaves her alone with the man, and she starts to cry, she's scared, *so scared*, and she tries to scramble away across the bed, but the man is too quick for her, he catches her by her skinny ankle and drags her back across the bed and pins her down, and she closes her eyes tight, tight. If she keeps them shut, maybe none of this will be real.

She'll wake up in her pretty bed with the pink sheets and none of this will be real.

Chapter 12

Saturday noon

She couldn't stop screaming. She refused to look at the cold, dead baby in the crib, the full enormity of her loss finally hitting home. Lucas wrapped his arms around her, but she thrashed against him, unable and unwilling to be comforted. In the end, one of the doctors prescribed some kind of tranquilliser for her, Valium or Xanax, by this stage Maddie didn't care; she simply took what they gave her, praying it'd knock her out, praying she'd wake up and find this had all been a hideous nightmare, nothing but a bad dream.

But everything stayed savagely real. She and Lucas left the hospital without Noah, her arms horribly empty, travelling home together in silence in the back of a taxi. Mercifully, the driver didn't try to talk to them, depositing them outside their house with a sympathetic discretion that suggested he'd worked the hospital route before.

Maddie glanced up at the nursery window as they got out of the cab. It was still thrown open from where she must have flung it wide to shout down to Lucas for help.

Was that really just six hours ago? Already, it seemed to belong to a different life.

The house was grimly quiet when they let themselves in. Emily and Jacob were at her mother's and the police had gone. It all seemed so eerily normal. Dirty plates from last night still lay soaking in greasy water in the sink. Damp washing sat in a plastic laundry basket, waiting to go into the dryer. Sarah had put Noah's changing bag away out of sight, but his bottles were still lined up on the kitchen windowsill and his bouncer remained in its usual place in a safe, draught-free corner of the kitchen, his favourite blanket folded neatly across it ready for him.

Maddie snatched it up and buried her face in it.

Lucas touched her shoulder. 'Darling, don't. You'll just make it worse.'

She raised her head. 'How?' she said dully. 'How could it be *worse*?'

Shrugging him away, she drifted through the silent house, roaming from room to room, randomly picking things up and putting them down as if she'd never seen them before. Nothing seemed familiar. Lucas followed her, but didn't try to comfort her again.

'Don't,' he repeated, as she reached the foot of the stairs.

She ignored him, heading upstairs to Noah's nursery. 'You can turn this room back into your office, if you like,' she said over her shoulder as he followed her. 'I know how much you've hated having to share the downstairs study with me.'

'Maddie ...'

'Or we could make this into a spare room. It's a bit small, but you can fit a single bed in here and a dresser, once we get rid of Noah's changing table. And the rocking chair,' she added, her voice suddenly bitter. 'I want that chair out of the house.'

She yanked open the little blue chest of drawers and grabbed a neat pile of Babygros and threw them on the floor and then opened a second drawer and started emptying that too.

Lucas shut the drawer. 'Leave this.'

'You can take the stair-gate down, now. Noah's never going to need it, and it makes getting up and down the stairs so awkward when your arms are full of clean washing.'

'You're in shock, Maddie. Please, come back downstairs.'

'The world doesn't just stop because Noah died. Things still need to get done. Someone has to sort them out.'

She wrenched the drawers open again and emptied their contents onto the floor. She didn't know if it was shock, like Lucas said, or the medication they'd given her, but she was completely, blessedly, numb. She had to get rid of Noah's clothes and toys, she had to erase every sign he'd ever existed, now, while she still could. She didn't know if she would survive the pain of walking into Noah's nursery, of seeing all his things still here, once that numbness wore off.

She crouched down and began to pull sheets and blankets and towels off the shelf beneath Noah's changing table, until Lucas knelt beside her and put his hands on hers.

'Maddie, *please*. You have to stop.'

Maddie stilled. 'I'm afraid to stop,' she whispered.

'I know.'

'If I stop, I might have time to think.'

'I know,' he said again.

'How can he be gone, Lucas?' she asked, bewildered. 'How can this have happened?'

'I thought we were safe now,' Lucas said thickly. 'I thought, we've had our share of grief and tragedy. That's it now. I lost both my parents; you lost Benjamin. I thought at least that meant we were owed some good luck. At least it meant the children would be safe.'

She had no room for pity. She knew that when the drugs wore off, the pain would return. It was actual, physical, as if her chest had been sliced open and her heart smashed into a thousand pieces. Heartbroken was no longer a metaphor but a description.

'How do we survive this?' she whispered. 'How do we even get up tomorrow morning?'

'We get up tomorrow because we don't have a choice. Emily and Jacob need us.'

She extricated herself from his arms and stood up stiffly. She couldn't even begin to imagine how to tell their children that their brother had died. She rested her hands on the rail of Noah's cot, staring at the mattress as if she could still see him there. 'I was the one looking after him. I was the one who let him down. You weren't even here.'

'I should have been!' Lucas shouted suddenly. 'I should have been here!'

'It wouldn't have made any difference.'

'How do you *know*?'

She looked at him. 'Are you saying there's something you could have done, that I didn't?'

His shoulders sagged, the fight suddenly leaving him. 'No,' he said wretchedly. 'No, of course not.'

'We can't keep doing this, Lucas. It's going to tear us apart.'

Even as she said the words, she wondered if it was already too late. You were born alone and you died alone. And now she realised you grieved alone, too.

Chapter 13

Sunday 6.30 a.m.

Maddie opened her eyes, and for a few merciful moments, as she hovered between sleep and wakefulness, she'd forgotten. And then remembrance slammed into her like a freight train.

She hadn't known how savagely physical grief was. Losing Benjamin had been bad, but it was nothing compared to this. Her body felt brutalised. She curled herself into a tight ball, hugging her knees to her chest, and pressed her pillow over her ears as if she could use it to block out her thoughts. If she could just get back to sleep, maybe she'd wake up again in her own life, instead of a nightmare that belonged to somebody else.

Her breasts were burning. It was time for Noah's feed. Except Noah was dead.

She threw back the covers and ran into the bathroom, retching violently into the lavatory bowl. She hadn't eaten in thirty-six hours; she was bringing up nothing but bile. She couldn't block the image in her head of Noah lying cold and white and still in that hideous plastic crib. Try as she might, she couldn't summon an image of her son alive.

She rocked back on her bare heels and wiped her mouth with the back of her hand. The phone was ringing, but she ignored it. She couldn't imagine going to answer it. She couldn't imagine leaving this bathroom at all.

The ringing stopped. She heard the muffled sound of Lucas's voice as he spoke to someone, and moments later, he appeared in the bathroom doorway. He'd pulled on a pair of jeans and a cotton sweater, but he looked haggard and unkempt and at least twenty years older than yesterday. She'd never seen him unshaven, she thought irrelevantly. She hadn't realised he was going so grey.

'That was the hospital on the phone,' he said.

She looked at him blankly.

He rubbed his hand over his stubble. 'They said if we want to take Emily and Jacob in, we need to go today.'

'What for?'

'To see Noah,' Lucas said bleakly. 'We talked about this yesterday, Maddie. The children need to see him, so they can say goodbye. It'll help them understand what's happened and that he isn't coming back.'

'No. I'm not ready.'

Lucas hesitated. 'They have to conduct a post-mortem,' he said finally. 'It's a sudden death. They don't have any choice. It's ... it's better if Emily and Jacob see him now. Before.'

A noise like the sound of a thousand bees filled her

97

head and she reached out for the cold porcelain solidity of the lavatory, her knuckles whitening. A post-mortem. They were going to cut her baby up. Cut into his fragile little body with their sharp knives and scalpels, dig around his insides, saw open his skull and cut out his heart.

'I can't,' she whispered. 'I can't have them hurt him. They can't touch our baby, Lucas.'

'It's not Noah anymore,' Lucas said miserably. 'It's just the husk of him. The wrapping he came in. The real Noah is with us, in our hearts. No one can touch that.'

'I can't remember what he looks like,' she said suddenly. 'I keep trying to picture him, and I can't remember what he looks like.' Her voice had an edge of panic. 'I keep seeing him in that room. Cold and white and dead. I don't want to do that to Emily and Jacob. I don't want that to be the way they remember him.'

'They need to understand what's happened, Maddie. We can't hide it from them. Maybe it's good that Noah doesn't look like he's asleep, even if it is a bit scary. They need to know the difference between death and sleeping, so they're not terrified every time they go to bed.'

'They don't need to know about death!' she cried. 'They're nine and two years old!'

'Maddie, I don't want them to know about death either. At their age, they shouldn't have to deal with anything more traumatic than the death of a goldfish.' He crouched down beside her. 'But I've been through this. I was thirteen when my parents died and I couldn't make sense of it until my Aunt Dot took me to see them in the funeral home. It was smoke that'd killed them, not the fire, so it was OK. They weren't burned. They didn't look like they were sleeping, they looked like they were dead, but I could handle that. It made sense.' He touched her cheek, turning her to look at him. 'Candace was only four, and everyone thought she was too young to see them. They thought it'd give her nightmares. Aunt Dot told her they were dead, but Candace thought that just meant they'd gone away somewhere. She waited for years for them to come back, long after she'd stopped asking for them. I think a part of her is still waiting.'

She knew Lucas was right: even after all this time, Candace had never really turned the page on the traumatic events of her childhood. Perhaps seeing her parents in death, however dreadful, would have helped her to accept they had truly gone. Maddie didn't know what was best for Emily and Jacob, but she trusted Lucas on this.

'I can't bear it,' she whimpered. 'I can't bear that they have to deal with this.'

'You don't have to go in with them. I'll do it.'

She clasped his hand against her cheek. 'We should both do it. It'll be the last time we're together as a family, all five of us. I want to be there.'

She nearly changed her mind when they arrived at the hospital, where Lucas had arranged for her mother to meet them with the children. She'd only managed to get there at all by focusing on one simple task at a time, refusing to let herself look even a single step ahead. *Find underwear. Pull on sweater. Drink the coffee Lucas is thrusting into my hand.* Don't think about what comes next. One step at a time, one foot in front of the other. Just do what needs to be done. Don't think, don't think at all.

Lucas stopped at the entrance to the hospital car park and opened his window to take a ticket. He circled the multistorey until he found a free parking bay at the end of a row, near the wall.

'Maddie, are you coming?'

Unbuckle seat belt. Get out of car.

But she couldn't move.

Lucas closed his door again. 'You don't have to come in, Maddie. You can wait here while I take them.'

'Give me a minute,' she managed. She couldn't make him do everything on his own. How he'd found the strength to get them this far, she didn't know, but she couldn't let him down now.

She forced herself to get out of the car.

Sarah was waiting with Emily and Jacob in the hospital lobby near the gift shop. As soon as the children saw them, they shouted and ran over. Lucas scooped Jacob into his arms, while Emily threw herself at Maddie, wrapping her arms around her mother's waist and burying her face against her stomach.

'How have they been?' Lucas asked quietly.

'Jacob doesn't understand,' Sarah said. 'Hardly

surprising, at his age. He's asked for Maddie a bit more than usual, but that's all. Emily hasn't said much since I told her. She's been very quiet.'

At the mention of her name, Emily raised her head from her mother's waist. 'Mummy, can we go home now?'

'In a little while. I promise.'

She spotted Jessica, the bereavement counsellor, coming across the hospital lobby, another clutch of folders and paperwork in her hands. Jessica greeted them and introduced herself to Sarah and then dropped into a crouch so that she was on eye level with the children. 'And you two must be Emily and Jacob,' she said. 'I have a couple of books for you to read later that I thought you might like.'

'Mine!' Jacob exclaimed, bouncing in Lucas's arms.

Jessica smiled. 'They have lots of pictures. Let me see if I can find some crayons so you can colour them in.'

'Are we going to see Noah now?' Emily asked.

Maddie felt her heart turn over. The closest her little girl should be coming to death was the tiny mouse corpses the cat left as a gift at the foot of the stairs. Right now, Emily should be out playing in the sunshine or watching some nonsense on her phone – anything but saying goodbye to her dead baby brother in a hospital morgue.

'Remember what I told you?' Sarah asked her grand-daughter, as they all followed Jessica. 'Noah isn't really Noah anymore. He won't look the same. The bit that makes him Noah isn't there. It's like when you turn off your computer. You can still touch the screen and the keys, but nothing will happen and the screen won't light up. It's just an empty box.'

'I don't believe in Heaven,' Emily said unexpectedly. 'If there was a Heaven, NASA would have found it by now.'

'How do you know about NASA?' Lucas asked.

She shot him a look of contempt. 'We did it in school. The International Space Station is way higher than Heaven. They've put robots on Mars and taken photos all the way out to Saturn and Jupiter. No way would they have missed Heaven if it was there.'

'It's not a place you can travel to, like Mars or Jupiter,' her grandmother said. 'It's not really a place at all. It's more like another dimension.'

'Doctor Who can travel through dimensions,' Emily said thoughtfully, as the lift doors opened. 'Maybe Heaven is just a different dimension, where Noah is still alive. I'm not buying God, though,' she added firmly. 'No way would God let so many bad things happen in the world, like polar bears getting extinct. He'd have to be a pretty mean person, if he was real.'

Maddie had never been religious. Sarah was an atheist, in a low-key way; she'd brought her daughter up to be curious and open-minded about everything, including the existence of a God she didn't believe in herself. Maddie had been agnostic before, not really believing in anything very much, other than the general idea of 'something out there', but she refused to countenance the idea that she'd never see Noah again, in this or any other life; she had to believe her child would be returned to her one day or she'd go mad. But that meant accepting there was a God and that he had deliberately allowed her baby to die.

'I like your idea,' she said, giving her daughter a fierce hug. 'Noah's not in Heaven, he's in another dimension. We just can't see him right now.'

'I hope he's not crying so much there,' Emily sighed.

Jessica showed them into the same lilac room they'd visited before. Lucas went in first, carrying Jacob, and Sarah followed, holding Emily's hand. Maddie noticed her mother stiffen slightly when she saw Noah's still form in the plastic crib, but her composure didn't slip.

Jacob looked around the room, clearly bewildered. 'Where Noah?'

'He's here, Jakey,' Lucas said, moving closer to the plastic cot so the little boy could see down into it. 'Do you want to say goodbye?'

'Where Noah?' he asked again, confused.

'Noah's right here, Jacob. Look.'

Jacob lurched violently in his father's arms, squirming away from the crib and burying his face in his father's shoulder. 'Not Noah! Not Noah!'

'He's right here, son …'

'Not Noah!'

'Take him back outside,' Maddie cried over Jacob's screams. 'It's upsetting him. He doesn't understand.'

Emily hadn't moved since her first sight of her brother. She stared at his small body, her expression curious rather than distressed. 'He doesn't look like Noah,' she pronounced. 'That's why Jacob doesn't understand. He looks like a doll.'

'Remember what I told you about the computer?' Sarah asked.

'What's that purple mark on his face?'

Sarah put her arm around her granddaughter as Emily peered into the crib. 'He got squashed up against the side of his cot a few days ago, remember? It gave him a bit of a bruise, that's all.'

'Is that why he died?'

Maddie flinched. That stupid lie was going to haunt her forever. Noah's accident couldn't have had anything to do with his death, she was sure of it. Only not quite sure enough.

'We don't know why he died,' Jessica said gently. 'The doctors will try to find out, Emily, but sometimes it just happens. Something is broken inside a baby and we just don't know what it is.'

'I don't see how he got such a big bruise just from squashing up against his cot,' Emily shrugged. 'Are you sure he didn't get stuck, Mummy?'

'I don't know,' Maddie said faintly.

Emily nodded firmly. 'I think that's what it is. I think he got his head stuck and that's why he died.' She slipped her hand into her mother's and looked up, her blue eyes filled with anxiety. 'Please, Mummy. I promise I won't get my head stuck and die. Can we go home now?'

Chapter 14

Tuesday 2.00 p.m.

Maddie didn't even glance up when she heard a vehicle pull into the driveway. There had been a steady stream of flowers arriving for the past two days; the front of the house was starting to look like Kensington Palace after Princess Diana had died. Lucas refused to let her bring any of the bouquets inside. He'd always loathed cut flowers; he said they reminded him of the banks that had filled his aunt's house after his parents died. She understood now what he meant. She didn't think she'd be able to smell flowers again without thinking of death.

She picked up another card from the pile on her desk. Everyone was being so kind. There were dozens of letters and cards, not just from friends and neighbours, but from people she barely knew, colleagues from Lucas's office, parents of children in Emily's class, friends she hadn't spoken to in years. Most of them didn't really know what to say, falling back on the same familiar clichés Maddie herself had relied on in similar circumstances in the past: *time is a great healer, he's in a better place, at least he didn't feel any pain.* But she supposed it wasn't what they said that really mattered. It was the fact they'd cared enough to try.

Jayne had come round to be with her as soon as Sarah had broken the news, but Maddie hadn't been able to face her. She wasn't ready to see anyone yet, to deal with their awkwardness and pity, not even Jayne. She was beginning to realise she was now part of an exclusive club, a club no one ever wanted to join. She was a mother who had lost her child and that set her apart from everyone else. It was like an invisible wall had gone up around her, cutting her off from the life she'd known.

There was the sound of running footsteps overhead, then a thump, followed by wailing. She heard Lucas run up the stairs, calling out that he was coming. She should go too, but she didn't have the will to move. It took an effort just to keep breathing. She'd wanted to send Emily back to school and Jacob to nursery yesterday, to try to maintain some semblance of normality, but Lucas had insisted on keeping them both home. He said Emily and Jacob needed to be with their parents, but she suspected he was the one who needed them. He hadn't let them out of his sight since they'd come home.

She closed the card and stared at the angel pictured on the front, unable to connect it with Noah. He wasn't a cherub or an angel. He was her baby, her flesh-and-blood baby. Death hadn't changed that. She put the card aside and reached for another. Lucas sought refuge from his grief in the children, but she found their reaction to Noah's absence unbearable. When they'd got back from the hospital two days ago, Jacob had run from room to room looking for his brother, excitedly lifting sofa cushions and checking cupboards and peering beneath his bed, as if they were playing a game of hide-and-seek. Lucas had wretchedly reminded him they'd said goodbye to Noah in the hospital and Jacob had flown into a terrifying rage, sobbing and screaming that the 'white baby' in the hospital wasn't Noah. Maddie had shut herself in the study, unable to listen to Lucas having to explain it all again.

But Emily hadn't asked about Noah once, which worried Maddie more. Her daughter had been eerily cheerful, getting up early to make her own breakfast and playing with Jacob for hours – two things she never normally did except under strict protest. Maddie didn't know if her daughter was in denial or just terrified that if she didn't behave, something bad would happen to her, too.

At least her children's reactions were normal. Rage, denial, bargaining; these were all recognisable stages of grief. And ever since she'd returned home without her baby, Maddie hadn't been able to feel any of them. She was utterly detached from it all, as if it was happening to someone else. Intellectually, she understood the enormity of her loss. Her baby had died. For the rest of her life, a part of her heart would be missing. Every time she kissed her two living children goodnight, every time they had a birthday, at every Christmas and school play and Mother's Day and football game, she would be reminded afresh of the child she had lost. And yet she didn't even feel *sad*. She couldn't summon a single tear for the death of her own son.

The study door opened. 'Lucas told me I'd find you in here,' her mother said. Maddie hadn't even heard her arrive.

Maddie gestured towards the pile of cards and letters on her desk. 'People have been so kind. All these cards and letters. I don't even know half the people sending them. And the flowers. Did you see them outside? People have been bringing us meals, too. Leaving them on the doorstep. Shepherd's pie and lasagnes and stews. We can hardly get the freezer door shut.'

'It was the same after your father died,' Sarah said, sitting on the small love seat beneath the window. 'People don't know what to say, so they do what they can. But you don't have to read them all now. No one expects you to reply. Look at them later, when you're ready.'

'Listen to this: "There is no foot too small that it cannot leave an imprint on this world." Isn't that beautiful?' Maddie said.

'Yes, it is.'

'It's from Emily's teacher, look. She's got the whole class to sign it. How sweet of her.'

Sarah gently took the card from her. 'Lucas said you've been holed up in here all day. Yesterday, too.'

'There's so much to do. All these cards—'

'None of it needs to be done now.'

'Did you know we can't have a funeral?' Maddie asked abruptly. 'We can't bury him till after the inquest.'

'I know,' Sarah said steadily. A beat fell. 'Maddie, I know the pain you're in, but you can't hide in here forever. The children need you. Lucas needs you. Shutting them all out isn't going to help—'

Maddie had stopped listening. She couldn't think about Lucas or the children, because then she would have to think about carrying on for them, about finding a way to go back to being normal, when there *was* no normal, and never would be again. She had to distract herself, to keep busy. To think about anything but the thing she couldn't think about.

She grabbed another card. 'Oh, look at this one. I've always loved this poem. *Death is nothing at all. I have only slipped into the next room*—'

Then she read the signature at the bottom of the card.

'I need to get some air,' she said suddenly, dropping the card as if it burned. She stood up and grabbed her jacket from the back of her chair. 'I'm sorry, Mum. I have to get out of here. I'll be fine, don't worry. Tell Lucas I'll be back soon.'

Sarah picked up the card. 'Maddie? Who's Bill O'Connor?'

But she was already halfway out the door. She could hear her mother calling her name as she banged out of the house, but she didn't stop. She threw the Land Rover into gear and tore off down the drive without bothering to put on her seat belt, her own personal *fuck you* to the universe.

Was it really only four days since she'd spoken to her accountant? It seemed like a lifetime. She pitied the woman who had thought discovering her husband had borrowed money without telling her was the end of the world. The loan didn't matter anymore; it was so irrelevant she couldn't believe she'd ever cared about it. But the only way she was going to survive *the thing she couldn't think about* was with Lucas, and she couldn't do that if she couldn't trust him. She needed to clear her head, and there was only one thing that ever did that for her.

Ten minutes later, she was jolting over the long, muddy track into the sanctuary's yard. She parked and got out. The yard was deserted; it was another tauntingly beautiful spring day and she guessed Izzy and Bitsy had probably taken advantage of it and had gone hacking for the afternoon. She was relieved they weren't here, so she didn't have to face their kindness and sympathy.

There was a soft whicker from the end stall as she walked across the cobbles. 'Oh, Finn. I've missed you, boy,' Maddie sighed, as he poked his head over the half-door. She stroked his velvety nose. 'I could use your company. Fancy a ride?'

Finn whinnied and gently nuzzled her shoulder. She opened the stable door and he stood patiently as she tacked him up, shortening the stirrups and looping his bridle over the saddle as she led him out. She and Finn usually took a gentle route through the woods, but today she needed to feel the wind in her hair.

She mounted and guided Finn along the lower paddock towards the bridle path over the downs. There was a long section where she'd be able to give him free rein; it'd been a while since they'd enjoyed a good gallop together, but she sensed Finn was as ready for it as she was. She didn't bother with her hard hat, for the same reason she'd eschewed her seat belt.

Finn was already snatching at the bit as they reached the bridle path. She rose and fell in the saddle as he broke into a trot, the two of them moving in a perfect syncopation of movement and strength and energy. They complemented each other effortlessly. It was what she had always believed her marriage to Lucas was like.

The path suddenly widened as they came out of the trees. Finn's stride lengthened into a canter and then, as she let him have his head, a gallop. She shut out everything but the thunderous pounding of his hooves beneath her, the exhilarating, terrifying rush of the landscape around her, the fierce burn of the wind against her cheeks. For the first time in four days, the suffocating blackness lifted and she could almost breathe again.

When Finn finally pulled up, she collapsed against his neck, panting as if she'd been the one running. She kicked her feet free from the stirrups and slid off, burying her face against Finn's neck and inhaling the pungent smell of horse sweat.

Suddenly her grief hit her like a tidal wave, a tsunami of sorrow and loss. Raw, wrenching sobs tore through her with brutal savagery. She found herself gasping for air, choking on her own tears, and had to hang on to Finn just to stay standing.

When it was finally over, she straightened up and wiped her face with her sleeve. Her desolation and pain were unbearable and yet it was still better than the soul-sucking numbness of the last few days. She *wanted* to mourn Noah. Her grief was a mark of her love for her child.

Wearily, she put one foot in the stirrups and swung back into the saddle. She had taken the first step into *after*, but this was only the beginning, she knew that. She had a long road ahead yet and she didn't want to take it alone. She needed Lucas beside her. But she couldn't live with his lie hanging between them. Even if it meant the end of her marriage, she had to know the truth.

Chapter 15

Wednesday 8.00 a.m.

Maddie poured herself a cup of coffee and sat down at the kitchen table, waiting for Lucas to come downstairs. Her hands were shaking and she was sorely tempted to add a slug of whisky to her coffee. She hadn't slept in days. The doctor had given her sleeping pills, but she was reluctant to take them on top of the antidepressants she was already on. She was exhausted, which made it even harder to think. If she could just *focus*, she was sure she'd find a way to make sense of it all.

She'd arranged for her mother to take the children, so she and Lucas would have the house to themselves for a couple of hours. She desperately didn't want to have this conversation, but she had to clear the air, one way or another. Her mistrust had created a wall between them just when she needed him most.

She jumped as her husband thundered down the stairs and stormed into the kitchen. 'What the hell have you been doing in Noah's room?'

Maddie was taken aback. 'What?'

He slammed the flat of his hand on the table, spilling her coffee. 'First you get rid of all his clothes, and now *this*? It's obscene! It's like you're trying to pretend he never existed!'

'Lucas, please! What are you talking about?'

He was angrier than she'd ever seen him. 'Don't play dumb with me, Maddie. I know you're hurting. We're all hurting. But you don't get to make all the decisions without even *asking* me. He was my son, too! The least you could have done was talk to me first!'

She still had no idea what he meant.

Abruptly, he grabbed her wrist and yanked her up from the kitchen table so hard she nearly kicked over her chair. 'Lucas, stop! You're hurting me!'

He loosened his grip but didn't let go. 'I don't know what's going on in your head, Maddie, but you don't have exclusive rights to grief,' he said, propelling her up the stairs. 'What message do you think it sends Emily and Jacob, trying to wipe out all sign Noah existed? And like this! What the hell were you *thinking*?'

They reached the nursery and she gazed around in disbelief. The Winnie-the-Pooh frieze had been crudely scraped from the walls and now hung in tattered shreds against the chair rail. The beige carpet had been ripped away from the skirting, exposing the underlay and tacking. Most shockingly of all, a broad roller had been taken to the walls, covering the warm, creamy yellow Maddie had spent hours painting when she was newly pregnant, with broad, grotesque sweeps of dark red. To her appalled eyes, they looked like grisly splashes of dried blood.

Her hand flew to her mouth. 'Oh my God. What happened?'

He stared at her incredulously. 'What *happened*?'

'Who did this?' she whispered as she took in the ugly vandalism. '*Why*?'

'Don't mess with me, Maddie. I'm not in the mood.'

'I'm not—'

'I can't let the children see this!' Lucas shouted. 'It'll scare them half to death!'

The penny finally dropped. 'Lucas, you can't think – Lucas, I didn't do this!' She grabbed at his shirtsleeve. 'You can't think I'd do this!'

He shook himself free. 'Come on, Maddie. Who else would it be?'

She swung back to the walls. She recognised the ox-red paint; it was left over from the accent wall they'd tried out in the dining room a year ago. She hadn't liked it then, either. They'd repainted it a few months later in a softer shade of burnt umber.

She touched the paint. It hadn't quite dried; the walls had been painted within the last couple of hours, at the most. A feeling of dread gathered in the pit of her stomach. Even in one of her blackouts, she'd never have done something like this. She'd remember if she had. Wouldn't she?

'Someone else must have done it,' she said wildly, grasping at straws. 'A – a neighbour, or something. Jayne or Mum, even! I don't know! Maybe they were trying to help!'

'While we were asleep?' Lucas said incredulously. He

rubbed his face, the fight suddenly leaving him. 'Look, Maddie, there's no right or wrong way to deal with what we're going through. We're all having to find our way. I shouldn't have shouted at you, I'm sorry.' He sighed heavily. 'But I wish you'd just talk to me. You don't have to hole up in your office and shut me out. I love you. I want to help you, and I need you, too. I can't do this on my own.'

'But I didn't do it, Lucas,' she said tearfully.

'You have paint on your arm.'

She twisted her forearm up to look. Dried paint the colour of blood was smeared from wrist to elbow.

His expression softened. 'Look, maybe it's the drugs the doctor gave you. Perhaps you were sleepwalking when you did it, I don't know. Some kind of fugue state or something.' He pinched the bridge of his nose. 'I'm sorry I lost my rag. I shouldn't have yelled.'

She started to shake. How could she not remember doing something like this? This went beyond a few hours she couldn't recall. Even when she'd lost time before, she'd never done anything odd or out of character. This level of anger and violence – it wasn't her.

'I'm frightened, Lucas,' she whispered. 'It feels like I'm losing my mind.'

'You're in shock. Maybe this is your mind's way of dealing with the trauma. You're literally trying to obliterate what's happened.' He spread his hands helplessly. 'God, Maddie, I don't know how this works. Grief doesn't come with a rule book. I know you don't want to hear this, but maybe it's time to see Dr Calkins again. He'll know better than me how to help.'

'He'll just give me more pills,' she said bitterly.

'Perhaps that's not such a bad thing, if it'll help you feel more like yourself.'

'The tranquillisers turn me into a zombie. I can't think when I'm on them.'

'Maddie, you got up in the middle of the night and wrecked our son's bedroom and you don't even remember doing it! Please, we need to get ahead of this thing before it gets out of control. Tell me you'll at least talk to Dr Calkins.'

She stared up at the gory walls. The last thing she wanted was to disappear into the medicated, foggy numbness she'd fought so hard to escape after Jacob was born. But this loss of memory was worse than anything that'd gone before. This wasn't just one of her 'episodes'. She must have spent *hours* wrecking the nursery last night and she couldn't remember a single second of it. How was that even possible? She was terrified at the thought of what she might do next. Suppose she had a blackout when she was driving or out with the children somewhere? She might abandon them by the side of the road and have no recollection of it. She couldn't take the risk.

She nodded reluctantly.

He looked visibly relieved. 'We're going to get through this, Maddie.'

She shivered as she followed her husband back downstairs. She felt as if the ground was shifting beneath her feet. What was wrong with her? *Why* couldn't she remember? If she couldn't trust her own memory, there was no knowing what she might do.

Or what she might already have done.

The doorbell buzzed as they reached the hall.

'I'll get it,' Lucas said.

He opened the front door. Two police officers stood there. There were no sympathetic glances or kind smiles today.

One of the officers stepped forward. 'Mr and Mrs Drummond. We've had the results of the post-mortem on your son,' he said.

Lydia

She doesn't resist anymore. She knows there's no point screaming and crying, because they're just going to do it to her anyway. Some of them actually like it when she puts up a fight, and she refuses to give them the satisfaction. It's not much, but it's something; it's a way to salvage her pride.

Mae has to let her go to school now, the stupid cow from the social checks up that she attends, like she gives a damn what happens to her. But Lydia doesn't tell anyone what goes on at home. Don't you breathe a word, Mae says, or I'll skin you alive. She believes her, she knows what Mae's capable of, but that's not why she doesn't tell. She doesn't tell because, like Mae says, who'd believe a dirty little bitch like her? If they knew what she was really like, Mae says, how wicked she really was, they'd take her away and lock her up and throw away the key. She knows she must truly be the lost cause Mae says she is, or Jean would have come back for her, Davy would have come back for her.

She's not a baby anymore. She knows her own name

from school. She's eight years old and she understands how the world works now. You have to look out for number one, like Mae says, because nobody else is going to do it for you. She doesn't hate Mae for what she makes her do. Mae's just trying to survive, like everyone else. But the men – that's different. She hates the men with every ounce of her scrawny being.

The things they've done to her. Awful things, terrible things, things that feel bad, and taste bad and hurt and leave scars. She's not big enough to stop them, not yet, but she will be one day. And then she'll cut off their little white worms and shove them in their slobbery mouths and watch them choke and she'll laugh. She'll laugh and laugh while they choke and bleed to death and she won't care.

She hears Mae on the stairs. Her bedroom door opens, and when she sees who's with her mother, when she catches sight of the white, narrow face and dead eyes, she shrinks back against the wall. Of all Mae's men, she hates and fears Jimmy the most.

He smells her fear, and he smiles. He's one of those who gets off on other people's pain. Mae jerks her head for her to come with them, and she reluctantly gets to her feet, feeling the bugs crawling all over her. She hates Jimmy and his long, pale fingers, his shark eyes, she especially hates his wet red lips, lips that suck the life out of you and leave you dead and empty. But she's not going to let him see how scared she is, she's not going to let him win.

She empties her mind of everything, floating high

above herself, and she doesn't cry out once, no matter how much it hurts. Only when Jimmy puts his hands to her throat and squeezes does she struggle, she can't help it, she can't breathe, but then the room begins to blur and black spots dance before her eyes and she yields to it, to the wonderful sense of release, as everything fades away into blessed nothingness.

She comes to, alone on the floor of her own bedroom. She feels sore all over and it's hard to swallow. It's always like this after a visit from Jimmy. She looks down at herself, at the scratch marks on her legs, the welts and the bruises and the bite marks. She knows from past experience it'll hurt for days when she goes to the toilet, and she'll have to wear her collar turned up at school tomorrow to hide the bruises around her neck.

Wearily, she gets up and goes into the bathroom to scrub herself clean. The house is silent, her mother has probably passed out drunk, so she risks filling the bath with hot water, as hot as she can stand it, and climbs in, leaning back and closing her eyes. She wishes she hadn't woken up, that Jimmy had finished the job. One day, he will.

Suddenly, the bathroom door bangs open and Mae storms in screaming and yelling, who do you think you are, lolling around like the Queen of Sheba, you've used all the hot water, you selfish dirty bitch! She leans over the bathtub and seizes her by the shoulders and pushes her down, pushes her under the water. Lydia splutters and coughs and takes in a lungful of water,

121

but Mae doesn't stop, her face is red and contorted with fury and a sadistic kind of pleasure.

Her lungs are bursting with the need for air as she fights her mother, her limbs flailing against the sides of the bath. She grabs at Mae's arms, trying to prise her off, but her mother's too strong. Lydia feels her strength begin to fail, the room is going dark again, and she is about to let go, to give up, give in, when something stirs deep inside her: a spark of the old anger, of resistance, a refusal to let Mae win. Mae has been trying to get rid of her since before she was born, but she won't be rubbed out, she won't be dismissed and ignored.

Instead of pushing against Mae, she pulls, and the move catches Mae off balance. She falls into the bath with a loud screech, and Lydia seizes the chance to squirm upright, breathing in deep gulps of air as she kicks and hits her mother as hard as she can, wriggling free.

She clambers out of the bath and stands on the bare boards of the bathroom, naked and dripping wet. Mae struggles to sit up in the tub, and the two of them glare at each other. Something has changed, and they both know it.

'I don't want Jimmy to come anymore,' Lydia says.

Mae doesn't say anything. She doesn't scream or shout or threaten to flay you alive, you little cunt. There is something new in her eyes along with the familiar hate and resentment, a grudging respect, an acceptance, and Lydia realises her mother knew this day was coming, was waiting for it.

122

Mae nods shortly and Lydia picks up her threadbare towel and wraps it around herself. All these years she's tried to appease Mae, to be a good girl and do as she was told and keep Mae happy. But Mae is a bully, and like all bullies, there is only one language she understands. Lydia is not as strong as Mae physically, not yet, but she knows now that her will, her anger, is stronger. Despite everything Mae has done to break her body and crush her spirit, she is still here.

She's not going to be Mae's good little girl any longer. She'll be as hard as Mae, as ruthless. She'll watch, and she'll wait. And one day, when she has the chance, she'll get her own back on everyone who let her down.

Chapter 16

Wednesday 11.30 a.m.

Lucas and Maddie followed the two police officers outside. For a moment, she wondered if they were going to be handcuffed and driven away in the back of the police car, like criminals, but when Lucas asked if he should follow them to the station in his own vehicle, they simply agreed.

The two of them drove there in silence. The officers had given them no more information, other than that the post-mortem results were back; they'd refused to provide any specifics. Maddie's mind whirled with questions. Noah had died from cot death. The paramedics had said so. The doctor at the hospital had told them he couldn't officially be sure until the post-mortem, but she'd assumed – they'd all assumed – it was just a formality. So why were they being dragged down to the police station now? Had they done something wrong? Lucas had called the ambulance as soon as they'd found Noah. Should they have tried CPR? Or did it have something to do with the bruises on his cheek? Were they going to be arrested for child abuse?

'Do we need to call a solicitor?' she asked Lucas suddenly.

'Why would we need a solicitor?'

'They must think we've done something wrong. Why do we have to go to the police station to talk to them? Why couldn't they just ask us their questions at home?'

'I don't know,' he said wearily. 'Procedure, I suppose.'

'What do you think was in the post-mortem? Why wouldn't they tell us?'

'I don't know, Maddie. Let's just get there and find out.'

He'd shaved this morning for the first time in days, but he still looked tired and drawn, his skin almost grey. He hadn't ironed his shirt properly, either; there were uneven creases down the front and he'd missed his cuffs entirely.

'You've got paint under your fingernails,' she noticed suddenly.

'I don't have time to worry about that now,' he said tersely, as they pulled into the police station. He unbuckled his seat belt. 'Come on. They're waiting for us.'

She stared up at the building. It was a sixties red-brick build, charmless and boxy. She'd never been inside a police station before. She'd never even had a parking ticket. 'I'm scared, Lucas,' she said.

'Don't make so much of this,' he said, getting out of the car. 'They only want to ask us a few questions. Let's just get this over with, so we can go home.'

Reluctantly, she followed him. Inside, it was bland and institutionally anonymous; it reminded her of the reception office at Emily's junior school. A young, bored-looking policeman sat at a glassed-in counter; behind him, two secretaries were laughing as they shared a blueberry muffin. On the walls, posters exhorted the public to beware of pickpockets and report suspicious packages.

One of the two officers who'd come to their house indicated a row of orange plastic chairs. 'Take a seat. DS Ballard will be with you shortly.'

Maddie sat down obediently. She'd never claimed to be one of life's rebels; she had an innate respect for authority and anyone in a uniform. Lucas, however, had no such limiter in place. He paced up and down the small reception area, not troubling to hide his impatience. She had to fight the urge to tell him to sit down before they got into more trouble.

Finally, after about twenty minutes, a door to the side of the reception desk opened and the red-haired woman they'd seen at the hospital emerged, an open manila folder in her hands. 'Mr and Mrs Drummond? I'm DS Natalie Ballard. I'm sorry to have kept you waiting.'

'What's all this about?' Lucas demanded, ignoring her outstretched hand.

She closed her folder. 'If you'd like to come with me,' she said, more formally.

She didn't wait for them to reply. They followed her past the reception desk and along a narrow, windowless corridor. It smelled of stale biscuits and burned coffee and floor polish.

'Your officer said you'd got the results of the post-mortem?' Maddie said, struggling to keep pace.

The woman ignored her question, stopping and opening the door to a small interview room. 'If you wouldn't mind waiting in here, Mr Drummond,' she said. 'DS Shortall will be with you shortly.'

'Couldn't you just tell us what's going on first?' Maddie begged.

'Just a moment, Mrs Drummond. Please come this way.'

She felt a wave of panic. 'Why can't I stay with Lucas?'

'It'll be much quicker this way.'

Maddie turned to Lucas in bewilderment. 'I'm not going anywhere without you!'

'It's fine, Maddie. Just let them ask their questions, and I'll see you soon.'

The woman touched the small of her back, ushering her along the hall. She was shown into an interview room which was both nicer and more intimidating than she'd expected. It had a window that looked out onto the car park and a picture of a sailboat on the wall. A box of tissues sat on a pale ash table, on either side of which were a couple of matching chairs. But the picture was screwed to the wall and there was a large panic button by the door.

Maddie sat down, neatly tucking her chair into the table as if she was back in pre-school. DS Ballard took a seat opposite her.

'Mrs Drummond, this interview will be recorded. Do you wish to have a solicitor present?'

'Am I being arrested?'

'We just want to chat to you, Mrs Drummond, to hear your side of the story. But it is your right to have a solicitor present if you choose. Obviously, this will take longer to arrange, and I'm sure you want to clear everything up as much as we do.'

Maddie nodded eagerly. 'Whatever I can do to help.'

DS Ballard smiled. 'Thank you. I should caution you, however, that you do have a right to silence. Whatever you say can be used against you in a criminal case in court, and if you don't mention something now which you mention later, a court might ask why you didn't mention it at the first opportunity.' She smiled again, but Maddie had no idea if it was genuine or not. 'Can I get you anything to drink? A cup of tea, perhaps?'

Maddie thrust her hands beneath her thighs to still their trembling. 'I'd just like to get on with this, if that's OK?'

'Of course. Before we start, Mrs Drummond—'

'Please, call me Maddie.'

'Maddie, thank you. Is there anything you'd like to tell me, Maddie, about what happened to Noah the night he died?'

'I told the other officer everything already,' she said, praying the woman wasn't going to ask her about the bruises again. They didn't have anything to do with Noah's death. The accident had happened days ago, and he'd been fine afterwards, she reminded herself. There was nothing else to tell.

DS Ballard tilted her head to one side. 'There's nothing you'd like to add, now you've had a chance to think about it?' she asked kindly. 'We often find people forget things in the heat of the moment. They don't mean to, but it's important we get as full a picture as possible before things go too far.'

Maddie's heart beat a little faster at the thought of what 'too far' might mean. She looked away. 'I can't think of anything.'

'Can you tell me who was with Noah the day before he died?'

'Well, I was with him, obviously. Lucas was working in Poole that day, and he had a late work dinner, so he stayed overnight. I don't know if he saw Noah in the morning before he left; it was very early. Emily and Jacob had chickenpox, so I kept them off school. My husband's sister stopped by with some scones, but she didn't stay long. Otherwise, it was just me.'

'And what is your sister-in-law's name?'

'Candace Drummond.'

'Did she see Noah while she was visiting?'

'He was asleep when she arrived, but she did help settle him down when he woke up. I was looking after Jacob; he was so itchy with the chickenpox and it took a while to get him settled.'

'Was she left alone with Noah?'

'Yes.' Maddie suddenly got what the detective was driving at. 'You can't think Candace had anything to do with what happened to him? She adores Noah! She'd never hurt him!'

'Mrs Drummond,' DS Ballard said softly, 'what makes you think anyone *hurt* Noah at all?'

Maddie stared at her. 'But you just said—'

'I understand from PC Tudhope you had postnatal depression after your second child was born,' DS Ballard interrupted, suddenly switching tack. 'That must have been very difficult for you and your husband.'

'It – it was, yes.'

'Tell me, how did you feel when you found out you were expecting another baby so soon after Jacob?'

'How did I feel?' Maddie repeated, wondering where this was going.

'Were you excited? A bit nervous, perhaps?'

Maddie hesitated. 'A bit, yes.'

'You must have been anxious. It'd only be natural, after such a difficult experience. The chances of developing postnatal depression are much higher if you've already suffered from it with a previous child, am I right?'

'The doctors knew what to look out for this time,' Maddie said uncomfortably. 'I'm on antidepressants. I'm stable now.'

'So everything's been fine? No sudden mood swings or anything like that?'

'No, nothing like that.' She thought briefly of the paint on the nursery walls. If they found out about that, she'd end up in a padded cell. But there was no reason for Lucas to tell them. It'd been the grief talking, that's all. She forced a smile. 'Maybe I could have that cup of tea now, after all?'

'I just have a few more questions,' DS Ballard said.

Maddie tried not to panic. Why was the woman

interrogating her like this? Trying to trip her up, catch her out. She hadn't done anything wrong! And she was so tired. She just wanted to go home.

'What about Lucas?' DS Ballard asked. 'How did he feel about the new baby?'

'He was pleased,' Maddie said quickly, relieved to be on safer ground. 'A bit worried about me, of course, after what happened when I had Jacob, but he's always wanted a large family.' She smiled. 'We'd have a football team if I let him.'

DS Ballard smiled back. 'So he was supportive, then?'

'Yes, of course. Please, can't you tell me what this is about?'

'That bruise on Noah's cheek,' DS Ballard said, briefly glancing at her notes again. 'Remind me, how did he get that?'

Maddie's stomach plunged. The woman's tone was deceptively casual, but her eyes didn't leave Maddie's face. 'It happened a few days before Noah died,' she said uneasily. 'I found him wedged in a corner of the cot one morning. His face was pressed up against the bars.'

'He must have been lying face down, then?' DS Ballard said. She indicated the top of her own cheek. 'To get those marks.'

'Yes, I suppose so.'

'You didn't put him to sleep on his back?'

Maddie nodded firmly. 'Oh, yes, we did. Always. They tell you to in the prenatal classes. I made sure Lucas knew to put him to sleep on his back, too. We were both very careful about that.'

131

'Noah was ten weeks old, is that right?'

'Yes.'

DS Ballard looked surprised. 'Goodness. My sister's two couldn't turn over by themselves until they were at least four or five months old.'

Too late, Maddie saw the trap. She flushed, caught in her lie. 'Maybe one of us forgot that night and laid him on his front,' she backtracked. 'Look, I'm sorry, but I've got an awful headache. I've told you everything I can. Please, I'd like to see Lucas and go home now, if that's OK.'

DS Ballard leaned forward, her expression sympathetic. 'Maddie, I can't begin to imagine what you're going through,' she said. 'To lose a child. It's every mother's worst nightmare. Even when they're keeping you up all night and you're so exhausted you can't even see straight, you never, ever, want anything bad to happen to them.' She sighed. 'My niece had colic. She cried for hours every single night for three months. There were times my sister had to leave her in the cot and just get out of the house because she was scared she'd do something she'd regret. And she didn't have two other children to look after.'

Maddie felt a rush of relief. Only another woman could understand the shameful mix of anguish and frustration at not being able to comfort your own baby. 'I just couldn't help him,' she confessed. 'No matter what I tried. Nothing made it better.'

'I know. It's awful seeing them in pain, isn't it? And the endless crying, it's enough to drive you to distraction. You end up not knowing if it's in your head or if they're really crying.'

'He used to wake up the whole house,' she confided. 'My nine-year-old, Emily, was falling asleep in school. There were nights when it was so bad, Lucas would take the baby out in the car and just drive around for hours until he fell asleep. But you can't do that every night, can you?'

'Of course you can't,' DS Ballard agreed. 'Sometimes it just all gets on top of you. No one would blame you for that. They'd understand.'

Maddie stiffened. 'There's nothing to understand,' she said sharply. 'I was fine, I told you.'

DS Ballard spun her folder round and pushed it across the desk towards Maddie. 'That's not what the post-mortem tells us,' she said, her voice suddenly steel. 'Would it surprise you to learn, Mrs Drummond, that Noah's wasn't a cot death after all?'

Chapter 17

Wednesday 2.00 p.m.

The expression in the policewoman's eyes was suddenly unfriendly. Gone was the soft sympathy of just moments ago. 'In fact, Mrs Drummond, would it surprise you to know that the preliminary post-mortem found that Noah exhibited a number of pathological features suggestive of a non-accidental head injury?'

'What?' Maddie gasped.

'The pathologist found evidence of retinal haemorrhages – that's bleeding into the linings of the eyes,' DS Ballard said relentlessly, 'and subdural haemorrhage, which is bleeding beneath the dural membrane.'

Maddie flinched. 'Please, stop.'

DS Ballard tapped the doctor's report. 'And there, you see? Encephalopathy, that's damage to the brain affecting function.'

'It's not possible—'

'I'm afraid it is. This was not a cot death, Mrs Drummond. Your son died from serious intracranial injuries.'

The room swam in front of her, and for a moment

Maddie thought she was going to pass out. Brain damage? Could her own carelessness in falling asleep have done this to Noah? He'd only been trapped against her rocking chair for a few seconds! He'd been fine the next day. How could it have *killed* him?

'The pathologist's verdict is clear,' DS Ballard said. 'Individually, perhaps, each of these clinical findings might be explained away, but all three taken together? You can see why I'm having trouble believing Noah's injuries were accidental. The only question is, who caused them?'

'But I loved my son!'

'Of course you did. Perhaps you didn't intend to hurt him. Maybe you just snapped. You and I both know what it's like looking after a colicky baby.' Her voice softened. 'Did you shake him, Maddie? If you didn't actually *mean* to hurt him, if it happened in the heat of the moment, that might put a different spin on things. But you have to tell me the truth now. No more lies and excuses.'

She felt trapped, like a cornered animal. The policewoman was making it sound like she'd hurt him on purpose. 'You said these results are preliminary,' she said desperately. 'So they might be wrong?'

'Who hurt Noah, Maddie?' DS Ballard pressed. 'You need to tell me. If it wasn't you, you must know who it was. You can't protect them any longer. If it was an accident, that'll be taken into consideration—'

She couldn't bear it. 'No! The pathologist is wrong!'

'Maddie, it's all right here. The post-mortem findings,

the bruises on his cheek. And then there are your own mental health issues, the depression and so on. What am I supposed to think?'

The policewoman had already made up her mind, Maddie realised. They'd heard her medical history and that was it. As far as they were concerned, depression was only one short step away from infanticide. They'd never believe it was an accident now if she told them what had really happened. She hadn't meant to hurt him. She'd just fallen asleep with her child in her arms, like thousands of mothers did every day. She hadn't even dropped him. He'd been right next to her in that chair the whole time.

'They were just a few red marks!' she cried, more to herself than the policewoman. 'You could hardly see them!'

'Oh, I'm not talking about the bruises on his cheek, though I don't think you're telling me the whole story about those,' DS Ballard said. 'But that's not how he died, Maddie. Being trapped against the side of his cot wouldn't be sufficient to cause these types of brain injuries, according to the pathologist. No matter how hard he jammed himself against the bars.'

Maddie reeled. 'I don't understand. You just said—'

'I said he died from his head injuries. But they weren't caused by the side of his cot or whatever really made those bruises. The damage to his brain was far too violent and deliberate to have been caused by that.'

She felt as if she'd been punched in the gut. '*Deliberate*?'

'Oh, yes. The pathologist was quite certain on that

score. Talk to me, Maddie. Tell me what really happened.'

Her head spun. She couldn't take it all in. Someone had deliberately hurt her baby? Who? *Why?*

'Come on, Maddie,' DS Ballard urged. 'Why don't we start with the truth about how Noah got those bruises?'

Before she could reply, the door opened, and the young constable from reception put his head around the jamb and coughed awkwardly. 'Excuse me, ma'am?'

DS Ballard looked up in irritation. 'Yes?'

A smartly dressed black woman in her mid-fifties pushed past the constable. 'Mrs Drummond, don't say another word.'

'Ms Piggott,' sighed DS Ballard. 'A pleasure to see you again.'

'Likewise, Detective Sergeant Ballard,' the woman said dryly.

'I'm sorry,' Maddie stammered. 'Who are you?'

The woman held out her hand. 'Rebecca Piggott. Your solicitor.'

Maddie looked bewildered. 'But I didn't call a solicitor.'

'Your mother did. Your husband spoke to her a short time ago and she called me. We've worked together a number of times on the hospital board. Now, let's clear up this ridiculous clusterfuck and get you out of here.'

DS Ballard stood up. 'Mrs Drummond, you're free to go. I'm sure we will be talking to you again soon.'

'*With* your solicitor present,' the woman said crisply.

Maddie smiled at her with gratitude. 'Thank you so much,' she said, as DS Ballard left the room. 'This is

137

all a terrible mistake! The police say Noah didn't die from a cot death, that someone hurt him, but that's just not possible—'

Rebecca held up a hand. Her long red nails perfectly matched her suit. 'Let's not discuss this now,' she said firmly. 'We'll set up a meeting in my office later. I had to cut short a conference call when your mother rang me and I need to get back. In the meantime, I don't want you to talk to *anyone* about this case without me present, is that clear?'

'Have you spoken to Lucas? He'll tell you—'

'Mrs Drummond, I'm *your* solicitor. I haven't spoken to your husband. And when I say I don't want you to talk to anyone about this case, that includes him. If necessary, your husband may have to find his own solicitor, whose job will be to protect him, not you. That creates an automatic conflict of interest, so please do not discuss the case with anyone, *especially* your husband.'

'But we haven't done anything!' Maddie protested, dumbfounded. 'Can't you just talk to the police and explain?'

'Mrs Drummond, I really need you to understand the seriousness of the situation,' Rebecca said in a tone that brought Maddie up short. 'The pathologist found a triad of intracranial injuries that are considered typical of what used to be called shaken baby syndrome. Now, before you panic,' she added, as Maddie felt ready to faint, 'these cases are extremely controversial and very difficult to prove. But you need to take this investigation very seriously. The police will be looking for evidence that either you or your husband harmed Noah in some way, possibly the two of you together. This is not something that's just going to go away.'

'I can't believe this is happening,' Maddie said, dazed.

'I sympathise, but I really don't have time to talk about this now,' the solicitor said. 'Before our next meeting, you should think very carefully about who else had contact with Noah in the day or two immediately prior to his death. If the police find any kind of evidence to support their theory, it will be my job to provide reasonable doubt and point the finger of suspicion away from you.'

Maddie was near to tears. 'How can they think I'd do anything to hurt my own baby?'

Rebecca sighed. 'This isn't about you, Mrs Drummond. The police have a child who has died from a suspected head injury. It's up to them to investigate. And the sad fact is that, in many of these cases, the injuries *are* inflicted by someone close to the child.' She paused, her hand on the door. 'One other question I'd like you to think very seriously about before we meet again, Mrs Drummond. How well do you *really* know your husband?'

Chapter 18

Wednesday 4.30 p.m.

They drove home from the police station in silence. Maddie still couldn't take it in. The idea that someone had deliberately harmed their child, had physically shaken him to death, was so horrifying she couldn't begin to get her head around it. She felt sick and clammy, as if she was about to throw up. Who? *Who* would hurt Noah? Who would hurt any baby?

Rebecca's parting words rang in her ears. *How well do you really know your husband?* Maddie shot him a sidelong glance as they waited at a set of traffic lights. The answer was not as well as she had once thought. But borrowing money was a long, *long* way from killing their child. Lucas would never hurt anyone. Despite his intimidating size, he was a gentle man, tolerant and patient. He wasn't violent in any way. He didn't even swat wasps, preferring to trap them in a glass and free them outside. She couldn't imagine him shaking their baby, even in a fit of rage. She hadn't ever seen him lose his temper in all their years together. He talked things out; he didn't even raise his voice, never mind his fist. It was simply inconceivable that Lucas had done anything to Noah. He hadn't even been there that night.

Who, then? Noah hadn't gone to daycare for a couple of days before his death, because of the chickenpox; apart from Maddie herself, the only people he'd come into contact with had been Lucas and Candace, fleetingly, the day she came around with the scones. And Maddie was certain she'd never hurt her own baby, *never*. No matter what else she might do when she had one of her episodes, she knew in the very bones of her that she wouldn't harm her children. She'd give her life to protect them. The pathologist had to have made a mistake. It was the only logical explanation.

But that policewoman had seemed so *sure*. Rebecca had bought Maddie a little time, but DS Ballard wasn't just going to let it go. She clearly thought Maddie was guilty. She'd come after her again.

Maddie chewed nervously on her thumbnail. 'What did they say to you?' she asked her husband. 'They let you go much earlier than they did me, didn't they? They must think it's me.' Her voice cracked. 'How could they think that, Lucas?'

'It's routine. They have to ask.'

'It's not routine to me! I don't care what their pathologist says! Did you tell them I'd never hurt him?'

Lucas swung recklessly onto a roundabout without bothering to check for traffic first. 'Of course I did! What d'you think I've spent the last hour doing? The whole thing is bloody ridiculous and I told them so. I wasn't even there, for God's sake!'

141

'But I was, wasn't I?'

'Don't, Maddie. That's not what I meant.' He pulled into their cul-de-sac and parked outside their house, turning off the engine but making no move to get out of the car. 'Of course I don't think you hurt him,' he sighed. 'But given what the pathologist found, the police had no choice but to question us both. They wouldn't be doing their jobs if they didn't.'

Maddie kneaded her fingers nervously. 'I've read about cases like this in the paper, women who've been sent to jail for killing their babies, even when they didn't do it. Remember that nanny in America? What if—'

'Maddie, stop.' He put his hand over hers to still them. 'I've read the same stories you have. Your mother was right to call a solicitor. These things can get out of control very quickly. But this will all get sorted out. You just have to be patient.'

'You believe me, don't you, Lucas?'

He didn't hesitate. 'Without question.'

The tightness in her chest eased a little. 'I'd never do anything to hurt the children.'

'I know that. And I hope it goes without saying I'd take a bullet before I let anything happen to any of them, either.'

'I'm scared, Lucas.'

He squeezed her fingers. 'There's no need to be. I've got you. I'm not going anywhere. We'll get through this, I promise.'

A beat fell. 'Do you think the pathologist could be

right?' she asked haltingly. 'All those injuries he found. He must have a reason for thinking someone hurt him, mustn't he?'

'Honestly, Mads, I don't know.' He exhaled slowly. 'Never mind what the experts say, pathology isn't an exact science. Everything is open to interpretation. Maybe something happened when the paramedics were trying to bring him round. Or perhaps Noah had a seizure. That could have mimicked shaking injuries. We're just going to have to wait and see what happens next.'

'You don't think ...' She trailed off.

He paused, his hand on the door handle. 'What?'

'You don't think someone did hurt him?'

'Someone else? Like who?'

'I don't know. At nursery, maybe,' Maddie said. Another reason to feel guilty. She'd never put Emily in daycare, taking her to the sanctuary until she was old enough to start nursery school. But she'd had no choice with Jacob, needing to focus on her own recovery, and had been relieved when Lucas had insisted Noah go to daycare too when he was eight weeks old, so that she didn't get overwhelmed.

He sighed heavily. 'I suppose it's possible. I'm sure the police are looking into it. I don't know what kind of time period is relevant. A few days? A week? I'm sure they'll want to talk to everyone who came into contact with him recently.'

'It's awful,' Maddie whispered. 'Everyone under suspicion like this. I can't bear it.'

His phone rang suddenly. 'It's Candace,' he said, climbing out of the car.

She followed Lucas into the house, drifting into the kitchen as Lucas disappeared into the study. They couldn't even plan Noah's funeral, not until his body was released, and the police weren't going to do that until their investigation was cleared up, one way or another. How could she grieve properly when she wasn't allowed to bury her baby? What was wrong with the world, that the first port of call when a child died was its own parents?

Lucas came into the kitchen. 'Maddie, I have to go out. Candace needs me.'

'Now? Can't it wait?'

'She's been drinking,' he said tersely.

Maddie gasped. 'Oh, Lucas, no.'

'I might have to stay with her overnight. It depends how bad she is. I'm sorry. You know I wouldn't leave you if it wasn't an emergency.'

'Why, after all this time? She's been doing so well.'

'I don't know.' He grabbed his coat from the hall cupboard. 'Here's Sarah with the children,' he said, as he opened the front door again. 'I'll call you later.'

Maddie watched from the doorway as her mother and Lucas negotiated their vehicles around each other on the narrow drive. Candace had been on the wagon for four years now, ever since she'd moved back down to Sussex to be near them. As far as Maddie knew, she hadn't had a single slip in all that time. She wondered if it had something to do with Noah's loss. It must have stirred all sorts of dark memories. But she needed Lucas herself right now. She couldn't spare him to nurse Candace through rehab and recovery.

Her mother shooed the children into the house and kissed Maddie's cheek as Jacob flung his plump arms around his mother's legs. 'Where's Lucas rushing off to?' Sarah asked.

Maddie scooped her son into her arms and rested him on her hip. 'Candace called. She's started drinking again.'

Sarah put her hand on her granddaughter's shoulder. 'Why don't you take your brother outside and play while I talk to Mummy?' she said, in a tone that brooked no argument.

Maddie put Jacob down, and dropped a kiss on her daughter's head. 'Thank you, Emily. I'll come out and play with you in a little while, OK?'

Emily nodded, taking her brother's hand. It was still cool for April, but the sun was out, and Maddie watched from the kitchen window as the two children ran down the lawn to the swing set at the bottom of the garden. 'Emily's being so good with Jacob,' she said fretfully. 'She never had much time for him before.'

'That's a good thing, surely?'

'Yes, of course, but it's *why* she's being so sweet that worries me. She asked me yesterday if I thought Jacob might die too.'

'Look at what she's been through. I'd be more worried if she acted as if nothing had happened.'

'Do you think she needs to see a counsellor?' Maddie asked.

'Maybe. But let's just give it time, first. She's young. You'd be amazed how resilient children can be.' Sarah put the kettle on and got out two mugs. 'I don't want you worrying about Candace,' she said firmly. 'She's a grown woman, and Lucas needs to remember where his priorities lie. Now then, what did Rebecca have to say?'

'I can't believe I just got back from the police station,' Maddie said, pulling out a kitchen chair. 'It doesn't seem real. None of it. They're saying Noah died from some sort of brain haemorrhage, did Lucas tell you? They think one of us *hurt* him.'

Sarah put a mug of strong, sweet tea in front of her. 'Drink this. I bet you haven't eaten all day, have you?'

'I'm not hungry.'

'You need to eat, Maddie.'

'I'll have something with the children later.'

Sarah pushed the tea another inch towards her. 'Drink this, at least.'

Maddie cupped her hands around the mug, fingers threaded backwards through the handle. 'Rebecca was great. She marched in like the cavalry and told that awful policewoman to leave me alone. I don't know what I'd have done without her.' She stared down at her tea. 'She told me not to talk about what happened with anyone, even Lucas.'

'That's probably sensible, in the circumstances,' Sarah said evenly.

'She seemed to be implying Lucas might have hurt Noah,' Maddie said, without looking up. 'You know him, Mum. I've never even seen him lose his temper. He's just not like that.'

'We're all like that,' Sarah said quietly. 'I'm not accusing him of anything. I'm just saying the line is easier to cross than you think, that's all. It only takes a split second. You think a man wakes up deciding this is the day he's going to batter his wife to death in a jealous rage?' She sat down opposite Maddie, her hands clasped neatly in front of her on the table. Maddie was too surprised by her mother's words to respond. 'You hear on the news about teenagers who shoot their parents in their own beds, and mothers who drive into a river with their children strapped in the back of the car, and you tell yourself they're different from the rest of us, there must have been signs there that everyone missed, but the truth is, they're the same. They just take a wrong turn somewhere, and sometimes, that wrong turn can happen in a single moment. One mistake, that's all it takes.'

Maddie shivered, as if someone had walked across her grave. 'What are you trying to say, Mum?'

'I'm not judging you, Maddie. You're my daughter and I'm on your side. I'll be on your side no matter what. Emily and Jacob need their mother and that's more important to me than anything else.'

It took a moment for her to understand. 'Mum, I didn't do anything,' she said, too exhausted to be angry.

'Are you *sure*, Maddie? Because I'll support you, no matter what.'

There was something telling in her mother's expression, almost as if she knew something Maddie didn't. Maddie had never told her mother about her memory lapses, she'd never told anyone except Jayne. But the way Sarah was looking at her now, it was as if she somehow *knew*.

Was it possible she'd hurt Noah that night?

She dismissed the thought immediately. She'd never deliberately hurt Noah, *never*, whether she was in some sort of fugue state or not. She'd never shake him so violently his brain bled and swelled inside his skull. She wasn't some sort of Jekyll and Hyde. Even when she had one of her episodes, she was still the same person. She couldn't remember shaking Noah because *it'd never happened*.

She tried not to think about the nursery, the violent red sweeps of paint on the yellow walls.

She shoved back her chair and put her mug in the dishwasher, staring out of the kitchen window, her hands resting on the edge of the sink. She could see Emily peacefully sitting on the swing at the bottom of the garden, scuffing the ground with the tops of her trainers as she swung slowly back and forth.

'Mum,' she said suddenly. 'Where's Jacob?'

Lydia

Mae has turned over a new leaf. Well, maybe not a new leaf, but she's mellowed. She's had to; Lydia is eleven now, and she won't be made to do anything she doesn't want to do by anyone. Especially not her mother.

Mae shacked up with one of her regulars two years ago. She didn't have much choice: when Lydia refused to service her mother's clients, most of them stopped coming, so she had no choice but to switch to Plan B. Lydia doesn't mind Frank. He's no oil painting and he snores so loud you can hear him from the street, but he treats Mae nice, he doesn't drink or knock her about. Best of all, as far as Lydia is concerned, he's got no interest in *her*. He has a daughter about her age, though he hasn't seen her since his ex ran off with a travelling salesman and took the kids with her. Sometimes she catches him looking at her, not in a pervy way, but with a sad look in his eye, and she knows he's thinking about his own daughter.

Frank insisted Mae come off the game. He's a long-distance lorry driver; it's not glamorous, he says, but it's honest work, and it means he can support his family without her having to turn tricks. Mae's a cleaner now for a posh family on the outskirts of town. Sometimes she takes Lydia along to help out. The big house reminds Lydia of somewhere, but she can't think where. She dreams of a house like it sometimes, a house with lots of rooms and a bed with pink sheets. In her dreams, there's a lady with grey hair who wears a pearl necklace and smiles a lot. Lydia told Mae about her once and Mae went flipping berserk. After that, she didn't mention her dreams or the lady again.

Mrs Taylor, the woman Mae works for, wears smart skirt suits and goes out to a job in an office, even though she has a rich husband and doesn't need to work. She has three children: two teenage boys away at boarding school and a little girl called Julia, who's nearly four. Julia has a full-time nanny who has to wear a fancy grey uniform, but sometimes, like today, the nanny slips Lydia a few quid to keep the little girl out of her hair so she can sneak off to see her boyfriend.

Lydia likes playing with Julia. It's nice to sit on the soft pink carpet in her bedroom and pretend she lives here, that this is her room and these are her toys. It's hard not to feel jealous, though. Julia's room is painted pink and white and it has long pink velvet curtains all the way to the floor and a white four-poster bed with a pink satin canopy. There's a white wardrobe packed tight with pretty dresses, most of which Julia's never even worn. It's like the bedroom of a princess in one of Julia's picture books. (There are no books at Lydia's house, not even ones with pictures. Sometimes she wonders if Mae can even read.)

Julia has so many toys, it's a wonder you can see the pink carpet. But her favourite game is Let's Pretend. She likes to play princesses and doctors and nurses, but her absolute favourite is when she pretends Lydia is her mummy. Secretly, it's Lydia's favourite game too. She never hits Julia, though, or shuts her in the cupboard. She calls Julia my darling child and cuddles her and reads her stories. When Lydia grows up and has a real baby of her own, she will never be mean to it like Mae. She will love her baby and feed it and look after it properly. If any of those old pervs comes near it, she'll slit their fucking throats.

Julia wants to play hide-and-seek today and Lydia indulges her, because she's in a good mood, thanks to the cash from the nanny burning a hole in her pocket. Julia is only three and three quarters; she still thinks if she covers her eyes so she can't see you that means you can't see her. Lydia makes a big show of lifting the cushions on the sofa and looking behind the curtains, pretending she can't see Julia crouching in the corner of the sitting room and peeking between her hands. Julia giggles and Lydia peers beneath the piano and into the fireplace and eventually Julia can't contain herself, she peals with laughter and Lydia swings round, her mouth a big O of astonishment, and swoops the little girl into a hug.

When Mae calls out that it's time to go, Lydia

reluctantly scrambles to her feet. Julia throws her arms around her waist and begs her to stay. Lydia pats the soft golden curls and promises to come again soon. Julia's only a baby, and she's very spoiled, but her unwavering adoration makes Lydia stop feeling quite so angry about everything for a little while. Her anger is almost like a living thing now, a beast she feeds and pets. Sometimes she wonders what will happen if she ever stops holding it in.

As soon as they're out of the house, Mae starts yelling at her. Lydia storms off down the pavement, ignoring the shrill stream of swear words that follows her. She hates it when Frank's away on one of his trips. Mae can still get vicious, especially when she's had a few, though she's always careful to make sure the bruises won't show. Lydia's been known to get in a few punches of her own, so it doesn't happen often these days. Not like it used to.

Mae gets her own back in other ways. There was a project at school last term, a science project about volcanoes; all the kids had to make models out of clay or papier-mâché for a special display. One of the local councillors was coming to judge them and everything. Lydia doesn't normally like science, but she'd worked really hard on this, Frank had helped her, and the two of them had spent hours moulding the soggy newspaper and then painting it when it was dry. Mae knew how proud she and Frank were of it. The night before the project was due, Lydia carefully set it on the kitchen counter, ready to take to school. When she came down the next morning, it was on the floor, crushed beyond recognition. The wind must have caught it, Mae said.

The wind, my arse, Lydia thinks, marching furiously down the street. Spite, that's what it was. Mae and Frank nearly came to blows over it, but he's never raised his hand to a woman and he's not about to start now.

As soon as they get home, Lydia runs upstairs and bolts herself in her room (she asked Frank to put a bolt on her door soon after he moved in; she said she was old enough to deserve some privacy, but the truth is she's just scared of what might happen if Frank ever leaves) and refuses to come out no matter how much Mae rants and raves. It means she goes to bed hungry, but she's used to that. Better that than being Mae's punchbag for the evening.

She's woken in the middle of the night by the unmistakeable sound of Mae's heavy brass bedhead thumping rhythmically against the wall. Frank must be home. She's surprised; he only left yesterday morning on a trip to Istanbul. She thought he'd be gone at least a week.

She peers out of the bedroom window to check for his lorry cab. It's not there. But parked in its place is a dark red Ford she recognises, a car that has her rushing to her bedroom door to double-check the bolt.

Jimmy's back.

Chapter 19

Thursday 9.00 a.m.

The space next to her was empty when Maddie woke up. She'd heard Lucas come home from Candace's in the middle of the night, struggling with the double-lock on the front door before finally letting himself in through the kitchen. But he hadn't come up to bed, presumably because he hadn't wanted to wake her. He usually slept on the sofa if he was late back; one of the many ways he'd always been the perfect husband.

Maddie threw back the duvet and then lay staring at the ceiling, unable to bring herself to get out of bed. A trickle of dampness pooled in her ears and she realised she was crying again. She made no effort to stop it. The tears came all the time now, even when she was sleeping, a constant flow of grief and sadness over which she had no control. She didn't even bother to wipe them away.

The front doorbell rang at the same moment as her phone buzzed on the bedside table. She ignored them both. She was overcome with inertia, as if a lead blanket was weighing her down. She couldn't think of a single reason to get up.

She wasn't fit to call herself a mother anymore. One child had already died on her watch and she had very nearly lost another yesterday. She had no idea how Jacob had got through the side gate and into the street; it was always kept locked and bolted, but somehow he'd opened it. She couldn't blame Emily for taking her eye off him; her daughter was only nine. Maddie was the one who was supposed to be looking after him. If Jayne hadn't found him wandering along the main road, he could have been kidnapped or hit by a car.

Her phone buzzed again. She let it go to voicemail but finally swung her legs sideways and sat up, checking the screen. Candace: she'd called three times, once very late last night and now twice this morning.

She didn't really want to hear what her sister-in-law had to say, but Candace would only keep calling. Wearily, she played the first message, the one from last night. At first there was a long silence and she was about to hit delete, when Candace's voice suddenly echoed loudly in her ear. 'Maddie, are you there?' There was a clatter as she dropped the phone. 'Oops, sorry about that. You still there? Lucas just left. Sorry it's so late. He's such a wonderful brother, you know. I'm so lucky to have him. He's a wonderful brother. Did I tell you that already?'

'Oh, Candace,' Maddie said softly. Four years sober, and now this.

'I did something,' Candace blurted suddenly. 'Something terrible. I'm so sorry, Maddie. I should have told you. Lucas wanted to, but I made him promise.'

155

The message abruptly ended. What on earth did Candace mean? She'd done something terrible? What sort of terrible? Maddie stared at the phone for a minute in frustration and then played the second message, the one Candace had left a short while ago.

'It's me again,' Candace said, now sounding sober and suitably contrite. 'Sorry I kept your husband out so late. Look, ignore whatever I said when I phoned last night. I'm sure I was talking all sorts of silly nonsense. Give me a call when you're up. Sorry again.'

She heard the sound of voices downstairs and Lucas calling up to her. 'Maddie! Are you awake?'

She ignored him and played Candace's last message. 'Look, Mads. Can you call me. Please.'

She had no idea what her sister-in-law was talking about, but it sounded ominous. She replayed the first message again, her sense of foreboding growing. Candace could be erratic when she'd been drinking, Maddie remembered that from before she got sober, but this was different. What could Candace have done that was so terrible, other than fall off the wagon? And that was hardly a state secret.

Candace was there that day, a voice whispered in her head.

No. Candace was no more capable of hurting Noah than she or Lucas. She couldn't imagine anyone she knew deliberately harming her child.

Maddie hated the fact that this cloud of suspicion was hanging over them all. Regardless of what the pathologist said, she still clung to the belief that it was all a mistake.

Lucas appeared in the bedroom doorway. 'It's the police again. You need to come down.'

'I'm not dressed.'

'Never mind that. Just come down, would you? It's important.'

She pulled a bobbly old cardigan over her pyjamas. More questions. More accusations. Why couldn't the police just leave them alone?

DS Natalie Ballard was waiting in the hall downstairs, her red hair pulled back into a neat ponytail. 'I don't believe you've met DS Shortall,' she said, indicating a tall, skinny man in his mid-thirties with an unpleasant expression. 'He spoke to your husband yesterday at the station.'

Maddie ignored the man's outstretched hand and wrapped her cardigan more tightly around herself.

'We just wanted to take a look round,' DS Shortall said. He had a strong south London accent and his pale blue gaze made Maddie feel distinctly underdressed. 'Get a feel for things.'

'I think I should call my solicitor,' Maddie said uncertainly, fearful of what the police would think when they saw the state of the nursery. Lucas had tidied up the mess, but the red paint was still there, garishly striping the walls.

'Oh, let them look,' Lucas sighed. 'We've got nothing to hide.'

DS Shortall headed towards the staircase. 'Your son's bedroom's up here, is it?'

'First door on the left,' Lucas said.

'Please, don't let us keep you,' DS Ballard said briskly. 'Just get on with whatever you were doing. We'll call you if we need you. This shouldn't take long.'

Maddie could hear the television blaring in the sitting room, even with the door tightly closed; no doubt the children were sitting square-eyed in front of it, breaking all the normal rules. But these were hardly normal times. Better they overdosed on CBeebies than saw the police searching the house for evidence their parents had murdered their baby brother.

'What are they looking for?' she said anxiously, following Lucas into the kitchen. 'What do they expect to find?'

Lucas put his finger to his lips, then reached up to the baby monitor on top of the fridge and switched it on. Maddie was taken aback. It would never even have occurred to her to listen in on someone else's conversation and she was a bit shocked that it'd occurred to Lucas. 'Is that even legal?' she whispered nervously.

'Sssh. It's our house. Why wouldn't it be?'

'... according to the paramedic,' DS Ballard was saying, her voice crackling slightly over the monitor. 'he'd been dead some hours before they were called.'

'Christ!' DS Shortall exclaimed. 'What the fuck happened in here? That's one hell of a paint job.'

'Mind those plastic bags, Mike.'

'They didn't waste much time clearing up, did they? It hasn't even been a week.'

'Give them a break,' DS Ballard said sharply and Maddie felt a brief flash of gratitude. 'They're probably in shock.'

'You've changed your tune.'

'I'm keeping an open mind. You should be, too.'

'It's the mother,' he said cynically. 'It's always the mother or the nanny, and there wasn't a nanny, so that leaves Mum. Drummond wasn't even there the night it happened.'

Maddie could feel Lucas's eyes on her. She glanced at him, but he had already looked away. She had no idea what he was thinking.

'Those injuries could have happened two or three days before he died,' DS Ballard continued.

'Yeah, in theory, but it's not likely, is it?'

They heard the two officers circulating the room and the sound of furniture being moved. When DS Ballard spoke again, her voice sounded distant, and Maddie guessed she must be at the opposite end of the room from the monitor, beside Noah's dismantled cot.

'Come over here, Mike.'

'What am I looking at?'

'Something about those bruises on his cheek doesn't add up.' There was another rattle of furniture. 'Hold this side rail, would you? Look. How could he get himself wedged that tightly against it? Ogilvy said there's no way he could have got bruises like that without considerable pressure. There's nothing here that'd wedge him that hard against the bars.'

'Unless they got rid of it?'

'Why get rid of something that backs up your story?'

DS Shortall exhaled noisily. 'Shit, who the hell knows?'

Maddie felt sick. She should have admitted what had happened the moment she was asked about the bruises. Better yet, she should have told Lucas the truth in the first place. She realised now that she wouldn't have had to tell him about the blackouts; she could simply have said she'd fallen asleep. He'd have understood. Instead, she'd panicked. The marks on Noah's cheek had nothing to do with his death, even the police pathologist acknowledged that, but bruises on the face of a dead child set alarm bells ringing. If she was in their shoes, she'd be asking questions, too. And that policewoman was like a dog with a bone.

'My gut tells me the mother's not an abuser,' DS Ballard said. 'There's no sign of neglect, the other two kids seem loved and well cared for. She's just not ticking the right boxes.'

Maddie glanced at Lucas, waiting for him to squeeze her hand, to give her a reassuring smile, to let her know he agreed with the policewoman and believed in her, too. But he didn't look at her, folding his arms as he stared fixedly at the baby monitor, subtly but distinctly distancing himself from her.

DS Shortall snorted. 'Yeah, well. It's always the quiet ones.'

'You spoke to the husband yesterday. He said she had serious postnatal depression after the older boy, but there was never any question of her hurting the kids, was there? I can see her topping herself, maybe, but not killing the baby. It doesn't add up.'

'OK. So why are we here?'

'Why lie about the bruises?' DS Ballard mused, her voice suddenly loud again. She must be standing right by the monitor. 'She's hiding something. The question is, what? Are the bruises part of a pattern of abuse, or is she covering up something else? That's what I want to know.'

Maddie couldn't bear to listen to any more. She'd boxed herself into a corner with her lies: first to Lucas and now to the police. It was going to come out: that policewoman would prod and poke until she got to the truth. Lucas had never questioned her version of events, but he had to be wondering about it now. It was never the sin that tripped you up; it was the cover-up.

Lucas turned to her and she saw the dawning realisation in his eyes. 'Maddie,' he said suspiciously. 'What did you do?'

Chapter 20

Thursday 10.00 a.m.

'Let me get this straight,' DS Natalie Ballard said. 'Noah *didn't* get his bruises from being wedged against the side of his cot, as you initially told us. You *now* say you fell asleep nursing him and he slipped out of your arms and became trapped between you and the side of your chair?'

Maddie nodded unhappily as she sat at the kitchen table. She didn't blame the policewoman for sounding sceptical. If she was DS Ballard, she'd have trouble believing her story, too. 'It was an accident,' she said tearfully. 'I know I should have told you before, but I didn't think it mattered. He was only stuck for a few seconds.'

'You can see why we'd find this all a bit confusing, can't you, Maddie?' DS Ballard said softly. 'First you tell us one thing and then you change your story and tell us something else. Why did you lie to us, Maddie?'

She glanced at Lucas, standing beside the sink, his back to her. She hadn't wanted to tell the police the truth, but he'd insisted. When she'd finally broken down in tears and confessed to him, he hadn't shouted at her, or lambasted her for lying to him. He'd simply informed her, in curt tones that brooked no argument, that they had to tell the police what had really happened. He'd refused to answer when she'd begged him to say if he believed her. She had no idea what he was really thinking, or what was going on behind his shuttered expression. Lucas had always been so transparent with her, so easy to read, and his opacity now frightened her far more than if he'd yelled at her.

'I was scared,' she said miserably, turning back to the two police officers. 'I didn't want everyone thinking I was a bad mother. And I didn't think it mattered how he got the bruises. I thought he died from a cot death! We all did!'

She could hear how feeble her excuses sounded. But she *hadn't* thought anything of the red marks on Noah's cheek. He'd seemed perfectly fine after his mishap; if she'd had any doubt, any doubt at all, she'd have come clean to Lucas and taken Noah to hospital. But the baby had seemed his usual self and so she'd told Lucas a single little white lie so that he wouldn't look at her with that wariness she'd come to dread in the months after Jacob was born. Of course she regretted it now, but she couldn't have known how much it would come to matter.

'What about your husband?' DS Ballard asked. 'Why didn't you tell him the truth, at least? You had a new baby with colic, two other young children to look after, you were exhausted from all the sleepless nights. Surely he wouldn't blame you for falling asleep?'

Maddie was too shamed even to look at Lucas. 'I don't know why I didn't tell him,' she said helplessly.

'Was it because he might think you'd dropped Noah on purpose?'

'Of course not!'

'By your own admission, you weren't very happy at the idea of another baby,' DS Ballard pressed. 'Lucas knew that, didn't he?'

The detective sounded so sure of herself, Maddie started to doubt her own motives. *Had* she been afraid, deep down, that Lucas might think she'd hurt Noah on purpose? *Was* that why she'd been so quick to cover up the accident?

'He knew I loved Noah!' she exclaimed. She turned to Lucas, desperate now for some support, but he remained silent, staring out of the window and refusing to catch her eye.

DS Ballard frowned. 'Well, surely he'd understand a simple mistake, then? You see, this is what's puzzling me, Maddie. If what you say is true and you just fell asleep in the middle of a very long and exhausting night with a crying baby, I don't see why Lucas – or anyone else for that matter – would blame you. Unless there's something else you're not telling me.'

She couldn't tell them about her memory lapses. She *couldn't*. Another lie, on top of everything else? Lucas would never trust her again. They'd take the children away from her, say she couldn't keep them safe. It was bad enough the way they were all looking at her now, when they thought all she'd done was fall asleep.

'I've told you,' she protested. 'It was an accident! I just fell asleep for a moment, that's all. You said yourself, it could happen to anyone!'

Lucas finally turned from the window. 'My wife's told you what happened. Your own expert says this had nothing to do with Noah's death.'

'Technically, maybe,' DS Shortall snapped. 'But there's often a pattern of abuse in cases like this. By your wife's own admission, she's already lied to us once. Who's to say she's telling the truth now?'

'I asked my wife to tell you the full story so that we could clear up any misunderstanding there may have been,' Lucas said shortly. 'Not so you could use it as an excuse to attack her again. This is exactly why she didn't tell you before. You need to stop wasting time chasing shadows and find out what really happened to our son.'

Maddie was grateful he'd finally intervened, but she was under no illusion that meant he'd forgiven her. She knew him well enough to pick up on the anger and hurt in his voice, even if it wasn't evident to the two detectives. What she still didn't know was whether it was due to the fact she'd lied to him, or because he believed her capable of something far more sinister.

DS Ballard got to her feet. 'That's exactly what we're trying to do, Mr Drummond. Rest assured, we will get to the bottom of this. In the meantime, please don't hesitate to contact me if you think of anything else that might be helpful.' She looked at Maddie, her expression unreadable. 'We'll be in touch.'

Lucas showed the two officers out. Maddie pressed

the heels of her hands against her eyes. Of course they didn't believe her. She wouldn't have done either, if she were them. They didn't know her, or what kind of mother she was. All they had to go on was a dead baby covered in bruises and a mother who'd confessed to lying about how he'd got them.

But Lucas knew she'd never harm their children. Didn't he?

She stood up as he came back. 'Lucas, I—'

He cut her off. 'Why did you lie to me?'

'Please, Lucas. Try to understand. I didn't mean to. It just slipped out. If I could take it back, I would.' Her voice thickened and she fought back tears. Lucas *had* to believe her, even if no one else in the world did. He was her rock. She couldn't bear it if he doubted her, too. 'It was so awful after Jacob, everyone watching me and second-guessing me all the time. I couldn't bear that again. If I'd told you the truth, would you have trusted me with Noah? It was such a little thing, I didn't think it'd matter.'

'How does lying make it easier for me to trust you?' he asked exhaustedly. 'Come on, Maddie. We're better than this.'

She'd rather he shouted at her than this weary disappointment. 'You don't know what it was like for me after Jacob was born,' she pleaded. 'Everyone looking at me like I was some kind of lunatic, waiting for me to slip up and do something crazy. You even hid all the painkillers, Lucas! You and Mum watched me like hawks every second of the day.'

'Have you got any idea what it was like for *me*, never knowing what I was going to come home to?' he asked, his voice raw. 'There were days you never even got out of bed, and I'd come home to find Jacob sobbing in his cot! Of course I was worried about you. We all were. Does that make me a bad husband?'

She was suddenly ashamed. Lucas had never once doubted her, all through those terrible months, when many other men would have left. She should never have doubted him. If she'd just told him the truth from the start, he would have supported her. It was her own pride that had got in the way.

'Maddie, I've always believed in you,' Lucas said earnestly. 'But your depression was very real. Of course I watched you after Jacob. I had to. I needed to be sure you really were better. I was just looking out for you.' He put his hands on her shoulders and waited until she looked him in the eye. 'I'm on your side, Mads. You can tell me anything. I'm not going to judge you. But I can't have you lying to me. What about the next time, when Jacob cuts his lip or Emily sprains her wrist? Are you going to make up some story about that too?'

She felt very small. 'Of course not.'

'We're in this together,' he said. 'No more secrets from now on. Promise me?'

She stiffened. *No more secrets*. Now was the perfect opportunity to ask him about *his* secret: about the second mortgage, eighty thousand pounds he'd borrowed without telling her. She didn't want him to think she was deflecting or trying to shift the blame. And in comparison to what had now happened to their family, it seemed ridiculously trivial. But it still mattered. Marriage was a question of trust, and trust went both ways.

'Lucas, I'm not as fragile as you think,' she said. 'You don't have to protect me all the time. If there's anything you're not telling me, any secrets *you're* keeping, I'd rather know now.'

He looked genuinely puzzled. 'I tell you everything.'

She suddenly felt incredibly tired. She'd given him a chance to come clean and he'd doubled down on his lie. A week ago, she would never have believed her honest, principled husband capable of deceiving her once, never mind twice. It was as if the ground was shifting beneath her feet. She'd thought she'd known Lucas inside out but clearly she was wrong.

She remembered Candace's phone call. 'Your sister phoned me last night,' she said abruptly.

Lucas's hands on her shoulders were suddenly very still. 'When?'

'Just after you left to come home. She said she'd done something terrible and needed to apologise.' She searched his face, looking for any flicker that might betray him. 'She said you'd know why.'

Lucas dropped his hands and turned towards the garden again. She could normally read him well, but she had no idea what he was thinking now. It was unsettling, as if a stranger were standing in her kitchen.

The odd moment passed as swiftly as it had come. Lucas swung round and gave a brief, weary smile, himself again. 'I have no idea what she's talking about. She was almost comatose by the time I got there and still pretty drunk when I left. She was probably calling to apologise for dragging me away.'

He was lying. She knew it instinctively. She had no idea what he and Candace were hiding, but it had nothing to do with her sister-in-law's drinking, she was certain of that. In the space of two minutes, he'd lied to her twice. And she was little better herself: she'd come clean about Noah's bruises, but she still hadn't confessed to her memory lapses. What was happening to them? When had they become the kind of people who lied to each other?

She remembered reading once that when a couple lose a child, ninety per cent of marriages don't survive. She was beginning to understand why.

Lydia

Frank hasn't found out about Jimmy yet, Mae's careful only to bring him home when Frank's away on a long-distance trip, but Lydia knows it's only a matter of time before the stupid cow gets caught.

In the meantime, she lives in fear. Jimmy likes them very young, she knows from experience that's his preference, and Lydia is eleven now – but any port in a storm. She doesn't just bolt her bedroom door when Frank's away now, she pushes her heavy chest of drawers against it.

She's so angry, she could kill Mae. They had such a good thing going before Jimmy came back. Enough money coming in the door, a real chance at a proper family life. Frank had even offered to try to find Davy. He'd tracked her half-brother first to Liverpool, where Davy's dad was from, and then on to Birmingham. Frank'd promised to ask around next time he had a trip there. He'd already put the word out. Truckers looked out for each other, he said. They'd find him sooner or later, Frank had promised.

And now Mae has put it all on the line because of that bastard Jimmy. Lydia's seriously thought about sticking him when he's in one of his drunken stupors, but he sleeps with one eye open, does Jimmy. He's got good reason, the amount of people who'd like to see him dead. Anyway, she doesn't trust Mae not to grass her up. The rancid bitch would do it out of spite.

She drags her feet as she follows Mae up the hill to the Taylors' big house. She doesn't feel like playing with Julia today. Jimmy caught her in the bathroom this morning, when she was still half-asleep. The bastard had her pinned between the bath and the washbasin with his hand up her nightdress before she'd known what was happening. She can still feel the raw ache from his thick fingers between her legs. She hates him so much, but she hates herself more for letting her guard down.

Julia runs towards her as soon as she sees her, flinging her arms around her legs. Lydia picks the little girl up and hefts her onto her narrow hip as Mrs Taylor rushes out of the house without even bothering to say goodbye. I'd never treat *my* little girl like that, Lydia thinks bitterly. I wouldn't go out to work in an office when I could stay home and play with my daughter instead. I'd hug and kiss her every day and I'd never dump her with other people to look after. Mrs Taylor doesn't deserve to have a little girl. It'd serve her right if somebody came and took Julia away.

She takes Julia upstairs to play, but it's bright and sunny outside and the little girl soon gets bored with her dolls and puzzles. She wants to go outside, and frankly, that's fine by Lydia; the more distance she puts between herself and Mae, the better.

Julia runs into the back garden, straight past the greenhouse and the potting shed to the fence at the end that separates the garden from the old disused railway cutting running along the bottom. She waits for Lydia to catch up and then points to a house high on the opposite embankment, clinging to the edge like a ship's barnacle. It's been derelict since before Lydia was born, condemned when the crumbling escarpment became unstable. Over the years, locals have gutted it, scavenging everything from floor joists and roof tiles to doorknobs and bog seats. Frank even built a chicken coop out of old doors he wrenched off their hinges, though the hens didn't last long before the fox got them. These days, even the dossers don't much bother with the place. It's damp and stinks of piss. But Julia begs and begs to go and explore it and in the end Lydia thinks, what the hell.

Julia may only be four years old, but she's determined. She wriggles through a gap in the fence, her sturdy little legs pumping as she scrambles up the railway embankment. Her pretty new dress is already torn and muddy and Lydia thinks, serve you right. The kid has far too many new dresses, more than she can possibly wear. When she was Julia's age, she wore Davy's jumble sale hand-me-downs, little better than rags by the time she got them.

Lydia gives the little girl a boost over the top of the escarpment and they go round the side of the old house to the back door. Lydia hesitates suddenly. There are

172

rotting boards over the windows, some of which have been wrenched away and the blank, black holes look eerily like half-lidded eyes. The house feels oddly threatening and she doesn't want to go inside. She turns to tell Julia they're going home, but the kid is already ducking under her arm and charging into the house.

Cursing, Lydia follows her, yelling at her to come back. It's almost pitch-black inside and it smells like some strange dead thing. Even Julia is brought up short. They can hear the sound of dripping water in the darkness and something scuttles in the shadows. There is something about this place that chills her blood. She shivers. Let's go, she says, taking Julia's hand, but Julia giggles and pulls away, running into the darkness. Lydia shouts at her, it's not safe, she cries, you'll trip and hurt yourself, but the little girl just laughs.

Lydia hates the dark. But she goes after her, holding her arms out in front of her like a TV zombie so she doesn't walk into anything. Broken glass crunches underfoot. Something brushes her face, a huge cobweb, and she yelps in fear. She could kill Julia, she thinks, plucking it from her face. It'd serve her right if she left the kid here.

Suddenly there's a tremendous crash ahead of her, the sound of timber cracking, a tumble of plaster, a loud *whoosh!* and Julia gives a terrified scream. Lydia freezes, her heart pounding. She calls the girl's name, and for a long horrible moment there's silence, but then Julia starts to wail.

She's alive, at least. Lydia gropes her way towards the sound as fast as she dares, terrified that one wrong step will plunge her headlong into the darkness after the little girl.

She pauses at the doorway of what was once the kitchen, daylight visible through the gaps in the boarded-up windows. The floor in the centre has given way, exposing the raw splintered wood of the joists. She edges towards the dark maw and peers down into the old cellar. She can't see a thing, but she can hear Julia's whimpering sobs. *Great*, she thinks crossly. *Now I'm going to have to go down there among the rats and the spiders and get her out.*

She shouts to the girl she's coming and searches for a way down to the cellar. There must be a staircase of some sort. It takes her a few moments to find it, but her eyes are finally starting to adjust to the gloom. She goes down the stairs carefully, testing each tread for soundness before trusting it with her full weight. She has to step over several stairs that are soft or rotted away and nearly falls, but she reaches the bottom safely, her body pulsing with adrenalin. The urge to get out, to run away, is almost overwhelming.

Julia calls her name again and she snaps that she's coming. She can hear the kid moving about, stumbling in the darkness, which means she's not badly hurt. Keep still, she tells her, you'll only hurt yourself, but once again the girl ignores her and then yowls when she bumps into something in the dark.

For God's sake! Lydia shouts. Keep still!

She can see the kid clearly now, caught in a stab of dim light from the hole above. She's filthy and covered in plaster dust, but she seems OK, more or less. She won't stop crying, though, her tears making train tracks on her dirty cheeks. Strings of snot hang unappealingly from her nose and her primped blonde curls are matted with dust. Mummy's going to be so cross with you, Julia hiccoughs, my dress is ruined, you're going to get into big trouble!

Lydia wants to shake her. And she does, she kneels on the filthy basement floor and shakes the girl by the shoulders. Stop crying! she yells. I told you not to go in, it's your fault, she shouts, you did this!

Julia's head snaps back and forth, she's not crying now, she's too scared, and Lydia knows she should stop. She can feel her heartbeat pulsing in her ears. All around her is a deadening silence, as if she's wrapped in black cotton wool. She lets go of the girl's shoulders and her hands close round the small throat. An abyss opens beneath her feet and the anger and fear drain away. She is in a void beyond rage, beyond pain. She doesn't stop. She *can't* stop. It is no longer a choice. The quiet is absolute. Julia doesn't make a sound.

Afterwards, she is calm as she covers the child's body with rubble and broken beams, checking to be sure that no part of her is visible. She feels oddly protective of the little girl again. She doesn't want rats or a fox to find her, she must make sure she's properly covered up.

She goes back upstairs to the sunshine, wiping off the dust and dirt from the basement on the long grass. She is already the keeper of so many secrets. One more won't make any difference.

Chapter 21

Saturday 10.00 a.m.

Maddie was standing in the supermarket aisle, surrounded by bottles of Johnson's shampoo, tubs of Sudocrem, boxes of nappies and packets of wet wipes. She felt groggy, as if she'd just woken up from a deep, drugged sleep. She blinked hard, trying to get her bearings. She had absolutely no idea how she'd got here. She couldn't even remember leaving the house. The last thing she could recall was making breakfast for Emily and Jacob. Boiled eggs and Marmite soldiers. After that – nothing.

Her head hurt. It was like having a hangover, only a thousand times worse. Her mouth was dry and cottony and she ached all over, as if she was going down with flu.

'Oi!'

She jumped. A security guard was making his way down the shopping aisle towards her as fast as his thick body would allow. 'Oi!' he yelled again.

The aisle was surprisingly empty for a Saturday morning, apart from a young mother who studiously refused to meet her eye. The security guard was clearly addressing Maddie.

He was panting by the time he drew level with her. 'What the hell is your problem, lady?'

'I don't know,' she said, confused.

His eyes narrowed. 'That supposed to be funny?'

'I'm sorry. I think I zoned out for a minute ...'

'We've got you on CCTV,' he interrupted rudely. 'Throwing a bloody hissy fit in the middle of the aisle! Chucking things all over the place! We could prosecute you for criminal damage!'

She looked around her. Someone had knocked down a shelf of disposable nappies; at least a dozen boxes lay scattered across the floor. 'It wasn't me!' she protested.

He pushed his face uncomfortably close to her own, and she backed away. 'They've decided to let you off with a warning,' he said unpleasantly. 'You're bloody lucky, if you ask me. It's not you who's got to clear this mess up, is it? If it was up to me, I'd throw the book at you. Crying and shouting and carrying on!'

'I don't know what you're talking about!'

'It's on tape!' he snarled.

Maddie gripped the handle of her shopping trolley, suddenly really scared. She'd learned to work around her memory lapses, but this was different. Until this week, she'd never acted out of character or done anything she wouldn't normally do. But vandalising the nursery had been so angry, so *violent*. And now this.

She'd obsessively googled *blackouts and memory loss*, even though she'd known Dr Google was hardly likely

177

to put her mind at rest. She'd discovered they could be caused by brain damage, drugs, excessive alcohol consumption, disorders affecting brain function, emotional trauma, stress – in other words, anything. In her case, the only thing she could rule out was alcohol, since she hadn't had a drink since she'd found out she was pregnant with Noah. It had to be the pills she was on. The after-effects felt too pharmaceutical for it to be anything else. If she didn't know better, she'd think she'd been slipped a roofie. She knew she should go back to Dr Calkins, but she was too frightened. They'd take the children away from her. They'd think she was the one who'd hurt Noah.

Maybe she had.

No. She'd never harm her own child.

She knew it deep in her soul. Her instinct to protect her children was visceral; had been from the moment she'd discovered she was pregnant with each baby. No matter what else she might do during one of her fugue states, she would never hurt her children. She would, quite literally, step in front of a train for them. Once, when Emily had been about two, Maddie hadn't quite put the brake on her pushchair down properly when she'd stopped to talk to a friend in the high street and the stroller had started to roll away towards the busy road. Without even thinking, Maddie had thrown herself into the road to stop it, heedless of the large lorry bearing down on them. It'd missed them both by just inches.

The security guard grabbed her shoulder and frogmarched her from the building, forcing her to leave her half-filled trolley behind. Her cheeks burned with humiliation as he left her on the pavement outside, with a final nasty warning not to try coming back.

She gazed at the sea of cars in front of her. She had no idea where she'd parked. She searched her memory for some hint, but she couldn't even remember driving here. One minute she was spooning egg yolk into Jacob's mouth, and the next she was standing in the supermarket surrounded by boxes of Pampers—

Oh, God, the children! Had she brought them with her? *Left* them somewhere?

She speed-dialled home as she ran back inside the supermarket to look for them, exhaling audibly when Emily picked up the phone. 'Oh, Emily, thank heavens! Is Jacob there?'

'Yes,' Emily said, sounding puzzled. 'Daddy's playing with him in the garden. He's taking us to Auntie Jayne's in a minute. Do you want me to get him?'

'No, no, it's fine. I just wanted to check everything was all right. I'll be home soon.'

She went back outside before the security guard spotted her. Clutching her bag to her side, she began running along the rows of parked cars, trying to spot her battered Land Rover amid the shiny people-carriers and smart German engineering. She couldn't see it anywhere. Her pace quickened as she turned into the next row. She wasn't sure how much more she could take. She was holding it together by the thinnest of threads for Emily and Jacob's sake, when all she really wanted to do was curl up into a ball and die. But the blows kept coming. The pathologist's report, the police interrogations, the growing distance between her and Lucas; and now it seemed she was literally losing her mind.

Oh, God, where was the car? She just wanted to go home. *Where was the damn car?*

She was running blindly now. A black Audi pulled abruptly out of its parking spot and she stumbled against it, sprawling across the bonnet. The driver swore at her and she backed away, spinning in circles as she scanned the car park. She still couldn't see the Land Rover. She had no idea where she was or what she was doing. Her throat closed and she struggled to catch her breath. Black spots danced before her eyes. She had to get out of here.

A silver-haired woman pushing a trolley stopped beside her. 'Excuse me, dear, are you all right?'

Maddie gave a hysterical half-laugh, half-sob. 'No. I've lost my car. I've lost my baby and my car, and quite possibly my husband. I'm not all right.'

'You've lost your baby?' the woman exclaimed, looking around as if expecting to see a pram hidden among the cars. 'How long has he been missing? Have you called the police?'

'The police know all about it,' Maddie said bitterly. 'They think I did it. They think I killed him.' She gazed at the woman, whose eyes were wide with disbelief. 'He just died! I don't know why. How could they ever think I did it? I loved him! Why don't they believe me?'

The older woman's startled expression softened. 'Oh, my dear. Your baby died?'

'It wasn't me!'

The woman hesitated. 'Let me put my shopping away and I'll help you find your car,' she said gently. 'Wait here, dear.'

Maddie was incapable of doing anything else. She stood like a child exactly where the older woman left her, oblivious to the curious stares of other shoppers eddying around her. Her good Samaritan returned and led her back to the safety of the pavement.

'Now, dear,' the woman said, surveying the car park. 'What sort of car do you have?'

'A Land Rover. One of those old ones.'

'Well, that shouldn't be too hard to find. Don't worry, dear. I've done the same thing myself a dozen times. One of the joys of getting older, I'm afraid. I don't suppose your car has one of those remote-clicker things so we can make it beep?'

'It's too old,' Maddie said, pulling out her keys. 'You have to unlock it with— Oh. Oh, God, I'm so stupid!'

'My dear?'

'These are my husband's keys! I must have come in his car, not mine. I do that, sometimes, if he's parked behind me.' Her eyes filled. 'I'm so sorry, I don't know what's wrong with me.'

The woman smiled kindly. 'Never mind. Let's just find it, shall we? What is it, your husband's car?'

'It's a silver Honda – wait, I see it. There, with the rug on the parcel shelf.' Her words fell over each other

181

in her rush to be gone. 'Thank you so much for helping, you've been so kind. I really appreciate it. But I'd better get home now, I've been gone too long already.'

She ran towards Lucas's car, suddenly frantic to escape. She climbed in and locked the door behind her, then leaned her forehead against the steering wheel, her heart pounding like it would explode from her chest. It took her several minutes before she brought her panicked breathing under control sufficiently to be able to drive.

When she was ready, she put the key in the ignition and reached beneath the seat to move it forward to a more comfortable position. Something was jammed in the mechanism. She gave it a gentle tug. A wedge of crumpled envelopes and bills addressed to Lucas spilled into her hands. He was hopeless with paperwork; his idea of filing was to shove everything into a drawer and jam it shut. She was about to shove it all back under the seat again, when something caught her eye.

She unfolded the paper and flattened it out against the steering wheel, her disbelief mounting as she read the page.

Chapter 22

Saturday 11.30 a.m.

She leaned on Candace's doorbell, not lifting her finger even when she heard running feet inside. She'd driven here straight from the supermarket and was in no mood to calm down, her inertia finally dispelled by fury. She'd had enough of being lied to and taken for a fool. She wasn't leaving until she got some answers.

The door opened and Maddie pushed past her sister-in-law without waiting to be invited inside. She hadn't been to Candace's house for months and was shocked how dirty and untidy the place was. 'Where's Lucas?'

'In the kitchen. Is everything all right?'

Lucas leaped up from the kitchen table when he saw her, scattering paperwork. 'What are you doing here? I took the children over to Jayne's. She said she'd drop them back this afternoon.'

'I know,' Maddie said tersely. 'I got your text.'

Candace pulled out a chair. 'Why don't you sit down while I put the kettle on?'

'I don't want any more damned tea!' Maddie erupted. 'Jesus! I've had enough tea in the past week to float the *Titanic*! Why does everyone think a gallon of Typhoo is the answer to everything? Arm shot off, have a cup of tea! House burned down, have a bloody cup of tea!'

'I don't know what's upset you,' Lucas said soothingly, 'but let's calm down and talk about it sensibly.'

She thrust the letter she'd found in the car at him. 'All right, if you want to talk, let's talk about *this*.'

He scanned it, confused. 'Why are you giving me this?'

'What did you think you were doing, going behind my back like this? Did you really think I wouldn't find out?'

'Find out what? It's just a confirmation letter from the insurance company. They insisted we increase our coverage when we got the loan, that's the way it works. I know the premiums are more expensive, but we didn't have a choice. We can drop them again when we pay off the loan. I thought I'd told you.'

'The loan you took out behind my back!' Maddie cried.

He looked genuinely shocked. '*What*?'

'You took a second mortgage out against the house without even telling me and then secretly doubled my life insurance!' She snatched back the letter. 'What are you up to, Lucas? Are you planning to bump me off? Or just drive me mad so you can lock me up and sell the sanctuary to developers?'

'Are you insane? We discussed it! You signed the paperwork!'

'I did no such thing!'

He gaped at her. 'Maddie, what the hell? Of course you did! We were at the bank for bloody hours! You bitched about it all the way home!'

It was her turn to look startled. 'I didn't,' she said, but her tone was suddenly less certain.

'Maddie, I don't know what you think is going on, but I'd *never* do something like this without telling you,' he said vehemently. 'You weren't happy about it, neither of us were, but we agreed it was the only way to get the bank off our backs. Haven't we got enough to deal with without going through all this again?'

'When?' she demanded. 'When did all this happen?'

He threw up his hands. 'I don't know. A few months ago, before Noah was born. Come on, Maddie. You *must* remember.'

She felt as if she had vertigo. Lucas sounded so *sure*. She searched his face, looking for the slightest hint he was hiding something. He seemed tired, impatient, anxious – but if he was lying, he deserved an Oscar.

Was she actually going mad? Not just ditsy, not just forgetful, actually *mad*? If Lucas was telling the truth, then she *had* signed off on the loan and she'd completely forgotten. How was she supposed to function if she couldn't remember something this big, this important? What on earth was *wrong* with her?

Candace was scrolling through her phone. 'Here,' she said, showing Maddie the screen. 'Look. A text from you just before Christmas, asking me to babysit the kids while you went to the bank with Lucas.'

Maddie stared at the screen. 'I don't *remember*!' she

cried, forcing down a surge of panic. 'I don't remember going to the bank, I don't remember any of it. What's wrong with me, Lucas?'

She didn't miss the wary glance he exchanged with his sister. 'It's those damn pills. The doctor said this might happen. Come on, Maddie.' His voice gentled, the way hers did when she soothed a skittish horse. 'This is me you're talking to. Do you really think I'd do something like that and not tell you?'

Candace thrust a mug of tea into her hands as Lucas guided her to a chair. She sank into it, the room swimming around her. Even to herself, she sounded paranoid. Lucas had never let her down, never lied to her before. What reason did he have to do so now? It was the stress of losing Noah, it was sending her out of her mind. Nothing seemed the way it should. She took a sip of tea. Even that didn't taste quite right. 'Am I going crazy?' she begged.

Lucas squeezed her arm. 'Of course not.'

'Why did we need the money, anyway?' she asked desperately. 'What was it for?'

Was she imagining it, or was there the slightest hesitation before he replied? 'I can't buy into the partnership without it,' he sighed. 'We discussed it, remember? You didn't want to sell any land at the sanctuary, so we decided to borrow against the house instead. We were going to clear our overdraft and use the rest for my partnership. The company will be able to expand and bid on bigger projects. We'll be able to pay the loan off within the next two to three years.'

'Why didn't my accountant know about it, then?'

'Why would he? It has nothing to do with the sanctuary.'

He was right, of course. Her accountant had only discovered the loan when she'd asked him about using their house as collateral. There was no reason for him to have known about it otherwise. She was being ridiculous. She was accusing Lucas of fraud and embezzlement, but her only 'evidence' was her own very unreliable memory.

She looked from Lucas to his sister. Something still didn't ring true here. She couldn't put her finger on it, but something wasn't right.

She closed her eyes briefly. She was so confused. She couldn't seem to get anything straight in her head. She was going mad. It was the only explanation. The violence in the nursery and the supermarket, the blackouts like the one she'd had this morning, and now this.

What else? asked a small voice inside her head. *What else did you do?*

'Lucas,' Candace said suddenly. 'Lucas, I can't do this to her anymore. I think it's time we told her the truth.'

Lydia

The police don't find Julia for four days. They do a 'fingertip' search of the area, covering every inch of ground for a mile around the Taylors' house, they search the woods and alongside the railway line and the allotments, and even the derelict house on top of the escarpment, but they don't find the little girl. (Heads will roll for that, later.)

They waste days searching for the tall, thin man with his arm in a sling whom Lydia described hanging around the Taylors' back gate just before she went inside to get Julia an ice lolly. They put out bulletins on the news asking for people to contact the police if they see the blue van with one door painted green that Lydia told them the tall thin man was driving. They sit her down with a police sketch artist and she describes the man's odd eyes, the wall eye that looks right even when he is staring straight at you. She describes the scar above his eyebrow and his straggly grey moustache and the chipped front tooth, and the artist draws it all, just as she describes.

It's a good likeness. Too good, in fact, because Jimmy is recognised; several friends and neighbours grass him up and the police haul him in for questioning. But Jimmy is able to prove he was nowhere near the Taylors' house the day Julia went missing, for once he has a cast-iron alibi: he was in the police cells in Birmingham, held on charges of GBH. He was safely behind bars hours before Julia disappeared, it couldn't possibly have been him.

Which suddenly makes the police consider Lydia's story with fresh eyes.

It doesn't take long for it to fall apart. Once they know the tall, thin man with the sling is a lie, they view everything she has said with suspicion. They press her about when she last saw Julia, *exactly*, they demand to know everything she said and did in the time leading up to Julia's disappearance. She covers up her lies with more lies, she says that Julia 'might' have gone out of the back garden chasing a lost puppy. At first she swears she didn't follow her, she never left the garden, but then a neighbour comes forward and says she saw Lydia alone in the railway cutting that afternoon, and so then Lydia admits that, yes, she did follow Julia, just to bring her home, but she fell down and hurt her knee and the little girl ran on ahead without her and after that she never saw her again.

It's a tissue of lies and the police know it. They think she's just trying to cover up the fact she wasn't watching Julia, like she was supposed to; they think she sneaked away to meet a friend, they have no idea what she's really hiding. But they search the local area again, more thoroughly this time, now they know Julia didn't disappear into the back of a blue van with a strange man, and this time they find her, buried

189

under the rubble in the basement of the derelict house.

Until now, Lydia hadn't quite believed Julia was actually dead. Hadn't Lydia always woken up after Jimmy's visits? Sometimes it'd taken hours, but she'd always woken up in the end. She understands dead is different from unconscious or asleep, she does *know* that, but until this moment some part of her had still believed Julia would wake up and come safely home.

At least, that's what she tells herself.

A special detective comes in to talk to her, and she knows immediately he's not going to be fooled as easily as everyone else. He's older than the other policemen and he's got a tired look in his eyes that reminds her of Frank, like he's seen too many terrible, ugly things. He asks her so many questions, on and on at her with his questions. Asking the same thing in different ways, trying to trip her up. They get her a solicitor who they say is on her side, but when Lydia gets tired and asks if she can go home now, the solicitor gives her a sad look and says no, she has to answer the detective, she has to tell him everything if she ever wants to go home again.

She sticks to her story, even when a policewoman comes in all excited and says they've found a button off her dress in Julia's dead little fist, a button Lydia guesses the little girl must've torn off when … at the end. Mae hasn't taught Lydia much, but she's taught her when to keep her mouth shut. She swears on a stack of bibles, on her mother's life, that Julia ran off after the puppy, she won't be shaken from her story: she'd tried to follow her, to catch up with her, but she'd fallen and hurt her ankle—

You told us it was your knee.

It was my knee. My knee and my ankle. I told you. Julia ran and when I tried to follow her, I couldn't find her, I looked everywhere and then I came home and told Mae and she called you.

The detective doesn't believe her, of course, but like Mae always says, it's not what someone believes, it's what they can prove. It's Mae, not the stupid, sad solicitor, who finally storms into the interview room and tells the police enough is enough, they've got nothing, her Lydia hasn't done anything wrong, this is police harassment, you can't treat a kid like this, she's got rights!

It's nearly two in the morning before they let her go home. She's tired and scared but she likes the way Mae is looking at her now, like she *matters*.

For a week she thinks she's got away with it, she even goes to the Taylors' house with Mae and Frank the day of the funeral to pay her respects, she stands with the huge silent crowds outside their big house. Julia's in that box, she thinks. She's in that box and they're going to put her in the cold, hard ground and cover her with dirt and the worms will get her and I did it.

Suddenly, the reality of what she's done hits her and she's seized with a cold, blinding terror. She can't help it, she tries to stop it, but a dreadful, nervous snort of laughter bursts out of her, and she covers her face with her hands and pretends to be crying, but the detective sees her, she feels his sharp eyes on her, *he knows*, and she realises her time of reckoning is coming.

Chapter 23

Sunday 2.30 p.m.

'Would you have agreed to the loan if Lucas had told you what it was really for?' Sarah asked.

Maddie rubbed her temples. She hadn't slept a wink all night; she'd had so little sleep in the last two weeks, she was almost starting to hallucinate. 'I don't know, Mum,' she said wearily. 'But that's not the point. He *lied* to me.'

'And I'm not excusing that, but his heart was in the right place—'

'Why are you taking his side?' she exclaimed. 'He lied to my face, Mum! I knew there was something going on with him and Candace, and he made me think I was just being paranoid! If she hadn't forced him to tell me the truth yesterday, he'd still be lying to me about it now!'

Sarah lifted a cardboard box of donations onto her kitchen table and began to sort through it. 'I'm not taking his side, Maddie. What he did was wrong, but surely not unforgivable? You agreed to the loan when you thought he wanted it to buy into a partnership at his firm, so it's not about the money, is it? Is it the fact that he lied to you that's bothering you, or that he gave the money to his sister?'

Maddie hadn't told her mother she didn't remember agreeing to the loan in the first place. She was so tired of being on the back foot, of being a problem everyone else had to fix. 'I love Candace, Mum, I do, but I'm the one Lucas is married to,' she said. 'He should never have done this without talking to me first, and he knows that or he would have told me the truth in the first place.'

'I realise Candace isn't the most reliable person, but from what you've said, they were very businesslike about it, drawing up a repayment plan and everything,' Sarah said. 'I'm absolutely not condoning the fact that he lied, but surely you can understand him wanting to help his sister?'

Maddie did understand. That was part of the problem. As angry as she was that Lucas had lied, she was also hurt that he hadn't had more faith in her. She'd never tried to come between him and Candace. If he'd told her he wanted to borrow the money to help his sister buy her flat, she wouldn't have been happy about it, but she would have agreed. Candace was family, after all. And Sarah was right, they'd put it on an official footing, with Candace agreeing in writing to pay back the loan within two years, once her business had been up and running long enough for the bank to agree to give her a mortgage. But there was no getting away from the fact that Lucas had put the roof over their heads in jeopardy without telling her. Candace might have the best of intentions, but if she fell off the wagon permanently, what then? Regardless of how fond she was of her sister-in-law, Maddie was tired of always coming second to her needs. Now, of all times, she needed Lucas to put their family first.

'Does he normally lie to you?' Sarah asked.

'Of course not!'

'Do you think he set out to hurt or upset you?'

'No, but—'

'Life isn't black or white, Maddie. You should know that by now. Most of us live in the grey areas. He told you he didn't want to worry you. He was foolish, but give him the benefit of the doubt and take him at his word.' She fished around in the box for some teacups and frowned in dismay. 'Oh, dear. Not even a matching pair.'

Maddie bridled. 'I'm not a child, Mum! I run the sanctuary without his help and I handle nearly all the household finances. It's not just the fact he told me an outright lie, it's that he's making decisions for both of us, as if I don't matter. We've already lent Candace more than we can afford to start her own business, but it's barely had time to get off the ground. Now he's given her more to buy her own flat.'

Sarah picked up another cardboard box. 'Candace may have had a rackety few years, but as I understand it, by and large she's got her life back on track. Lucas knows his sister. If he's so sure she'll be able to pay him back, you have to trust his judgement.'

194

'It's easy for you to say. How would you feel if Dad had mortgaged this house without telling you?'

Her mother's hands stilled. She rarely talked about Maddie's father. Maddie had no real idea of the kind of man he'd been, or even how her parents had met. There was no secret about it; on the odd occasion she'd asked about him, Sarah had answered readily enough. It was more that she felt as if she was intruding on her parents' privacy, entering a room that had been theirs alone. Sarah had loved her husband very much, and three decades later, she still grieved for him.

'I'd have trusted he knew what he was doing,' Sarah said quietly. 'Maddie, Lucas lied to you, but by your own admission, it was a one-off. Why does it matter to you so much? Is something wrong between the two of you?'

'I don't expect Lucas to be perfect, Mum. I'm not asking him to tell me every little thing that's going on in his life.' She picked fretfully at her fingernails. 'The papers I found in the car,' she said in a sudden rush. 'Lucas has doubled our life insurance. He said the mortgage company insisted on it, because of the loan.'

'You think he plans to kill you for your life insurance?' Sarah asked calmly.

It sounded preposterous now her mother had said the words aloud. Delusional, even. 'No, of course not!'

'Do you have any reason to think Lucas might hurt you?'

'Mum, how can you even say that?'

'You're the one who mentioned the insurance.'

195

'That's not what I meant!' she cried, wondering exactly what she *had* meant.

'Does this have something to do with Noah?' Sarah asked shrewdly.

Maddie hated herself for even thinking it. But was it possible ... just possible ... that Candace *had* hurt her son, and that Lucas knew about it? Candace wouldn't have done it deliberately, of course. But perhaps there had been some sort of accident. It would certainly explain why Candace had started drinking again and the odd confession in that voicemail: the 'terrible' thing she said she'd done. Lucas had covered for his sister about the loan. It was a small stretch to imagine him covering for her again.

An even darker thought occurred to her. Lucas knew how much she'd suffered with her depression after Jacob. He must know how destabilising it would be for her to lose her child. If he really wanted the sanctuary sold—

It was unthinkable. And yet there must be some part of her that considered it a real possibility or she wouldn't have been up half the night trying to convince herself she was just being paranoid.

It suddenly occurred to her that she had no real idea what her mother thought of Lucas. She'd always assumed Sarah loved him, but in six years her mother had never actually ventured an opinion on her son-in-law, acting instead as an echo chamber for Maddie's own emotions. Perhaps that's what parents were supposed to do for their children, but it was a little disconcerting to discover that she had no idea what was really going on in her mother's head.

She was so confused. It felt as if she were blundering around in a fog, hopelessly trying to find her bearings. She had gone from thinking no one she knew could have hurt Noah to thinking everyone could have done, including herself. And she was so *tired*. She simply didn't have the emotional bandwidth to deal with this right now.

'I googled Lucas last night,' she said abruptly. 'Lucas and Candace.'

Sarah gave her a long, level look, but said nothing.

'I don't know anything about his life before we met,' she added defensively. 'I never asked before, because I didn't think it mattered, but now …'

'So what did you discover?' her mother asked. 'On Google?'

For a split second, Maddie considered telling her. There had been numerous entries for both Lucas and Candace, dating back a dozen years: accolades for Lucas's architectural designs, LinkedIn recommendations for Candace's IT expertise, a newspaper profile from when she'd run the London Marathon, telephone and email listings – the usual virtual footprints everyone left nowadays. Beyond that, nothing. *Nothing at all*.

It was as if Lucas and Candace Drummond had materialised fully formed out of thin air twelve years ago. These days, with the internet, it was easy to research someone's background, but she couldn't find a single reference to either of them before then; no previous jobs held, no colleges attended, no voter registration, nothing. None of their social media profiles mentioned their schools or where they'd grown up. There were no photographs of them with old school friends or at college reunions. Most ominous of all, there was no record of their parents' death in a house fire, the kind of story that would have definitely made at least the local newspaper. She was no investigative journalist, but it was odd. More than odd, in fact.

She didn't want her night terrors given substance. She didn't want to wake up in the middle of the night, wondering if the man lying next to her was plotting to kill her or – perhaps even worse – have her committed to a madhouse.

'Nothing,' she said. 'I found nothing at all.'

Chapter 24

Monday 12.30 p.m.

Emily pirouetted on the small round dais in front of the three-sided mirror, holding out her skirts. 'What do you think, Mummy?'

There was an unexpected lump in Maddie's throat. Seeing Emily standing there in her white first communion dress, fair hair tumbling around her shoulders beneath the frothy lace veil, she had a sudden vision of her daughter as she would look on her wedding day. 'You look beautiful, Emily. Absolutely beautiful.'

Emily glowed and spun back towards the mirror. 'I look like I'm getting married.'

'You do,' Maddie said softly.

Sarah hadn't been particularly religious, but Maddie's father had been Catholic, and in his memory, Sarah had raised her in his faith. Maddie had lapsed when she was a teenager, but she and Lucas had married in their local Catholic church, and all three of their children had been baptised there – Noah's christening had been less than four weeks before he'd died. At the beginning of the school year, she'd signed Emily up to make her first communion with the rest of her class at her small Catholic primary school, but it'd been more about the dress and the party than a religious sacrament.

The saleswoman returned with a tiny pearl tiara. 'We've had a lot of little girls from Holy Cross Primary in this week,' she smiled, taking the tiara out of its box. 'This one's a little bit more expensive than some of the others, but it's definitely a favourite.'

Emily's eyes widened with delight. 'I can have a tiara?'

Maddie nodded at the saleswoman, who carefully placed it on Emily's head. She worked the veil around it, draping it delicately over Emily's shoulders and standing back to admire her work. 'You look just like one of our brides,' she sighed.

Emily twirled again, admiring her reflection over first one shoulder and then the other with innocent vanity. Impulsively, she leaped off the dais and threw her arms around Maddie's waist. 'Thank you, Mummy. I love it.'

Maddie hugged her back. It was rare for Emily to be so outwardly affectionate; like her grandmother, she was generally self-contained and undemonstrative, rarely seeking hugs or cuddles. Since Noah's death, however, she'd been much more tactile, as if in constant need of reassurance.

Maddie helped her daughter change back into her normal clothes and watched as the saleswoman boxed the communion dress carefully between sheets of tissue paper. It felt so wrong to be carrying on with life as if nothing had happened; celebrating Emily's first communion when they hadn't even been able to hold

Noah's funeral. But her daughter needed some normality, and Maddie needed a reason to go on living. Somehow, she had to pick up the pieces of her life, for the sake of the two children she still had.

Emily skipped beside her as they walked back to the car park by the library. 'Can we go for an ice cream now, Mummy?'

'I'm sorry, darling,' Maddie said reluctantly. 'I know I said we would, but that's before I knew you were going to try on ten dresses! We're running late to pick up Jacob. We don't have time for ice cream.'

Her daughter stopped skipping. 'But you promised.'

Maddie felt the familiar tug of maternal guilt. 'I know I did, and I'm so sorry. But Auntie Jayne has to go out and I said we'd be back to collect your brother by one o'clock.' She put her arm around Emily's shoulders. 'I'm sorry, sweetheart. We'll do it tomorrow.'

Emily shrugged. 'It's OK.'

'I promise, we'll get ice cream tomorrow. We'll go and get cones and feed the ducks, how about that?'

'It's all right, Mummy,' Emily said. 'I understand.'

She seemed like a little old lady, Maddie thought uneasily, so polite and considerate. She said as much to Jayne, as they stood in her friend's kitchen a little later.

'It's like she's aged forty years overnight,' she explained, watching Emily walking solemnly around Jayne's new rose garden like a Victorian matron taking the air. 'A month ago, she'd have thrown a hissy fit if I reneged on a promise to buy ice cream. And now she

201

just calmly gets in the car and offers to help me with dinner when we get home.'

'It doesn't take a shrink to know why,' Jayne sighed. 'She's scared something bad will happen to her if she steps out of line. What do they call it? Survivor guilt?'

Maddie switched Jacob to her other hip as he grizzled fretfully in her arms, straining away from her. She understood how he felt; she was so tired, she wanted to cry, too. 'But what do I do about it?'

'Just give it time,' Jayne said.

By the time they got back home, Jacob's grizzles had given way to full-blown crying. He was gnawing on his fist, drool dampening his T-shirt, and his cheeks were bright red and shiny. He was teething again; he'd been up most of the previous night.

Maddie gave him a spoonful of Calpol and took him upstairs to settle him down, sitting with him until he fell asleep, his favourite plastic dinosaur clutched in his hand.

Emily was colouring at the kitchen table when Maddie came back downstairs. 'Emily, will you be all right for an hour? I thought I might lie down for a minute. Just while Jacob's having a nap.'

Her daughter didn't glance up. 'OK, Mummy.'

'Don't answer the door, or—'

'Use the stove or answer the phone. It's OK, Mummy. I know what to do.'

Maddie kissed the top of her daughter's head and

went upstairs, sliding gratefully between the cool sheets. She just needed to close her eyes for a few minutes. Now that the Easter holidays had started, she was juggling the children along with the sanctuary and everything else. If she could just get some rest, maybe she could make sense of the confusion in her head ...

It seemed just moments later she was being shaken awake. 'Maddie!' Someone shook her shoulder again. 'Maddie, please wake up!'

Groggily, Maddie opened her eyes. A woman's face loomed over the bed and Maddie screamed in shock.

'It's OK, Maddie. It's Jessica Towner. We met at the hospital?'

Maddie struggled up against the pillows. 'What are you doing here?'

'I'm with the social worker assigned to your case. It's just routine,' she added, as Maddie scrambled out of bed. 'Please, there's no need to get upset.'

Maddie glanced at the clock beside her bed. It was four-thirty in the afternoon. She'd been asleep for hours. 'What are you doing in my house?' she demanded. 'How did you get in?'

'Your daughter Emily. Don't worry, she insisted I push my ID through the letter box before she opened the door. You should be proud of her.'

Maddie flushed, embarrassed that the social worker had caught her in bed. What must the woman think of her, allowing her nine-year-old daughter to answer the door?

'I don't understand. Why didn't anyone call me and tell me you were coming?'

'We like to make informal follow-up visits in situations like this. Maddie, I don't want to worry you, but we need to take Jacob to hospital.'

Maddie's heart stood still.

'There's no need to panic,' Jessica called out belatedly, as Maddie bolted down the hall to Jacob's room. 'He's going to be fine. But there is a chance he's taken an overdose of paracetamol—'

His room was empty. Maddie whirled round. 'Where is he?' she shouted.

'My colleague Carol is downstairs with him. An ambulance is already on its way.'

Maddie raced down the stairs. Emily sat at the kitchen table, her blue eyes huge in her pale face. A short, overweight woman with close-cropped grey hair stood behind her daughter, dictating directions to the house into the mobile jammed beneath her double chin. Jacob was unnaturally quiet in the woman's arms, his eyes half-closed, his head lolling against her shoulder. Maddie's heart skipped a beat. *Not again. It couldn't be happening again.*

Maddie rushed over to her son, but the woman turned away so she couldn't get to him.

'Give him to me!' she cried.

'Let Carol talk to the paramedics,' Jessica said, putting her arm on Maddie's. 'She knows what she's doing.'

She shrugged the woman off. 'Let me have my son!'

'I'm afraid that's not possible just now,' Jessica said

steadily. 'As I've already explained, Maddie, it's normal procedure to make unscheduled follow-up calls after a suspicious death. You didn't answer the door, and your daughter told us you were in bed—'

'Jacob's teething, I was up all night! I haven't slept! I just wanted to close my eyes for five minutes!' Her voice rose and the two women exchanged glances. Maddie forced herself to sound calm. 'Look, I'd put Jacob down for his nap, and Emily was colouring in the kitchen, it's not like I left them alone or anything.'

'I understand that. But when we checked on your son, as we were duty-bound to do, we found him in a dazed state in his bedroom with an empty bottle of Calpol in his cot. Obviously, his safety and well-being is our first priority.'

The older woman put her phone away. 'They'll be here in a few minutes.'

'Did you give him Calpol, Maddie?' Jessica asked.

She immediately felt defensive. 'Yes, but only a teaspoon, like it says on the bottle.'

'But you left the bottle in his room?'

'No!' She hesitated, suddenly unsure. She'd been so tired. It was possible she'd left it on the windowsill, which was near enough for him to reach. 'He couldn't have got the lid off, anyway, it's got one of those child-safety tops. He's only two, he could never have opened it himself.'

'You never know,' Jessica said. 'Maybe you didn't screw it on properly. Can you remember how much Calpol was left in the bottle?'

Maddie shook her head helplessly.

'Never mind. We'll work on the assumption it was full. Better safe than sorry.'

They were judging her, she could feel it. One dead baby and another child half-unconscious. They must think she was a psychopath or one of those women with Munchausen's by proxy, who hurt their own children to get attention.

'Is Jacob going to die, too?' Emily asked suddenly.

'No, darling!' Maddie said quickly. 'He's going to be absolutely fine.'

The woman holding Jacob opened the back door. 'Ambulance is here.'

Maddie started towards the door, but Jessica discreetly blocked her way. 'Why don't you follow behind? You can't leave your daughter alone and she can't come in the ambulance.'

Maddie wanted to scream with frustration, but she didn't have a choice. She and Emily watched as the woman carrying Jacob climbed into the back of the ambulance, panting heavily. Jessica got into a red Prius parked in the drive, presumably the car in which the two women had arrived.

She called Lucas as she got into the car. He picked up immediately.

'I'm on my way to the hospital,' he said tersely. 'The social worker called me. I'll meet you there.'

He hung up. Maddie tossed the phone onto the front seat. She couldn't believe it was happening again. The paramedics, the ambulance, the desperate dash to the hospital. How was it even possible? There's no way she'd have left an open bottle of Calpol in Jacob's reach. She was certain of it.

Except she wasn't certain of anything anymore.

Lucas was already in the Emergency Room when she arrived and Jacob had been taken to triage.

'Can we go through?' Maddie asked anxiously.

'We're to wait,' Lucas said. 'Someone will be through in a minute.'

'Is he all right? Are they pumping his stomach? What did they tell you?'

Lucas looked grey with anxiety and exhaustion. 'You know as much as I do.'

'I don't like it here,' Emily said suddenly. 'I want to go home.'

'I know, sweetheart,' Maddie said distractedly.

'What on earth happened?' Lucas asked her quietly. 'How did he get hold of a bottle of Calpol, for God's sake?'

She heard accusation in his tone. 'I put the top on, I know I did.'

'I never said you didn't. But you must have left the bottle in his reach. You were the only one there.'

His voice was cool. He'd apologised for lying to her and she'd accepted it and apologised herself for her wild accusations, but there was a tension between them, a wary mistrust that neither of them seemed capable of dispelling. They'd barely spoken since the row on Saturday, and this morning he'd left for work before she'd woken up.

The strained silence was broken by the arrival of the doctor. He was tall and very thin, with a pronounced Adam's apple. 'Mr and Mrs Drummond? We've run some preliminary tests on your son, but we need to take a blood test to determine his levels of paracetamol,' he said. 'We can't do that until at least four hours after ingestion. I gather it's been less than two, so we've got a bit of a wait on our hands.'

'You're not going to do anything?' Maddie exclaimed. 'Don't you need to pump his stomach or something?'

'It doesn't work that way, I'm afraid. I realise how worried you must be, but we will monitor Jacob carefully. Can either of you tell me how much Calpol was left in the bottle the last time you remember seeing it?'

Maddie looked wretched. 'I don't know.'

'It wasn't much, Mummy,' Emily said suddenly. 'Not even half.'

'Let's hope you're right,' the doctor said, smiling down at her. 'As I say, all we can do is wait.'

'Can we see him now?' Lucas asked.

The doctor glanced over at Jessica and the social worker, who were talking to the nurse by the admissions desk. 'If you'll just excuse me for a minute, I'll be right back.'

They watched him confer with the two women. After a few moments, he returned and gave them a brief nod.

'You're welcome to sit with him while we wait it out, as long as you don't mind Ms Avery and Mrs Towner joining you. Or you can take your daughter and Jacob to the playroom to help pass the time if you prefer. We don't need to monitor him if he stays awake. As long as you don't leave the floor, that'd be fine.'

Maddie tried to block the hideous sense of déjà vu as they followed the doctor across the lobby and through the double doors to the triage centre. History wasn't going to repeat itself. Jacob wasn't going to die. It couldn't happen, not again.

As soon as they reached his cubicle, she scooped him out of his hospital cot before anyone could stop her and he buried his face in her shoulder, clinging on to her like a limpet.

'What do you think I'm going to do to him?' she demanded, as the stout older woman pulled out a plastic chair and sat down facing her, her hands resting on her spread knees like a prison warden. 'Smother him with a pillow the moment your back's turned?'

'They're just trying to help,' Lucas said wearily.

'Mummy,' Emily said anxiously.

Maddie forced a smile, stroking Jacob's back as she swayed from side to side. 'It's all right, darling. Everything's going to be fine.'

'Look, why don't I take him for a bit,' Lucas said, reaching for his son. 'You and Emily can go and get a cup of tea, or something. Come on,' he urged, as she hesitated. 'It's not good for Emily to stay here. It's making her nervous.'

Maddie reluctantly handed Jacob to his father. Emily scurried alongside her as she stormed down the corridor and back into the hospital lobby, fuelled by anger and frustration. She couldn't afford to let self-doubt creep in or she'd be lost. Maybe her memory was hopeless, but she was sure she'd never leave an open bottle of medicine in a child's room.

But she *wasn't* sure, that was the point. She was so tired; she could have made a mistake. She was beginning to wonder if she should be allowed to look after her children, if she couldn't keep them safe ...

'Mummy,' Emily said, tugging her hand as they exited the hospital. 'I need to tell you something.'

'Not now, darling.'

'It's about Jacob.'

She stopped. 'Emily, what is it?'

'Lucas said you must have left the medicine in Jacob's room, because no one else was there, but that's not true.'

Maddie looked confused.

'You weren't the only one at home,' Emily burst out in a rush. 'Aunt Candace was there too.'

Lydia

It's Davy. She sees him as soon as she enters the court-room, high up in the front row of the public gallery, and she gasps in pleasure and surprise and starts towards him, but of course they hold her back, she's not allowed to go to him, they usher her instead to a chair in front of a big desk with her back towards her brother.

She twists round in her seat to gaze up at him. He looks just the same as she remembers. Older and thinner, of course; he was thirteen when she last saw him and he's twenty now. Stubble shadows his jawline, she can see it from here, and his shoulders are broad and strong, like he's been working outdoors. She has a thousand questions for him: where have you been? What have you been doing? *Why didn't you come back for me?* But she can't even speak to him.

Mae is sitting right behind her; stop fidgeting! she hisses, slapping her with the flat of her hand between her shoulder blades and making her turn back towards the front of the room again.

She wonders for a moment how Davy even knew

she was here and then realises that of course he knows, everyone knows who she is and why she's here. It's been in all the papers, her photo and everything. The headline writers had a field day with her name, Lydia Slaughter.

She'd thought at first that Mae was being supportive at the police station because she actually cared, but she should have known better. Mae is revelling in her new-found notoriety as the mother of a child on trial for murder. She's sold stories about Lydia to anyone who'll pay, sobbing her crocodile tears and describing how wild and uncontrollable Lydia has always been, how she knew she was wicked from the moment she was born. Today she's wearing a short, bright red dress, her bleached blonde hair piled high, teetering into court on skyscraper heels as if it's her own personal catwalk.

Lydia looks around as she waits for something to happen and notices two rows of people on her left, gazing intently at her. She leans towards her sad-faced solicitor; why do they keep staring like that, she asks, don't they know it's rude? That's the jury, he says, and Lydia looks puzzled, so he explains, they're the people who're going to decide what's going to happen to you, and she asks how, but he just tells her to shush.

Everything is such a blur, so many faces, all of them turned towards her, all she can see is a swirl of pink smears. She tries to focus on the judge, the man in the big chair in the red robe that everyone keeps telling her is the most important man in the room, but she's tired and hot and uncomfortable, and everyone keeps *staring* at her. She twists up again to look at Davy, and he smiles and nods encouragement, and she feels a little better.

Her solicitor told her she had to pay attention and look like she was taking the trial seriously, but it's so *boring*, all this talking, lots of men droning on and on, using long foreign-sounding words she doesn't understand, and her eyelids flutter and her bottom goes numb from sitting for so long. She wishes they would hurry up and get on with it, so she can go home again. She never thought she'd say this, but after four months locked in a single room on her own with no one to talk to because they won't let her mix with the older girls, she actually misses home. Well, Frank, anyway.

Poor Frank. Unlike Mae, he doesn't relish his new celebrity. When Lydia spots him at the back of the public gallery, a few rows behind Davy, she almost doesn't recognise him. He's aged twenty years overnight. He and Mae split up when it all came out about Jimmy during the police investigation, and she's touched that he's even here. She knows he's hoping to hear something that'll prove she didn't do this and she wishes she could give that to him. Frank doesn't deserve this. She and Mae, they're no good, rotten apples the pair of them, but Frank's a decent man.

The trial goes on for nine days, every day the same, just talking and talking. Every day, Davy and Frank are in their places in the public gallery, and every day Mae sits behind Lydia, pinching and nipping her on her arms and the skin of her back when no one is looking. Mae

213

puts on a show, her dresses getting shorter and tighter, laying on the crocodile tears every time she turns to face the press box. Whenever the solicitors say something she doesn't like, which is often, she storms dramatically out of court, only to return just as showily twenty minutes later.

Lydia tries to sit still and pay attention, like her solicitor told her, but it's so dull and she doesn't understand most of it. No one explains what anything means. She listens to the prosecution describe her as a bad seed, the very essence of wickedness, a vile huntress preying on innocence, a monstrosity of nature. That last one actually makes her laugh out loud, *a monstrosity of nature*: it sounds like something off a science-fiction show on the TV. The jury people look shocked by her outburst and she wants to tell them, I didn't mean to laugh, but it's just all so silly, I mean, honestly, a monstrosity of nature?

They say she lured Julia to her death, that she was jealous of the little girl, of her pretty dresses and toys and gold curls, that she deliberately enticed her to the derelict house so she could murder her in cold blood. Lydia starts at that, *no I never! it was an accident!* and her solicitor tells her sharply to be quiet.

They'll get their chance to explain, her solicitor tells her. But even she can see it's going to be too late by then. The jury have made up their minds. It doesn't help that she changed her story so many times. They don't understand she was just scared, she only lied to the police because she didn't want to get into trouble.

She should have just told them it was an accident from the beginning. Now it looks like she's only saying that because she was caught out in her own lies.

When it's his turn, her solicitor gets up and talks about her troubled childhood, her neglectful mother, *a common prostitute* (Mae storms out again at that), her absent father, a petty criminal who'd died in a prison brawl while on remand for manslaughter – Lydia hadn't known that, but she doesn't much care either way – and an older brother who'd run away and spent most of his teenage years in juvenile detention after being convicted for the arson of a notorious vice den. She twists round in her seat then, staring up at the public gallery, and Davy gives her a tiny shrug, a rueful what-can-you-do? smile, and she smiles back, filled with happiness because he hadn't abandoned her, he hadn't just left her to Mae's tender mercies, after all.

She knows her solicitor is just trying to help, painting a picture of deprivation and neglect, trying to get the jury's sympathy: it's not her fault she grew up this way, it's not her fault she was born, but it's making her look like the bad seed the prosecution described, *bad blood*, and she can see the jury shaking their heads, deciding she's a wrong 'un, guilty by birth.

Will they hang me? she whispers to her solicitor, and he looks shocked. We don't hang people anymore, he says, and certainly not little girls.

Can I go home, then? she asks.

He looks at her with pity and doesn't answer.

The jury come back the next afternoon with their

215

verdict. Guilty of manslaughter by virtue of diminished responsibility, they say gravely, though she doesn't understand what that means. Mae screams and sobs for the benefit of the press box, and when Lydia turns to the public gallery, she sees Frank bent over, covering his face with his hands. I'll see you after, Davy mouths. Chin up, peanut.

The Taylors are weeping in relief a few feet away. Have they been here every day? She hadn't even noticed them until now.

What happens next? she asks her solicitor. Can I go home now?

The judge leans forward. *The sentence of the court upon Lydia Slaughter is a sentence of detention and the detention will be for life.*

What does that mean? she says. No one answers her. No one will even look at her. The court is in an uproar.

What does that mean?

Chapter 25

Monday 11.30 p.m.

Maddie sat down at her dressing table and dragged a brush through her hair with quick, angry tugs. 'Candace was the one who left the Calpol in Jacob's reach, not me. Emily *saw* her in his room.'

'She was just giving him back his dummy,' Lucas sighed. 'She'd never give him medicine without telling us and she certainly didn't leave an open bottle where Jacob could get it. She'd never be that irresponsible.'

'Oh, so I would?'

'Come on, Maddie. That's not what I said. I just meant she's not his mother. She wouldn't give him drugs without asking one of us first.'

'Assuming she was sober,' Maddie said bitterly.

'That's a low blow, Maddie, and you know it.'

She knew nothing of the kind. She was trying very hard to be rational and not leap to conclusions, but even if she pushed her wilder conspiracy theories aside, she was still left with the fact that Candace had been present when both her boys had got hurt. But sniping at Lucas wasn't going to get them anywhere. They'd been fighting ever since they'd got home from the hospital with Jacob. His blood tests had shown his levels of paracetamol had been elevated, but not dangerously so. The doctor believed he'd probably drunk no more than a quarter of a bottle of the Calpol; he'd advised them not to give their son any more medicine for at least seventy-two hours, but otherwise, there was nothing else they needed to do, medically speaking.

Since there was no proof it had been anything other than a mistake, and in view of their recent bereavement, the social worker had agreed – reluctantly – to let Jacob go home, but she'd made it clear she considered Maddie on notice. She'd be following up with her supervisor in the morning, she warned, and Maddie could expect further unscheduled home visits. There was no escaping the subtext: whether by accident or design, you are a danger to your children, and we're going to prove it.

She put her hairbrush down and swivelled to face Lucas. 'What was Candace doing sneaking into the house while I was asleep, anyway?'

'She wasn't *sneaking* anywhere. Emily let her in. Candace didn't want to wake you because she was being considerate.' He pulled off his tie and threw it on the bed. 'She was dropping off a cheque towards the loan that *you* keep making such a song and dance about!'

'Because you *lied* to me about it!'

'Really, Maddie? You really want to get into this now?'

It didn't matter where they started, they always seemed to end up here. She was suddenly tired of it all. 'Lucas, I don't have the energy to keep fighting with you,' she said bleakly. 'Jacob's going to be fine. That's all that really matters.'

'I'm as relieved as you are,' Lucas said tersely. 'But this should never have happened in the first place.'

'What do you want me to say? I'm a bad mother? It's my fault this happened? Fine.' He started to protest, but she angrily cut across him. 'I shouldn't have gone to bed, even though I'm so tired I can hardly see straight. I should've sat by his cot while he slept and made sure he was still breathing. I should keep all medicines under lock and key, to be doled out by you. To be honest, I'm not sure I should ever be left alone with the children.'

He pinched the bridge of his nose. 'Come on, Maddie. You're being ridiculous.'

'Am I? I'm beginning to wonder if everyone's right. Maybe I *am* a danger to my own children. Perhaps I should be locked away.'

Lucas exhaled slowly. She could see him reining in his impatience, forcing moderation into his tone, which just annoyed her even more. 'I know it doesn't seem like it, but none of this is personal,' he said. 'I'm not saying that bloody social worker is right,' he added, before she could interrupt again. 'But we still don't really know what happened to Noah. Maybe the pathologist has got his facts wrong, but what if he's *right*? What if someone did hurt him on purpose? They have to consider it might be us. And then Jacob ends up in the hospital with a suspected overdose. What are they supposed to think?'

'Yes, I know all that. I'm not an idiot, Lucas. They

don't know me. I can see how it looks to an outsider.'

He sat down on the bed. He'd lost more weight, she noticed suddenly. He seemed shrunken within his shirt, deflated. Had it really only been ten days since they'd lost Noah?

'Maddie, I know you love the kids,' he said heavily. 'That's never been in doubt. Losing a child is enough to break most people – how you've managed to stay standing, I have no idea. You've been amazing.' His voice unexpectedly softened. 'Not just during the last few days, either. I know how difficult it was for you after Jacob was born and how hard you had to fight to pull yourself out of the depression. You have the heart of a lion and I love you for it.'

Her throat was suddenly tight. All she needed was to know that Lucas was on her side, fighting her corner. She could cope with anything, as long as she had that.

He patted the bed beside him and she flew to him, burying her face against his chest as he enfolded her in his arms. 'I know the strain you've been under,' he murmured, his chin against the top of her head. 'It's not surprising you've dropped the ball a few times. It'd be more surprising if you hadn't. You're human, Mads. And you're not the only one.' He sighed. 'I'll be in the middle of a meeting and suddenly realise I've got no idea what anyone's said to me for the last half an hour. I got all the way to Homebase the other day and sat for twenty minutes in the car park trying to figure out what it was I'd gone there for.'

'I'm not crazy,' she said thickly.

He gave her a hug. 'Of course you're not crazy! But the stress we've both been under is unbearable. And we all react to it in different ways. I've seen the way you zone out sometimes. I'll be talking to you and it's like you're in a world of your own. Honestly, I think a bomb could go off under you and you wouldn't notice.' His smile took the sting from his words. 'You lost a *child*, Maddie. I'm not a doctor, but if I had to guess, I'd say that business with the nursery was some kind of PTSD.'

Post-traumatic stress. It had never occurred to her that's what her blackouts might be. But now that Lucas had suggested it, it made sense. Losing track of time, zoning out, memory loss: PTSD would explain everything.

Except, of course, her blackouts had started *before* Noah died.

'Have you thought about talking to Calkins again?' Lucas asked gently. 'I know you don't want to, but you need to talk to someone who knows how to help you, before this gets any worse.' He hesitated, clearly afraid of upsetting her again. 'What you did to Noah's room, Mads, with the paint, ripping up the carpet, that frightened me. There was so much *anger* there.'

Abruptly, she pulled away from him. 'You think I hurt Noah, don't you?'

He hesitated just a fraction too long.

'You think I had some kind of breakdown and killed Noah. I can see it in your eyes!' She leaped up from the bed, feeling utterly betrayed. 'How *could* you, Lucas?'

'I didn't say—'

'That's what all this has been about, isn't it?' she cried. 'All this sympathy and understanding. You're softening me up, trying to get me ready for the men in white coats, so I don't kick up a fuss when they come to take me away!'

'Maddie, calm down. This isn't a conspiracy. I just want what's best for you, what's best for all of us.'

'What's your end game, Lucas?' she demanded furiously. 'Is the plan to get me out of the way, have me arrested or committed, and then sell the sanctuary? Is that it? Was taking out a mortgage on our house and putting everything we have at risk not enough for you?'

He stared at her in disbelief. 'Maddie, do you have any idea how delusional you sound?'

He was right. She sounded paranoid, utterly crazy. She didn't make sense, even to herself. And that was exactly what he'd wanted all along, wasn't it?

Chapter 26

The smell of smoke woke Maddie first. She'd been dreaming of bonfires and fireworks, laughing with the children as they waved their sparklers and jumped up and down in their wellies, the flames catching the Guy Fawkes effigy on top of the bonfire.

She jolted awake, blinking hard to clear her head. She must have fallen asleep at her office desk. It took her a few moments to realise she could still hear the crackle of flames, even though she was wide awake and Bonfire Night was months away.

She leaped out of her chair. Thick coils of grey smoke were already roiling beneath the door of her office, filling the small Portakabin with shocking speed. She pulled up her sweatshirt to cover her mouth and nose, coughing as she inhaled a lungful of acrid smoke. Outside, she could hear the horses whinnying with terror in their boxes, their hooves banging against the walls.

She groped for the door handle, then let it go with a gasp as the hot metal burned her hand. Heat radiated through the thin cabin walls. For a moment, she was too terrified to move, but the sound of Finn's frightened whinnies gave her courage and she yanked the door open.

A wall of flames greeted her. The stable block was fiercely ablaze, fire leaping a dozen feet high into the sky. A sweet, nauseating smell filled the air. The horses were burning alive.

Sparks flew from the burning building, raining down around her. She was already cut off by a sheet of flames ahead of her and to her left. Her only option was the alleyway to her right, leading towards the old barn where they stored the feed and farm implements. If she could make it to the barn, she could get through to the upper meadow and safety. From there she could double round to the back of the stable block and reach the horses that way.

She was almost blinded by smoke. She could hardly breathe, the hot, gritty air searing her lungs. She briefly glimpsed a figure on the other side of the yard, behind the burning stable block, though she couldn't see who it was. A violent fit of coughing forced her to bend double, her hands on her knees as she gasped for breath. When she looked up again through streaming eyes, the figure had gone, and she wondered if she'd imagined it.

She wiped her eyes, trying to see through the smoke. For a brief moment, it cleared, and with a shock, she realised the figure was Lucas. He was just standing there with his back towards her, gazing at the blazing stables.

Why wasn't he opening the back gate to let the horses out? Why wasn't he *doing* anything?

The barn roof collapsed with a mighty crash and he turned and stared straight at her. She knew he'd seen her. And still he did nothing.

She was cut off, now. Flames surrounded her on all four sides. The oxygen was being sucked up by the fire and her lungs heaved with effort. She couldn't get enough air, she couldn't breathe, *she couldn't breathe—*

'Maddie! Maddie! Wake up!'

Izzy was shaking her awake. Maddie gasped in a deep lungful of air, her heart pounding, the image of the flames still dancing behind her eyes. 'Oh, God, Izzy! I was having such a terrible nightmare. The stables were on fire, and Lucas was just *standing* there—'

'Never mind that now. The police are here to see you.'

'It was so *real*,' she insisted, still only half-awake. 'Everything was on fire. I couldn't get the horses out—'

'Maddie, pull it together. The police want to talk to you.'

With an effort, she cleared her head and shook herself awake. It was a measure of how unreal her life had become that she didn't even question why the police were here. She'd been expecting them, after Jacob's near miss yesterday. She was surprised they hadn't arrested her in a dawn raid at home, even though she'd done nothing wrong. 'Where are they?'

'Outside by the ring. Do you want me to send them in?'

'No. I could use some fresh air.'

She stood up, trying to force the harrowing images from her mind. She'd had nightmares ever since Noah's death, dreadful dreams in which she ran down endless dark corridors in search of her son, her legs moving horribly slowly as if she were struggling through quicksand. But she'd never dreamed of a fire like this, of feeling her own skin melt around her bones. The horses; it made her sick just to think about it. And Lucas, standing there with that awful smile on his face, doing nothing as he watched her burn.

The red-haired detective was leaning against the split-rail fence by the upper paddock.

The bright afternoon sunlight caught the woman's hair and gave her a fiery halo that reminded Maddie queasily of her dream.

'Sorry to bother you at work,' DS Ballard said.

She didn't sound sorry. 'What do you need?' Maddie asked shortly.

'I heard about the scare you had with Jacob yesterday. That must have given you quite a fright.'

Maddie opened the door to Finn's box as he nickered and rubbed a whiskery pink nose against her face. Her heartbeat started to return to its normal rate, the nightmare fading in Finn's reassuring presence. 'Before you ask, no, I don't know how Jacob managed to get the bottle open, and yes, I'm sure I screwed the lid on properly. It's one of those things you do automatically when you have kids, like tugging their seat belts after you buckle them in.'

'You'd be amazed how many parents don't even bother with car seats,' DS Ballard said.

Maddie stroked Finn's long nose. 'Well, I'm not one of them.'

She adjusted his hay net and checked his water. It was low, so she picked up the heavy black plastic bucket and headed towards the standpipe in the centre of the stable yard.

DS Ballard followed her, like a bad smell she couldn't leave behind. 'Remind me, Maddie, who else was in the house yesterday afternoon?'

'I'm sure you've already checked,' she said testily. 'It was just me and the children. Lucas was at work.'

'I believe his sister stopped by, too?'

Maddie hefted the full water bucket and turned back to Finn's box. 'Yes, but I didn't see her. I was asleep.'

'Can I help you with that bucket?'

'I'm fine.'

She gave Finn his water. DS Ballard fell in step with her as she headed towards the lower paddock to check on two new rescue ponies who'd arrived at the weekend, pointedly acting as if the policewoman wasn't there.

'It's not the first time Jacob has been admitted to casualty, is it?' DS Ballard asked.

Maddie didn't break her stride.

'According to his medical records, he's been treated there twice in the past year,' the woman continued, keeping pace. 'Last summer, he was admitted with a broken arm, apparently from falling while climbing a bookcase at home, and then just before Christmas, he allegedly shut his hand in the door.'

'He's a little boy,' Maddie snapped, infuriated by the policewoman's obvious scepticism. 'It's what they do. They climb trees and play with matches and stick their heads through railings.'

She was so tired of everyone questioning her mothering. She didn't know if Lucas really thought she'd hurt Noah and Jacob or if he just wanted her to doubt herself for some dark reason she couldn't fathom, but deep in her bones she *knew* she'd never deliberately harm her children. She wasn't perfect and she made mistakes, like every other mother, but that's all they were: mistakes.

'Do you have children?' she asked DS Ballard suddenly. She needed this woman to understand.

The woman looked surprised. 'No. I'm not married.'

'A brother, then?'

'Two brothers and a sister.'

'And how many times did your mother end up in casualty?'

'She probably lost count,' the detective admitted.

'If you combed through their medical records, I'm sure you could make a case for abuse, but that doesn't mean your mother was guilty of anything other than having two normal little boys.'

DS Ballard suddenly stepped into her path, forcing her to stop. 'Frequent visits to casualty are also a common indicator of domestic abuse, Mrs Drummond. It's my job to look into them and determine if an investigation is warranted.'

'I wasn't even with Jacob when he broke his arm,' Maddie retorted. 'You can check with the hospital if you don't believe me. My mother had arranged for me to go away for a few days, to give me a break. The Burgh Island Hotel in Devon, if you want to check. I was depressed, she and Lucas thought it'd be a good idea. The accident happened while I was away. They didn't even tell me until I got home, because they didn't want me to worry.'

The detective's interest sharpened. 'Who was looking after Jacob, then? Your husband?'

'No, I don't think so. It was a weekday trip, the hotel was doing some kind of two-for-one deal. He'd have been working.' She stepped around the other woman and opened the gate into the lower paddock. 'I think my mother was looking after Jacob, but it might have been Candace.'

'Your sister-in-law was babysitting Jacob when he broke his arm?'

She suddenly got what the policewoman was driving at. A chill settled in the pit of her stomach. All roads seemed to lead to Candace. 'I don't know,' Maddie said. 'Maybe. I wasn't there, I told you.'

'And when Jacob got his hand stuck in the door. Who was with him then?'

Maddie pulled a carrot from her pocket as the ponies trotted across the paddock, her mind working overtime. Could her sister-in-law really be capable of hurting her own brother's children? *Why?*

'We were all there,' she said slowly. 'It was two days

before Christmas, everyone was in the house – Lucas, the children, my mother, Candace, Izzy and Bitsy, plus a couple of friends from down the road. I wasn't in the room, so I didn't see what happened, but somehow Jacob got his hand shut in one of the kitchen cupboard doors.' She gave each of the two rescue ponies a carrot, gentling them as they nuzzled against her. 'I didn't think it was broken, but it was really swollen, so I took him to hospital just in case. The swelling had gone down by Christmas morning.'

The detective rummaged in her pockets and produced a pack of Polos. 'May I?'

Maddie looked surprised, then nodded.

'I used to go riding every Sunday when I was a child,' DS Ballard said, unwrapping the mints as the ponies whickered and butted their heads against her shoulder. 'I always kept a packet of Polos in my pocket. This takes me back. I don't think I've been on a horse in years.'

'We do refresher lessons for returning riders,' Maddie said absently. 'Talk to Izzy. She could arrange something for you.'

'I might do that.' The detective gave the ponies the last of the mints and patted their noses. 'So, your sister-in-law, Candace, was with you at Christmas, too?'

'Of course.'

'And you get on well with her?'

'I've always loved Candace. She's kind and very sweet with the children.'

'But?'

Maddie hesitated, her loyalties torn. Despite everything

Candace had put them through with her drinking over the years, she *did* love her sister-in-law. She'd never questioned Candace's love for her niece and nephews in the past, and even now she found it impossible to picture her ever wanting to harm them. But she knew Lucas's sister had been irrevocably scarred by the loss of her parents. How deep did that damage really run?

'She's had problems in the past,' she said finally. 'With alcohol. She lost her job a few years ago and Lucas has had to help her out quite a lot.'

'She has financial troubles?'

'She's never been very good with money, but, obviously, after she lost her job, things were a bit tight. She had to sell her flat in London and move down here. Lucas lent her the money to start her own IT company about a year ago and she's got some good clients, but she's still getting it off the ground.'

'You must have quite a lot of financial commitments yourself, running this place,' DS Ballard observed. 'You don't mind your husband lending his sister money?'

Maddie shrugged noncommittally.

'Would it be fair to say this isn't an issue on which you and your husband see eye to eye?' She took Maddie's silence as assent. 'I understand the two of you took out a second mortgage recently. Your husband told us it was to help his sister buy somewhere to live.'

Maddie looked startled. 'He told you about that?'

'It's all part of our wider investigation,' DS Ballard said blandly. 'So your husband has lent his sister money for her company and you've both helped her to buy a flat. Do you have plans for any further loans? If your sister-in-law needed additional funds to keep the business going, for example.'

'No,' Maddie said shortly.

'I also understand your husband recently doubled your life insurance,' the detective said.

'Because of the mortgage, yes. The bank insisted on it.' Maddie dug her hands into the pockets of her padded vest. 'Look, where are you going with this?'

'And of course he also arranged cover for your three children,' DS Ballard continued. Her gaze didn't leave Maddie's face. 'Ah,' she said softly. 'You didn't know.'

Lydia

They don't know what to do with her. When she was being held before her trial, they stuck her in an ordinary care home for teenage girls, then refused to let her mix with them in case her wickedness was catching. After she's sent down, smuggled out of the courthouse under a scratchy grey blanket, they take her to an adult prison where she is kept in isolation in the hospital wing while they try to work out where to send her next. They don't have a prison uniform small enough to fit her, so they give her an adult one that trails on the floor and makes her seem even younger than she really is.

It's as if it hasn't occurred to anyone until now that she might be convicted and they'll have to find somewhere to keep her. She knows she isn't the first child to be jailed for murder, or even the youngest, but the whole notion is so unpalatable, so unthinkable, they've all been burying their heads in the sand and hoping she'd go away.

But she didn't, so here she is, in her baggy uniform with the cuffs turned over and the legs rolled up, stuck in a bare cell with a window too high for her to see out and a plastic bucket in the corner for her to piss in.

Being locked up doesn't bother her. She quickly gets used to the sounds of the prison: the keys, the barked orders. At night, the lights are turned out and she's alone but not frightened. She has regular meals and hot showers, and best of all, there's no Mae and no Jimmy. She feels more free in jail than she ever did at home. In a way, the rules make her feel safe.

But of course she can't stay in an adult prison. They still don't know what to do with her, so after two weeks, they move her to a short-term remand facility for young offenders with high-security provisions – she laughs when she sees the razor wire: do they think she's going to go on the lam, at eleven years old? – but at least this time they don't lock her up on her own.

To her surprise, the other girls welcome her like she's one of them, sharing their cigarettes and pointing out the decent screws. They know who she is, why she's here, and for the first time, she discovers the benefits of her notoriety. In here, she's a celebrity, like Jack the Ripper.

The girls are filled with morbid curiosity. They want to know what it felt like to kill someone. At first she doesn't want to talk about it, but then she realises this is her currency now, her infamy, this is what she has to trade for friendship and cigarettes. These girls are here because of family and personality conflicts, not because they've committed any serious crimes. She's in a league of her own.

She lies in her narrow bed and stares up at the ceiling the first night, listening to the grunts and murmurs of the other girls. Until now she hasn't really thought about Julia, she's blocked what happened from her mind. She knows she should feel remorse and guilt, that's what any normal person would feel, but she doesn't feel anything. Something inside her is dead or broken, the part of her that feels sorry for people, the part that should tell her not to do something bad. She doesn't want to be this way. She wants to be normal. She wants the girls to like her, she wants to have friends. She realises that if she wants to fit in, she has to learn to compensate, to train herself to behave as if she hears the warning voice that other people hear. It's not her fault that a part of her is broken, but she can use her wits to work around it. She's smart; Frank always said she was a quick study. She'll be like those people with no arms who learn to paint with their feet.

Six weeks after her arrival, she's called into the Governor's office and curtly told she's being transferred the next morning. The Governor doesn't explain where she's going, he doesn't tell her anything else, only that it's a permanent juvenile detention facility where she'll be staying until she's grown-up and can be moved to an adult prison.

She doesn't sleep a wink that night. She's well aware her new place isn't going to be a cushy number like the remand home. She'll be in amongst teenagers who've been in the system their whole lives, toughened and brutalised by years of fighting for survival. She's

235

no pushover, she's survived Mae and Jimmy and all the rest, but she's eleven years old, fresh meat. Easy prey.

But Font Hill isn't what she expected at all. It doesn't even look like a prison; she's reminded of a large country hotel Frank took her to once, on one of his lorry deliveries. There are locked doors and rules, of course, but there's also a large garden, and proper classrooms. There's a well-equipped art room and even a pottery kiln. In the garden, there's a greenhouse and allotments which they're expected to tend, and a shed for pets. Lydia is surprised they're allowed to keep pets; you'd have thought it'd be tempting fate, she thinks, putting a lot of defenceless animals in with a bunch of hardened criminals.

But of course they're not hardened criminals at all. They have certainly committed serious crimes – one or two have even killed someone, like her – but they're also children, even if, as usual, she's the youngest by quite a few years. She's also the only girl.

She loves Font Hill. She loves the gardens and the classrooms and the straightforwardness of boys: when they disagree, they punch each other, and then it's over and done with. There's none of the slyness of girls, the subtle exclusions and betrayals. What you see is what you get with boys. They treat her like she's one of them, and for the first time in her life, she makes some real friends.

And she loves Mr Tallack, the Governor at Font Hill, though he doesn't like anyone to call him that. He says it smacks too much of prison and cabbage (she laughs when he says that, everywhere else they've sent her *does* smell of cabbage) and he insists this isn't a prison, it's a reform school in the truest sense of the word. He tells her Font Hill is a 'tightly run ship' and there's no preferential treatment. By that, he says, he means they're all equal, staff and children; they all eat together, the same food, and they work together. He promises that if she keeps her head down and does her best, she'll be allowed to leave one day. Not just to go to another prison, but to be set free.

Free. It's the first time anyone has offered that hope to her, even her solicitor didn't tell her that, and she is suddenly filled with determination. She will do whatever it takes to win back her freedom. She didn't think she wanted it, she'd told herself she didn't mind being locked up, it was better than what had gone before, but the prospect of walking out of here, of being able to go and live with Davy, to be free, makes her realise she wants it more than anything.

If she can't fix the broken piece inside her, she will find a way to make them think she has.

Chapter 27

Tuesday 6.00 p.m.

Vomit rose again in Maddie's throat, and for the second time, she had to pull the car over to the side of the road. She tumbled out of the door and bent double, retching into the long grass. The thought that Lucas might have deliberately hurt Noah for money was literally too horrific to stomach.

When she'd finally stopped heaving, she leaned against the side of her Land Rover and wiped her mouth with the back of her hand. She'd spent the last three hours trying to pull herself together enough to drive home from the sanctuary and confront Lucas. But every time she tried to frame the question in her mind, her stomach lurched again.

She could barely get her head around the notion that Lucas might have hurt Noah by accident. A split second of temper, a momentary loss of control; it was hard to imagine that happening to Lucas, but she could just about accept it was possible. She knew better than most how anyone could be driven to the edge by frustration and exhaustion. But the idea that he might have harmed their baby on purpose, that he could deliberately set out to kill him, to *murder* him, was simply unthinkable.

And yet here she was.

She climbed back into the Land Rover but didn't start the car again. Instead, she stared unseeingly through the grimy windscreen as dusk gathered. Everything she knew about Lucas told her DS Ballard was wrong. To kill a child, you'd have to be devoid of the most basic sense of humanity. You'd have to be a psychopath, completely lacking in empathy and utterly amoral. That was so far from Lucas, it would be laughable – if it wasn't all so bloody, *bloody* awful.

Because in the midst of all this, in the midst of the police investigation and the financial intrigue and the revelations about how and why Noah had died, at the centre of it all was the fact that she had lost her child.

Maddie rested her forehead on the steering wheel, consumed anew by the terrible, aching grief that leached the life from her and hollowed out her soul. There was something fundamentally wrong with outliving your own child. It went against every natural law. In moments like this, she didn't really care why her baby had died. Nothing would bring him back. Somehow, she had to learn to accommodate the enormity of her loss, to live in the spaces around it. Reason told her time would teach her how to survive, but right now it was hard to imagine it ever being possible.

She jumped as her mobile rang on the passenger seat

next to her and glanced at the screen. Lucas. She let it go to voicemail.

Had she really been sleeping with the enemy for six years? Lying next to a handsome sociopath capable of murdering her child in cold blood? She'd made a point of not prying into Lucas's past when they'd met, allowing him to share pieces of his history with her over the years as he was ready. It wasn't that she didn't care; it just hadn't seemed relevant.

She remembered joking to her mother, when she'd first met Lucas, that at least she didn't have to worry about vetting him. 'They don't let just anyone serve on a jury,' she'd laughed. 'Lucas Drummond is one of the good ones, Mum.'

This afternoon, DS Ballard had made her feel like a naive fool. She'd been unable to answer some of the most basic questions about the man with whom she shared her life: where he'd been born and gone to school, what jobs he'd held before they met, even if he'd ever been married before. But it had never occurred to her until this week that these things mattered. She'd known – she'd *thought* she'd known – that Lucas was good and honourable and had integrity stamped through him like a stick of rock. She'd known he rubbed her feet when she had a cold and stood up for her when she left the table at a restaurant and laughed when she told him how Finn had filched a carrot from her pocket. *I know my husband,* she'd wanted to shout at DS Ballard. *I know the things that matter!*

But she didn't really know him, did she? At least, not the way she'd thought she had. He'd lied to her about the loan, which drove a coach and horses through her previous assumptions about the kind of man he was. And what possible reason could he have for taking out life insurance on their *children*? Who *did* that? All that talk yesterday about PTSD, when Lucas seemed so solicitous and concerned – was it really all an act?

Her blood chilled as another horrifying thought occurred to her. If he had something to do with what had happened to Noah, was it also possible he was responsible for her memory blackouts?

She'd read a story only a few weeks ago about a woman who'd woken up on the Eurostar to Paris with absolutely no idea how she'd got there. It turned out her boyfriend had put the date-rape drug, Rohypnol, in her drink. Her symptoms were identical to Maddie's. It'd certainly be easy enough for Lucas to drug her: he could just add it to the cup of tea he brought her every morning. Maybe he was deliberately trying to drive her mad. It sounded ridiculous, fantastical, even, but she was already trapped in an alternate reality where the inconceivable was all too real.

She was spinning in dark circles. She turned the key in the ignition, suddenly anxious to be home. She needed to look Lucas in the eye and see the truth there.

Dusk had fallen and it was raining by the time Maddie got home. Emily had left her pink bicycle slewed in the driveway on its side, blocking the garage, and the banal normality of it nearly undid her. Everything all looked so *ordinary*. It was hard to believe that in a matter of just two weeks, her entire world had been turned upside down as carelessly as if a child had upended a box of toys.

Almost on autopilot, she picked up Emily's bike and wheeled it around the side of the house to the shed. The chain had come off and was tangling in the pedals; she stopped and worked it free, getting oil all over her hands. Propping the bike against the side of the shed, she heaved open the door and rummaged around Lucas's workbench for a rag to wipe off the oil. She pulled out an old T-shirt shoved in the toolbox at the back, and then paused, surprised, as she saw the logo on the chest pocket. She'd only bought this T-shirt for Lucas at Christmas. She knew he'd liked it, so she was puzzled he'd thrown it out so soon.

She shook it out. It was stuck together with what looked like dried blood. Her heart started pounding. This was way too much blood for a small gardening scratch. She couldn't remember Lucas injuring himself recently, certainly not this badly. So whose blood was it? And why had her husband hidden the shirt at the back of the shed?

She peered at the T-shirt more closely and realised with relief it was paint. Just paint! She wasn't living some suburban horror story. There was a perfectly normal, ordinary explanation, as there would be for everything else …

Paint. *Red* paint.

The same colour that had been used to vandalise the nursery walls.

She dropped the T-shirt as if it burned. That day they'd gone to the police station: Lucas had had paint under his fingernails. She remembered because it had been so unusual for him. He didn't paint. He wasn't an artist or a handyman. He couldn't even put up a shelf. If she hadn't been so distracted by everything else that was happening, she'd have been curious how he'd ended up with paint on his hands.

Lucas had vandalised the nursery. How else had he got red paint on his T-shirt and beneath his nails? He'd vandalised it, and he'd wanted her to believe *she'd* done it.

What possible reason could he have for trying to manipulate her into questioning her own sanity? It didn't make any sense. Nothing made any sense. If he was so desperate to get his hands on her money, there were easier ways, surely? Maybe *he* was the one losing his mind. Maybe Noah's death had disturbed him far more than she'd realised. For both Lucas and Candace, Noah's loss must have reawakened the trauma of their parents' terrible deaths. Perhaps Lucas was the one suffering from PTSD and projecting it on to her.

She snatched up the T-shirt and shoved it back into the toolbox. Lucas didn't seem mad. He was distraught over their son's death, of course, but otherwise, he had been his usual rational, normal self. No nightmares or mood swings, nothing to suggest he was anything other than her grieving, devoted husband. Unless he had suddenly developed some kind of split personality disorder, she had no idea or explanation for what was going on.

She left the shed and stopped as she passed the kitchen window, gazing from the dark at her family sitting in the pool of light, the symbolism of the moment not lost on her. Emily was at the table, poring over a thick textbook. Beside her, Lucas jiggled Jacob on his lap as he leaned over and pointed to the page in front of her, evidently explaining something. It looked like a portrait of the perfect family: Engaged Dad At Home With His Bright-Eyed Children. No doubt the cynical DS Ballard would say he was *blending in* and remind her that psychopaths could be charming and manipulative, just look at Ted Bundy; but Maddie only saw a decent, loving father doing his best to hold his family together in almost unbearable circumstances.

Lucas glanced up suddenly and saw her standing outside the window. He smiled, and despite everything, she automatically found herself smiling back.

The red-haired detective was wrong. *She* was wrong. Her husband wasn't a killer, for God's sake! He wasn't mad *or* bad. There would be some logical explanation for the paint, she knew it. She'd lived with him for six years, he'd fathered two boys with her. She *knew* him. Shame on her for letting herself get sucked into whatever twisted mind games the policewoman was playing. No doubt the woman had been whispering into Lucas's ear, too, pitting them against each other, telling him his wife was deranged, unhinged, that she couldn't be trusted with her own children. Well, she wasn't going to let DS Ballard destroy her marriage with lies and insinuations. Lucas had made mistakes, lying about the loan, but so had she. That didn't make either of them cold-blooded killers. She'd ask him about the paint, and he'd tell her, and it would all be fine. They had to stick together if they wanted to get through this.

The back door opened. 'Maddie?' Lucas called. 'Everything all right?'

'Just putting Emily's bike away,' she replied. 'I'll be right there.'

Lucas had a cup of hot tea waiting for her. He helped her out of her wet coat and hung it up by the back door. 'You look soaked through,' he said, handing her the steaming mug. 'Come on, sit by the radiator and get warm. You'll catch your death otherwise. It might be the end of April, but this is still England, remember.'

'Thank you,' Maddie said, slightly surprised. He didn't usually fuss over her like this, but she wasn't complaining. It would make this conversation easier. 'Lucas, can I ask you something?'

'Let's get you sorted, first. Can I get you something to eat? The kids and I have already had dinner, but there's some lasagne in the oven. It should still be hot.'

'That'd be lovely—'

'Drink your tea. It'll warm you up.'

She shot him a look. 'Is everything all right, Lucas? You seem a bit twitchy. Where have the children gone?'

'They're fine,' he said quickly. 'Emily's just taken Jacob upstairs to give him his bath.'

The front doorbell rang and Lucas shot down the hall as if he'd been waiting for it.

Maddie put her tea down and followed him. 'Are we expecting someone?'

He hesitated, then turned back to her. 'Maddie, you know I love you. I only want the best for you, you understand that, don't you?'

'I know that,' she said uneasily. 'Lucas, what's going on?'

The doorbell rang again. Lucas looked like he wanted to say something else, but instead he gave her arm a quick squeeze and opened the front door.

'Dr Calkins,' Maddie exclaimed, when she saw who was standing there.

'I just thought I'd stop by and see how you were doing. How are you, my dear?'

'Fine.' She shrugged. 'Well. You know.'

'Good. That's good.'

A cold draught blew through the open door. Maddie didn't miss the brief glance the two men exchanged as they all stood awkwardly in the hall. Clearly Lucas had asked Calkins to come round, even if neither of them were prepared to admit it. 'I'm sorry, but why are you here, Doctor?'

'Your husband's been very worried about you, Maddie. We all have. I can't begin to imagine what you've been going through. You both have my deepest condolences on your loss.'

Maddie shot Lucas a glance. Was he really worried about her, or was this another ploy to suggest she was unstable and needed medical help? 'Thank you,' she said warily.

'I want you to know I'm here to help in any way I can.'

'That's very kind of you,' she said automatically, 'but I'm doing OK. My mother has been wonderful, and Lucas, too, of course.'

The doctor nodded. 'Family are very important at a time like this. But sometimes we need a little bit more help than they can provide. No one wants to see you slip back to where we were a couple of years ago,' he added kindly. 'A traumatic event like this could undo all the progress we've made. We want to make sure that doesn't happen.'

'We're here to help,' Lucas said.

Chapter 28

Tuesday 8.30 p.m.

Maddie took a wary step back. 'Why are you really here?'

'No one is going to force you to do anything you don't want to do, I promise,' the doctor said.

'What are you talking about? Like what?'

'Please, Maddie. We only want to help.'

She felt a flare of panic. There could be only one reason Lucas had secretly arranged for the doctor to turn up at her house. He wanted her sectioned. Either he really thought she was crazy, or he wanted her out of the way for some reason of his own after all. She thought again of the paint on his T-shirt, and his insistence that she'd been the one who'd wrecked the nursery. 'I'm not crazy!' she cried. 'You can't just lock me away!'

'No one's locking you away,' Calkins said soothingly. 'I just want to talk to you. There's no need to get upset.'

Lucas looked wretched. 'Maddie, you're my wife and I love you. We simply want what's best for you. Please, let us help.'

She wanted to believe him. She had to hold fast to the fact that he loved her and not let that detective's insinuations mess with her head. If he truly thought she was having some kind of breakdown, he was right to call in expert help. It didn't have to mean anything sinister. She had to stop thinking about that T-shirt, covered with red paint.

'Maddie, you've suffered a tremendous loss,' Calkins said. 'Of course you're upset. You're grieving for your child.'

She glanced at Lucas. 'We both are.'

'Yes, of course. But grief affects everyone differently. With your history, it's only natural Lucas is concerned about you. He just wants us to get ahead of this and for you to know we're here to help you through it.'

'I know, and I appreciate it,' she said carefully.

The doctor looked visibly relieved at her sudden tractability. 'We have a wonderful new facility available at Alexander House,' he said. 'The therapies we offer have been extremely helpful to many of our patients and have proven very effective. You'd have the opportunity to work through your feelings in a neutral, safe space with trained professionals and grief counsellors.'

A current of shock rippled through her. 'A facility? You mean, I'd have to stay there?'

'On a purely voluntary basis, of course. But we find that many patients welcome the chance to get away from the stresses of their day-to-day lives and concentrate on healing themselves without any distractions,' he added encouragingly. 'It's a private facility. You'd have your own room and bathroom and would be free to come and go as you choose, though we generally discourage it in the early stages, to allow as complete a break from stress as possible.'

Lucas squeezed her shoulder. 'You'd be free to come and go whenever you want,' he repeated, as if she was a slow-witted child.

'Once you're through the first period of assessment,' Calkins put in quickly.

She suddenly felt uncertain. She was so tired and so confused. She had no idea what had been causing her blackouts, and the idea of being alone, and having some time to heal, to come to terms with the terrible gaping hole at the centre of their family, felt incredibly tempting.

'It'll give you a real chance to sort yourself out,' Lucas urged.

Maybe it was for the best. She could take a few weeks, put herself back together. And that awful policewoman wouldn't be able to get at her there. 'But what about the children?' she asked weakly.

'I'll take some time off work, and I'm sure your mother will help out. You haven't been yourself since we lost Noah, Maddie, you know you haven't. It's not your fault, I'm not blaming you, but what happened with Jacob yesterday, what you did to the nursery, it's got to stop. It's not good for the children, seeing you like this.'

The nursery. Her self-doubt was abruptly swept away on a tide of fury. Lucas wasn't suffering from PTSD or shock, he was deliberately gaslighting her, trying to make her think she was going mad. 'I didn't do anything to the nursery!' she cried. '*You* did it, and you damn well know it!'

Lucas looked nonplussed. 'What?'

He was a good actor, she had to give him that. 'The red paint,' she snapped. 'I saw it on your T-shirt, the one you shoved in the toolbox. *You* vandalised the nursery. You wanted me to think *I'd* done it.'

'Seriously, Maddie. I don't know what you mean.' He turned to Calkins, who was frowning with concern. 'You see, this is what I'm talking about. She's not making any sense. You can understand why I'm so worried.'

Maddie couldn't believe she'd ignored so many red flags, when the truth had been right in front of her all along. 'You wanted me to think I was going mad, didn't you? You thought if you could get me out of the way, you'd have free rein to do whatever you want.'

'For God's sake! Why would I *do* that?'

The doctor gave Lucas a quelling glance. 'Maddie, why do you think your husband would want to make you think you were mad?' he asked gently.

'He wants me out of the way.'

'Why would he want that, my dear?'

'She's paranoid,' Lucas snapped, his patience at an end.

'I don't know. But it's something to do with Candace, I know it is!' Her voice rose. 'I don't know why, I don't know if it's something to do with the insurance money, or if he's just covering up for his sister, but they want me out of the way!'

251

Lucas looked incredulous. 'What insurance money?'

'That policewoman told me about it. You took out life insurance on our *children*! How much will you get for Noah? Fifteen thousand pounds? Twenty? Is that all he was worth to you?'

'You're seriously suggesting I'd kill my own son for *money*?'

'Do you have any proof of this, Maddie?' Calkins asked.

She could tell he was just humouring her. 'I can show you his T-shirt,' she said desperately. 'It has red paint all over it.'

'I got paint on my shirt cleaning up the mess *you'd* made,' Lucas said tersely. 'Look, William, you can't possibly take any of this seriously. It's like something out of a bad novel. Sneaking around painting rooms in the middle of the night, trying to drive my wife mad for the insurance money! Maddie, you do know how insane this all sounds, don't you?'

She knew exactly how insane it sounded, but that didn't make it any less true. 'What about yesterday, with the Calpol? You arranged the whole thing so I'd get the blame, didn't you?'

Lucas threw up his hands in exasperation. 'I wasn't even *here* when that happened!'

'But Candace was! She came over when I was asleep, Emily saw her!'

The doctor frowned. 'Are you suggesting, Maddie, that Lucas and his sister knowingly conspired to put Jacob at risk just to implicate you?'

Maddie looked from one man to the other. She felt cornered: the more she protested the truth, the crazier she sounded. 'I know how mad it seems, but that's the whole point,' she said, close to tears. 'They know no one will believe me. They *want* me to sound crazy. I just don't know why. I think it's because Candace did something. I think … I think she's the one who hurt Noah, and Lucas is covering up for her.'

'Maddie, my dear, I think perhaps it's all been too much,' Calkins said gently. 'With everything that's happened, it's not surprising you're struggling to cope. I really think it might be best if you came with us now, so we can get you the help you need.'

Panic flared again. Lucas had been so clever, setting her up like this. He held all the cards. She had to tread carefully, or she'd find herself locked up. 'You said I don't have to.'

Calkins hesitated. 'That's right, I can't insist on it, Maddie, but I really think it'd be best,' he said. 'Clearly you've been under tremendous strain. A short break—'

'Perhaps I could stop by Alexander House in a day or two and have a look around?' she said quickly, trying to buy time. 'Let me sleep on it and see how I feel in the morning?'

'Well, we can't force you to come with us,' Calkins said doubtfully. 'Not as things stand. And I'd much rather you came because you wanted to. All right, Maddie. We can talk again in a day or two. But if things get any worse, if you start to experience depressive or suicidal thoughts, I want you to come in straight away.'

'That's it?' Lucas demanded disbelievingly. 'You heard what she said! She thinks I'm some kind of psychopath! God knows what she's going to accuse me of next!'

'Lucas, we can't make her accept our help if she doesn't want it,' Calkins said. 'I think perhaps we need to reconsider the antidepressant medications you're on, Maddie. In some cases, certain prescriptions can cause paranoia and similar feelings of persecution. I'm not saying you're paranoid,' he added hastily, 'but we should consider your treatment holistically, rather than compartmentalising our therapeutic and pharmaceutical responses.'

For a moment, Maddie was thrown. It hadn't even occurred to her to consider the effect her pills might be having on her judgement.

But she quickly recovered herself. The pills hadn't put that paint-spattered T-shirt in Lucas's toolbox. Nor did they explain why he'd taken out life insurance on a ten-week-old baby, or why Candace had been present for every single accident that had happened to either of her sons in the last year. She might not have all the answers yet, but she wasn't crazy.

The doctor said goodbye, his reluctance to leave evident. Lucas showed him out, and Maddie could hear the murmur of their voices as they talked in the hall, though she couldn't make out what they were saying. She could guess, though. Lucas wasn't going to give up that easily. She might have won this skirmish, but the doctor had clearly bought into Lucas's version of events. The next time, she might not be able to talk her way out of it.

She heard the front door close, and a moment later Lucas came back into the kitchen. 'Did you mean what you said?' he asked. 'You'll consider going to Alexander House?'

'No, of course not,' she snapped. 'You know, for a while there, you almost had me going. I actually started to wonder if I was going mad. But I'm not going to let you get away with it. I've let Noah down, but I'm not going to let you hurt Jacob or Emily.'

Lucas crossed the room in seconds. Maddie was reminded suddenly how big he was, how easily he could overpower her. She was trapped in the corner of the kitchen with no way to reach the door. 'You really believe that?' he demanded furiously. 'You really think I'm capable of something this ruthless, this *insane*?'

She stood her ground, trying to keep her legs from shaking. 'I don't know who you are, Lucas. I don't even know if that's your real name.'

He held her gaze for a long moment and there was something in his eyes that suddenly made her doubt herself again. Then he bent his head so that his mouth was just a fraction of an inch from her ear.

'Did it ever occur to you,' he whispered, the menace in his tone unmistakeable, his breath warm against her skin, 'did it ever occur to you, Maddie, that when you told the good doctor to leave, you just sent your last lifeboat away?'

Lydia

She's sixteen, and she knows she's going to get out soon. There's a boy a year older than her at Font Hill called Marion who killed a teacher. ('Bastard took the mick out of my name one too many times,' he says, 'it's not my fault my mother was a bloody John Wayne fan.') He's done really well at Font Hill, and Mr Tallack got permission for him to go to the local community college to study mechanical engineering. He can't stay on campus, he has to come home every night to Font Hill, but he's allowed to live in a special flat within the grounds with a couple of other boys, and once he gets his qualifications, he'll be released on licence.

Mr Tallack promises the same for her. He's not supposed to have favourites, no preferential treatment, that's what he always says, but she knows he's got a soft spot for her. She was a disturbed little girl when she came to Font Hill, he says, an angry little girl, but she's growing up now, she's clever, she can do anything with her life if she puts her mind to it, if she decides to make the rest of her life a *good* life.

She does well in her exams in the summer (she sits them at the local community college, they give her another name, *Miss Jones*, they call her), and Mr Tallack says she can do her A-levels next and then go to college, get some proper qualifications, go into a real profession. She'll be allowed to move out of the secure unit and into a flat in the grounds, like Marion. Eventually, she'll be released, too. She was only eleven years old when she did what she did, she can't be held responsible forever. She'll leave with an education, which is more than she'd have got if she'd stayed with Mae, and a future. A real future.

She's made friends at Font Hill, too, for the first time in her life. As far as the boys are concerned, she's one of them, doing her time, just like they are. They don't treat her any differently because she's a girl. It's just like having forty brothers. Now and again, a new boy arrives, and gets bowled over by her startling blue eyes and developing curves, but the other lads soon put him straight. She can't be doing with any of that romantic nonsense. She's had enough of men to last her a life-time.

Davy is allowed to visit her one Sunday a month, and he drives down from Manchester, where he's working part-time as a nightclub bouncer while he goes back to school. He can't let her be the only one with qualifications, he laughs, she'll get a swelled head.

The two of them plan what they're going to do when she gets out, where they're going to live. Nowhere near Mae, they're both agreed on that. She likes the idea of the West Country, Cornwall maybe, it sounds so romantic (she had to read *Jamaica Inn* for her exams), but Davy says they need to go to a big city, somewhere it'll be easier for her to blend in and disappear, and anyway, she'd be bored rigid in Cornwall. She's young, he says, she's got her whole life ahead of her. She needs bright lights and people. She needs to learn what it's like to have *fun*.

Davy says they should go to London, so she agrees. She'll do whatever Davy thinks is best. He's stuck by her through thick and thin when no one else did, and she worships the ground he walks on. He's the only one who's never let her down. Frank wanted to come, but they wouldn't let him. He's not even allowed to write, Davy says. According to the police, he's just another one of Mae's johns. Even when she asks her solicitor, they still won't let him visit.

Mae came to see her at Font Hill once just after she'd moved there, and stupidly she thought it was because her mother cared – will she never learn? – but of course Mae just went straight out and sold the story to the papers again. Lydia told Mr Tallack she didn't want to see her mother anymore, but that hasn't stopped Mae talking to the press, inventing stories about her childhood and plastering Lydia's name all over the front pages every time the story shows signs of beginning to die down. It's as if she *wants* to make sure no one can forget what Lydia did.

A couple of weeks after her seventeenth birthday, the staff at Font Hill get together for their monthly case conference, so all the kids go to the common room to watch a film as they always do when there's a staff meeting. As the only girl, she nearly always gets outvoted on what to watch, the boys always want something like *Star Wars* or some stupid spaghetti western, so she curls up in an armchair by the window to catch up on her reading. She's read *Pride and Prejudice* already, it's one of her A-level set books, and frankly she thinks Elizabeth Bennet is kind of lame, her namesake Lydia has much more get-up-and-go; but Mr Tallack says the book is a classic and he's offered to give her extra English lessons, and she wants to make him proud of her, so she's giving it another go.

She looks up as the staff file out of their meeting past the common room. Mr Blake, one of the masters, glances at her through the open doorway and then looks quickly away. He's white as a sheet. One of the art teachers rubs her eyes, looking suspiciously as if she's crying. There's a very strange atmosphere as the staff scuttle away and Lydia wonders if someone has died.

Mr Tallack beckons to her from the doorway. He doesn't smile and she gets up and follows him to his office, wondering nervously what's going on.

There's no other way to tell you this, he says, as soon as she sits down, so I'm just going to come straight out with it: you're leaving tomorrow and you're going to prison. He swallows hard, struggling to speak. He's tried his best, he says, as his eyes fill with tears, he's tried for a week to get them to change their minds, the authorities, he's told them about college, all the plans he has for her, her A-levels and everything, but none of it has worked, they won't listen, it's all been decided.

She's almost too stunned to speak. She gives a shocked laugh. No, she says, no. Why would they send me to prison? I haven't done anything!

He looks at her sadly.

I was eleven years old! she exclaims, starting to cry. I didn't understand what I was doing! That's not who I am anymore! Did you tell them that?

Of course, Mr Tallack says. He's been fighting for her all week, he explains, that's the only reason he didn't say anything before, didn't give her more warning, he was talking to the Home Office, trying to get them to reconsider, until that afternoon he'd still hoped he'd succeed, but then—

Then what?

Your mother, he says reluctantly.

It turns out Mae picked this week of all weeks to go to the papers again, stir up a new story. Some nonsense about Lydia's cushy life at the 'Font Hill Hilton', her art classes and private bathroom – of course it's private! she cries, I'm the only girl! – and swimming lessons on day release at the local pool. They've even managed to get hold of a photograph of her sunbathing in her bikini on a picnic rug in the grounds, a pair of sunglasses propped on her head and a drink (lemonade, but the photo's black and white, so you can't tell) in her hand. The photographer must have climbed a tree and taken it with a long lens, Mr Tallack says grimly.

The Home Office doesn't care that it was her birthday, the staff had made a special occasion of it. They don't care about her A-levels or college, they only care that it's making them look bad, letting her live the good life when she's supposed to be behind bars. Besides, she's seventeen now. It's not appropriate for her to be locked up with forty boys.

How long will I have to stay in prison? she asks, but he can't answer that.

This is all my fault, he says, for getting your hopes up. I was so sure, after Marion. But you'll go forth as Font Hill's ambassador. You'll show them, you'll show all of them. It'll be all right, you'll see.

She doesn't believe that any more than he does. Font Hill is her home, the people here are her family. She's been in the system long enough to know what she can expect in an adult prison. She'll be the youngest again, a fresh teenage girl in a world of isolated women. There's no time or money in jail to educate and encourage prisoners. Inmates are there to be contained and punished, not pampered and rehabilitated. She can forget about A-levels and college. She can forget about a flat in London with Davy.

She's back where she started.

Chapter 29

Tuesday 9.30 p.m.

Maddie's eyes darted to the kitchen door. There was no way for her to reach it with Lucas blocking her way. 'The children are upstairs,' she said hoarsely, trying to dodge around him. 'Please, Lucas. Let me go.'

He stepped back suddenly, throwing his arms up in disgust. 'For God's sake, Maddie! I was just trying to show you how ridiculous you're being! What do you think I'm going to do? Batter you to death with a frying pan and bury your body under the patio?'

She fled to the other side of the kitchen table, although the menace that had been such a tangible presence in the room just moments ago was already dissipating. 'Stay away from me!'

Lucas stopped in his tracks. 'I don't get it. Do you really think I'd ever do anything to hurt you or the children?' He sounded genuinely confused. 'Where is this coming from, Maddie? Why are you acting like I've suddenly turned into a monster?'

They stared at each other from opposite sides of the table. Maddie couldn't quite believe it'd only been three weeks since they'd sat at this same table, his arm affectionately draped around her shoulder as they'd planned their summer holiday. Her head filled with white noise, questions buzzing so loudly in her mind she could hardly think.

Despite everything, she couldn't believe he'd murder their own son. But she knew his loyalty to his sister ran deep. And their marriage had been sorely tested in the year after Jacob's birth, and she knew her depression had pushed him to his limits. She'd thought they'd emerged stronger than ever, but was that when the damage had been done? Their marriage may have seemed unharmed on the outside, but inside, had it been silently haemorrhaging? In the end, was his bond to Candace stronger than his ties to her?

He started around the table towards her again, but she moved to keep it between them. 'You think I'd protect anyone, even my own sister, if they'd hurt our son?' he asked. 'Please, Maddie. Look at me. *Look* at me. You *know* me. I'm still the man you married. I don't know what's going on in your head, but I haven't changed!'

She was so confused. Every time she thought she'd touched the bottom, the seabed shifted. He seemed so sincere, but wasn't that what psychopaths did? 'I don't know what to think anymore,' she said weakly.

'Then don't think,' he urged. 'Trust your instincts. Trust *me.*'

'I want to,' she said slowly.

'Please, Maddie. I know how much you're grieving.

263

We lost our *son*. But you need to stop lashing out and looking for someone to blame. I don't know what happened to Noah, but it had nothing to do with me or Candace. You *have* to know that, deep down.'

'I don't even know who you are,' she said hollowly. 'I've searched, but I can't find any record of you or Candace that goes back beyond twelve or thirteen years.' She suddenly found her voice again. 'There's nothing, no old address, no college friends, nothing. It's like you were beamed down from outer space. There's only one reason you'd appear out of nowhere like that, and that's if you'd changed your name. Why would you do that, Lucas?'

He shrugged. 'Because Candace asked me to.'

She was taken aback. Of all the responses he could have made, she hadn't expected him to come straight out and admit it.

He saw her surprise. 'I've never tried to hide it, Maddie. If you'd bothered to ask me about it, I'd have told you! I hate to burst your conspiracy bubble, but there's no dark, dreadful secret in my past. I'm not in witness protection or running from the law, if that's what you're thinking.' He smiled wryly. 'I changed my name because Candace asked me.'

'Why?'

'It was this thing she had.' He hesitated a moment, lost in the past. 'After our parents died, my mother's sister took us in, but she never formally adopted us. When Candace was about twelve, she got a bee in her bonnet about the three of us not being a proper family because we had a different surname. She wanted both of us to change ours to Drummond, Aunt Dot's name. But Aunt Dot said Candace had to wait till she was eighteen, in case she changed her mind.'

Maddie felt herself weakening in the face of his calm, rational explanation. He made her fears seem like night terrors exposed as nonsense by the cold light of day.

'When she turned eighteen, she switched her name by deed poll and asked me to change mine, too.' He sighed. 'I didn't care. The name I'd been born with, Carter, had nothing but bad memories for me. Lucas Carter was the thirteen-year-old boy who watched his parents burn to death. I was happy to leave him behind. So I agreed to change my name to Drummond, too. It made Candace and Aunt Dot happy and cost me nothing. The only reason I didn't tell you before is because it had nothing to do with *us*. You and me. It never even occurred to me to mention it. Why would it?'

She searched his face, alert for the false note that would tell her he was lying. He seemed genuine, but she no longer trusted either him or her own judgement. She'd believed him when he'd lied to her face about the loan. 'Even if this is true—'

'Of course it's true!'

'You've just admitted you've been lying to me for six years,' she said in a rush. 'I don't even know who you are.'

'I'm Lucas Drummond. I haven't lied to you! I've never pretended to be anyone I'm not, Maddie. I don't

265

understand why you're making such a big deal about this. Drummond is my legal name. Maybe I should have told you before, but I honestly didn't even think about it. I've been Lucas Drummond for so long. It's who I am now.' He shrugged helplessly. 'It's just a *name*.'

'You *have* pretended to be someone you're not!' she cried. 'I'm not talking about the different name, Lucas! You made me think you were honest and trustworthy, that I could rely on you. But you lied about the loan, you've lied about your name – what else have you hidden from me? Is your birthday your real birthday? How do I know Candace is even your sister?'

He looked repelled. 'Of course she's my sister. I don't know where this paranoia is coming from, but you can't keep using me as your punchbag, Maddie. I'm not a robot. I'm grieving too.' His voice grew bitter. '*You* were the one there that night, *you* lied about how Noah got those bruises, but never once did I blame you when all the evidence pointed in your direction. I gave you the benefit of the doubt. I cleaned up your mess when you trashed the nursery so the kids didn't see it, and the only thanks I get for it is to be accused of wrecking it myself. You're twisting and turning like a rat in cage so you don't have to face the truth, which is that the only person who's a danger to this family is *you*!'

She flinched, as if the blow had been physical. Never mind the business with the nursery. She'd been the one there the night Noah had died, and she hadn't been able to keep him safe. She'd dropped him, given him those bruises, and even now, despite the fact the pathol-

266

ogist had said they hadn't caused his death, she still felt guilty about it. She might not be a danger to her family, but she hadn't been able to protect her baby when it mattered.

Lucas looked suddenly contrite, his anger draining away as quickly as it had arrived. 'Maddie, I'm sorry, I didn't mean that—'

'I think you should leave now,' she said, her voice wobbling. 'I want you out of the house tonight.'

'Maddie, please. I'm sorry. I should never have said that. I don't know what I was thinking—'

His phone rang suddenly, startling them both. Lucas ignored it. A few seconds later, it rang again. The third time, he pulled it out of his pocket, glanced at it and ended the call.

'It was her, wasn't it?' Maddie demanded.

'Maddie—'

'Go on, go to her! I'm calling my mother. If you're not gone by the time she gets here, she'll call the police.'

'No, she won't,' Lucas said tiredly. 'Fine. I'm too exhausted to argue anymore. If this is really what you want, I'll go. Just for tonight. We can talk about this tomorrow, when you've had a chance to come to your senses.' He grabbed his coat from the hook by the back door and turned to face her. 'You know, I never thought you were crazy before, whatever you might think. But I do now.'

Lydia

They summon her to the Governor's office. She's twenty-two years old now; she's been in prison more than five years and hauled in to see the Governor at least three times a year, every time her mother sells a story or some do-gooding campaigner decides to launch a petition to set her free. They have no truck with her celebrity in here; not the screws, anyway.

Among the inmates, it's different. She's faced her share of hostility, especially from the younger women, the ones inside for drugs or theft, who call her a monster and spit in her food; but the older women and the lifers have always been kind to her, protective, really. They don't see her as a child-murderer. She was only eleven, they say, a child herself. She can hardly be held responsible for what she did.

She doesn't believe that, though. Not anymore. The one good thing about prison is that they made her see a shrink, a proper shrink, not a kid-gloves soft-touch counsellor like she saw at Font Hill. She ran rings around that woman, feeding her the whole sob story about

Mae and Jimmy and all the rest. It's not your fault, the counsellor used to say, oozing liberal understanding and handing her a box of tissues. It's your mother who should be in jail.

But the prison shrink isn't having any of it. She has to take responsibility for what she did, he says. Plenty of kids have a shit-awful childhood, just take a look around you, half the women in here came from similar backgrounds to you, or worse, and they don't go around strangling toddlers. Maybe it's my bad blood, she says, glibly parroting what she read in the papers, Mae's wicked and she passed it on to me, along with my blue eyes, I can't help it, it's in my genes. Bullshit, he says unsympathetically. You made a choice when you strangled Julia. You're not a helpless little puppet. Which is a *good* thing. It means you can choose to be different, going forward. You can choose *not* to be like Mae.

She kicks over the coffee table when he says that the first time, storms out of the session. But she comes back. Even so, it's not Damascene, her change of heart, it doesn't come as a sudden lightning bolt from the blue. She sees the shrink every week for years, and most of the time, it's two steps forward, one step back.

The realisation that she took a life, that all of this – being spat at, prison, everything – isn't something that happened *to* her, it's something she *caused*, is hard to face. She suffers panic attacks, nightmares, she finds it almost impossible to sleep. The prison doc offers her antidepressants, but she refuses to take them. As hard as this is, she knows she has to square up to what she's done or she'll be no better than Mae.

Even so, she still shies away from the savage reality of what she did. When the shrink asks her to describe the fatal moment, all she sees is darkness. But she has at least accepted that Julia died because she made the choice to kill her. It doesn't really matter why: she can blame her mother, she can blame her genes, her 'bad blood', but like the shrink says, in the end, the only person who had control over what happened that dreadful day was her.

She isn't the monster the press makes her out to be; she refuses to see herself as a *murderer*, even now. But she killed a child; she is, in fact, a child-killer in every sense of the phrase, and she will have to live with that knowledge for the rest of her life. *That's* her real punishment.

She knows she won't ever be let out. There's too much public anger and hatred towards her, even now, over a decade later. Thanks to her mother's frequent forays into print, she's a household name. They'll never let her go free. She'd probably be lynched if they did. She doesn't crave her freedom anymore, not like she did when she was at Font Hill. She's given up hope. She's been in the system now for as long as she was out of it, and frankly, she's not sure how she'd cope if they did let her go.

So when the Governor says, without preamble, without even looking up from her desk, your parole has been granted, we're moving you to a halfway house tomorrow, you need to go and pack, she simply sits there, uncomprehending. The Governor might as well be talking Dutch, for all the sense she makes.

She's suddenly eleven years old again, bewildered and disoriented as she's smuggled out of the courthouse beneath an itchy grey blanket.

Parole? she repeats, stupidly.

You'll be on licence, the Governor says tersely. She has never liked Lydia and she doesn't trouble to hide it. You'll be at the halfway house for six weeks, and they'll find somewhere permanent for you to go after that. They'll set you up in a flat. Find you work. You can't go back home, she adds. Someone's bound to recognise you. Even with a new name, it's too much of a risk. You've got to stay away from the area. Once news breaks you've been let out, the world and his wife will be looking for you.

A new name?

You can hardly keep the old one, the Governor says derisively. In case you hadn't realised, you're not Miss Popular out there. We can't have someone taking matters into their own hands, she adds, sounding regretful.

Lydia walks back to her cell in a daze. Her solicitor has applied for parole every year since she became eligible, but she never thought she'd ever get it. Not after they took her out of Font Hill and sent her here. She thought they'd locked her up and thrown away the key, like all the newspapers said they should do. She'd thought she'd die in here.

She doesn't know what to feel as she sits on the edge of her narrow bed and stares blankly at the wall. She's had no time to prepare for this. All her friends are here, on the inside. She's never had a real home outside prison; she hasn't had a friend who wasn't an inmate. Davy is her only family, and even though he's visited her every month without fail, she knows he has his own life now.

How is she supposed to function outside? She's never even caught a bus on her own, much less driven a car. The last time she was free, she was eleven years old. She hasn't bought a packet of cigarettes or gone to the cinema or ordered a drink in a pub. She's never been to a library or gone out dancing or even shopped at the supermarket. How's she supposed to juggle electricity bills and rent and doing her own laundry, never mind get a job? What's she even qualified to do? She never finished her A-levels, not after they dragged her out of Font Hill. She's not trained for anything. For eleven years, she's never had to worry about where her next meal is coming from or what to do with her day. It's all decided for her, even what clothes to wear. She feels a rising tide of panic just thinking about being cut loose from everything she knows.

And it won't be real freedom, will it? She'll be looking over her shoulder for the rest of her life. The Governor is right: there'll be plenty of people who'd be happy to see her swing and would consider lynching her a public service. Even with a new identity, she'll never really be safe.

But she doesn't have a choice. She has twelve hours to pick a new name and say goodbye to all her friends. She has been oddly popular in prison and her talent for friendship has given her a feeling of self-worth.

As she passes out through the prison gates, it all drains away, leaving nothing but a hollow void.

She arrives at Wellington House with one small bag that contains everything she owns. She feels more angry and abandoned and frightened now than she did even when they sent her down. She has six weeks to learn what she's missed out on for the last eleven years. A new name isn't going to fix that.

She stares at herself in the mirror as she brushes her teeth that night. She doesn't look broken, though she knows that, deep down, nothing has changed. She sees without vanity that she's beautiful, with her slanting blue cat's eyes and creamy skin. She's kept her fair hair cropped short out of convenience ever since Font Hill, but it gives her a delicate, Audrey Hepburn air. Much good her looks have ever done her, she thinks bitterly. If she'd been ugly, maybe Jimmy and all the rest would've left her alone.

She's twenty-two, and she feels a hundred. She could live for another fifty years, seventy, and she'll have to carry around what she did for every single one of them. How is she supposed to make friends, when she can never tell anyone who she is? At least in prison she could be herself.

Hastings, they tell her. That's where they're sending her. Some dull little town on the south coast where old people go to die. London is out of the question, as is Manchester or Edinburgh or anywhere lively she might actually want to go. No to the West Country, too; she'll stand out a mile, they say; she needs to go somewhere no one's going to ask questions. They veto the new name she chose, too, they tell her it's too similar to her old one, nothing with the same initials is allowed. They give her another one, a name that doesn't feel like her, doesn't sound like her, feels foreign on her tongue; that's the point, they say, we want it as far from *Lydia Slaughter* as we can manage.

At first they tell her she's to have no contact with Davy, she's effectively going into witness protection. It's for her own good; the first thing the journalists will do once they find out she's free is put a tail on her brother, but she throws a complete fit at that, says she'd rather slit her wrists or strangle another kid so they have to put her back inside. They listen to her *then*.

It takes several weeks of wrangling, but in the end they agree to let her live with Davy. He has to promise to change his name, too, move to bloody Hastings with her, but he says why not, it's a chance for him to start over as well, wipe the slate clean. He's done so well while she's been inside, passed his exams, got his qualifications, but his record is holding him back, no one wants to hire an arsonist, of course, as soon as they find out he's an ex-con the door slams shut.

She's introduced to her probation officer, Michael Conway, a retired policeman in his early forties who lives in Hastings, not far from the flat they've found

274

for her. He reminds her a lot of Mr Tallack, and of Frank; he treats her like a normal human being, not shit on the sole of his shoe. He tells her they've found her a job at a local travel agents, it's not much, he says, she'll be in the back room writing up bookings and making phone calls, she's not allowed to work with the public, not yet; but it's a job, a real job, she'll be earning her own money, she'll have her independence.

She knows Michael must have gone out on a limb to get her this job. It's hard finding anyone willing to employ a former felon, and she knows he must've called in a favour to sort this for her. She's lucky she's got a decent probation officer. She's heard some horror stories from the girls on the inside: POs who demand sexual favours, show up drunk, take a cut of their earnings, force them to run drugs. She can tell Michael is a good man. It makes her feel a bit less terrified, knowing he'll be there to keep an eye on her. It's going to be tough, she knows that, but she's starting to see a future now, for the first time since she left Font Hill.

A week before her release, one of the staff at the halfway house says she's wanted in the warden's office. She puts down her book and goes downstairs. Michael is waiting for her along with the warden, and she smiles, wondering if he's got the new library card he promised her.

But he doesn't smile back. The warden asks her to sit down, and then Michael unexpectedly crouches down next to her, and in a voice warped by pity, he gives her the worst news of her life.

Chapter 30

Thursday 4.30 p.m.

Maddie turned off the ignition and stared at her house, still holding her phone. In a few minutes, she would have to go in and paste on a smile for the children, explain to her mother what had happened, pick up the threads of life and try to carry on. But this one small moment was Noah's.

She could still smell her baby when she closed her eyes, feel the weight of his small warm body in her arms. The ache in her heart was physical, a crushing pressure in her chest that threatened to suffocate her. She longed to yield to her grief, to stop fighting and let it submerge her. But this moment was all she could allow herself. She had two other living children she had to protect.

Emily had already started to ask questions about Lucas, wanting to know why he hadn't been home for two days. Maddie had told her he was away working, but her daughter was smart; she wouldn't buy that for long. Even two-year-old Jacob had been asking for his daddy. She hadn't spoken to Lucas yet, and he hadn't called, but they'd have to talk soon and come to some arrangement about the children. She guessed he was staying with Candace. There was no way she was letting that woman near Emily or Jacob, but Lucas had the right to see them. It still hadn't sunk in yet that he'd moved out. Even though she'd had no choice but to tell him to go, she missed him with every fibre of her being. Last night, she'd reached for him, and instead of the familiar, warm bulwark of his body, there was only cold, dead space beside her.

Her fingers curled around the phone in her lap. On her way home from the sanctuary, Rebecca Piggott had called and given her the news she'd been waiting for: the police were dropping their investigation. But not because they thought the post-mortem had been wrong.

'Forensic pathology is not an exact science, Maddie,' Rebecca had said carefully. 'As with so many things presented as indisputable fact, when it actually comes down to it, it's all a question of interpretation. That's actually a *good* thing for us. Their experts say black, our experts say white, and reasonable doubt lies in shades of grey.'

Reasonable doubt. It sounded like a line from a television drama, not a phrase that could ever be applied to her. Rebecca obviously dealt with cases like this every day, women accused of murdering abusive husbands, college students on trial for date rape, but Maddie felt as if she'd fallen through the rabbit hole and found herself in a parallel universe.

'I don't understand,' she'd said, unable to hide her

frustration. 'If the police are dropping the investigation, surely that means they think it was a cot death after all?'

'It's not quite that simple. As you are now unfortunately aware, the basis for bringing a charge citing Shaken Baby Syndrome is the so-called "triad" of head injuries: retinal haemorrhages, subdural haemorrhages, and damage to the brain affecting function. Luckily for us, because of the controversy over other cases like this that've been thrown out, the Court of Appeal says that if the outcome of a trial depends *solely* on this triad, it's unsafe to proceed. In other words, unless there is corroborative evidence of trauma, or other non-medical facts that are relevant, the CPS will refuse to prosecute.'

'But they couldn't find any other evidence, could they?'

'Maddie, I don't want to upset you, especially after all you've been through,' Rebecca had said. 'But DS Ballard was very keen for me to point out that just because they don't have enough to move forward at the moment, it doesn't mean they don't believe Noah was shaken to death. They simply can't prove it.'

'She thinks I did it,' Maddie had said flatly.

'Not you,' Rebecca said.

It had taken a moment for her to understand. Rebecca had been *warning* her. Noah's injuries might not be enough for the police to be able to prosecute, but that didn't mean they had an innocent explanation.

She hadn't known whether to laugh or cry. The police

finally believed her story and were dropping the investigation. But that meant whoever *had* killed her baby would be getting off scot-free.

'There's a high chance that someone close to you is responsible for Noah's injuries,' Rebecca had added quietly. 'Someone who was alone with him in the seventy-two hours before his death. The police can't do anything, not as things stand. Which means it's up to you to keep Emily and Jacob safe.'

It's up to you to keep Emily and Jacob safe. She wanted justice for Noah, of course she did. But he was dead, and there was nothing more she could do for him right now. She had to focus on Jacob and Emily.

She picked up her bag and left the cocoon of the car to go inside. Her mother had been staying with her ever since Lucas had left, and she found her now in the kitchen, filling a saucepan with water and setting it on the stove, next to a packet of spaghetti she was about to cook for the children's tea.

'Did you manage to speak to Rebecca?' Sarah asked.

'The police aren't going to press charges against me,' Maddie said.

'Oh, darling. What a relief.'

Maddie glanced out of the window and watched the children playing outside on the swing set at the bottom of the garden. 'They don't think it's a cot death,' she said, without turning around. 'They just don't have enough evidence to charge anyone, that's all.'

'Pathologists make mistakes,' Sarah said. 'It's always easier if there's a rational explanation, but sometimes awful things happen for no reason, no matter how horrible and random and unfair that sounds.' Her voice softened. 'Cot death is tragic and terrible, but it's no one's fault, Maddie.'

She couldn't understand why her mother was so quick to suggest there was an innocent explanation. Did she still think Maddie had had something to do with Noah's death, was that it? Was she trying to seize on this chance to rewrite the facts because she was afraid of the truth?

'Did you not hear me?' Maddie demanded, swinging around. 'It's not a mistake, Mum. The police don't think the pathologist was wrong, and nor does Rebecca. They're sure Noah's injuries aren't accidental. They just don't know who caused them, that's all.'

'No one caused them,' Sarah said firmly. 'Just because the so-called experts want to find a reason, it doesn't mean there is one. Dozens of these cases have been thrown out on appeal—'

'I don't want to believe it any more than you do,' Maddie said. 'But someone close to Noah hurt him. *Deliberately* hurt him. It might not have been Lucas, but I think he's covering for Candace. I can't let him come home. I can't trust him anymore.'

'I know Lucas hasn't been entirely straight with you,' her mother said. 'Of course he should have told you why he really wanted that bank loan, I'm not making excuses for him. But lying is a long, *long* way from condoning murder, darling.' She squeezed her daughter's hand. 'He shouldn't have lied to you, but he's apologised, and you need to let it go. Come on, darling. He wouldn't cover up the death of his own child, not even for Candace. You're not thinking clearly.'

For a moment, she was tempted to do as her mother said. She *wanted* to believe in Lucas, she *so* much wanted to believe in him; he was her husband, the father of her children, the man she still loved. But there was simply too much at stake. She couldn't gamble Emily and Jacob's lives on giving him the benefit of the doubt. She hadn't told her mother the real reason why Lucas had moved out two days ago, allowing her to assume it was over the second mortgage; Sarah had always tended to side with Lucas, as she had over the loan, and Maddie hadn't been ready to have her reasoning questioned yet again.

'He tried to have me sectioned,' she said bitterly. 'He called Calkins and tried to get me locked up.'

'Lucas didn't call Calkins,' Sarah said.

'Mum, stop trying to defend him. He *did* call Calkins, he—'

'I was the one who called him, not Lucas.'

Maddie's jaw dropped. '*What?*'

'Darling, no one thinks you're crazy. But you *are* traumatised. Who wouldn't be, with what you've been through? You need time and space to heal. Dr Calkins can help you do that.'

'How could you, Mum?' she shouted. 'Lucas is trying to make everyone think I'm going mad, and now you're helping him! I found his T-shirt hidden in the shed, it had red paint all over it, *he* was the one who vandalised

Noah's room!' She sounded crazier than ever, she knew that, but she couldn't stop. 'He and Candace, they're in this together, Mum, she was here the night before Noah died, and she came to the house when I was asleep and gave Jacob the Calpol—'

'Maddie, stop.'

'I know it sounds insane, but—'

'Stop,' Sarah said forcefully. '*You* were the one who painted Noah's nursery. Emily *saw* you.'

Maddie was literally rendered speechless.

'Emily told me this weekend,' Sarah said, more calmly. 'She was very upset. She heard a noise one night a few days after Noah died, and when she got up to see what was going on, she saw you ripping up the nursery carpet and rolling red paint all over the walls. She said you were crying and saying Noah's name over and over again. She didn't know what to do, the poor child must have been terrified. In the end she just crept back to bed.'

Maddie's head spun. *She* had done it? *She'd* been the one who'd wrecked the nursery.

'I can't have,' she said, shocked. 'I'd remember.'

'Grief does strange things to us all, darling.'

Maddie groped for a chair and collapsed into it. Just as she'd thought she'd made sense of the madness engulfing her, her world was upended yet again. Lucas *had* been telling the truth. He'd been cleaning up the mess she'd made of the nursery, just as he'd said. He hadn't been plotting to get her locked up: her mother had been the one who'd called Calkins, not her husband. And if he'd been telling the truth about all of that ...

282

She'd been wrong. She'd been wrong about everything.

She was the one who was going mad. She covered her face with her hands. 'Lucas will never forgive me, Mum. I said such terrible things to him—'

'He'll understand. He knows you're not yourself, sweetheart.' Sarah sat down next to her and took her hands. 'Grief takes many forms. Sometimes it can lead you to think things that aren't true and get strange ideas into your head. It doesn't mean you're crazy. But you're not thinking straight either. That's why I told Lucas we needed to get Calkins to see you. There was nothing sinister about it. No one's plotting to get you out of the way.' She smoothed Maddie's hair away from her forehead. 'This is my fault. If I'd had any idea you were blaming Lucas for calling him, I'd have told you before.'

'What about Emily?' Maddie said wretchedly. 'She must have been so scared when she saw me in the nursery.'

'Emily and I had a long talk. She understands now you were just very sad about Noah, and seeing his room upset you. Maybe it'd be nice if I took her to spend a few days with me. I think she needs some alone time, away from Jacob—'

She broke off as the doorbell rang.

'I'll get it,' Sarah said.

Maddie sat frozen in her chair as her mother went into the hall. Her mother might think Lucas would forgive her, but Sarah hadn't been there; she hadn't seen the look of hurt and betrayal on his face. Maddie had accused him of being complicit in the murder of his own son, based on nothing but suspicion, paranoia and what she saw now were a few flimsy – at best – pieces of circumstantial evidence. What in God's name had she been thinking? She felt as if she'd been groping around in the dark, and someone had suddenly switched on the light. She had to call him and explain. Beg for his forgiveness, agree to see Calkins, promise to do whatever it took to get her head straight and put her family back together.

She shoved back her chair and ran towards the front door. 'Mum, I need you to mind the children. I'm going—'

She broke off as she saw the red-haired detective on the doorstep. They must have come to tell her officially that the investigation was over. Either that, or they were here to arrest her after all.

But DS Ballard didn't even look in her direction. The woman's eyes never left her mother's face.

'Hello, Lydia,' she said.

Lydia

Davy is driving down the M6 on his way to see her at the halfway house when a fifty-three-year-old mother-of-two tries to undertake him on a rain-slicked stretch of road and loses control. The woman clips Davy's car, sending him spinning into the central reservation. The car flips onto its roof, killing him instantly. Seven other cars are caught up in the crash and more than a dozen people are injured, though no one else dies. The woman gets away with a broken ankle and sprained wrist.

Her blood alcohol level is twice the legal limit.

The accident makes front-page newspaper headlines. Of course it does, it's an irresistible story. There's a strong suggestion of karma in some of the editorials, as if it serves Lydia right to lose someone she loved. They bring up Davy's own criminal record, too, like it somehow makes what happened to him less terrible.

The drunk driver is initially accused of causing death by careless driving, but she pleads guilty to a lesser charge, some bullshit about being in charge of a vehicle while unfit through drink, instead of *murder*, which is what Lydia thinks she bloody well should be charged with. The judge sentences her to three months in jail, suspended for two years, bans her from driving for thirty-six months and fines her £2,500. She's a respectable Surrey housewife, after all; her husband is some rich wanker in the City, her mother has just died, her kids need her. If she'd been a single mother from Peckham, maybe the judge wouldn't have been so understanding.

Lydia wants to throttle the woman who killed her brother. She wants to squash that drunk driver like a cockroach, to look into the woman's bulging eyes as she squeezes the life out of her, and if she had the opportunity, she'd do it without a second's thought. Mae is right, and the shrink is wrong. She *is* a bad seed. There's a wickedness inside her she can't control. She can bury it like nuclear waste, encase it in well-intentioned concrete, but sooner or later, it'll burst to the surface. All it needs is the right trigger.

She isn't even able to go to Davy's funeral, because of the press. Instead, her probation officer takes her to visit his grave a few weeks later, under close protection, just in case.

She knows Michael Conway is already half in love with her. Unlike most people, it isn't her looks that attract him. He's simply one of those men who's drawn to damaged souls. His mother was an alcoholic, his first wife a schizophrenic who eventually committed suicide. Michael wants to fix people. And she clearly needs fixing.

Three months after her release, he resigns as her probation officer and takes her to dinner. Another three months after that, on her twenty-third birthday, he proposes and she says yes. They marry in a very quiet ceremony at a register office, no guests and two strangers off the street as witnesses. It's the first time she's officially used her new name.

She marries Michael, because he's a nice man, a decent man, because he plainly loves her and makes it easy for her to love him back, because, despite everything he knows about her, he still wants to marry her; and because, after Davy's death, he is the only person left in the world who cares if she lives or dies.

Children aren't part of the plan. That deadness inside her, that lack of conscience: she won't be responsible for passing that on. Michael can't have children anyway, thanks to a case of mumps when he was twelve. He'd grieved their absence when he'd been married to his first wife – though given her diagnosis, it was probably a good thing – but he's reconciled to it now. Lydia asked the doctor who'd signed off on her release if she could be sterilised, but he'd looked shocked and said no, they couldn't do that to a young girl, no matter what she'd done, it wouldn't be allowed. So she's relieved when Michael tells her he's infertile; one less thing to worry about.

And then, just six weeks after their wedding, she finds herself pregnant.

To his credit, Michael doesn't doubt the child is his. The doctors obviously got it wrong, he shrugs, they're only human. His sperm count may be low, but it only takes one little swimmer. He neither pressures her to have the baby, nor urges her to terminate. Whatever she wants is fine by him, he says. He warns her, however, that she'll face the fight of her life to be allowed to keep the baby, given who she is. He'll do everything he can to help her, after all, this is his child too; he'll call in every favour, make whatever promises are required, but at the end of the day, social services might take the baby away from them and there'll be nothing either of them can do to stop it.

She doesn't want a child. She never has. Given her own experience of mothering, how can she possibly raise a normal, well-balanced child herself? She's spent half her life behind bars; she's only been out of prison a year. She's still trying to figure out the way the world works. And if there *is* some gene for wickedness, if it can be passed on, she doesn't want to be responsible for bringing more evil into the world.

But the terrible irony isn't lost on her: here she is, a convicted child-killer, and the first real decision she has to make since her release is whether or not to take a child's life.

She can't start over again by killing another child. She has to break the cycle. She can be the kind of mother to her child that Mae never was to her. This baby will have half her genes, yes, but it'll have half Michael's too, and he is the most decent, honest, *good* man she's ever met. That'll outweigh whatever badness the child inherits from her and Mae. It has to.

It makes no logical sense, her baby is no more than a bunch of cells the size of a pinhead, but she already feels overwhelmingly protective towards it. If this is love, if she feels like this now, what will it be like when her baby is born? When it goes out into the world, vulnerable to the kind of wickedness that she'd once shown?

She realises then that having this child will bring home what she did to Julia's parents with brutal clarity. The guilt will be unbearable. And she'll deserve every second of it. It will be her way of atoning.

They decide that if the baby's a boy, they'll call him Davy, and if it's a girl, they'll name her after Michael's mother.

Maddie.

Chapter 31

Thursday 5.30 p.m.

Maddie looked confused. Her gaze moved from DS Ballard on the doorstep to the unpleasant male officer glowering behind her. Both officers were staring at her mother with something akin to fascination. She turned back to her mother.

'Mum?' she said uneasily. 'What's going on?'

Sarah didn't look at her. 'Please,' she said to DS Ballard, her voice strangely thin. 'Not here.'

'We tried you twice at your home,' the policewoman said awkwardly. 'We didn't want to have to do this in front of your family, but you didn't leave us any choice. It would have been better if you'd told us the truth in the beginning, Lydia. So much easier, in the long run.'

'Why do you keep calling her Lydia?' Maddie asked sharply.

DS Shortall abruptly shouldered past them all into the hallway. 'Enough of this bullshit,' he said nastily. 'Lying to the police is a serious offence. We could have you both up for perverting the course of justice.'

'Mike, please,' DS Ballard said. She followed her

290

colleague inside and took Maddie's elbow. 'I'm so sorry.
I had no idea you didn't know. I just assumed ... Is
there somewhere we could talk in private?'

Maddie pulled away. She'd never seen her mother
like this, submissive and uncertain. A pit of foreboding
opened in her stomach. 'Mum, what's this about?'

'I'm so sorry,' Sarah said helplessly. 'I was just trying
to protect you.'

'Please,' DS Ballard urged Maddie, as the sound of
running feet and laughter came from upstairs. 'Let's go
into the kitchen, where we won't be overheard.'

A knot of fear built in Maddie's chest as she led the
four of them into the kitchen. The pan of water her
mother had put on for the children's spaghetti had
almost boiled dry. On autopilot, she turned off the stove
and moved the spitting saucepan to a back burner. She
suddenly felt chilled to the bone. 'Will someone please
tell me what this is about?'

'This is going to be hard for you to hear,' DS Ballard
began. 'I think you might want to sit down.'

'Oh, stop pussyfooting around,' her colleague snorted.
'Your mother's a psycho, that's what she's trying to tell
you. She killed a kid!'

DS Ballard glared at him.

'What?' he said belligerently. 'You think you're doing
her a favour, dragging it out?'

'Mum had nothing to do with Noah's death,' Maddie
protested.

'Your mother's a convicted murderer,' DS Shortall
told Maddie contemptuously. 'And right now, I'm

wondering if the apple doesn't fall far from the tree.'

'I don't know how you think this is helping,' DS Ballard hissed furiously. 'Go outside and wait in the damn car!'

'What is he talking about?' Maddie asked, aghast. 'Why would he say that?'

DS Ballard glanced towards her mother, but Sarah was staring blankly through the kitchen window, kneading her fingers together with nervous intensity. It was clear no assistance would be forthcoming from that direction. 'Lydia Slaughter was convicted in 1974 for killing a four-year-old little girl she was babysitting, Julia Taylor,' she said reluctantly. 'Lydia herself was only eleven at the time.'

Maddie was more confused than ever. 'I'm sorry, but what does she have to do with Mum?'

DS Ballard looked like she'd rather be anywhere else than here. 'Lydia was sent to a young offenders' institution at first, and then to an adult prison when she turned seventeen. She served six years there before being released on licence and given a new identity.' She hesitated again. 'Lydia changed her name when she came out of prison. To Sarah.'

It took a second for Maddie to connect the dots. She laughed. 'I think you've got the wrong Sarah. Obviously it's not Mum! Someone's got their wires crossed.'

A beat fell. Neither her mother nor the policewoman spoke.

'Someone's made a mistake,' Maddie insisted again. Fear sharpened her tone. Why wasn't her mother saying anything? 'Don't you think we've been through enough without this? First you turn up at my home and accuse me of killing my own son, and now *this*? Maybe I should call my solicitor—'

'Enough,' her mother said suddenly. '*I'm* Lydia.'

Suddenly Maddie couldn't breathe. She knew the name, of course she knew the name. There'd been one of those true crime documentaries on Channel 4 just a couple of years ago, to mark the fortieth anniversary of the case. Emily had been only a few years older than the little girl who'd died and Maddie had watched it with a kind of horrified fascination. The case had been hashed and rehashed over the years by newspapers covering the trials of other children who'd killed children, like poor little Jamie Bulger: *Lydia Slaughter*, a name synonymous with wickedness and evil, alongside Myra Hindley and Rosemary West. Lydia Slaughter, the startlingly pretty eleven-year-old child who'd put her small hands around a little girl's throat and squeezed the life out of her, then covered her body with rubble and coolly concocted a story of a tall man with his arm in a sling to conceal her own crime.

Lydia Slaughter, who grew up and was set free and given a new name …

The ground tilted beneath Maddie's feet. 'You can't be,' she whispered. 'It's not … it's not possible. You can't be.'

Still Sarah didn't look at her.

'*Mum*,' Maddie said fearfully.

'I meant to tell you,' Sarah whispered. 'I meant to

293

tell you, when the moment was right. But by the time you were old enough to understand, it would have caused more harm than good.'

Maddie fought back a wave of nausea. She looked at her mother's hands, small and well-kept, the fingernails neatly painted with pale pink polish and trimmed to a sensible length. She pictured those hands around that little girl's throat, around Emily's throat, and nearly vomited where she stood. 'Old enough to *understand*?' she choked out. 'How could I ever understand?'

'You have to remember, I was only eleven—'

'Eleven is enough to know the difference between right and wrong,' she spat. 'Emily is only nine, but she knows! She'd never do anything to hurt her brothers, never!'

Sarah reached for her, but Maddie slapped her hands away.

'Don't!' she screamed. 'Don't touch me!'

'Maddie, please—'

How many times had her mother rocked her grand-children in her arms? Fed them and bathed them and smoothed their sweet, innocent faces with those pale, soft hands? Her babies had a killer for a grandmother and Maddie had trusted Sarah with their lives. 'How could you?' she shouted. 'How could you not tell me?'

Sarah looked ashen. 'Maddie, there isn't a day goes by I don't wish I could go back and change what I did,' she pleaded. 'I swear to you, I didn't mean to hurt Julia. Not the way they said. Not *on purpose*. I was just trying to make her be quiet. I was just a child myself, I didn't even understand what death *was*.'

'Did my father know?' Maddie demanded. 'Did he know what you'd done?'

'Yes. He was my parole officer. He knew everything.'

Her entire life was a lie. Everything she'd thought about her childhood, about her mother, about herself, was a lie. Whatever wickedness flowed in her mother's veins flowed in hers, too. She was tainted by what her mother had done. She wanted to rip the evil out of herself, to claw her own body and rip it to shreds.

'You should never have had me!' she yelled. 'How could you get married and settle down and have a baby like *nothing had happened*?'

'Maddie, I realise what a shock this must be,' DS Ballard intervened. 'I swear to God, I had no idea till we got here that you didn't know. I would never have sprung it on you like this if I had. I'm so sorry—'

'Why didn't you warn me before? She's been looking after my children!'

'We only found out today. It's been more than thirty years since your mother was released. Technically, she's still on licence, but in practice ...' She spread her hands. 'She hasn't even had a parking ticket in three decades. Her case officer has long since retired. It's a different department, it wasn't flagged on our computer system. I'm sorry. It should have been.'

'You know I would never hurt Emily or Jacob,' Sarah protested.

Maddie stared at her with repulsion. Her loathing was so visceral, it surprised even her with its intensity. Her mother hadn't just lied to her, she'd made a mockery of everything. All those years she'd looked up to her mother, tried to be like her, tried to please her. She didn't even know who she was anymore.

'You should never have been allowed to have a child,' she said bitterly. 'You're not fit to call yourself a mother!'

'This isn't helping,' DS Ballard said. 'Let's just calm down and talk this through—'

Maddie covered her ears. 'I don't want to know any more. I don't want to hear her sick excuses. I want her out of my house and away from my children!'

'Are you sure?' Sarah asked suddenly. 'Don't you want to ask me if I'm the one who hurt Noah?'

Chapter 32

Thursday 7.30 p.m.

Sarah sat down at the kitchen table and folded her hands neatly in her lap. All of a sudden, she was chillingly calm. Her entire world was crashing around her, and yet she appeared utterly composed. The panicked woman who moments ago had begged for Maddie's understanding had vanished. *This* was the mother Maddie had grown up with: controlled, contained, never impulsive, never melodramatic or irrational. She hadn't ever seen her mother lose her temper in her entire life. Even now, her self-control was terrifying. For the first time, Maddie was beginning to understand why that might be.

'I did not hurt Noah,' she said, slowly and clearly. 'I would never do anything to harm you or your children.'

'Why should I believe you?' Maddie hissed. 'I don't even know who you are! You've lied to me my entire life!'

'Only to protect you,' Sarah said evenly.

'Protect me? You're the one I need protecting *from*!'

Sarah nodded. 'You're right. It was never my intention to have a child. But if you'd just let me explain—'

'I told you, I don't want to hear it!'

'Maddie—'

'How could you have a baby, knowing what you are? How do you think it feels to have a mother who's a *murderer*?'

'I don't expect you to listen to me now,' Sarah said. 'But at some point you'll need to talk to me. I know you're hurt and angry, but I'm the same person I've been your whole life. What I did will always be a part of me, and I have to live with that every day, but it happened such a long time ago, before you were even born. I've changed. The person I am now, the person you've always known, that's not Lydia, don't you see?'

Maddie turned away from her. She groped for the kitchen sink and leaned on it, her legs shaking. She felt physically overwhelmed by the enormity of what she was trying to take in. Her mother had murdered a child. A little girl, just a few years younger than Emily. It didn't matter how long ago it'd happened. If she was capable of killing once, she could do it again. Could already have done so, in fact. Had her mother hurt Noah? Lost her temper, as she had so many years ago with that little girl? Was that why she'd been so insistent Lucas and Candace were innocent, because she'd known the truth? Or did she still believe it was Maddie herself who had killed her own child? Perhaps that was the real reason she'd called Dr Calkins. Maybe she thought evil was in her daughter's genes.

'How could you not tell me?' Maddie choked out. 'How could you let me find out like this?'

'Don't you think I've wanted to tell you, so many times?' Sarah pleaded. 'But I was so afraid of losing you. I couldn't bear for you to look at me the way you are now.'

'Every time I look in the mirror, I'll see you,' Maddie said bitterly. 'Half of me *is* you. No wonder the police thought I killed Noah.' She turned to DS Ballard. 'The apple doesn't fall far from the tree, that's what he said. Isn't that what you're all wondering?'

'Whatever DS Shortall might think, that's not the way I do police work,' DS Ballard said crisply. 'I look at the evidence in front of me. Evil isn't inherited. We're not talking red hair or blue eyes here. If you had anything to do with your son's death, trust me, I'll hold you to account, but you certainly won't avoid responsibility by blaming it all on your genes.'

Maddie was starting to feel light-headed. Black spots danced before her eyes and she gripped the edge of the sink more tightly for support. She needed to get out of here before she fainted. She needed air.

She needed Lucas.

'You have to leave,' she told DS Ballard abruptly. 'Take my mother with you. Lock her up and throw away the key for all I care. I'm going to find my husband.'

'What about the children?' Sarah said. 'Who's going to look after them?'

Maddie turned to her incredulously. 'I'll take them with me. You think I'll ever let you near them again?'

Maddie could hear her mother calling her name as

she locked herself in the bathroom and rested her head against the cool tiled wall. This couldn't be happening. Any minute now, she was going to open her eyes and discover it was all just a hideous nightmare. Her baby would still be alive. Her husband would still be the honest, trustworthy man she'd married. And her mother would be an ordinary grandmother, who organised charity raffles and made papier-mâché blowfish with her granddaughter, her most guarded secret the recipe to her Christmas rum cake.

Lydia had only been two years older than Emily when she'd strangled that little girl. Dear God, what could have driven her to do such an evil, unforgivable thing?

Maddie pressed the heels of her hands hard against her eyes and shook her head as if to clear the images away. She could feel the darkness threatening to engulf her. She couldn't allow it to win. She had Emily and Jacob to think of.

She opened her eyes again. Emily was shaking her shoulder. She was no longer hiding in the bathroom but sitting behind the wheel of her Land Rover, the two children buckled in behind her. She had no idea how she'd got there. Her mouth felt dry and cottony, as if she'd been drugged.

'Mummy,' Emily said. 'Why aren't you driving? You said we had to go and get Lucas. You said it was *urgent*.'

Maddie struggled to focus. Her brain was foggy, and she felt unbelievably tired, as if she'd run a marathon. Another memory blackout. Thank God she hadn't driven anywhere in her fugue state. If only she could forget everything that had happened in the last fort-night. Sleep, and never wake up.

'I'm sorry, Em,' she said thickly, starting the engine. The police vehicle and her mother's car were no longer in the driveway. She didn't know if the two detectives had arrested her mother, and she didn't care. 'I'll take you to Auntie Jayne's—'

'Auntie Jayne is in Scotland till Saturday,' Emily said. 'She promised she'd bring us back a haggis, remember?'

'Yes, of course she is,' Maddie said, flustered. 'I'll have to take you to the sanctuary, then. Bitsy and Izzy can look after you for a little while. I'll come and get you before bedtime.'

'I hate the sanctuary,' her daughter said mutinously. 'Why can't we come with you?'

'Because I need to talk to Lucas on my own.'

'Why can't Manga look after us, then?'

'Because she can't,' Maddie snapped.

Emily kicked the back of her seat. 'It's not fair. Manga was making us spaghetti. I'm hungry. When are we going to have something to eat?'

'Bitsy will make you something. Pizza, maybe. Please stop kicking my seat, Emily.'

'Pizza!' Jacob yelled joyfully from his car seat.

'Bitsy smells of horses,' Emily muttered. 'She makes everything smell like horses, too. I don't want pizza if she's cooking it.'

'That's enough!' Maddie shouted, crashing gears as she reversed jerkily onto the street. 'I don't want to hear another word!'

301

Both children were shocked into silence. She never usually shouted at them; it was one of her rules. Instantly, she was suffused with guilt. Emily and Jacob had both been through enough without having their mother go off the deep end. Another black mark in the ledger of good mothering.

Abruptly, she pulled over to the kerb. She couldn't do much about everything else, but she could do this one small thing for her daughter.

'If I take you with me, you need to be good,' she warned, twisting around in her seat. 'I have to go to Auntie Candace's house to get Daddy, but I need you and Jacob to sit quietly in the car and wait while I talk to him, OK?'

Emily nodded quickly. 'OK.'

There was an adult resignation about her daughter these days that worried Maddie more than the tantrums and seat-kicking. She knew she needed to spend more time with her. She'd been so consumed by her own grief, she hadn't given Emily the attention she deserved. She'd make it up to her. Somehow. The first step was to find Lucas, to apologise, and put their family back together. It wasn't too late. Lucas would understand. He'd forgive her. She still had time to put things right.

But then she arrived at Candace's house and saw the flashing blue lights of an ambulance on the drive.

Chapter 33

Thursday 8.00 p.m.

Maddie screeched to an uneven halt in front of Candace's house, hitting the kerb and bouncing up onto the pavement and then back into the road with a jarring thud. She was already unbuckling her seat belt before the car had stopped moving.

'I need you to stay here, Emily,' she said in panic. 'I'm going to go and find Lucas. You can't get out of the car. Promise me, Emily. No matter what happens. Stay here until I come back and look after your brother.'

Emily nodded, white-faced.

Maddie scrambled out of the car and ran towards the house. Her heart stopped as two paramedics emerged with a loaded stretcher, protective blankets preventing her from seeing who it was. Her entire body vibrated with a single thought: *please God, not Lucas*. The paramedics stopped briefly to talk to two police officers waiting outside, adjusted their patient's IV line, and then moved swiftly towards the waiting doors of the ambulance parked on the drive and loaded the stretcher inside.

She nearly collapsed with relief when Lucas appeared on Candace's doorstep.

'She locked herself in her bedroom and drank an entire bottle of vodka,' he said tersely, before she could get a word out. 'God knows what else she's taken. There's no question that it was deliberate.'

'Is she going to be OK?'

'I don't know. I only got back from work twenty minutes ago. We've no idea how long she's been unconscious.' He walked swiftly towards his Honda, parked neatly on the road. 'I was supposed to be at a work dinner tonight with all the partners. Candace knew I wouldn't be back till gone ten. She must have planned it like this deliberately. Another hour, and I'd have been too late. The only reason I came back early was because the police phoned to tell me about your mother—'

He broke off awkwardly. The two of them watched the police officers get back into their patrol car and leave.

'Is it true?' Lucas said finally.

Maddie nodded dumbly.

'I'm sorry,' he said stiffly. 'I can't imagine how you must be feeling.'

'I'm numb. I don't know what I feel.'

The paramedics slammed the ambulance doors.

'I have to go,' Lucas said. 'I need to follow them to the hospital.'

'Will you call me? Tell me how she is?'

'Of course.' He paused suddenly, one hand resting on top of his car door. 'Why are you here, Maddie?'

She hesitated, suddenly unsure of her ground. Her first instinct had been to turn to Lucas for help and support, automatically trusting that he'd be there for her, as always. Patient, dependable Lucas. But she'd said some terrible things to him; unforgivable things.

She swallowed. 'I came to ask you to come home.'

'You threw me out, remember?'

'I was wrong, Lucas. I'm so sorry. Please, can you forgive me?'

'You didn't even give me a chance to explain,' he said, sounding more hurt than angry. 'It's like six years of marriage counted for nothing.'

'I know you're angry. I'm not trying to defend myself,' she pleaded, realising wearily that's exactly what she was doing. 'Lucas, I love you. You're my husband. But you and Candace went behind my back. You lied about that loan to my face. I've always trusted you, but that turned everything I knew about you on its head. Surely you can see that?'

'It's a long way from there to thinking I'd condone the death of my own child, Maddie.'

He was right, of course. 'It wasn't just that,' she said miserably. 'Then I found out you weren't who you said you were, and there was the life insurance, and then I thought you'd brought in Calkins to try to get me shut away so I wouldn't find out about Candace—'

'I was trying to *help* you,' he sighed. 'It's all I've ever tried to do.'

'I realise that now, but I wasn't thinking straight. My baby had just died—'

'Our baby,' Lucas said. '*Our* baby, Maddie.'

She was shamed into sudden silence.

'You think you're the only one hurting?' he said painfully. 'I'm hurting, Emily's hurting, we're all hurting, Maddie. But your grief, it sucks all the oxygen from the room. It doesn't leave any space for me. You're not the only one in pain.'

'Lucas, I'm so sorry—'

He exhaled tiredly. 'Maddie, I love you too. But I'm overwhelmed right now. I don't know which end is up.' He rubbed his face. 'I can't talk about this here. I need to get to Candace.'

'Will you come home later? Once you're sure she's OK?'

'I don't know. Everything's such a mess. Maybe we both need some time apart to think through what we do next.'

She watched him get into his car and drive away, shaken to the core. Lucas had always been the reasonable one, the forgiving one, the first to say sorry when they had an argument, no matter who was in the wrong. It was his sense of justice and fair play that had first drawn her to him, all those years ago in the jury room. She'd taken his tolerance for granted, she realised suddenly. She'd always known Lucas would never let things escalate or get out of hand. They never went to bed on their anger because Lucas always made the first move to heal the breach.

But what if, this time, he didn't? It would take a lot to push him over the edge, but if he gave up on their marriage, she knew there would be no changing his mind.

A chill settled inside her. She hadn't grasped how much she'd been relying on Lucas's absorbent forgiveness. The thought that he might have reached his limit had never even occurred to her.

'Is it Auntie Candace?' Emily asked, as Maddie climbed wearily into the car. Her whole body ached as if she'd been hit by a bus. Shock was so *physical*, she thought to herself.

She glanced over her shoulder at the children. Jacob had fallen asleep in his car seat, tears drying on his ruddy cheeks. Her poor little boy. He might not understand what was going on, but that didn't mean it wasn't affecting him. And Emily looked so anxious and scared, her small face pinched and grey. An old woman in a little girl's body.

'Auntie Candace isn't very well,' Maddie said, buckling her seat belt. She felt light-headed and oddly removed from her own body. She looked at her hands on the steering wheel, chapped and reddened, the nails bitten down to the quick, and felt no connection to them whatsoever.

Emily was still talking, but her voice sounded strangely muffled, as if it was coming to her underwater.

'Mummy,' Emily said. '*Mummy!* Is she going to die?'

That odd metallic taste in her mouth again. 'No, she's not going to die,' Maddie said, swallowing with an effort. 'But she has to go to the hospital, so they can make her better.'

'But she still might die, mightn't she? Noah went to hospital, and he died.'

Maddie winced with pain. Children spoke such bald truths. 'Emily, please. She's not going to die.'

In her rear-view mirror, she saw her daughter close her eyes and press her small hands together in prayer. She was whispering something over and over again, but Maddie couldn't make out what she was saying.

Emily was fixated on death these days. Losing Noah had prematurely catapulted her into an adult world of grief and bereavement she wasn't equipped to face. Children were supposed to learn about death incrementally, in stages, Maddie thought unhappily. A goldfish, flushed down the toilet, or a gerbil buried with solemn reverence in an old shoebox by the rhododendrons. Then grandparents, loved and missed but old, in a child's mind, their deaths natural and understandable. By the time they lost their parents, they would, with luck, be adults themselves, fortified and able to cope. But for Emily, as for Maddie herself, the natural order of things had been abruptly turned on its head. If a little baby with his whole life ahead of him could die, asleep in his own bed, then death could strike anyone, at any time. No one was safe.

What would it do to Emily, to learn who her grandmother really was? How would it affect her sense of self? Her daughter had always been so close to Sarah. To *Lydia*, Maddie corrected herself bitterly. Emily might not grasp the full implications now, at nine, but in a few years, she'd start to wonder the same things as

308

Maddie herself. Was there something bad, some kind of wickedness, running through their family? Did that mean bad things would happen to her, too?

There had to be more to Lydia's story, she thought desperately. Sarah was right: the mother who'd raised her wasn't wicked or depraved. She wasn't a cold-blooded killer. And yet the same neat, capable hands that had stroked Maddie's forehead when she had a headache and put plasters on her skinned knees had also squeezed the life out of an innocent four-year-old little girl.

Maddie had to know *why*. It was the only way she could silence the voice inside her now asking if those gentle hands had also killed her son.

Chapter 34

Friday 2.00 a.m.

Maddie didn't sleep. As soon as she'd fed the children and put them to bed, she went online, feverishly pulling up anything and everything she could find out about the Lydia Slaughter case. The harsh irony of her mother's real name wasn't lost on her.

There were dozens of press articles from the late nineties onward, most of them detailing the various court injunctions that prevented the media from revealing Lydia's new identity and location, or citing her story in coverage of more recent cases like the death of Jamie Bulger. She was surprised how little hard information about the Slaughter case there actually was, but of course the contemporary coverage had been in a pre-internet age. Lydia was infamous, her name a literal byword for juvenile depravity, and yet there were almost no details about her beyond the stark facts of her crime and incarceration. Nothing that answered *why*.

Maddie made herself a pot of strong coffee and turned back to her computer. There had to be more to Lydia's story than the scant biographical details on her Wikipedia page, which mentioned only her mother, Mae Slaughter, and a brother who'd been killed in a car crash around the time of Lydia's release. Something that explained why she'd done something so wicked. A history of abuse, mental illness in the family, *something*.

Sometime around midnight, she had managed to find the names of the detective who'd worked the Julia Taylor case, and a journalist who'd covered the story for *The Times* and attended every day of the trial, but when she tried to follow the online breadcrumbs, she discovered both men were now dead. According to one opinion piece she'd found, the journalist had tried to write a book about the case in the late eighties, but it'd been shut down when it emerged he'd paid Lydia to co-operate, since it was illegal for prisoners to profit from their crimes. For all her digging, by the time it started to get light outside her office window, Maddie knew little more than when she'd started. She'd found no mention of what had happened to Lydia's mother, Mae, after her daughter's incarceration, or if she was still alive. What kind of woman had Mae been, to raise a child who could have done something so terrible?

She shoved back her chair and went to get more coffee. If a crime like this happened now, there'd be a mountain of stuff online, more than she'd ever have time to read. Hand-wringing pieces from liberal writers examining Lydia's upbringing, 'expert' opinions from armchair psychiatrists and criminologists, op-eds about nature versus nurture, articles in the *Guardian* about genetic predisposition to violence; so-called experts weighing in on all sides.

But Lydia's case had been more than forty years ago. It'd made headline news in 1976, even knocking the famous drought off the front pages, but all she could find online now was a blurry black-and-white photograph of the eleven-year-old Lydia that bore little resemblance to her mother and a montage of headlines that had had a field day with her bitterly apt last name: *Lamb to the Slaughter, Slaughter of the Innocent.* The original articles themselves were presumably buried in filing cabinets in newspaper basements or on library microfiche somewhere. If she really wanted to know more about Lydia, she would have to trawl through archives, and even then, she might still end up empty-handed.

She must have finally fallen asleep at her desk, because she awoke stiff and cold when Lucas phoned around seven. The hospital had pumped Candace's stomach and she was conscious and lucid, which he said was a good sign, but the doctors still didn't know if she'd done lasting damage to her liver. All they could do now was wait and see.

'Vodka and Xanax,' Lucas said grimly. 'It's not a good mix.'

Maddie didn't know whether to be relieved or not that Candace was OK. There was only one reason she could think of for Candace to attempt suicide: guilt. Despite what she'd learned about her mother, Sarah couldn't have been the one to hurt Noah. As soon as Maddie had sat down and thought about it, she'd realised the timeline simply didn't fit; Sarah hadn't seen Noah for more than a week before he'd died. Lucas might not be covering up for Candace, but that didn't mean she hadn't done it.

'I should have seen this coming,' Lucas sighed. 'She hasn't been herself for weeks, she's been depressed and anxious. If anyone should've recognised the signs, it's me.'

'Did you get a chance to talk to her?'

'Briefly.'

'And did she say why she did it?'

He sighed. 'Please don't start with your witch hunt again. This has nothing to do with Noah. She has demons, Maddie. She always has.' He sounded distracted and exhausted. 'Look, I have to go. I'll call you when I can.'

She got up from her desk, wincing as she straightened her back.

Even in her darkest hour, she'd never come close to attempting suicide, though she'd have been lying if she said she hadn't thought about it when things had seemed at their bleakest. But she'd always had Lucas and the children to bring her back from the brink. Candace was alone.

Her phone beeped again, and she picked it up, assuming it was Lucas calling back. She flinched when she saw the name on the screen.

She had so many questions that only her mother could answer. *Tell me how it happened, Mum. Was it an accident? A game that went wrong? Did you really mean to*

313

kill her? Did you know what you were doing, or did you lose your temper, lash out? Tell me how one little girl could murder another, Mum, because for the life of me, I can't begin to understand.

She let the call go to voicemail. She was tempted to delete it without listening. But her mother had been right about one thing: at some point, she would have to talk to her.

She braced herself and played the message back.

'I'm here,' Sarah said simply. 'I'm here when you're ready to talk.'

Vomit rose in her throat at the mere sound of her mother's voice. She ran to the bathroom, unable to stop picturing her mother's neat hands – the same hands that had cradled Emily and Noah and Jacob when they were born – tightening around the throat of that poor little girl. It wasn't just the thought of what her mother had done that sickened her so much. It was what it might mean. There was a reason, Maddie realised, that she needed so badly to believe Candace was responsible for Noah's death.

The dark fear that'd stalked her since Noah's death now had shape. For weeks, she'd been trying to convince herself that her memory blackouts had had nothing to do with what'd happened to her baby. That they didn't matter, because she would never hurt her son, whether she remembered what had happened in those lost blocks of time or not. It simply wasn't in her nature.

But nor was taking a can of red paint and savagely destroying her baby's nursery. It was so out of character

314

she'd refused to believe it was true – and yet it'd happened. Both Lucas and Emily bore witness to that. It was hard to admit it now, but she hadn't wanted Noah, much as she'd adored him after he was born. What if that resentful, secret part of her had found its outlet during one of her blackouts?

Like mother, like daughter.

What if violence *was* in her nature, after all?

DS Ballard might dismiss the idea of an evil gene, but plenty of well-respected scientists had devoted their careers to researching it. Genes didn't just cover physical traits, like curly hair or big feet. As she'd learned online in the last twelve hours, scientists had already proved that behavioural disorders like autism had a genetic aspect, and many believed other traits like alcoholism and a predisposition to addiction could be passed on, too. The so-called 'warrior gene' had been scientifically linked to antisocial behaviour and violence: criminals in jail were far more likely to have it than the rest of the population. They might not have found the gene for murder yet, but why shouldn't psychopathy be inherited too?

It wasn't an excuse – DS Ballard was right about that. No one was saying rapists and murderers couldn't help it: everyone had a choice. But perhaps the tendency was there. An emotional disconnect. The right – or the wrong – set of circumstances: parental neglect, sexual or physical abuse, a traumatic childhood, and the same gene that propelled a child with a stable, loving upbringing to become a global business CEO could turn a damaged child into a monster. A perfect storm of genetics and circumstances, a fatal trigger, and evil was given wing.

Maddie flushed the lavatory and leaned on the bathroom sink, staring at her reflection in the mirror. What had made a pretty eleven-year-old child strangle the little girl she was supposed to be babysitting? She couldn't rest until she found out. If it had been an accident, a game that'd gone wrong, she could come to terms with that. But if it was something else, something darker, if there was wickedness in her own blood, she had to know.

She had to find it, and root it out.

Chapter 35

Saturday 7.00 a.m.

Maddie sat up in bed, not quite sure what had woken her. The doorbell buzzed again just as Emily's blonde head appeared around the bedroom door.

'Do you want me to get it, Mummy?'

'No, you shouldn't be answering the front door, not when we don't know who it is.' She flipped back the covers, careful not to rouse Jacob, who had woken crying in the night and refused to settle until she'd brought him into bed with her. Maddie hadn't slept for more than half an hour at a time; she was terrified to be alone with either of the children. She didn't trust herself anymore, not since she'd learned about her mother. It had only been the naive belief that violence wasn't in her nature that had allowed her to trust she wouldn't harm the children even if she had a blackout. Now, she didn't even have that security to cling to.

She struggled into her dressing gown and knotted it at her waist. 'Can you go downstairs and put the kettle on, Emily, while I see who it is?'

The doorbell rang again. Who on earth was here at

this time on a Saturday morning? Lucas had a key, and she wasn't expecting anyone.

She peered through the gap in the bedroom curtain. She was at the wrong angle to see the front door, but an unfamiliar green Volvo estate was parked in the drive. Not the police, then. As she watched, a second car pulled up behind it, this time a blue SUV with tinted windows. Two middle-aged men in jeans and sweatshirts got out and went around to the rear of the vehicle. From what she could see, it looked like they were unpacking boxes from the back of the car. They must have got the wrong address.

She dropped the curtain and hurried downstairs. The smudge of two figures was visible through the frosted glass pane in the front door. Before she had a chance to open it, one of the figures bent down and pried open the letter box.

'Mrs Drummond! Mrs Drummond, are you in there?'

She froze, and the letter box flapped again.

'Mrs Drummond, this is Aaron Wilson for the *Evening Observer*. I can see you're in there. I just wondered if we could have a word?'

Her stomach plunged, as if she'd fallen headlong down a flight of stairs. 'What do you want?'

'We'd just like to ask you a few questions.'

'What about?'

'I think it would be better if we talked about this in private.'

More shadows at the door. The letter box clanked as the journalist let go and stood up, and there was some jostling, and then a sharp knock on the glass.

'Mrs Drummond? Peter Squire-Taylor, *Daily News*. Any chance you'll be making a statement this morning?'

'Why are you here?' she called anxiously. 'What do you want?'

'Mummy!' Emily shouted from the kitchen, her voice high with panic. *'Mummy!'*

Maddie ran down the hall to her daughter. Emily was cowering in a corner of the kitchen, scrunched into a tight ball, her arms wrapped tightly around her knees, her bare feet poking out from beneath the hem of her nightie. She looked about four years old.

There was a rap at the kitchen window as she crouched down beside Emily. A young man with a camera slung around his neck peered in at them. 'Mrs Drummond?' he called, raising his camera to the glass. 'How do you feel about a quick picture with your daughter?'

Maddie leaped up and rattled the kitchen blind closed. The young man simply went around to the back door and shook the handle.

'Come on, Mrs Drummond. One picture, and I'll be out of your hair.'

'Go away!' she shouted.

'Look, Mrs D. Just one nice picture, maybe sitting out here on the terrace, won't take a minute, everybody's happy—'

Maddie was suddenly consumed by unfamiliar fury. How dare these people come to her home, traumatise her daughter, invade her privacy and intrude on her grief, just to sell a few newspapers? Abruptly, she yanked open the back door, grabbing the shocked photographer's camera and hauling him sideways by its strap before he had a chance to react. 'What's *wrong* with you?' she cried. 'You can't come round to people's houses like this, harassing them in their own homes! You're trespassing! Go away before I call the police!'

'And tell them what?' the young man sneered, scrabbling at the camera strap.

'How about we start with you trying to take photographs of my nine-year-old daughter in her *nightie*,' she snapped, flinging the camera back at him so it thumped him hard in the chest. 'Let's see how keen your paper is to buy pictures taken by a registered sex offender!'

He looked alarmed. 'There's no need to be like that—'

'Get out of my fucking garden! If I see you here again, I'll call the police and have you arrested. And that's if my husband doesn't get to you first!'

'All right, all right, keep your hair on. I'm leaving. But you can't hide forever,' he yelled, as she slammed the door on him. 'This is a free country! People have a right to know if there's a monster next door!'

Maddie leaned against the door, her heart hammering. She'd got rid of one cockroach, but there would soon be a dozen more to take his place. She knew why they were here. Someone had leaked the news about her mother; maybe someone from inside the police investigation. Soon everyone would know.

They'd be lucky if they weren't run out of town. No one wanted the family of a baby-killer living next door, or their children sitting in the same classroom as their precious offspring. She'd read about sex offenders hounded out of their homes, bricks thrown through their windows and petrol poured through their letter boxes. A doctor in Wales had had his house wrecked by ignorant vigilantes who didn't know the difference between a paediatrician and a paedophile. What would happen to Emily when her classmates found out who her grandmother was?

'Why was that man trying to take pictures of us?' Emily asked tearfully.

'Ignore him, darling. And I'm sorry about Mummy's swearing.'

'What did he mean about monsters next door?'

'He was just being silly, Emily. There's no such thing as monsters, you know that.'

Her daughter looked troubled. 'Is he here to take photos of it?'

'Emily, listen to me.' She dropped down onto her haunches, so that she was at eye level with her daughter, and put her hands lightly on Emily's shoulders. 'There are no monsters, not here, not next door, and not anywhere else. That man was just trying to take photographs for a newspaper story. I promise you, there is nothing to be frightened of.'

'Is the story about us?'

Her daughter was too smart to be deflected for long. With a weary sigh, Maddie sat down on the kitchen floor, pulling Emily onto her lap. 'Do you remember last summer, when your friend Becca's daddy went away for a while?'

Emily nodded. 'He went to prison.'

'Remember all those silly stories about him at school?'

Maddie asked, stroking her daughter's blonde head. 'People said he was a bad man, that he followed girls to the gym and murdered them on their way home. Remember? There was even that story in the newspaper about him, the Gym Killer, they called him.'

Emily twisted around to look up at her mother. 'But it was true. He *did* kill someone, didn't he?'

'Yes, but that wasn't the whole story, was it? He'd knocked a poor girl off her bicycle when she was cycling home from the gym and she died. He'd been drinking, so the police arrested him and sent him to prison for a while. But he hadn't murdered anyone. It was an accident, he hadn't done it on purpose.' She tucked a strand of hair behind her daughter's ear. 'He'd made a terrible mistake. He'd done a terrible thing and he was punished for it. But he wasn't a bad man. We all knew he wasn't a monster, like they said in the newspaper, that's why Daddy stayed friends with him after he came out of prison.'

'So the newspaper people made it all up?'

She hesitated, choosing her words carefully. 'They wanted to make the story sound more exciting, so more people would read it. They didn't lie, exactly, but they made a big drama out of something that was very ordinary and very sad. Then people who hadn't even read the story, who'd just heard about it from friends or seen something on Facebook, repeated it, and every time, the story got bigger and bigger, and in the end no one really cared what was true and what wasn't.'

'Becca had to leave school,' Emily said sadly. 'Is someone going to make up a story about us?'

'I don't know. I hope not, but I think they might, yes.'

'Because of Noah? Are they going to say we killed him?'

God, she was smart. 'It doesn't matter what they say,' Maddie answered staunchly. 'We know what's true, don't we?'

The doorbell rang again. Moments later, she heard the metallic chink of the letter box opening and people calling her name.

She stood up, and ushered Emily towards the stairs. 'I need you to get dressed, darling, as quick as you can,' she said quietly. 'Put Rabbit in your backpack and anything else you want to bring with you. I'll pack your clothes and your toothbrush.'

'Where are we going?'

'Somewhere these vultures can't find us.' She chivvied her daughter up to her room. 'Quickly now, Emily.'

She packed a holdall with Emily's clothes, then went into Jacob's room and added what he needed. Leaving Emily to fill her backpack, she returned to her own bedroom. Jacob was still sleeping in her bed, and she checked on him quickly, then left him to sleep while she threw a few things into a second bag for herself. Jeans, a couple of T-shirts, underwear. She had no idea where she was going to take the children, but she couldn't subject them to this. They'd have to hole up in a hotel somewhere, until the frenzy died down.

She hooked back the edge of the curtain with one finger and peered down into the drive. She was shocked to see how many people had gathered outside. At least a dozen journalists and photographers were hanging around the front door, trampling the flower beds as they tried to see into her downstairs windows, heedless of the fact they were trespassing. Maddie felt a growing sense of outrage as she counted five cars blocking her driveway, with others double-parked on the main road. She hadn't done anything wrong, yet these ambulance chasers were invading her privacy and terrifying her children for the sake of selling a few newspapers. It was still not quite eight o'clock on a Saturday morning, but the disturbance had brought curious neighbours out into the street, some still in their pyjamas, where they huddled in small knots, staring openly at her house. She wished Jayne wasn't in Scotland, if only so she'd have one person on her side.

Someone must have spotted her at the window. There was a sudden shout, and the journalists swarmed across the small front garden in a pack, shouting her name.

She dropped out of sight and crawled to the bedside table, unplugging her phone and pulling up her list of contacts. Her car was blocked in and she had no intention of running the media gauntlet on foot, especially with Emily and Jacob.

DS Ballard answered on the first ring. 'You don't have to explain,' she said wearily. 'We've already had several calls from your neighbours. We'll have someone over there as soon as we can.'

'This had to have come from someone in *your* team,' Maddie snapped. 'Someone leaked it to the press, and now I have journalists poking cameras through my windows, trying to take pictures of my *children*!'

'Maddie, I am truly sorry. I'm trying to get someone

there as soon as I can. It's the weekend, it's not easy. I'd come myself, but I'm in Birmingham.'

'What am I supposed to do in the meantime?'

'Just sit tight. I know that's easier said than done, but try to be patient. To be honest, Maddie, there isn't much we can do anyway. We can remove them from your property if they're trespassing, but unless they're posing a danger they have a legal right to be in the street.'

'So I just have to put up with it?'

'I'm sorry. They'll get bored eventually.'

'They'll get *bored*? That's the best you can do?'

The detective sighed. 'What do you want me to say, Maddie? I told you, the press has a legal right to be there.'

There was a sudden crash of breaking glass, and Emily screamed.

Moving faster than she ever had in her life, Maddie scooped her sleeping son from the bed and ran into her daughter's bedroom. 'Are you all right?' she cried. 'Are you hurt?'

'It was downstairs,' Emily said, her eyes huge with fear.

From the top of the stairs, Maddie could see broken glass spilling across the floor of the sitting room.

'You see what you've done?' she shouted into the phone. 'Bricks through my window! What next, petrol through the letter box? You need to get someone here *now*!'

'A patrol is on the way,' DS Ballard said tersely. 'Stay inside, Maddie, and stay away from the windows.'

Chapter 36

Saturday 8.00 a.m.

Maddie sank onto the top stair, doing her best to calm Jacob as Emily pressed herself against her mother's side. She put her arm round her daughter, the three of them clinging together in fear as the noise outside intensified. They could hear angry shouting, the rattle of gravel against the windows, the shatter of more glass. She didn't know if some of her own neighbours had turned against her, or if word had got out online and vigilantes were taking up arms from far and wide. They were under siege, here in their own home in an ordinary cul-de-sac in the middle of the English countryside. But she was so inured to shock now she didn't even have the energy to be surprised.

A particularly loud bellow outside made them all jump, and Emily screamed as the front door flew open. Lucas stood in the doorway, a hulking great bear of a man, roaring at the assorted photographers and journalists and rubbernecking neighbours like the fairy tale giant who'd scented the blood of an Englishman. Maddie had never been so glad to see him in her life.

Emily's blonde hair streamed behind her as she flew down the stairs, launching herself at Lucas two steps from the bottom and clinging onto him like a human limpet. Lucas hooked one huge arm around her waist, swinging her up and settling her on his hip as if she were no heavier than Jacob, and then swung back towards the driveway. 'Get those cars off my property!' he roared. '*Now*!'

Journalists scrambled over each other like Keystone Cops. Lucas had never thrown a punch in his life, but they weren't to know that. She guessed the respite wouldn't last long, and they'd regroup and gather again on the street, but she savoured it anyway.

Her husband strode out to his car with Emily still in his arms, glowering ferociously at the photographers, daring them to take pictures. Maddie loaded the two holdalls she'd packed into the back of her Land Rover, then strapped Jacob into his car seat. There hadn't been time to switch the seat to Lucas's car, and she needed her own vehicle anyway. She watched Lucas roar off down the road, then jumped in her own car and reversed out of the drive to follow him.

She called Lucas and put him on speakerphone. 'Where are you?'

'Heading over to the Edenbridge Hotel. Meet me there, and make sure the bastards don't follow you. I've already booked a junior suite for tonight, with a roll-away for Emily and a travel cot. It's in Jayne's name, just to be on the safe side. We can figure out once we're there what we do next.'

'How did you know the press were at the house?'

'I didn't.'

It took her a moment to realise what that meant. 'You were coming home,' she said, her throat suddenly tight. 'You forgive me.'

'You're my wife,' he said simply. 'There's nothing to forgive.'

It was the first time since Noah had died that she felt they were truly on the same side.

She parked the distinctive Land Rover out of sight at the back of the hotel and walked around the front to check in, waving away the teenage porter who offered to take her luggage. She could manage a single overnight bag and a backpack on her own, even carrying Jacob.

Her own holdall she had left in the car.

'You're going there *now*?' Lucas exclaimed, when she got to the hotel suite and explained what she planned to do. 'Maddie, you saw the media circus back there! You think those journalists won't have had the same idea as you?'

'I'm hoping they'll be too busy running my mother to ground for the next day or two to worry about me,' she said, lowering Jacob to the floor with a sigh of relief. He was getting too heavy to carry far these days. 'And as long as the reporters stay away from you and the children, they can follow me to Timbuktu for all I care. In fact, I hope they do, if it keeps them away from you.'

Lucas ushered Maddie into the hotel corridor and shut the door behind them. 'You don't even know if this woman is still alive,' he said, in a low undertone so the children wouldn't hear them. 'Even if she is, how are you going to find her? She's probably changed her name or married or moved away. It's been more than forty years. Come on, Maddie. This is a fool's errand.'

'I can't just sit here and do nothing,' she said impatiently. 'There has to be a reason my mother did what she did. Children aren't born monsters! Something drove her to it. It can't just have happened in a vacuum!'

'I'm sure it didn't, but do you really think this woman is going to give you answers, if by some miracle you *do* manage to find her?' Lucas asked reasonably. 'What kind of woman raises a child who does something like that?'

'That's just the point. I don't *know* what kind of mother she was. And I need to, Lucas, I really need to. Otherwise …' her voice broke suddenly, 'otherwise how do I know I won't end up the same?'

'That's not even a possibility,' Lucas said, without a second's doubt.

'You don't know that,' she said thickly. 'You can't.'

'I know *you*, and that's enough.'

'But I don't, Lucas, don't you see? I need to know where I came from. Where my mother came from. I need to know who I really am, what kind of genetic inheritance I really have, don't you understand?'

He paced back and forth in the hotel corridor. 'Do

329

you really believe this woman is going to want to help you?'

'I'm not naive, Lucas. Children who grow up in stable, happy families don't turn around and murder little girls.' She swallowed. 'Something terrible happened to Lydia, and her mother probably had a lot to do with it. I don't expect the woman to suddenly sit down and confess her maternal shortcomings. But if I can talk to her, at least see where Lydia came from, what kind of life she had, maybe it'll give me some answers. Some closure, at least.'

'What if it turns out she was just an ordinary mother, no different from you?' he said quietly. 'What if Lydia was just born evil? What then?'

'I don't believe anyone is born evil, and nor do you.'

He pulled her aside as an elderly couple made their way down the hotel corridor. 'Are you absolutely sure about this?'

'After everything that's happened, I wouldn't blame you for not wanting to be a part of it,' she said. 'But I don't have a choice. I have to go.'

'OK,' he sighed. 'I'll take the children to stay with Lucy and Giles in the morning, if this is really what you want. He's an ex-Para; no one's going to get past him. I doubt the press will think to look for us at a client's house.'

'Thank you. I'm so sorry to put you through this—'

'Don't apologise, Maddie. None of this is your fault.'

She knew she was hardly to blame for her mother's sins, but she felt guilty nonetheless for dragging Lucas into this. 'Maybe you should warn the hospital, in case they come after Candace,' she said. 'If they can't find us, she'll be an easy target.'

'Sarah didn't hurt Noah,' Lucas said abruptly. 'If that's what this is all about. You do *know* that, Maddie, don't you?'

She stared at him, startled. She knew it couldn't have been her mother, but how could he be so sure? 'Lucas,' she said slowly. 'Have you spoken to Candace yet? About why she took those pills?'

'She won't talk about it. I've tried so many times to get inside her head, but I don't think even she has a handle on why she finds life so difficult.' He leaned back against the wall and stared at the ceiling. 'That night, the night we lost our parents, I pulled her out of the fire,' he said softly. 'But I didn't really save her. I've spent my whole life trying, but I don't know now if I ever can.'

Maddie hesitated. She didn't want to fight with him again, not now, but she had to ask. 'Lucas, there could be another reason she did this,' she said carefully.

He looked at her. 'You still think she hurt Noah?'

'Not deliberately.'

He exhaled slowly. 'I've thought it,' he admitted. 'Maybe. I don't know anymore. But this isn't the first time she's done this, taken pills. She tried once before, when she was about nineteen, after she split up with her boyfriend. She went to therapy for years afterwards, but it didn't stop the drinking.' He rubbed his face wearily. 'I don't know why our parents' death hit her so much harder than me. Maybe it's because it was her nightlight that started the fire. It wasn't her fault, obviously – she covered it with her blanket because she liked the glow. She was only four, she couldn't have known what would happen. But she's always blamed herself. And she was so young, she has no memory of our parents. She's always felt she doesn't belong anywhere, and nothing I do helps.'

She wrapped her arms around him, reaching up to stroke his huge back. 'Oh, Lucas. I didn't know.'

'I promised her I wouldn't tell anyone.' He hugged her hard. 'I kept hoping that I could be her family, *we* could be. I thought we'd give her roots. But losing Noah seems to have churned everything up again.'

'Lucas—'

'I love you, Maddie,' he said fiercely, burying his face in her hair. 'I never stopped. You and the children, you're all that matters to me. We nearly lost each other, and I don't want to risk that happening again. If I have to choose between you and Candace, I choose you.'

Now was the time to tell him the truth: she was racing two hundred and fifty miles north to Manchester not because she thought his sister had killed their baby, but because she was deathly afraid *she* had. It wasn't Lydia she needed to exonerate, but herself. She needed her mother to be innocent, for there to have been a reason for what she'd done, because if her mother was innocent, then Maddie might be, too.

Chapter 37

Saturday 2.15 p.m.

It took Maddie more than five hours to reach the outskirts of Manchester. She checked the satnav on her phone as she drove into the city, praying the battery wouldn't die before she got to the Central Library. Thirty-two per cent. She should make it.

Her certainty that she was doing the right thing had dimmed with every mile. Lucas was right: she was on a fool's errand. The chances of tracking down Lydia's mother after all this time were infinitesimally small. She had no idea what she'd do if she failed. Maybe she could find a social worker who'd known the family, friends, neighbours; anyone who'd met Lydia and might be willing to talk about her. But it was a long shot. Forty years after the event, there would be few adults alive who'd known Lydia as a child, and those who had would have spent the last four decades trying to forget her. This was a waste of time.

But she was here now. She parked the car in an underground car park and walked to St Peter's Square. She'd been to the library once before, when she was a student. It was an impressive building, with its domed rotunda and columned portico. Lucas had always admired it: he'd once told her it was loosely based on the Pantheon in Rome. But she didn't have time to appreciate its architecture today. It was already after two, and the library shut at five.

She made her way to the newspaper archives and narrowed down her search to the *Manchester Evening News* for late May 1976. Julia Taylor had disappeared on Tuesday May 25th. For the next four days, the frantic search for her had made front-page news.

Maddie stared at the artist's sketch of the tall, thin man with his arm in a sling whom Lydia had described as hanging around the Taylors' back gate the day the little girl disappeared. He *looked* like a paedophile, with the sinister scar above his eyebrow and his wall eye and straggly grey moustache and chipped front tooth. No wonder people had believed Lydia's story. There had been no reason to think the distraught eleven-year-old was lying. The police had asked people to contact them if they saw the thin man or the blue van with one door painted green that Lydia had said he was driving. For four days, they'd scoured Manchester, running down false leads and hitting dead ends. And then, on Saturday, Julia's broken body had been found buried beneath a pile of rubble in a derelict house just yards from the Taylors' back garden.

Maddie couldn't bear it. She knew what it felt like to lose a child. But to lose one like this, knowing how your baby must have suffered, to imagine her last moments, terrified and alone, crying out for you, wondering why you didn't come – how could any parent live with that knowledge?

She read every edition of the *Manchester Evening News* from the 25th May onwards. She read about the arrest of Jimmy Resnick, a lowlife with a long criminal record, whose police mugshot bore a striking resemblance to the man Lydia had described. She saw the photographs of the hundreds of mourners who'd gathered to pay respects at Julia's funeral, and learned about the £25,000 reward for any information leading to the conviction of her killer.

And then she read of the arrest of the angelic-looking little girl who had been Julia's babysitter and was now accused of her brutal murder. Even now, more than four decades on, in a world wearily familiar with acts of terror and cruelty, it still had the power to shock.

She couldn't take her eyes from Lydia's grainy black-and-white photograph. It could easily have been Emily, except for her mother's distinctive widow's peak. *This* was what a real monster looked like, sweet-faced and innocent, not a pantomime villain like Jimmy Resnick.

Except her mother had been far from innocent, that much was now clear. Lydia had put the Taylors through four days of indescribable agony before their daughter had been found. She'd described her own mother's boyfriend and wept crocodile tears as she'd coolly sent the police off on a wild goose chase after the sinister thin man to save her skin. Those weren't the panicked actions of an innocent little girl caught up in a tragic accident. They were the self-serving lies of a cold-blooded killer.

Maddie's heart ached by the time she reached coverage of the trial in October 1976. She no longer wanted to talk to Lydia's mother. She'd seen and heard more than enough of Mae Slaughter to last her a lifetime. The woman had shamelessly sold her story to anyone willing to pay, with no regard for the Taylors' grief, posing for photographs in plunging tops and short skirts, peroxide hair piled high on her head, clearly revelling in her daughter's notoriety. Despite the brassy exterior, she was an exceptionally beautiful woman, and the newspapers loved her. According to Mae, Lydia had always been violent and uncontrollable. 'She was born with the devil in her,' Mae said, almost triumphantly. 'I always knew she'd end bad.'

When Lydia was sentenced to life behind bars at the end of her nine-day trial, Mae had given a self-pitying interview lamenting the cost of travelling to visit Lydia in jail and the 'embarrassment' her daughter had caused her. She didn't spare a thought for the Taylors, who'd lost their child in the most unbearable way possible, or even for her daughter, whose life was also over before it had really begun. Maddie felt sick with the tragedy and waste of it all.

A woman like Mae Slaughter wouldn't have just disappeared from view, she realised. She'd have gone on milking her notoriety for as long as people were willing to pay for it. She must be dead, or she'd be popping up on *Jeremy Kyle* even now, lapping up another fifteen minutes of fame.

On a sudden hunch, she searched for Jimmy Resnick, Mae's on-again, off-again boyfriend, whom Lydia had used as her inspiration for the mythical thin man. And there it was. He and Mae had married a month after the trial, generating yet more newspaper headlines and no doubt getting paid handsomely for it. And it was Mae *Resnick*, not Mae Slaughter, who'd been found dead in 1997, having choked to death on her own vomit after a drug- and alcohol-fuelled weekend. Resnick himself had died while on remand for rape shortly afterwards, killed in a brawl with another inmate. They'd died as they'd lived – in the gutter, despised and unmourned.

So that was it, then. The end of the line.

A librarian passed through the stacks, quietly reminding everyone that the library shut in fifteen minutes. Maddie wearily rolled her shoulders. Once again, Lucas had been right. She should never have come. Even if Mae had still been alive, Maddie could see in that beautiful, spiteful face that she wouldn't have given her any answers. Mae would have delighted in twisting the knife, rubbing salt into the wound. She was a monster. And so was her daughter, just as everyone had said.

Or almost everyone. One person had tried to speak in Lydia's defence, although the papers hadn't run the story until after the trial was over. An ex-boyfriend, who'd lived with Mae and Lydia for several years. 'My regiment was one of the first into Belsen in 1945,' he'd told the interviewer. 'I was only eighteen, but I've never forgotten the look I saw in the eyes of the children in the camp. Like they were dead already, only their bodies didn't know it yet. That's the same look I saw in Lydia's eyes.'

Maddie suddenly turned back to the newspapers, speed-reading as the librarian came back down the aisle towards her.

'It's after five,' the librarian said, glancing pointedly up at the clock.

'One more minute,' Maddie pleaded.

She'd seen it just five minutes ago. *There*.

Frank Brzezina, that was his name.

Chapter 38

Sunday 9.55 a.m.

Brzezina. It wasn't exactly a common name; once she'd got back to the cheap hotel where she was spending the night and started searching for him online, he'd been easy to find. The surprise was that he was actually still alive.

She was five minutes early, but the old man opened the front door straight away. He'd clearly only just finished his breakfast; he was wiping his mouth on a napkin as he came to the door, and the scent of bacon lingered on the air. 'Sorry about the smell,' he apologised, as he led her through to his sitting room. 'My sister always swore the fry-ups would kill me, if driving trucks didn't.' He nodded towards a blurry black-and-white photograph of two teenagers on the mantelpiece. 'Ruth never smoked, didn't touch a drop of alcohol her whole life. Got breast cancer when she was thirty-four. Died eight months later. And here I am, ninety-two and still going strong.'

Maddie returned his sad smile. He seemed like a respectable enough man. His bungalow was small but well kept, and he had the upright bearing of an old soldier. What had he been doing with a trampy woman like Mae? Try as she might, she couldn't picture the two of them together.

He gently shooed an elegant black cat off the dark green velour sofa and waved for her to sit down. 'May I get you anything, Mrs Drummond? A cup of tea?'

'No thank you. I'm fine.'

The old man lowered himself into a claw-scratched armchair opposite her. 'Well then. You're doing some background research into the Lydia Slaughter case. That's a name I haven't heard in a while.'

She couldn't quite meet his eye. When she'd phoned him and spun him a story about researching a book into violence and childhood trauma, she hadn't given the lie a second thought. She'd just been relieved he'd agreed to see her, especially since she'd foolishly given her real name, though so far she didn't think there had been anything about her in the newspapers and she doubted the old man went online. But now she was here, the deceit suddenly seemed shabby and dishonest.

The black cat leaped onto the old man's knees, kneading his trousers. He stroked it, and the cat arched its back and settled itself in his lap.

'I appreciate you seeing me, sir—'

'Please, call me Frank,' the old man interrupted. '*Sir* makes me feel even older than I am, and Mr Brzezina is a bit of a mouthful, wouldn't you say?'

She smiled. 'A bit.'

'Polish. On my father's side. My mother was Irish. Doesn't get much more Catholic than that.'

'No, it doesn't.' She hesitated, unsure where to start. She felt wrong-footed by Frank's evident decency. Whatever had led his and Mae's path to cross in the past, he didn't deserve to have it raked over again now, at his age. 'It's very kind of you to agree to talk to me, especially at such short notice.'

'I've been waiting for someone like you to call me for forty years,' Frank said unexpectedly. He leaned forward, unsettling the cat, which leaped indignantly to the floor. 'What happened to that child was a bloody scandal! I said so at the time, but no one wanted to listen.'

Maddie was taken aback by his sudden vehemence. He started to rub the flat of his hands back and forth against the arms of his chair, clearly agitated.

'The way they treated her, trying her in an adult court, no attempt to understand what had driven her to do such a thing,' he exclaimed. 'Her defence team were a disgrace! Lydia was a victim, just as much as that poor little girl!'

She hadn't realised how much she'd needed him to say that until this moment. Her whole body went limp with relief. She'd been right to come here. She'd known there was more to it than the official story. 'What do you mean, Frank?' she asked keenly. 'How was Lydia a victim?'

'That mother of hers. Mae. The things she did to Lydia. Unspeakable things.' He closed his eyes, as if to

341

block out the images. 'I knew she was no angel, but I had no idea. She used to lock the poor child in a cupboard for days at a time. No food, no water. And that wasn't the half of it. That woman was a monster! Lydia was *traumatised*. In shock. What do they call it now?'

'PTSD,' Maddie said softly.

He nodded. 'Beatings, sexual abuse, horrific things you can't imagine.' His mouth trembled, his distress evident even after forty years. 'She prostituted her own daughter. Her own child! Was it any wonder Lydia did what she did? She was so damaged, she didn't know what she was doing!'

Maddie blanched with shock. She couldn't imagine anyone doing something so heinous to a child, never mind the girl's own mother. For a moment she wondered if the old man had got it wrong, but this wasn't the kind of thing you made a mistake about. Her stomach roiled, and she felt a burning sense of outrage at what had happened to that poor child. Why had no one said anything, *done* something? How had Mae been allowed to get away with it?

'How do you know this?' she asked hoarsely.

'Lydia's brother Davy told me, at the trial. He was there every day, in the gallery. I knew Mae wasn't the perfect mother by any means, but I had no idea what'd really gone on until he told me. He didn't know himself until years later, when it was too late for him to do anything. If I'd known at the time—' He broke off, collecting himself with a visible effort. 'Lydia wasn't responsible for what she'd done, not in any real sense. She should have been given help, not locked up!'

'But if you and Davy had gone to the police and told them—'

'You think we didn't try?' the old man said angrily. 'Davy talked to solicitors, the police, journalists, but no one cared. With his criminal record? I tried to get them to listen, too, I begged till I was blue in the face, but it was like talking to a brick wall. Too many people were busy covering their own backs. The family was known to social services – Davy had reported Mae after Lydia took an overdose of sleeping tablets when she was four. He was convinced his mother had tried to kill her, but Mae managed to talk her way out of it. Davy ran away after that and went to the police, but no one wanted to know.' Frank shook his head. 'Bloody disgrace. That poor girl was let down by every damn adult in her life. They're the ones who should have been on trial, not her.'

Maddie felt sick to her soul. She'd been right to refuse to believe children were born wicked. Something had to have corrupted them, corroded their souls.

Or some*one*.

'Why didn't Lydia tell you herself what her mother had done to her?' she asked quietly. 'She obviously trusted you.'

'I've asked myself that for more than forty years,' Frank said, his rheumy eyes filling with tears. 'There isn't a day goes by I don't wonder if I could have saved them, Lydia *and* Julia, if I'd known. I'll never forgive myself for letting that child down. I should have seen what Mae was really like, I should have *known*. But she could put on a good show. She was charming when she'd a mind.' He shrugged helplessly. 'My wife had left me a few months before I met Mae, and I suppose I was vulnerable. Lonely. Mae could be good company. Life and soul of the party, when she was in the mood. And she was a beautiful woman.' He sighed. 'Photographs don't do her justice. She just had this way about her. Lydia was the same. She was a pretty little girl. Somehow that made it all worse. People looked at that lovely face and felt they'd been tricked.' He blinked away tears. 'It was only later I found out how vicious Mae could be, but by then, there was Lydia to consider.'

His voice softened. He'd clearly loved Lydia, despite everything she'd done. Perhaps the only person who ever had.

'So you stayed with Mae anyway, because of Lydia?'

'I tried to do my best for her. Build a family. I even tried to track down Davy, but he was in Borstal by then.' He shook his head. 'I couldn't bear to tell Lydia.'

The guilt he'd been living with, all these years, blaming himself for what had happened. He'd been caught in Mae's web of depravity, a good man doing his best to keep Lydia safe, unaware of the dark forces ranged against him. 'Did you ever go to visit her, when she was in prison?'

'They wouldn't let me. Relatives only, they said. Wouldn't even let me write. When Lydia was released, they gave her a new name, wouldn't tell me what it was.' His voice broke. 'She must have thought I'd abandoned her, too. I never even got a chance to tell her I was sorry.'

'It wasn't your fault,' she said gently.

He rubbed his palms against the arms of his chair with increasing urgency. 'I should have *known*. I should have protected her!'

Maddie wanted to get up and hug him, but was wary of hurting the old soldier's pride. 'You said yourself, Mae put on a good show. And even if you'd known, you could never have predicted what Lydia would do.'

He bowed his head. 'I think about her every single day, you know. Wondering what happened to her. If she's happy. If she's even still alive. Davy was killed in a car crash just after she was released, so she'd have had no one waiting for her on the outside. Poor kid. She never had a chance.'

Maddie couldn't lie to the old man any longer, not even by omission. 'I think she made a good life for herself, in the end,' she said softly. She hesitated, trying to find the right words. 'Frank, I'm not just researching the case. Well, I am, but not quite the way you think.'

He looked up sharply. 'Are you a journalist?'

'No, I'm not a journalist. I'm on Lydia's side, I promise you.'

'Those reporters, with their sensational headlines!' Frank cried, forcing himself to his feet. 'They destroyed any chance Lydia had to get a fair hearing. We told them the truth, Davy and me, and they didn't want to listen, didn't want to know what'd really happened.

345

They hung her out to dry, just to sell a few more of their damned papers!'

His whole body was shaking. For a moment, Maddie was genuinely afraid he was going to have a heart attack. He was ninety-two years old, after all. 'I'm not a journalist. I just want to know the truth, that's all.'

'Why? Who are you?'

'Please, Frank. Sit down, and I'll tell you.'

He hesitated. She nodded encouragingly, and after a long moment, he finally sank back into his chair. 'If you're not a journalist, why are you here?'

Maddie swallowed. It was the first time she'd said the words aloud, and she had to force them out.

'Because Lydia Slaughter is my mother.'

Chapter 39

Sunday 1.30 p.m.

The fuel light in the Land Rover came on just as Maddie was about to join the motorway. The indicator hadn't worked properly for years: the needle jerked from full to running-on-fumes without warning. If past experience was anything to go by, she had less than a quarter of a mile before the car coughed to a shuddering halt.

Abruptly swerving across two lanes of traffic, she sailed past the slip road and continued back around the roundabout the way she'd come. She'd passed a petrol station just a few minutes earlier. If the Land Rover conked out, at least she wouldn't have far to walk to fill up her spare jerrycan with petrol. Better than being stuck on the hard shoulder of the M6.

She was lucky. The engine stuttered and died just as she limped onto the garage forecourt. She coasted to a stop beside a vacant pump and got out, her legs still a little unsteady from her encounter with Frank. Her emotions were all over the place. Her hands shook as she unscrewed the petrol cap, the fuel nozzle clinking against the side of the car as she inserted it into the tank. Listening to the old man had been like scouring an open wound with steel wool and salt. The pain had been almost unbearable, and yet now that the layers of half-truths and rumour had been scraped away, the truth he'd exposed felt raw but clean. Her mother wasn't evil. Lydia had been a lost, damaged little girl, not a monster. She'd committed the most terrible crime and strangled a child, and that could never be undone or excused, but Lydia herself had been a child, too, a little girl who'd been viciously abused and whose early life had been warped by a vindictive woman and wicked men. Nurture – or the lack of it – had created her, not nature. There was no murderous gene, no inherited wickedness. Maddie had been reprieved.

She leaned against the side of the car, feeling suddenly light-headed. She couldn't remember the last time she'd eaten. Yesterday afternoon sometime, when she'd stopped for a sandwich at a motorway service station. She'd never make it safely back home if she didn't have some coffee and something to eat.

She finished filling the car with petrol and headed inside to pay. As she approached the till, a row of newspapers neatly stacked in perspex boxes caught her eye, and her stomach swooped. The Sunday tabloids all carried the same photograph: a petite blonde woman, her head ducked to avoid photographers, frozen mid-stride as she walked down the front steps of a Georgian house.

Maddie snatched up the nearest paper, and almost crumpled with relief. It wasn't her mother. Someone else's dirty washing was being aired for the delight of the nation. The cheating wife of a Cabinet minister, caught as she left the 'love nest' she shared with a young rap musician half her age.

She paid for her petrol and bought herself a cup of coffee that smelled burned, as if it'd been left sitting on the hotplate for too long, and a tuna wrap. Both remained untouched on the seat beside her as she sat in her car on the forecourt, thinking about what Frank had said when she'd told him Lydia was her mother. 'Everyone deserves one chance,' he'd sighed. 'Not a second chance, maybe, but at least *one*.'

He was right. Lydia had deserved a chance at life. A chance she'd never had, thanks to Mae. She'd been let down by every single person who should have saved her: the social workers, the police, her solicitors, even Frank and Davy, despite their best efforts. But *Sarah* had had that chance. She'd made something good out of her life. Perhaps she could never weight the scales in her favour; maybe nothing could truly atone for the death of a child. But she had saved scores more children with her charity work and fundraising and campaigning. Children who might otherwise have grown up in a world of violence and abuse, as Lydia had. Who might have gone on to hurt others in turn. Surely that counted for something?

Maddie bit her lip in frustration. The world wouldn't give a damn what Sarah had done when they found out who she was. Her mother hadn't been on the front page today, but it was only a matter of time. The court injunctions might stop newspapers from running their stories, but nothing could prevent online journalists and bloggers and gossip outlets from writing whatever they wanted. As soon as the solicitors stopped one, another would pop up, like some kind of malevolent whack-a-mole. There was no way to keep anything secret anymore.

And sooner or later, it would emerge that Maddie had been a suspect in her son's death, if it hadn't already. Even she could see the story was irresistible. *Like mother, like daughter.* To the world, she'd be guilty. It would become the truth.

Her phone beeped as she finally started the car. She fished it out of her bag and glanced at the screen. The text was from Lucas. **Candace needs to talk to you**.

She tossed the phone onto the front seat beside the untouched coffee and tuna wrap without replying. She knew what Candace was going to say. The circle of those close enough to have hurt Noah was small. She knew now it hadn't been her mother, or Lucas, and in her heart she'd always known it wasn't herself. There was only Candace left.

Perhaps she'd panicked when she hadn't been able to get Noah to stop crying and had shaken him harder than she'd intended. Maybe she'd simply dropped him. Candace wasn't used to being around small babies. Maddie didn't believe she'd hurt Noah on purpose. It'd been an accident. She'd made a mistake with devastating consequences – just as Lydia had done. Candace had tried to take her own life because of it. Punishing her now wouldn't bring Noah back. Her son would still be dead.

She headed back towards the motorway. She knew she should feel bitter, angry, but she simply didn't have it in her anymore. She wanted her husband back, her children gathered safely around her. She wanted her biggest problem to be worrying about the damn mortgage again.

It started to rain as she joined the slip road, and she flicked on the arthritic wipers, peering through the dirty streaks they left on the windscreen. She was so tired. Her eyes burned. Her head was throbbing, too, and she rested the side of her forehead briefly against the cool glass of the window. The metallic taste in her mouth was strong, even though her lip wasn't bleeding. There was a strange smell in the car, too, like peat or damp wood. Must be from the horse blankets in the boot. Funny, that she hadn't noticed it before.

She passed another service station and slowed slightly as a large caravan pulled from the slip road into the lane ahead of her.

Her phone beeped again. **Come home safe**.

Her headache was blinding now. Spots danced before her eyes. That smell was growing stronger.

And then suddenly everything turned black.

Chapter 40

Tuesday 7.30 a.m.

She hurt everywhere.

It hurt to move. It hurt to breathe. Every time she inhaled, skewers of pain pierced her chest. Maddie felt as if she'd been pounded by rocks, every muscle in her body bruised and aching. The pain in her neck was so intense, it hurt even to keep still.

She tried to swallow, but her mouth was too dry. When she opened her eyes, a bright light burned her retinas and she was forced to close them again.

With an effort, she tried to collect her thoughts. She had no idea what had happened to her, or where she was. Her head was pounding so much it was hard to concentrate. Jarring images flickered behind her eyes.

Rain.

Cars.

Blood in her mouth.

Black.

She coughed, and the pain was so bad she saw stars.

'Maddie?'

Lucas's voice. She swam towards it.

'Don't try to speak, darling. You've been in an accident. Just keep still, while I go and get the doctor.'

An accident?

Voices.

'She tried to open her eyes, Dr Walsh. I think she's coming round.'

'It's all right, Mr Drummond. Just give her a moment.'

'Maddie? Can you open your eyes?'

This time she braced herself for the brightness. She opened her lids a fraction, waiting for her eyes to adjust to the light. She licked her lips and coughed again, grimacing in pain.

'Mrs Drummond, I'm Dr Walsh. Don't try to move too much. You've been in a car accident, but you're going to be fine. You have a concussion and four broken ribs. You have some severe bruising to your upper torso, but you're a lucky woman. A very lucky woman.'

'I'm here,' Lucas said, leaning over the bed so that she could see him. 'You're going to be OK, Maddie. The doctor's right. You were incredibly lucky. You could have been killed.'

Her breath came in uneven gasps. 'What ... happened?'

'You were in a car accident. Don't you remember?'

She closed her eyes again. Fragments of conversation floated through her mind. *She needed help, not locking up! Everyone deserves one chance.* More images, jumbled and discordant. She struggled to put them into a coherent order. The library. An old man. She couldn't remember his name, she didn't know him.

'Where ...?'

'You're in hospital, Maddie. Manchester Royal Infirmary. You've been here for two days.'

Two days?

She struggled to sit up.

A grey-haired man in a white coat put his hand on her shoulder, gently restraining her. 'Mrs Drummond, please.'

The doctor pressed a button to the side of her head, and the top of the bed slowly rose. He adjusted the pillows behind her, and she settled against them with relief. It was easier to breathe now she was sitting up. 'Tell … me.'

'You were driving back from Manchester,' Lucas said, sitting on the bed beside her and taking her hand, careful to avoid the IV line taped to it. 'Do you remember that?'

She could see an old man standing in his doorway, waving as she pulled out of his drive. Suddenly she remembered. Frank Brzezina. It all came back in a rush. Driving to Manchester, the hours in the library, her conversation with Frank. *Everyone deserves one chance.* He had been talking about Lydia. Her mother. She could remember getting back into her car, waving to him, but after that, there was only blank tape where her memories should be.

'You crashed into the back of a caravan on the motorway,' Lucas said. 'You were incredibly lucky, Maddie. The caravan crumpled like cardboard and broke your impact. If you'd hit the back of another car or a lorry, we'd have lost you.'

The doctor pulled up a chair on the other side of the bed and sat down. Behind his wire-rimmed glasses, his eyes were kind. 'We believe you experienced a generalised tonic-clonic seizure, Mrs Drummond. Do you know if you've ever had one before?'

She looked shocked. 'A seizure? No, never.'

'We performed a CAT scan and an MRI when you came in, and there's no evidence of injury, other than mild concussion. We also ruled out any underlying organic cause, such as a brain tumour. Please don't worry. You should make a full recovery.'

'The accident ... caused ... a seizure?'

'No. It was the seizure that *caused* the accident,' Dr Walsh said. 'When you have a convulsion of this kind, your body stiffens and becomes rigid. Your foot jammed on the accelerator. According to witnesses who spoke to our paramedic, you hit the caravan at almost one hundred miles an hour.'

Lucas squeezed her hand. 'We've been so lucky, Maddie.'

'Why ... seizure?' Maddie managed. 'Never had ... before.'

'Have you had any other head injuries recently? Your husband said you work with horses. Maybe a fall?'

'No. Nothing ... like that.'

'Have you noticed anything else strange in the last few months? Memory loss, losing track of time, confusion, that kind of thing?'

Maddie caught Lucas's eye, and nodded, giving him permission to speak. 'She's had a few memory lapses, yes, but it's been a very difficult time,' he said defensively. 'After everything that's happened, it's not surprising.'

She coughed, clutching her side. 'Started ... before Noah.'

Lucas looked surprised. 'You never said anything.'

'Didn't want you ... to worry. Thought ... just tired.'

The doctor leaned forward. 'These memory lapses. Can you tell me a bit more about them? When did they start?'

'About ... a year ago.'

'You should have told me,' Lucas reproved softly.

'How often do they happen?' the doctor asked.

'Don't know,' Maddie said helplessly. 'Lose track of time. Mucking out horses ... next thing in my office, doing ... paperwork. Maybe two or three times a week, I don't know.' She was tiring with the effort of talking. 'More often since ... Noah died.'

'Do you have any other symptoms?'

'Tired, sometimes. Mouth ... is dry. Sometimes ... I taste metal.'

'Any odd smells?'

A shaft of memory briefly lit up the darkness in her head. She closed her eyes, trying to summon it back. 'Just before the accident. A peaty smell ... damp wood. Very strong. Thought it was a ... horse blanket in the boot.'

'Have you noticed any bruises or other injuries that might suggest you've been unconscious for a period of time?'

She hesitated. The night she'd dropped Noah, when he'd got stuck between her body and the rocking chair arm, her lip had been badly bleeding, and she'd had no idea why. 'Once or twice.'

'Mrs Drummond, I think you may have been suffering from what we call absence seizures,' the doctor said, taking off his glasses. 'Even though they only last a few seconds, the memory loss can be several hours, even days, in some cases. They more commonly occur in young children, and it's uncommon, but not unusual, for them to preface tonic-clonic seizures in adults, too.'

'But I've never had … a seizure before.'

'You wouldn't have known. They're called absence seizures for a reason.' He smiled. 'To a casual observer, it would look like you were simply blanking out or daydreaming. These types of seizures usually last no more than a few seconds in most cases. They're extremely difficult to diagnose – in children, the first sign is often trouble in school, since it appears as if the child isn't paying attention, and repeated absences can cause them to become confused.'

'Mine last longer than … few seconds,' Maddie protested, ignoring the searing pain in her ribs. 'Minutes … hours. Not *daydreaming*!'

'Memory is a funny thing, Mrs Drummond.' He put his glasses back on. 'There's a part of your brain in the temporal lobe called the hippocampus, which is responsible for receiving new information and storing it. However, it only stores that information for a short time. Then, if it's important enough to retain – where you parked your car, for example – it ships it to a different section of the brain for long-term storage. If not, it simply deletes it. When you need that information again, the hippocampus helps retrieve it. Think of it as a librarian, if you like.' He smiled again. 'But a very highly strung, temperamental one. It's extremely sensitive to changes in brain activity. Every time you have a seizure, it hardens and shrinks. Information may be stored, but in a disorganised way. It's as if your librarian has gone on strike. No one is there to find what you need, so it's effectively lost.'

Maddie struggled to digest what he was saying. 'I don't understand. Why isn't ... my memory working?'

'Each time you have a seizure, the short-term information in your hippocampus gets wiped.' He gestured towards the monitor beside her bed. 'Imagine a computer crashing. Whatever was on the page since it was last saved gets lost and your memory reboots to the last saved information you had. So you might be hanging out the washing and then you go inside to make the beds. You're halfway through changing the sheets and you have an absence seizure, so short you don't know it's even happened. No one with you would even notice. But your hippocampus has just been wiped. Everything that you've done for the last five or ten minutes, since you were out pegging the washing is lost. You have no memory of what happened in between, because it's never been permanently stored.'

'Why is she having these seizures?' Lucas asked. 'What's triggered them?'

The doctor shrugged. 'They can be triggered by certain health issues, such as extremely low blood sugar or a high fever, but the majority of seizures are caused by epilepsy, which is what I think happened in your wife's case.'

'*Epilepsy*?'

'She'll need to have more tests, when she returns home, just to make sure we haven't missed anything, but I don't think you should worry, Mr Drummond. The onset of epilepsy is most common in early childhood or after the age of sixty, but it can occur spontaneously at any age. With the right medication, it's eminently treatable.'

'The bits of time I can't remember,' Maddie said suddenly. 'I wouldn't do anything ... *odd* ... during them? Out of character?'

She could feel Lucas staring at her.

'It's unlikely. We're not talking about some sort of psychotic break, Mrs Drummond. Your brain has just made a small edit, a jump cut, in your memory. To anyone watching, your behaviour would seem absolutely normal. It *is* normal. You've just forgotten a few frames.'

Not a psychotic break.

Absolutely normal.

She wasn't going mad. She wasn't having a mental breakdown. Her memory lapses had a logical, organic, *physical* explanation.

She buried her face in her hands and sobbed. She might have wrecked the nursery in a moment of crazed

359

grief, but the reason she couldn't remember it was because her memory had crashed and rebooted, as the doctor put it. She wasn't losing her mind. She wasn't schizophrenic or deluded. She hadn't hurt her baby in some crazy psychotic episode. It wasn't her fault.

It wasn't her fault.

'Mrs Drummond, please,' the doctor said, alarmed. 'Now that we know you're having them, the seizures are extremely treatable. There are a number of medications we can try. Please, try not to worry. We've had some excellent results—'

'Dr Walsh, is there any reason my wife can't go home now?' Lucas interrupted.

'I'll need to complete some paperwork, but there's no reason why not,' the doctor said. 'I'll write you a prescription for some painkillers, and, Mrs Drummond, you'll need to take it easy for a bit. You've had a nasty bump on the head, and your ribs will be painful for a few weeks. But there's no reason to stay here any longer. I'll refer you to a specialist for the seizures.' He patted her arm as he got up. 'Please don't worry. You'll be as right as rain in no time.'

She waited until they were alone again. 'We can't go home,' she said anxiously. 'It's not safe … not with all those … journalists.'

'Your solicitor applied for an emergency court hearing yesterday,' Lucas said. 'The judge extended the initial court injunction preventing the press from naming your mother or you so that it includes Emily and Jacob as well. They're not allowed to mention or otherwise identify any of you in any way. It won't stop some of the online stuff, but it should contain things, at least.'

'You spoke to my solicitor?'

He hesitated briefly. 'Your mother did. We thought you were dying,' he added, as she stared down at her hands. 'She's your mother. I had to let her know.'

Maddie shifted in the bed, trying to ease the pain in her ribs. It was worse than being kicked in the chest by a pony, which had happened to her more than once. 'Where are the children?'

'Still with Giles and Lucy.' He sighed. 'I'm not going to lie, Maddie. It's not going to be easy to go back home. A lot of the neighbours spoke to the journalists and heard the rumours. It'll help that nothing's appeared in the papers, but there may be some unpleasant days ahead. The police are going to maintain a discreet presence, so there shouldn't be any more bricks through the window, but it's not going to stop the gossip. If you don't want to go back, we don't have to. We can rent somewhere, until we sort things out—'

'No,' Maddie said firmly. 'We haven't done anything wrong. I'm not going to hide, like I'm ashamed of who I am.'

Lucas looked surprised, and then impressed. 'Good for you. Whatever you want, I'll support you. Anything you need, just tell me.'

'There is one thing,' she said.

Chapter 41

Thursday 3.00 p.m.

Maddie opened the door to Finn's stable, smiling as the horse whinnied with pleasure. 'I'm glad to see you too, boy,' she said, stroking his soft nose as he butted it against her shoulder. 'Hey, be gentle there! I'm a bit fragile at the moment. But you know what that's like, don't you, darling?' He nudged her again, and she winced and laughed at the same time, reaching for the Polos in her Barbour pocket. 'Cupboard love, that's all this is. OK, here you are. If only everyone was this easy to please.'

She glanced round at the sound of another horse clattering into the yard. Bitsy was leading a small grey pony across the cobbles, its stomach rolling like a wide barrel on the waves. Maddie gave Finn the last of the Polos and bolted the door of his stable behind her as she went out to greet the grey with an affectionate pat.

'Is this the new rescue from Arundel?'

'Complete with bloody "adoption basket" for her new owners,' Bitsy snorted. 'Pink ribbons for her mane, I ask you! They couldn't afford to keep her, but they "want her to go to a good home". Looks like they're giving a good home to a new Mercedes, from what I could see when they made their fond farewells.'

'Never mind the Mercedes, I'm not surprised they couldn't afford to keep her. Look at the size of her. They must have been feeding her six times a day.'

Bitsy looped the reins over the pony's head and unclipped them. 'They'll all be on a bloody crash diet if we don't get some money coming in soon.'

Maddie looked stricken. 'It's my fault. Izzy said three donors have pulled out since the weekend and others aren't returning her calls. I thought we'd be OK, since we managed to keep everything out of the papers, but the rumour mill has been working overtime. I'm so sorry. I've let you all down.'

'You've done no such thing,' Bitsy retorted. 'None of this is your fault. Bloody idiots. Spooking at the first sign of trouble. How long have those donors known you? They should have more bloody gumption.'

Maddie sank onto an upturned feed bucket and leaned back against the stable wall. Her ribs were killing her, despite the painkillers, and she was exhausted. Lucas was right, she should be in bed resting. But she couldn't just sit at home doing nothing while Bitsy and Izzy were fighting to keep all their heads above water. She needed to keep busy, so that she didn't spend all her time thinking about Noah. And she missed being at the sanctuary. She missed Finn, she missed being needed and useful. She knew who she was here. It wasn't just horses the sanctuary rescued.

'At least the reporters never came here,' she said wearily. 'The sanctuary hasn't publicly been linked with Lydia Slaughter. If Izzy can get in front of the right people, we may be able to contain it.'

Bitsy scowled. 'Don't hold your breath. A lie travels halfway round the world before the truth gets its boots on.'

'Well, they're leaving us alone for now. Whatever my solicitor did, it seems to have worked.' She winced as she changed position. 'In fact, a couple of the neighbours have come over to apologise for "jumping to conclusions" and buying into "fake news". The media isn't exactly popular these days. Silver lining, I suppose.'

'What about your mother? You spoken to her?'

'No,' Maddie said shortly. She had huge sympathy for the child who'd been Lydia, though it wasn't her place to forgive her for what she'd done: that tragic privilege belonged to the parents of the little girl she'd strangled. Maddie understood, too, why Sarah had needed to turn the page on her past and start again. But her mother had owed her the truth. Maddie wasn't yet ready to forgive her and move on, although she was closer than she had been before her trip to see Frank Brzezina in Manchester. She just needed time, that was all.

She watched Bitsy settle the new pony into its stall. 'Do we have enough in the account to cover the next set of feed bills?' she asked.

'You'd have to check with Izzy.'

She knew neither Izzy nor Bitsy had taken wages

themselves in months. Izzy had a trust fund to fall back on, and Bitsy lived in a small flat above the stables and didn't need much, but that wasn't the point. Things at the sanctuary had been hand-to-mouth before this scandal, and she knew things would probably get worse before they got better. She couldn't let it go under on her watch.

A car appeared in the lane at the bottom of the hill as Bitsy stamped off to the upper paddock. Maddie watched Candace park at the top of the yard and get out, hovering by the open car door as if any moment she might leap back in and drive off again.

Maddie struggled to her feet and walked up the hill towards her.

'Are you all right?' Candace exclaimed, taking in her battered appearance. 'Shouldn't you be at home in bed or something?'

'It's mostly just bruises. Looks worse than it is. The Land Rover was way too old for airbags, so the steering wheel broke my ribs. Hurts like you wouldn't believe, but it could have been a lot worse.'

'Shame,' Candace said. 'I know you loved that car.'

Maddie couldn't help a small smile. Only Candace would offer condolences over a Land Rover. 'Those things are built like tanks, but I guess it met its Waterloo. I've got a Jeep rental for now, but it's not the same.'

They stood for a moment in awkward silence. Maddie resisted the urge to break it.

'So,' Candace said finally. Her hands were trembling. 'Lucas said you wanted to talk to me.'

Maddie met her gaze head on. 'I think it's time, don't you?'

Candace swallowed and nodded.

'I thought it was better to have a conversation here at the sanctuary,' Maddie said. 'Somewhere where we wouldn't be interrupted.' She indicated her office. 'Let's go in and sit down. I think both of us could use the rest.'

Inside the dusty Portakabin, she cleared away a teetering stack of paperwork from a chair and Candace sat down, her tall frame swamping the furniture and the room and making it look like she was in a child's playhouse. Extraordinary how a woman could seem so solid and resilient and yet be as fragile as spun sugar. Maddie surprised herself with a sudden surge of empathy. She should hate Candace for what she'd done to Noah, even if it had been a moment of madness, a flare of anger or impatience in the heat of the moment. And yet somehow she couldn't. She looked at the ungainly woman before her, the woman who so much resembled her husband in all the wrong ways, and saw her mother – saw Lydia – there. Both Candace and Lydia had had traumatic childhoods, for very different reasons. Lydia had almost ruined her life with one act of senseless wickedness, and yet she'd been given a chance to make amends, and so much good had come from that. Maddie was too tired, too drained by grief, to have room for hate.

She sat down, their knees almost touching in the confines of the tiny space. 'Candace,' she said gently. 'Why did you take those pills?'

Her sister-in-law looked away. 'I wasn't trying to *off* myself. I'm not that brave.' She bit her lip. 'I just … I just wanted it all to *stop*.'

'What did you want to stop?'

For a long moment, Candace said nothing. 'Feeling,' she said finally. 'I wanted to stop *feeling*, just for a while. You can understand that, can't you?'

She understood that.

Candace twisted the silver ring on her finger. Maddie recognised it as the one Lucas had given her on her twenty-first birthday. 'I know what you think,' Candace said miserably. 'You think I did it out of guilt, because I hurt Noah.'

Maddie waited. She knew what Candace was going to say, but she needed to hear it from her, to finally put to bed all the doubts and suspicions that had plagued her family since Noah's death.

'I went upstairs that day to settle him for you because he was crying and you had to deal with Jacob.' Candace closed her eyes as if replaying the scene in her head. 'I picked Noah up and cuddled him and then I changed him, but he wouldn't stop crying. I did everything I always did, everything that usually worked, I winded him and gave him his dummy, but he kept crying. So I put him back in his cot and … and I turned the baby monitor off, so you wouldn't know. And then … and then I left.'

'You turned the monitor off? Why?'

'You always thought I was so good with him!' she exclaimed. 'I've always been useless with babies, but it

367

was different with Noah. I could always get him to sleep.' Her eyes were suddenly bright. 'I know it sounds stupid, but I couldn't bear you to think I'd failed. If I hadn't wanted you to think I was the bloody baby-whisperer, maybe you'd have heard him that night. Maybe he wouldn't have died.'

'You turned off the baby monitor?' Maddie repeated.

Candace dashed her sleeve across her nose. 'I left him to cry himself to sleep, with no one to hear him. It's *my* fault he died!'

Maddie stared at her. She'd been so certain Candace would finally tell her the truth. 'You didn't do anything else?' she pressed. 'You didn't shake him when you were trying to get him to be quiet, maybe even just … just rock him a little too hard? Please, Candace, I'll understand if you did. I won't tell anyone.' Her voice was raw. 'I just need to know what happened to my son.'

'I swear to you. On my brother's life. I would never do anything to hurt Noah!'

Maddie sat back. There was something in Candace's voice that made her believe her, the ring of truth that instinct told her was genuine. '*This* is what you wanted to tell me, the night you phoned?'

Candace started to sob. 'I haven't slept since Noah died. I kept thinking the guilt would go away, but it just gets worse. Every time I close my eyes, all I can see is Noah. I promise you, Maddie, I didn't do anything to hurt him. If I had, I'd tell you. But I left him to die alone and I'll never forgive myself for that, *never*!'

'He wouldn't have known anything,' Maddie said, praying it was true. 'He just fell asleep and didn't wake up. It wasn't anyone's fault. There's nothing any of us could have done.'

For the first time since that dreadful morning when she'd discovered Noah, the band around her chest loosened, and she could breathe. Her mother had been right all along. It was no one's fault Noah had died. It couldn't have been prevented. She couldn't have kept him safe, no matter what she'd done. No one wanted to believe that a beautiful, healthy baby could just stop breathing. Pathologists were trained to look for reasons, to determine cause and effect. It led them to see things that weren't there. They made mistakes; sometimes with catastrophic results. She should have trusted her instincts, but her grief had caused her to cast about for someone to blame – Lucas, Candace, her mother, herself – anything to make sense of it all. Noah's had been a cot death, nothing more.

And yet.

Candace may not have hurt Noah, but what if her baby *had* cried out that night? What if she'd heard him, gone in to him, picked him up to soothe him? Maybe that's all it would have taken, and Noah would still be alive. The thought that he might have been crying for her, waiting for her to come to him, feeling alone and abandoned in his final few moments, was too terrible to contemplate.

She loved Candace, but she didn't know if she could ever forgive her.

Chapter 42

Friday 2.30 p.m.

Maddie was in the sitting room, cleaning up the last vestiges of the damage from the previous weekend, when she saw the police car pull into the drive. She paused, cradling dried putty from the new window in the palm of her left hand. She was surprised to see DS Ballard get out of the car alone. They usually travelled in pairs, like Jehovah's witnesses or nuns.

She dusted the putty carefully into the wastebasket, readying herself for whatever blow was coming next, and opened the front door.

DS Ballard greeted her with a weary smile. 'May I come in?'

She was caught off guard by the tentativeness in the detective's tone. Until now, the woman hadn't asked for permission to do anything.

With a shrug, Maddie stepped back, waving her into the house. 'You know the way.'

'This won't take long. Is Lucas home?'

'He had to go back to work; he's taken so many days off recently. You can find him at the office, if it's urgent.'

DS Ballard shook her head. 'No. I had been hoping to tell you together, but I'll leave you to break the news to your husband.' She paused. 'We're officially closing our investigation into your son's death. I know your solicitor has already told you, but I wanted to let you know in person. You can have your son back, Maddie. You'll be able to say goodbye to him now.'

Maddie thought she'd braced herself for anything, but the news left her strangely unmoved. She should be relieved it was finally over, angry at what the police had put them through, but she just felt numb. It didn't bring Noah back, after all. He was still dead. And now she would have to bury him and somehow find a way to go on living.

'So you believe me?' she said abruptly. Legally, it might not matter, but she needed to hear the words.

'You didn't hurt your son, Maddie. I believe you.'

'Why?'

The detective gave a small shrug. 'Honestly? I can't tell you. I've been doing this a long time, and there've been times I've thought someone was innocent, only to find out they're as guilty as sin. Other times, I've charged someone, and then discovered evidence that exonerated them.' She sighed. 'But nineteen times out of twenty, I'm right. In theory, I don't believe in hunches. But I think it's possible to pick up on subconscious signals without even being aware of what we're doing. It's what makes a good detective. Call it intuition, if you like. And my intuition tells me you didn't hurt your son.'

'You still think someone else did, though, don't you?'

'I told you, Maddie. Officially, our case is closed.'

'And unofficially?'

Natalie Ballard stared out of the kitchen window for a long moment. There were fingerprints all over it, from where journalists and photographers had pressed up against the glass, trying to peer in. 'There have been a few high-profile cases where forensics got things wrong,' she said finally. 'Some tragic miscarriages of justice. But pathologists don't usually make mistakes. Not like this.'

After the detective had left, Maddie stayed sitting at the kitchen table for a long time. Maybe there would always be questions about why Noah had died, but it was time to let them go. She could finally bury her baby. She and Lucas would be able to grieve properly, without having to worry whether they were about to be arrested for the murder of their own child. Well-meaning friends would tell them they could move forward with their lives at last. But how did you ever move on from the loss of a child?

She thought of the parents of Madeleine McCann, who'd been forced to keep going after their little girl had disappeared for the sake of the twin toddlers they still had. How had they found the strength? Not just to get up in the morning and put one foot in front of the other, but to give their twins a normal, happy childhood? To celebrate birthdays and Christmases and go to McDonald's, without feeling they were betraying their lost daughter by daring to live without her?

She pushed herself back from the table, wincing once again as the pain shot through her ribs, and picked up her car keys to go and get the children from school. She and Lucas had sent them back yesterday when school resumed after the Easter break, in an attempt to get back into some sort of normal routine. They'd done their best to prepare Emily for what she might hear when she returned, explaining that some people might say bad things about her grandmother, about something she'd done when she was not much older than Emily herself. But despite their fears, the rumours hadn't reached the playground so far. Maddie prayed the reprieve lasted.

Jacob was fretful and grizzly when she collected him from nursery school and she had to wrestle him into his car seat, grimacing as his thrashing feet made contact with her ribs. There were bright spots of colour on his plump cheeks. She sighed. Two days back at nursery and he'd already caught a cold.

'He's crying *again*?' Emily complained as she got into the car. 'He woke me up, like, a million times last night.'

'He's got a cold,' Maddie said, braking as a woman in a Porsche SUV cut in front of her. 'Try to be nice to him. It's not his fault.'

Emily theatrically pulled up her school sweater to cover her mouth and nose. 'He'd better not give it to me,' she warned, her voice muffled. 'It's Sophie's party on Sunday. I can't be sick for that! It's a spa party, there's going to be a lady there to do pedicures and manicures and everything.'

Maddie briefly wondered what had happened to pin-the-tail-on-the-donkey and musical chairs. 'Calm down. You're not going to miss it.'

'I don't know why I have to have brothers. All my friends are only children. It's not fair.'

Maddie suppressed the urge to snap: *you only have one brother left!* Bickering with your siblings and complaining how much you hated them was *normal*. It was the first normal thing Emily had said since Noah had died.

Her daughter reached between the front seats and turned the radio up. Ariana Grande blared from the Jeep's surround-sound speakers.

'Emily! Turn that down!'

'I don't want to listen to Jacob!'

'And I want to be able to hear myself think!'

'What do you need to think for? You're just driving!'

'Emily!'

Her daughter folded herself into an angry knot against the side of the car. Maddie eyed her in the rear-view mirror. It was so unlike her daughter to let anything visibly upset her like this. She was usually an introvert, keeping her emotions bottled up inside. 'Emily, did something happen at school?'

Her daughter shrugged.

'Did someone say something to you?'

Another shrug.

'Was it about Manga?' Maddie pressed.

Emily scowled. 'No. Just stupid stuff about Noah.'

'What do you mean? What sort of stuff?'

'Everyone wants me to be sad all the time, because

of Noah!' her daughter cried suddenly. 'But I'm tired of feeling sad! Sophie wasn't even going to invite me to her party because she thought I wouldn't want to do anything fun. I told her I wanted to come, and she said OK, but she looked at me as if I was bad and mean and I know they all talked about me when I wasn't there!'

'You listen to me, Emily Drummond,' Maddie said firmly. 'You are neither bad nor mean, do you hear me? No one expects you to be unhappy all the time. It's sad that Noah died and sometimes you'll feel sad, but you're allowed to be happy, too. That doesn't mean you didn't love him.'

'I don't really miss him,' Emily said, lifting her chin defiantly. 'He was just a baby. He didn't do anything very much, except cry. I don't miss him like I'd miss you if you died, Mummy.'

'I don't blame you,' Maddie said, refusing to react. 'He was just a baby. Babies aren't very interesting when you're nine years old.'

Emily suddenly screeched and the wheel jerked in Maddie's hand. 'Mummy! Jacob just puked all over the car!'

'Don't shout like that when I'm driving!' She risked a quick glance over her shoulder as she pulled onto the dual carriageway. 'It's hardly all over the car, Emily. There's no need to make such a fuss.'

'Eeew! It's disgusting!'

'For heaven's sake,' Maddie sighed.

As soon as they got home, she extracted a sobbing

Jacob from the car and took him straight upstairs to the bathroom. Without even stopping to take off her coat, she started his bath running and helped him off with his soiled clothes.

'Emily!' she called down the stairs. 'I need you to watch him in the bath, so I can get your tea started.'

'Do I *have* to?'

'You always like playing with him when he's having his bath!'

'It's boring. None of my friends have to look after their brothers or sisters.'

'Give me strength,' Maddie muttered. If this was *normal*, she'd never survive the teenage years. 'Emily, I'm not having this conversation with you now. Come and mind Jacob, so I can get dinner started.'

Emily dragged her feet as she came upstairs, deliberately hitting each tread with her school shoes. Maddie held on to her temper with difficulty, ignoring her daughter as she thumped onto the lavatory seat and mulishly refused to engage with Jacob, who'd lit up at her appearance and was holding out his favourite green whale.

'Call me when he's had enough,' she said, sliding Jacob carefully into his bath seat, so that he could play in the water without losing his balance. 'Don't try to get him out of the bath yourself.'

'Fine,' Emily muttered.

Maddie went back downstairs. After a few minutes, she heard the sound of Emily's laughter and breathed a sigh of relief. She didn't know what had got her daughter so upset, but it seemed the storm had passed.

It took her a little longer to put together the children's tea than she'd planned. The fresh ravioli she had been going to give them had passed its sell-by date, so she had to whip up some sausages and mashed potato. Jacob didn't like sausages very much, but if she cut them up small enough, she might get away with it.

She pulled a load of clean towels from the dryer, folded them neatly and took them upstairs to put in the airing cupboard. There was a lot of splashing coming from the bathroom, she noticed wryly. The floor would be a swimming pool by now. Never mind. At least they were having fun.

She took a pair of towels into the bathroom. At first, she didn't realise anything was wrong. Emily was still sitting on the closed lavatory seat, watching Jacob playing in the bath with an expression of mild disinterest.

Except Jacob wasn't sitting up in his bath seat playing. He was face down in the water.

Chapter 43

Friday 4.30 p.m.

Maddie didn't even have time to scream. Jacob was trapped by the bath seat, unable to right himself, his fat little legs thrashing against the side of the bath. In one heart-stopping instant, she dropped the towels and scooped him out of the water, wresting the plastic seat off his lower body as she held him against her shoulder and banged his back, praying she wasn't too late.

'It's OK, darling, it's OK,' she exclaimed, as he coughed and gasped for air. 'You're safe now, sweetheart. It's OK. It's OK.'

Emily hadn't even moved.

'You were supposed to be watching him!' Maddie cried. 'What on earth happened?'

Her daughter turned her clear blue gaze towards her. 'He kept crying.'

She showed all the emotion of a block of wood. Was she in shock?

'How did he end up in the water?' Maddie demanded. 'His seat is supposed to keep him safe!'

She grabbed a towel from the floor and swathed Jacob

in it. His chest heaved as he buried his head against her shoulder, too frightened to actually cry. She took him into her bedroom and laid him gently on her bed, carefully patting him dry. He had red weals around his waist from the bath seat, and there were vivid red marks on the back of his shoulders, too. Marks that almost looked like handprints.

She glanced up. Emily stood in the doorway watching her. 'Did you leave him on his own?' Maddie challenged.

'No. You said I'm not allowed to.'

'Then what happened?'

'He kept crying,' she said again. 'It's annoying. He's always crying.'

Something about Emily was off. She'd always been a self-contained child, keeping her thoughts and feelings to herself, but this was different. Her brother had nearly drowned and she was acting as if he'd just stubbed his toe.

The counsellor at the hospital had warned them the children could react to the trauma of their brother's death in unexpected ways. But this deadness worried her. Emily might only be nine, but children suffered nervous breakdowns too. Jessica had given her the names of some paediatric counselling services. Maybe it was time to make an appointment.

'Emily, you're not going to get into trouble,' she said, keeping her voice neutral. 'But I need you to tell me the truth. Did you push Jacob?'

'We were just playing with his boats and hippos,' Emily said. 'He was laughing, and then he got splashed, and he started crying. It gives me a headache. So I pushed him to make him stop.'

It was her offhandedness that Maddie found disturbing. 'You pushed him over? Emily, you saw what happened! He could have drowned!'

'It was *his* fault.'

'Didn't you hear me? It doesn't matter how much his crying *annoys* you! Do you have any idea how serious this could have been? If I hadn't come in when I did, Jacob might have *died*!'

'I'm tired of looking after him,' Emily said impatiently. 'It's boring. You're always making me take care of him. If Noah hadn't died, I'd have had to look after him, too. It's not fair. I didn't ask for brothers. I don't *want* them.'

Maddie flinched. 'Don't say that, Emily, please. I know you don't mean it, but it makes me sad to hear you talk like that.'

'I *do* mean it,' Emily said truculently. 'It's nice when they're not here. I like it when I go to Manga's house and they don't come. I wish it could be like that all the time!'

Maddie's patience snapped. 'You need to go to your room and think about what you just said,' she said sharply. 'When you're ready to apologise to your brother, you can come back downstairs.'

'You're so mean!' Emily shouted, running down the hall. 'You don't care about me at all! You only care about the boys! I wish Jacob *had* drowned!'

'Emily—'

She stared helplessly as her daughter slammed the

380

bedroom door behind her. As exasperating as it was, at least tantrums she understood. The detached, strangely dissociated child who'd dismissed Jacob's drowning as an *annoyance* was far more troubling.

Maddie obsessively checked every inch of her son as she dressed him in his pyjamas, listening to his chest to make sure his breathing was normal, examining his skin for bruises or scratches, and even taking his temperature. Only when she was certain he was fine did she settle him in the sitting room with his favourite comfort blanket in front of *Peppa Pig*, mentally promising to atone for her bad parenting with extra mummy-and-me-time tomorrow as she left him staring mesmerised at the screen.

Upstairs, she knocked on her daughter's door and opened it without waiting for a reply. Emily was curled in a ball on her bed, facing the wall. Maddie guessed she'd been crying.

She sat on the bed next to her. 'What you said upset me very much,' she said evenly. 'Why do you think I don't care about you, Emily?'

Silence.

She tried again. 'Of course I've been sad because of Noah, but I promise you that's not because I love him more than you,' she said. 'Noah's gone, and I miss him. We *all* miss him. But I love you every bit as much as the boys, you know that, don't you, Emily?'

She stroked her daughter's hostile back, but the small shoulder blades flinched beneath her touch and she withdrew her hand.

'I know I haven't given you as much attention as I should have since Noah died, but that doesn't mean I don't care about you, Emily. I love you more than anything in the world.'

'You love the boys more,' Emily said, her voice muffled.

'Of course I don't! Why would you think that?'

'Because they belong to Lucas, and you love him. But you didn't love my dad, and you don't love me.'

For once, Maddie didn't know what to say. She felt her daughter's pain so acutely, her heart physically ached. 'Oh, Emily. Your daddy died. Of course I loved him. And I love you for *you*. How I feel about you has nothing to do with your dad or Lucas.'

Emily abruptly flipped towards her, and Maddie realised with a slight shock she hadn't been crying at all. Her daughter's face was red with anger. 'I'm *nine*! I've been your daughter for nine whole years! Noah was just a baby! How can you love us both the same?'

She was utterly taken aback. 'Emily, it doesn't work like that,' she said in bemusement. 'Love stretches and stretches. When a new baby comes along, that doesn't take away any of the love for the children you already have. It just gets bigger. I love you *more* now you're a big sister, not less.'

'You weren't supposed to be this sad!' Emily burst out.

'What do you mean?'

Her daughter fiddled with the ears of her favourite stuffed blue cat. 'For ages and *ages* we didn't have Noah

382

and you weren't sad.' She hugged the cat against her chest and buried her face in its turquoise plush fur. 'I thought if he wasn't here, everything would just go back to the way it was before he came,' she said, her voice indistinct. 'I thought it would be *better*.'

'Emily, you're not making any sense,' Maddie said uneasily.

'You weren't sad like this when Grendel died!'

'Grendel was a *hamster*.'

'But we had him for two years,' her daughter cried. 'We only had Noah for, like, two months! I played with Grendel every day, he was my *friend*. I taught him to climb up the ladders to get his carrots and everything. Noah couldn't do anything, he couldn't even roll over!'

Maddie stared at Emily's pretty face, contorted with spite and fury. She'd had no idea her daughter was jealous and resentful of her brothers. How could she have missed it? She and Lucas had talked about how to handle the issue of sibling rivalry before Jacob was born, they'd read all the books and done everything they could to reassure Emily she wasn't being displaced. They'd repainted her room the way she wanted, played up the idea of her as the Big Sister, and both Jacob and Noah had arrived home from the hospital laden with 'gifts' for her. But clearly somewhere along the line, they'd dropped the ball.

'I've loved you from the minute I knew you were in my tummy,' she said. 'It doesn't matter how old you are. It's not a competition, Emily. Are you listening to me? There's enough love to go round.'

'You weren't supposed to be this sad,' Emily repeated, her gaze on the blue cat in her lap.

'Why do you keep saying that?' Maddie demanded.

'I didn't want any more brothers or sisters,' Emily said. 'I told you and told you, but you didn't listen!'

A pit yawned at Maddie's feet. 'Emily,' she whispered, her throat constricted with fear. 'What did you do?'

The blue eyes that met hers were guileless. Maddie's stomach turned over. She'd seen that expression on a child's face before. Angelic and utterly without remorse.

Just like Lydia.

Chapter 44

Friday 6.30 p.m.

Maddie pounded on her mother's back door. She knew Sarah was there; Lucas had spoken to her half an hour earlier. By some perverse miracle, the press hadn't found her, and she'd stayed quietly at home as the storm had broken over Maddie's head. But then her mother was good at hiding. After all, she'd had more than thirty years of practice.

A light in the kitchen went on. Sarah stood by the back door, her expression unreadable as she stared at her daughter. Maddie rapped on the glass again.

Finally her mother opened the door, then wrapped her cardigan around herself and turned on her heel without a word. Maddie followed her into her small sitting room, hovering awkwardly in the doorway as her mother seated herself in her usual armchair and reached for a glass of what looked like whisky on the side table next to her. Maddie couldn't ever remember seeing her mother drink before.

'I need to talk to you about Emily,' Maddie burst out.

'Sit down, Maddie,' Sarah said wearily.

Something in her mother's tone alerted her. Ever since Noah's death, her mother had gone out of her way to spend time with Emily, offering to look after her, to give her some alone time away from Jacob. The two of them were so alike, so secretive and self-contained—

The realisation hit her like a punch in the stomach. *She knew.* Of course her mother knew. She'd recognised herself in her granddaughter.

'How long?' she whispered faintly. 'How long have you known?'

Sarah put the glass back on the table but didn't release it.

'*How long have you known*?' Maddie shouted.

'Since the business with the Calpol,' Sarah said finally. 'I didn't know, but I suspected then.'

'Why didn't you *tell* me?' Maddie yelled. 'She just tried to drown Jacob in the bath! I caught her, red-handed! Why didn't you *warn* me?'

Sarah closed her eyes briefly in dismay, but she didn't look surprised. It was as if she'd been expecting something like this to happen. 'Would you have listened to me?' she asked.

Maddie was brought up short. Of course she wouldn't have listened. It sounded insane, even now. Less than an hour ago, she'd sat there as her sweet-natured, pretty nine-year-old daughter had explained how she'd deliberately shaken her baby brother until his brain had swelled inside his skull because she didn't like his crying. Maddie still couldn't believe it. If her mother had come

386

to her with a horror story like this, she'd have slammed the door in her face.

She sank despairingly onto the sofa and buried her face in her hands.

'Lucas said you went to Manchester,' Sarah said abruptly. 'You found Frank.'

Maddie looked up. For a second, she was confused. She'd almost forgotten about Frank and Manchester. What her mother had done forty years ago suddenly seemed unimportant. The only thing that mattered was what her daughter had done in the here and now.

'You know what kind of childhood I had,' her mother said bleakly. 'My grandfather raped his own sister when she was twelve. She got pregnant with Mae. And then later, when she was old enough, he raped Mae too. Mae told me herself, she said if she could survive something like that, then I could too. I had it easy, she said. She never made me go with old men, or family. I should be *grateful*.' Abruptly, she raised her glass of whisky and drained it. 'I thought I could break the cycle with you, Maddie. You turned out well, you married a good man. You had three beautiful children. I was stupid enough to think I could put the past behind me. But I was wrong. I passed the bad seed on after all. Not to you, but to *Emily*.'

Maddie recoiled. 'Don't say that.'

'You said I didn't deserve a baby, and you were right. I didn't deserve to be happy.' She looked at Maddie, her eyes haunted. 'Your father threw me a lifeline after Davy died. Babies were never part of the deal. But

387

when it happened, when I found out I was pregnant, how could I kill you, too?' She shook her head. 'How would taking another innocent life have made things right?'

'You did your best,' Maddie said, getting the words out with difficulty.

'It wasn't enough, though, was it? I thought if I was a good mother, if I did everything right, the wickedness would end with me. But there's an evil in our blood. No matter what we do, it's not enough.'

Maddie shivered. 'Stop it. That's just superstition. Evil isn't hereditary. You said it yourself.'

'Isn't it?' Sarah said bitterly. 'What other explanation is there? Emily's got no reason to hurt her brothers. You've given her everything. A beautiful home, two parents who love her, everything she could possibly want. You've shown her nothing but love, you and Lucas. But it didn't make any difference, did it? She ended up just like me.'

Maddie had thought losing Noah had been the worst thing that could happen. But *this*? This was on another level entirely. How could you love someone and hate them this much at the same time? Emily had killed her baby. Her sweet, innocent Noah. But she was still Emily. Her need to protect and defend her daughter burned stronger than hate.

'Where's Emily now?' Sarah asked.

'At home with Lucas. I couldn't tell him.' She suddenly started to sob. 'I brought Jacob with me – he's asleep in the car. I couldn't risk Lucas leaving him alone with Emily.' She covered her face with her hands. 'Oh, God. What am I going to do? How can this even be happening?'

'You have to protect Jacob.' Sarah reached out and gripped Maddie's hand so hard it hurt. 'Emily did this just because she *could*. Mae and me, we had our reasons. We hurt others because we were hurt ourselves. But Emily did it without remorse or regret. That makes her so much more dangerous, don't you see?'

Maddie pulled away. 'What am I supposed to do? I can't tell the police! They'll send her to *prison*!'

'You have to keep Jacob safe!'

'And then what?' she demanded angrily. 'What about when she's grown up? What if she has a child, like you? A granddaughter like Emily? Then what do we do?'

Sarah stared at her. Maddie felt a weary sense of resignation. There was no point looking to her mother for answers. She was the one who had to decide. She needed to protect Jacob, but she had to save Emily, too. If she went to the police, her daughter would be sent away, given therapy and treatment, and eventually released, as Sarah had been. Even if she never put a foot wrong again, she would spend a lifetime looking over her shoulder and doing penance, just like her grandmother. And what about *her* children? And *their* children? What was to prevent evil cascading down the generations, as it had for so many generations before?

'You never should have had me,' Maddie said, getting to her feet. Her body was stiff and ached in a way that had nothing to do with her broken ribs. 'You knew what you came from. You shouldn't have taken the risk. You should have got rid of me before I was born.'

'That's an easy thing to say, but I'm your *mother*, Maddie. I loved you from the first moment I knew you existed.' She caught her daughter's arm. 'You know what it's like to love a child. Could you have got rid of Emily, even knowing what she would do?'

Maddie gently freed herself. 'You forget,' she said coolly. 'I'm Noah and Jacob's mother too.'

Chapter 45

The present

Maddie slipped into Emily's bedroom and closed the door gently behind her, waiting for her eyes to adjust to the darkness. She could see her daughter's strawberry-blonde hair spilling across her pillow and the gentle rise and fall of her chest beneath the duvet. Emily had always been a tidy sleeper, tucked neatly beneath the covers, no sprawling limbs or tangled bedsheets. Even in repose, she was controlled and composed. Maddie had always admired that about her, but now she found it chilling.

She stared down at her daughter. She couldn't ever remember Emily losing her temper, even when she was a toddler going through the 'terrible twos'. She hadn't killed Noah by accident. By her own admission, she'd known exactly what she was doing when she'd picked up her brother and shaken him. When Jacob was born, Maddie had warned her you had to be careful with babies, you could never shake them or drop them, you had to support their necks and never, ever hit them. She'd even heard Emily telling Jacob as much, when Noah arrived.

Her daughter's logic had been chilling, but perfectly reasoned. Noah had only been part of their lives for a few weeks. How could he possibly be missed? Once he was gone, things could go back to the way they'd been before.

She hadn't allowed for the grief her parents would feel, because she was nine years old. How could she have known? Despite everything, she was still a *child*. She had no real comprehension of bereavement. She'd been genuinely taken aback by the scale of their loss, by the police investigation and everything that had followed. *You weren't supposed to be this sad*.

But she'd known the consequences when she'd tried to drown Jacob. No excuses then. She'd been fully aware of the grief she'd cause, she'd seen it first-hand, and she hadn't cared. It was her daughter's utter indifference that Maddie found so terrifying.

She had no doubt now who'd given Jacob the overdose of Calpol. The open gate that had let him wander into the road – that must have been Emily, too. Her daughter had been the one playing with Jacob when he'd 'fallen' climbing the bookcase last year and broken his arm; she'd been with him when he'd shut his hand in the door, too. Knowing what she knew now, Maddie doubted either incident was an accident. Emily was just biding her time, waiting for the right opportunity. Sooner or later, if Maddie dropped her guard for a second, she'd try again.

She crouched beside the bed and gently stroked her daughter's forehead, her vision blurring with tears.

Emily was a psychopath in the truest sense of the word. She felt no guilt, no remorse for what she'd done. She was utterly lacking in either conscience or empathy. Lydia had lashed out in pain and rage, hurt and hurting, her violence stemming from the damage that had been done to her. She'd been rehabilitated, because once her pain had healed, so had she. But Emily had killed Noah simply because it suited her, and she'd do the same to Jacob if she got the chance.

During her online trawl for information about Lydia, she'd read you couldn't cure a psychopath. They didn't learn from either mistakes or punishments. They had no fear and no remorse, so retribution was lost on them. There was no medication to treat them, because they weren't sick. You couldn't teach them empathy and emotion because their brains weren't wired to feel them, any more than a typewriter was wired to cook pizza. Emily couldn't change. It wasn't her fault. It was just the way she was born. A genetic short straw, passed from Sarah to Emily through Maddie herself.

How was Maddie supposed to keep Jacob safe, without condemning Emily to a miserable half-life? She couldn't let them lock her daughter away. Emily wouldn't even understand why she was being punished. They'd pump her full of drugs and turn her into a zombie. If they ever let her out, she'd live her life in fear of discovery, as Sarah had done. And supposing she had a child? There was no guarantee she'd be allowed to keep it, and if she did, that might be worse.

If she could kill her own brother, what might she do to a baby who got in her way?

Emily sighed in her sleep and turned over. Maddie's tears fell hot and fast on her hands. Despite everything her daughter had done, she loved her more than life itself. Enough to do what was best for her, no matter the cost to herself.

She picked up a pillow that had fallen to the floor and turned back to the bed.

Six months later

Chapter 46

Saturday 11.00 a.m.

Maddie spread the tartan blanket on the sand, shading her eyes and smiling as Jacob ran excitedly towards the sea. It was unseasonably warm for early October and she leaned back on her hands and tilted her face to the sun, relishing its warmth on her skin. Not quite bikini weather, but there was no need for the cardigan she'd brought either, and she was beginning to wish she'd opted for shorts instead of jeans.

'This break was a good idea,' Lucas said, as he sat down beside her. 'Can't beat this weather.'

'After the wet summer we've had, we deserve a bit of sunshine.' She rolled her jeans up to her knees, digging her toes pleasurably into the sand. 'Devon is so beautiful this time of year. I love it when there are no bloody tourists.'

He laughed. 'Tourists like us, you mean?'

She ducked playfully as he tried to kiss her. 'I think your son wants some help with his sandcastle.'

'He's the son of an architect. He'll figure it out for himself.'

This time, she didn't avoid his kiss. Her mouth opened beneath his and she tilted her hips towards him as he fit his body against hers on the tartan blanket. He only had to touch her for her to want him.

Jacob ran back across the sand towards them. 'Daddy! Help me bucket!'

'Looks like you're needed,' Maddie grinned, giving him a little shove.

Lucas scooped their son up and swung him around in a wide arc, giggles trailing from the little boy like bubbles. Now that it was just the three of them, Jacob had come out of his shell and she was surprised daily by her funny, feisty little boy. Before, it'd been easy for him to get slightly lost in the shuffle, the middle child, a sniffly toddler overshadowed by his pretty older sister and the cute baby who'd replaced him. Now, with all his parents' attention to himself, he had finally come into his own.

Maddie watched Lucas as he crouched next to his son, helping him fill his yellow bucket with sand. Jacob patted it with his orange plastic spade, and together the two of them carefully upended it. The little boy clapped his hands delightedly, then abruptly smacked them down on top of the sandcastle, pealing with laughter. 'Again! Again!'

It was good to see her husband relax at last. He'd been working flat out for months. The dreadful floods along the Thames this summer had had an unexpectedly silver lining: Lucas had been commissioned to elevate several prime riverside properties above flood level and his innovative designs had sparked more work than his firm was able to handle. He'd been offered partnership without the usual buy-in, and this year's profit share had already put a significant dent in the sanctuary's debt. Maddie had protested over taking the money at first, but Lucas had been insistent, and she hadn't been in a position to refuse twice.

And Candace had done as she'd promised and repaid the second mortgage on their house in full. She'd joined AA and had just earned her green chip for six months' sobriety. There was even a man hovering in the wings, though Candace refused to put her recovery at risk by dating before she'd reached the twelve-month mark. Maddie still found it hard to be around her sister-in-law, but she was working on it. After all, she was hardly in a position to cast stones.

She'd agonised long and hard whether to tell Lucas about Emily. She'd known he might go to the police; at the very least, there was a strong likelihood he'd leave her. But they'd promised each other no more secrets. If their marriage was to have any future, she'd have to be honest.

She hadn't quite told him everything. But enough. As hard as it had been for her to say it, it had been even harder for him to hear. She knew it'd taken him many nights of soul-searching before he had been able to accept what Emily had done. But she'd gambled on his fundamental sense of natural justice, and her instincts had proven right. It had been the best thing to do, even if it hadn't been the right thing to do.

There was a shout behind her, and she turned, kneeling up on the picnic blanket and shading her eyes for a better view. Two figures were coming across the sand towards them. The smaller of the two suddenly started running, her strawberry-blonde hair streaming behind her. 'Mummy!' she shouted. 'We're here! We're here!'

Maddie held out her arms and Emily launched herself into them. She hugged her daughter, greedily breathing her in. Even a week was a long time in the life of a child. 'You're so brown!' she exclaimed, holding Emily at arm's length so she could see her properly. 'Look at you! What have you and Manga been doing for half-term?'

'We went crabbing yesterday!' Emily said excitedly. 'I caught four crabs, but we let them go. Manga said it's not fair to kill them if you're not going to eat them. And guess what?'

'What?'

'We went to see the Exmoor ponies and I got to ride one!'

Maddie looked astonished. 'You rode a *pony*?'

'I wasn't even scared!' Emily declared, glowing with pride. 'His name was Great Uncle Bulgaria and he was the oldest pony there, and we went out on the moors and he jumped over a little stream, but I didn't fall off! I fed him an apple after our ride to say thank you.' She shrugged nonchalantly. 'I think when we get home I might like to learn to ride at the sanctuary after all.'

'I'd love that,' Maddie said lightly.

'Can I go and play with Jacob and Lucas now? Manga bought me a bucket.'

Sarah handed her granddaughter a plastic wicker basket filled with beach toys, and Emily ran down to the water's edge, where Lucas and Jacob were building an impressively sprawling sand fort. As soon as he saw her, Jacob leaped up and shrieked with delight, throwing his arms around his sister's legs and nearly knocking her over. She laughed, then sat cross-legged in the sand beside him, smiling patiently as he showed off the finer architectural points of his sandcastle.

'He's missed her,' Sarah said.

'Of course,' Maddie replied, her tone neutral.

A beat fell. Maddie made no effort to bridge the awkward silence. She understood why her mother had concealed her past and lied all these years, and had forgiven her for it, but there was an undeniable distance between them now. Maddie had always known Sarah wasn't a natural mother, sensing even as a small child that Sarah's maternal attentions stemmed from duty more than joy. Now that she understood her place in Sarah's story, she realised that if her mother loved her at all, it was a very different kind of love from that which Maddie herself felt for her own children. For Sarah, love was a discipline she'd learned through years of painstaking determination. For Maddie, it was as effortless as breathing. She and Sarah would never be close, and for the first time in her life, Maddie was fine with that.

Sarah slipped off her sandals and sat next to her on the picnic blanket. 'Did you have a good drive down?'

'It was congested around Salisbury, but otherwise not too bad. You?'

'Well, we came down on Wednesday, so we missed the worst of the traffic. Emily's been looking forward to seeing you all. Spending some time together as a family.' She shaded her eyes and looked towards the horizon. 'How are you doing?' she asked lightly. 'No more blackouts?'

'Five months clear. The epilepsy medication seems to be working. No more seizures, and no more blackouts, as far as I can tell.' She sat up and brushed the sand from her hands. 'I'll be able to get my driving licence back in another month, which will make life a lot easier. Jayne's been amazing, driving me and Jacob around like she's my personal chauffeur, but it'll be good to get my independence back.'

'No side effects?'

Maddie smiled. 'Apart from making my hair go a bit curly, no. Apparently it's quite common, it happens with some chemo drugs, too.'

'My brother had curls like Shirley Temple,' Sarah said unexpectedly. 'He hated his hair, but I always loved them.'

Another silence fell between them. It was the first time Sarah had mentioned her brother, and although Maddie had come to terms with her mother's past, she still wasn't ready to talk about it.

'I can't believe you got Emily anywhere near a horse,' she said, changing the subject. 'You know how much she hates them.'

'It was nothing to do with me. She asked to go to the Exmoor Pony Centre, and then when we got there, she said she wanted to ride. She did it for you, of course,' Sarah added. 'She knew it'd please you.'

Maddie swallowed hard. 'She seems happy.'

'She is.'

Maddie watched her daughter upend a bucket on the sand with her brother, the two of them giggling as the castle fell apart. No one watching them would ever guess that six months ago, that solicitous big sister had tried to drown her little brother in the bath; that she'd already killed once and could easily do so again.

After that terrible night when, for a split second, Maddie had actually contemplated killing her own child, she'd known she couldn't keep Emily with her. Even now, the thought of what she might have done made her feel sick to her stomach. It had been a moment's madness, gone as swiftly as it had arrived, but the very fact that she had even been capable of thinking it had turned her view of herself on its head. She'd always thought of herself as a fundamentally decent person, the kind of person who rescued spiders from the bath; she'd once stopped traffic to let a mother lead her row of ducklings across the road. Yet for a few, insane moments, she'd considered committing the most heinous crime of all.

Sending Emily to stay with her grandmother had been a last-ditch, temporary measure while Maddie worked out what to do next. It was Sarah who'd suggested they make it permanent. 'I can teach her how to live in this world when you're made the way we are,' she'd said. 'How to compensate for the parts of her that are broken. She'll never learn that in prison. She may never feel empathy and compassion the way you do. But she'll adapt. I did.'

'Lucas thinks she should be punished,' Maddie had said doubtfully. 'He thinks she needs to understand what she did was wrong.'

'You can't punish her for behaving the way she was made. It's like punishing a lion for killing an antelope. Emily will probably never fully understand *why* what she did was wrong. Her brain isn't wired that way. But she knows now it won't be tolerated and I can teach her to behave in a way that will help her fit in.'

'But what if she hurts another child? I'll never forgive myself.'

Sarah had sighed. 'Where does blame get us, in the end? How far back do we trace fault? To me? To Mae? To my grandfather, or to *his* grandfather? In the end, we have to take responsibility for ourselves. It's the only way to find peace.'

'Have *you* found peace?'

'Emily will be my penance,' Sarah had said.

It hadn't been an answer, but Maddie had realised it was the only one her mother was able to give.

Any lingering fears Maddie had had that Emily would miss her had been quickly dispelled. Emily had been thrilled to be sent to live with her grandmother, and delighted when she was told she could stay there for good. She had Sarah's undivided attention, and didn't have to share her time or space with anyone. Maddie visited her there every week without fail, and Emily always seemed pleased to see her, but showed no sign of wanting to return to what she dismissively termed 'Lucas's house'. Her chillingly easy acceptance of an exile that would have devastated any normal nine-year-old told Maddie she'd done the right thing.

She watched Lucas now, watching Emily. He hadn't taken his eyes off the little girl since she'd arrived, his alertness evident in every stiffened muscle of his body. Lucas had only visited Emily twice since she'd gone to live with Sarah. It'd taken Maddie a month of pleading to get him to agree to this short break together, and he'd only acquiesced on the proviso they stayed in a separate B&B from Sarah and Emily.

Jacob came running up the beach towards her, a shell clutched in his chubby fists. Maddie scooped him up, throwing off her dark mood and admiring his find. He dropped it in her lap, and wriggled out of her grasp, reaching for another shell that had caught his eye. As he did so, he turned and smiled at her over his shoulder, and it suddenly struck her for the first time. Put aside the obvious differences, and the similarity was startling.

Emily wasn't the only one who looked like her mother. Jacob was just like Sarah, too.

Acknowledgements

For nearly two decades, my agent extraordinaire and very dear friend, Carole Blake, fought like a tigress to find wonderful homes for my books in more than a dozen countries. Three years ago, we discussed the idea for my thirteenth book, *A Mother's Secret*, over dinner one evening, accompanied as always by much laughter and plenty of champagne. By then, I'd written ten women's fiction novels, and wanted to take my writing in a different, darker direction. Carole was hugely supportive of the idea, and gave me the confidence to follow my instincts as a writer. No author could ask for more.

Sadly Carole died suddenly in October 2016, before the novel was finished. A doyenne of the publishing industry with more than fifty years' experience in the business, she was an astonishingly energetic and vivacious woman who relished life, and her death has left a gaping hole in the lives of everyone who knew her.

It was Carole's former protégé, Oli Munson, who introduced me to his colleague, my new agent, Rebecca Ritchie, at A. M. Heath. I consider myself exceptionally fortunate to have struck so lucky a second time. Rebecca's enthusiasm for the book is inspiring and infectious, and I am immensely grateful to her.

In Rachel Faulkner-Willcocks, I have an editor who is every writer's dream. The book is so much better for her detailed and constructive edits, and the time and energy she has invested in it is hugely appreciated. Together with copy editor Jade Craddock, she is part of a fabulous team at Avon and HarperCollins who have worked their socks off to make the book a success. That it has seen the light of day at all is due entirely to them. Every book is a joint effort, and none more so than this.

Closer to home, my wicked stepmother, Barbi, was the first to read the manuscript and we had great fun working out some of the plot intricacies together. She sets a high literary bar, and I knew that if the book entertained her, it was ready to go out into the wider world. Thank you, darling WSM.

Thanks, too, to my children, Henry, Matt and Lily – you're finally old enough to be allowed to read my books. And to my husband, Erik. I love you for your patience, your cooking, and especially the way you rub my feet.